I0592396

Francis Beaumont

The Dramatic Works of Beaumont and Fletcher

Vol. 6

Francis Beaumont

The Dramatic Works of Beaumont and Fletcher
Vol. 6

ISBN/EAN: 9783337337841

Printed in Europe, USA, Canada, Australia, Japan

Cover: Foto ©Andreas Hilbeck / pixelio.de

More available books at **www.hansebooks.com**

THE

DRAMATICK WORKS

OF

BEAUMONT and FLETCHER.

VOL. VI.

THE CAPTAIN.

Good Frederick, let me go; I would fain try
If that thing do not counterfeit.

Act V.

THE

DRAMATICK WORKS

OF

BEAUMONT and FLETCHER;

Collated with all the Former Editions,
AND CORRECTED;

With Notes, Critical and Explanatory,

BY VARIOUS COMMENTATORS;

And Adorned with Fifty-four Original Engravings.

IN TEN VOLUMES.

VOLUME THE SIXTH;

CONTAINING,

CAPTAIN;
PROPHETESS;
QUEEN OF CORINTH;
TRAGEDY OF BONDUCA;
KNIGHT OF THE BURNING PESTLE.

T H E

C A P T A I N.

A C O M E D Y.

———————————

The Commendatory Verses by Hills and Gardiner aſcribe this Play to
Fletcher alone; thoſe by Mains, to him and Beaumont. The
Prologue ſpeaks of but one author. This Comedy was firſt printed
in the folio of 1647. We do not know of any alteration of it, or
that it has been acted for many years.

PROLOGUE.

TO please you with this play, we fear, will be
(So does the Author too) a mystery
Somewhat above our art; for all mens' eyes,
Ears, faiths, and judgments, are not of one size.
For, to say truth, and not to flatter ye,
This is nor Comedy, nor Tragedy,
Nor History, nor any thing that may
(Yet in a week) be made a perfect play:
Yet those that love to laugh, and those that think
Twelve-pence goes further this way than in drink;
Or damsels, if they mark the matter thro',
May stumble on a foolish toy, or two,
Will make 'em shew their teeth. Pray, for my sake,
(That likely am your first man) do not take
A distaste before you feel it; for ye may
When this is hiss'd to ashes, have a play,
And here, to out-hiss this: Be patient then.
My honour done, you're welcome, gentlemen!

DRAMATIS

DRAMATIS PERSONÆ.

MEN.

Julio, *a noble gentleman, in love with Lelia.*
Angelo, *friend to Julio.*
Lodovico, } *two cowardly gulls.*
Piso,
Frederick, *brother to Frank.*
Jacomo, *an angry* Captain, *a woman-hater.*
Fabritio, *a merry soldier, friend to Jacomo.*
Father *to Lelia, an old poor gentleman.*
Host.
Vintner.
Drawers.
Servants.

WOMEN.

Frank, *passionately in love with Jacomo.*
Clora, *sister to Fabritio, a witty companion to Frank.*
Lelia, *a cunning wanton widow.*
Waiting-woman.
Maid-servants.

SCENE, VENICE.

THE

THE

CAPTAIN.

ACT I. SCENE I.

Enter Lodovico and Piso.

Lodovico. THE truth is, Piso, so she be a woman,
And rich and wholesome, let her be
of what
Condition and complexion it please,
She shall please me, I'm sure: Those men are fools
That make their eyes their choosers, not their needs.

Piso. Methinks, I would have her honest too, and
handsome.

Lod. Yes, if I could have both; but since they are
Wishes so near impossibilities,
Let me have that that may be.

Piso. If it were so,
I hope your conscience would not be so nice
To start at such a blessing.

Lod. No, believe me,
I do not think I should.

Piso. But thou wouldst be,
I do not doubt, upon the least suspicion,
Unmercifully jealous.

Lod. No, I should not;
For I believe those mad that seek vexations:
A wife, tho' she be honest, is a trouble.
Had I a wife as fair as Helen was,

That

That drew ſo many cuckolds to her cauſe,
Theſe eyes ſhould ſee another in my ſaddle
Ere I believe my beaſt would carry double.

Piſo. So ſhould not I, by'r lady ! and I think
My patience (by your leave) as good as yours.
Report would ſtir me mainly, I am ſure on't.

Lod. Report ? you are unwiſe ; report is nothing ;
For if there were a truth in what men talk,
(I mean of this kind) this part of the world
I'm ſure would be no more call'd Chriſtendom.

Piſo. What then ?

Lod. Why, Cuckoldom ; for we ſhould loſe
Our old faiths clean, and hold their new opinions :
If talk could make me ſweat, before I would marry
I'd tie a ſurer knot, and hang myſelf.
I tell thee, there was never woman yet,
(Nor never hope there ſhall be) tho' a ſaint,
But ſhe has been a ſubject to mens' tongues,
And in the worſt ſenſe : And that deſperate huſband,
That dares give up his peace, and follow rumours [1],
(Which he ſhall find too buſy, if he ſeek 'em)
Beſide the forcing of himſelf an aſs,
He dies in chains, eating himſelf with anger.

Piſo. Having theſe antidotes againſt opinion,
I would marry any one ; an arrant whore.

Lod. Thou doſt not feel the nature of this phyſic ;
Which I preſcribe not to beget diſeaſes,
But, where they are, to ſtop them.

Piſo. I conceive you :
What think'ſt thou, thy way, of the widow Lelia ?

Lod. Faith, thou haſt found out one, I muſt confeſs,
Would ſtagger my beſt patience : From that woman,
As I would bleſs myſelf from plagues and ſurfeits,
From men of war at ſea, from ſtorms, and quickſands,
From hearing treaſon and concealing it,
From daring of a madman, or a drunkard,

---

[1] *Follow* humours.] The variation in the text was made in 1750.
The whole converſation is on the ſubject of *report*, for which
rumour is ſynonimous, and conſequently genuine.

From

From herefy, ill wine, and ftumbling poft-horfe,
So would I pray each morning, and each night,
(And if I faid each hour, I fhould not lie)
To be deliver'd of all thefe in one,
The woman thou haft named.

 Pifo. Thou haft fet her in a pretty Litany.

Enter Julio, Angelo, and Father.

 Ang. Pray take my counfel.

 Jul. When I am myfelf,
I'll hear you any way; love me tho' thus,
As thou art honeft, which I dare not be,
Left I defpife myfelf. Farewell!   [*Exit.*

 Pifo. Do you hear, my friend? Sir! are you not a
   fetter
For the fair widow here, of famous memory?

 Father. Ha! am I taken for a bawd? Oh, God!
To mine own child too? Mifery, I thank thee,
That keep'ft me from their knowledge.—Sir, believe me,
I underftand you not.

 Lod. You love plain-dealing:
Are you not parcel bawd? Confefs your function;
It may be, we would ufe it.

 Father. Were fhe worfe,
(As I fear ftrangely fhe is ill enough)
I would not hear this tamely.

 Pifo. Here's a fhilling,
To ftrike good luck withal.

 Father. Here's a fword, Sir,
To ftrike a knave withal: Thou lieft, and bafely,
Be what thou wilt!

 Ang. Why, how now, gentlemen?

 Father. You are many: I fhall meet you, Sir, again,
And make you underftand, you've wrong'd a woman
Compar'd with whom thy mother was a finner.
Farewell!   [*Exit.*

 Pifo. He has amaz'd me.

 Ang. With a blow?
By'r lady, 'twas a found one! Are ye good

A 4   At

At taking knocks? I fhall know ye hereafter.
You were to blame to tempt a man fo far,
Before you knew him certain. H'has not hurt ye?
 Pifo. No, I think.
 Lod. We were to blame indeed to go fo far;
For men may be miftaken: If h'had fwing'd us,
H'had ferv'd us right. Befhrew my heart, I think,
We've done the gentlewoman as much wrong too;
For hang me if I know her,
In my particular.
 Pifo. Nor I. This 'tis to credit
Mens' idle tongues: I warrant they have faid
As much by our two mothers.
 Lod. Like enough.
 Ang. I fee a beating now and then does more
Move and ftir up a man's contrition
Than a fharp fermon; here *probatum eft.*

Enter Frederick and Servant.

 Serv. What fhall I tell your fifter?
 Fred. Tell her this;
'Till fhe be better converfation'd,
And leave her walking by herfelf, and whining
To her old melancholy lute, I'll keep
As far from her as th' gallows.   [*Exit Servant.*
 Ang. Who's that? Frederick?
 Fred. Yes, marry is't. Oh, Angelo, how doft thou?
 Ang. Save you, Sir! How does my miftrefs?
 Fred. She is in love, I think; but not with you,
I can affure you. Saw you Fabritio?
 Ang. Is he come over?
 Fred. Yes, a week ago:
Shall we dine?
 Ang. I cannot.
 Fred. Prithee do.
 Ang. Believe me, I have bufinefs.
 Fred. Have you too, gentlemen?
 Pifo. No, Sir.
 Fred. Why then, let's dine together.

                                                  Lod.

Lod. With all my heart.

Fred. Go then. Farewell, good Angelo.
Commend me to your friend.

Ang. I will.   [*Exeunt.*

SCENE II.

Enter Frank and Clora.

Clora. Do not diſſemble, Frank; mine eyes are
          quicker
Than ſuch obſervers, that do ground their faith
Upon one ſmile or tear : You are much alter'd,
And are as empty of thoſe excellencies
That were companions to you, (I mean mirth,
And free diſpoſure of your blood and ſpirit)
As you were born a mourner.

Frank. How, I prithee?
For I perceive no ſuch change in myſelf.

Clora. Come, come, this is not wiſe, nor provident,
To halt before a cripple. If you love,
Be liberal to your friend, and let her know it :
I ſee the way you run, and know how tedious
'Twill prove without a true companion.

Frank. Sure thou wouldſt have me love.

Clora. Yes, marry would I ;
I ſhould not pleaſe you elſe.

Frank. And who, for God's ſake?
For I aſſure myſelf, I know not yet :
And prithee, Clora, ſince thou'lt have it ſo
That I muſt love, and do I know not what,
Let him be held a pretty handſome fellow,
And young ; and if he be a little valiant,
'Twill be the better ; and a little wiſe,
And, faith, a little honeſt.

Clora. Well, I'll ſound you yet, for all your craft.

Frank. Heigh-ho! I'll love no more.

Clora. Than one ; and him
You ſhall love Frank.

Frank. Which him? Thou art ſo wiſe,

People

People will take thee fhortly for a witch.
But, prithee tell me, Clora, if I were
So mad as thou wouldſt make me, what kind of man
Wouldſt thou imagine him?

   Clora. Faith, ſome pretty fellow,
With a clean ſtrength, that cracks a cudgel well,
And dances at a wake, and plays at nine-holes.

   Frank. Oh, God!
What pretty commendations thou haſt giv'n him!
Faith, if I were in love (as, I thank God,
I do not think I am) this ſhort epiſtle
Before my love, would make me burn the legend.

   Clora. You are too wild: I mean, ſome gentleman.

   Frank. So do not I, till I can know 'em wiſer.
Some gentleman? No, Clora, till ſome gentleman
Keep ſome land, and fewer whores, believe me,
I'll keep no love for him: I do not long
To go a-foot yet, and ſolicit cauſes.

   Clora. What think you then of an adventurer?
I mean ſome wealthy merchant.

   Frank. Let him venture
In ſome decay'd crare of his own²: He ſhall not
Rig me out, that's the ſhort on't. Out upon't!
What young thing of my years would endure

---

   ² *In ſome decayed* crare *of his own.*] Thus rightly reads the copy
of 1647. The editor of 1679 has corrupted the paſſage, though at
the ſame time I own he has well explain'd it; for thus he reads,
        In ſome decayed crare *or* carrack:
Crare here ſignifies juſt what *carrack* does, being the name of a
trading veſſel then, though I believe at this time 'tis entirely difuſed.
   Mr. Warburton I hope will pardon me, if after him I endeavour
to correct a paſſage in Cymbeline from this line in our authors, act iv.
ſcene ii.
       Bel. *Oh, melancholy!*
         Who ever yet could ——*find*
         The ooze to ſhew what coaſt thy ſluggiſh care
         Might eaſieſt harbour in.
This reading our great critic judiciouſly rejects, and gives the paſſage
thus,
         ——— *thy ſluggiſh* carrack,
Which certainly continues and compleats the metaphor; but we may
yet come much nearer the traces of the letters, by reading thus,
         — *what*

To have her hufband in another country,
Within a month after fhe is married,
Chopping for rotten raifins, and lie pining
At home, under the mercy of his foreman ? No;
Tho' they be wealthy, and indifferent wife,
I do not fee that I am bound to love 'em.

   Clora. I fee you are hard to pleafe ; yet I will pleafe
      you.

   Frank. Faith, not fo hard neither, if confider'd
What woman may deferve as fhe is worthy.
But why do we beftow our time fo idly ?
Prithee, let's entertain fome other talk ;
This is as fickly to me as faint weather.

   Clora. Now I believe I fhall content you, Frank:
What think you of a courtier?

   Frank. Faith, fo ill,
That, if I fhould be full, and fpeak but truth,
'Twould fhew as if I wanted charity.
Prithee, good wench, let me not rail upon 'em ;
Yet I have an excellent ftomach, and muft do it :
I have no mercy of thefe infidels,
Since I am put in mind on't ; good, bear with me.

   Clora. Can no man fit you ? I will find him out.

   Frank. This fummer-fruit, that you call Courtier,
While you continue cold and frofty to him,
Hangs faft, and may be found [3] ; but when you fling
Too full a heat of your affections
Upon his root, and make him ripe too foon,
You'll find him rotten in the handling :
His oaths and affections are all one
With his apparel, things to fet him off ;

   —— *what coaft thy fluggifh* crare
    Might eafieft harbour in.   *Sympfon.*
   Mr. Sympfon is wrong in his affertion about the lection of the
fecond folio, for that exhibits
     Some decayed WARE, *or carrack,* &c.
Common fenfe and the firft folio both authorife *crare.*——Mr. Steevens
adopts Sympfon's variation in Cymbeline ; and adds, ' A *crare*, fays
' the author of *The Revifal*, is a fmall trading veffel, called in the
' Latin of the middle ages *crayera*.'

   [3] *Hangs faft and may be* found.] Corrected in 1750.

                             He

He has as many miftreffes as faiths,
And all Apocrypha⁴; his true belief
Is only in a private furgeon :
And, for my fingle felf, I'd fooner venture
A new converfion of the Indies⁵,
Than to make courtiers able men, or honeft.

 Clora. I do believe you love no courtier;
And, by my troth, to guefs you into love
With any I can think of, is beyond
Either your will, or my imagination :
And yet I'm fure you're caught, and I will know him.
There's none left now worthy the thinking of,
Unlefs it be a foldier; and, I'm fure,
I would ever blefs myfelf from fuch a fellow.

 Frank. Why, prithee?

 Clora. Out upon 'em, firelocks!
They're nothing in the world but buff and fcarlet,
Tough unhewn pieces, to hack fwords upon;
I had as lieve be courted by a cannon,
As one of thofe.

 Frank. Thou art too malicious;
Upon my faith, methinks they're worthy men.

 Clora. Say you fo? I'll pull you on a little further.—
What worth can be in thofe men, whofe profeffion
Is nothing in the world but drink and *damn me?*
Out of whofe violence they are poffefs'd
With legions of unwholefome whores and quarrels?
I am of that opinion, and will die in't,
There is no underftanding, nor can be,
In a fous'd foldier.

 Frank. Now 'tis ignorance,
I eafily perceive, that thus provokes thee,

---

 4 *All Apocrypha.*] Mr. Sympfon (and he acknowledges the variation!) reads, *apocryphal.* But *apocrypha* conveys the fame fenfe as
the adjective, and is rather a more elegant reading.

 5 ———— *I'd fooner* VENTURE
A new CONVERSION *of the* Indies.] Mr. Sympfon, thinking
that to *venture* a *converfion* is not a clear expreffion, propofes reading
Indians for *Indies.* The text certainly is beft.

And not the love of truth. I'll lay my life,
If God had made thee man, th'hadst been a coward.

Clora. If to be valiant, be to be a foldier,
I'll tell you true, I had rather be a coward;
I am fure with lefs fin.

Frank. This herefy
Muft be look'd-to in time; for if it fpread,
'Twill grow too peftilent. Were I a fcholar,
I would fo hamper thee for thy opinion,
That, ere I left, I would write thee out of credit
With all the world, and make thee not believ'd
Ev'n in indifferent things; that I would leave thee
A reprobate, out of the ftate of honour.
By all good things, thou haft flung afperfions
So like a fool (for I am angry with thee)
Upon a fort of men, that, let me tell thee,
Thy mother's mother would have been a faint
Had fhe conceiv'd a foldier! They are people
(I may commend 'em, while I fpeak but truth)
Of all the old world, only left to keep
Man as he was, valiant and virtuous.
They are the model of thofe men, whofe honours
We heave our hands at when we hear recited.

Clora. They are,
And I have all I fought for: 'Tis a foldier
You love (hide it no longer); you've betray'd your-
          felf!
Come, I have found your way of commendations,
And what I faid was but to pull it from you.

Frank. 'Twas pretty! Are you grown fo cunning,
          Clora?
I grant I love a foldier; but what foldier
Will be a new tafk to you? But all this,
I do imagine, was but laid to draw me
Out of my melancholy.

Clora. I will have the man,
Ere I forfake you.

Frank. I muft to my chamber.

Clora. May not I go along?

Frank.

Frank. Yes; but, good wench,
Move me no more with thefe fond queftions;
They work like rhubarb with me.

Clora. Well, I will not. [*Exeunt.*

SCENE III.

Enter Lelia and her Waiting-Woman.

Lelia. How now! who was that you ftay'd to fpeak
    withal?

Woman. The old man, forfooth.

Lelia. What old man?

Woman. The poor old man,
That ufes to come hither; he that you call father.

Lelia. Have you difpatch'd him?

Woman. No; he would fain fpeak with you.

Lelia. Wilt thou ne'er learn more manners, than
    to draw in
Such needy rafcals to difquiet me?
Go, anfwer him, I will not be at leifure.

Woman. He will needs fpeak with you; and, good
    old man!
He weeps fo, that, by my troth, I have not
The heart to deny him.   Pray let him fpeak with you.

Lelia. Lord!
How tender-ftomach'd you are grown of late!
You are not in love with him, are you? If you be,
Strike up the match; you fhall have three pounds
And a pair of blankets! Will you go anfwer him?

Woman. Pray let him fpeak with you; he'll not away
    elfe.

Lelia. Well, let him in then, if there be no remedy:
I thank God, I am able to abufe him;   [*Exit Woman.*
I fhall ne'er come clear elfe of him.

Re-enter Woman, with Father.

Now, Sir; what is your bufinefs? Pray be fhort;
For I have other matters, of more moment,

To

To call me from you.

Father. If you but look upon me like a daughter,
And keep that love about you that makes good
A father's hope, you'll quickly find my business,
And what I would say to you, and, before
I ask, will be a giver: Say that sleep,
(I mean that love) or be but numb'd within you,
The nature of my want is such a searcher,
And of so mighty power, that, where he finds
This dead forgetfulness, it works so strongly,
That if the least heat of a child's affection
Remain unperish'd, like another nature,
It makes all new again! Pray do not scorn me,
Nor seem to make yourself a greater business
Than my relieving.

Lelia. If you were not old,
I should laugh at you! What a vengeance ails you,
To be so childish to imagine me
A founder of old fellows [6]?—Make him drink, wench;
And if there be any cold meat in the buttery,
Give him some broken bread, and that, and rid him.

Father. Is this a child's love? or a recompense
Fit for a father's care? Oh, Lelia,
Had I been thus unkind, thou hadst not been;
Or, like me, miserable! But 'tis impossible
Nature should die so utterly within thee,
And lose her promises: Thou art one of those
She set her stamp more excellently on,
Than common people, as foretelling thee
A general example of her goodness.
Or, say she could lie, yet Religion
(For love to parents is religious)
Would lead thee right again: Look well upon me;
I am the root that gave thee nourishment,
And made thee spring fair; do not let me perish,

---

[6] *A* founder *of old fellows?*] Mr. Sympson proposes reading *fondler* for *founder*; but the latter word is certainly right, and very good sense, alluding to charitable foundations. See note 67 on Wit without Money.

Now I am old and fapless.

   Lelia. As I live,
I like you far worfe now you grow thus holy!
I grant you are my father; am I therefore
Bound to confume myfelf, and be a beggar
Still jn relieving you? I do not feel
Any fuch mad compaffion yet within me.

   Father. I gave up all my ftate, to make your's thus!

   Lelia. 'Twas as you ought to do; and now you cry
      for't,
As children do for babies, back again.

   Father. How wouldft thou have me live?

   Lelia. I would not have you;
Nor know no reafon fathers fhould defire
To live, and be a trouble, when their children [7]
Are able to inherit; let them die;
'Tis fit, and look'd for, that they fhould do fo.

   Father. Is this your comfort?

   Lelia. All that I feel yet.

   Father. I will not curfe thee!

   Lelia. If you do, I care not.

   Father. Pray you give me leave to weep.

   Lelia. Why, pray take leave,
If it be for your eafe.

   Father. Thy mother died
(Sweet peace be with her!) in a happy time.

   Lelia. She did, Sir, as fhe ought to do; 'would you
Would take the pains to follow! What fhould you,
Or any old man do, wearing away
In this world with difeafes, and defire
Only to live to make their children fcourge-fticks,
And hoard up mill-money? Methinks, a marble
Lies quieter upon an old man's head
Than a cold fit o' th' palfy.

   Father. Oh, good God!
To what an impudence, thou wretched woman,
Haft thou begot thyfelf again! Well, Juftice

------

7 *When children*] I have inferted *their* for the fake both of the
meafure and the fenfe.   *Symbfon.*

                                 Will

Will punifh difobedience.

Lelia. You miftake, Sir;
'Twill punifh beggars. Fy for fhame! go work,
Or ferve; you're grave enough to be a porter
In fome good man of worfhip's houfe, and give
Sententious anfwers to the comers-in;
(A pretty place!) or be of fome good concert,
You had a pleafant touch o' th' cittern once,
If idlenefs have not bereft you of it:
Be any thing but old and beggarly,
Two fins that ever do out-grow compaffion.
If I might fee you offer at a courfe
That were a likely one, and fhew'd fome profit,
I would not ftick for ten groats, or a noble.

Father. Did I beget this woman?

Lelia. Nay, I know not;
And, till I know, I will not thank you for't:
However, he that got me had the pleafure,
And that, methinks, is a reward fufficient.

Father. I am fo ftrangely ftrucken with amazement,
I know not where I am, nor what I am.

Lelia. You'd beft take frefh air fomewhere elfe;
'twill bring you
Out of your trance the fooner.

Father. Is all this
As you mean, Lelia?

Lelia. Yes, believe me, is it;
For yet I cannot think you are fo foolifh,
As to imagine you are young enough
To be my heir, or I fo old to make
A nurfe at thefe years for you, and attend
While you fup up my ftate in penny pots
Of malmfey. When I'm excellent at caudles,
And cullices, and have enough fpare gold
To boil away, you fhall be welcome to me;
'Till when, I'd have you be as merry, Sir,
As you can make yourfelf with that you have,
And leave to trouble me with thefe relations,
Of what you have been to me, or you are;

For as I hear them, so I lose them. This,
For aught I know yet, is my resolution.

Father. Well, God be with thee! for I fear thy end
Will be a strange example. [*Exit.*

Lelia. Fare you well, Sir!
Now would some poor tender-hearted fool have wept,
Relented, and have been undone: Such children
(I thank my understanding) I hate truly;
For, by my troth, I had rather see their tears
Than feel their pities! My desires and ends
Are all the kindred that I have, and friends.

Enter Woman.

Is he departed?
Woman. Yes; but here's another.
Lelia. Not of his tribe, I hope: Bring me no more,
I would wish you, such as he is. If thou seest
They look like men of worth, and state, and carry
Ballast of both sides, like tall gentlemen,
Admit 'em; but no snakes to poison us
With poverty. Wench, you must learn a wise rule;
Look not upon the youths of men, and making,
How they descend in blood, nor let their tongues,
(Tho' they strike suddenly, and sweet as music)
Corrupt thy fancy: See, and say them fair too,
But ever keep thyself without their distance,
Unless the love thou swallow'st be a pill
Gilded, to hide the bitterness it brings;
Then fall on without fear, wench; yet so wisely
That one encounter cloy him not; nor promise
His love hath made thee more his, than his monies:
Learn this, and thrive; then let thine honour ever
(For that's the last rule) be so stood upon,
That men may fairly see
'Tis want of means, not virtue, makes thee fall;
And if you weep, 'twill be a great deal better,
And draw on more compassion, which includes
A greater tenderness of love and bounty:
This is enough at once; digest it well.

Go,

Go, let him in, wench, if he promife profit,
Not elfe.—Oh, you are welcome, my fair fervant!

Enter Julio.

Upon my troth, I have been longing for you.
Woman. This, by her rule, fhould be a liberal man:
I fee, the beft on's may learn ev'ry day.   [*Exit.*
  Lelia. There's none come with you?
  Julio. No.
  Lelia. You do the wifer;
For fome that have been here (I name no man),
Out of their malice, more than truth, have done me
Some few ill offices.
  Julio. How, fweet?
  Lelia. Nay, nothing;
Only have talk'd a little wildly of me,
As their unruly youth directed 'em;
Which, tho' they bite me not, I would have wifh'd
Had lit upon fome other that deferv'd 'em.
  Julio. Tho' fhe deferve this of the loofeft tongue,
(Which makes my fin the more) I muft not fee it;
Such is my mifery [*afide*].—I would I knew him!
  Lelia. No, no; let him go;
He is not worth your anger.—I muft chide you
For being fuch a ftranger to your miftrefs;
Why would you be fo, fervant?
  Julio. I fhould chide,
If chiding would work any thing upon you,
For being fuch a ftranger to your fervant;
I mean, to his defires: When, my dear miftrefs,
Shall I be made a happy man?
  Lelia. Fy, fervant!
What do you mean? Unhand me; or, by Heav'n,
I fhall be very angry! This is rudenefs.
  Julio. 'Twas but a kifs or two, that thus offends you.
  Lelia. 'Twas more, I think, than you have warrant
      for.
  Julio. I'm forry I deferv'd no more.
  Lelia. You may;

But

But not this rough way, fervant : We are tender,
And ought in all to be refpected fo.
If I had been your horfe, or whore, you might
Back me with this intemperance ! I thought
You had lov'd as worthy men, whofe fair affections
Seek pleafures warranted, not pull'd by violence.
Do fo no more.

Julio. I hope you are not angry ?

Lelia. I fhould be with another man, I'm fure,
That durft appear but half thus violent.

Julio. I did not mean to ravifh you.

Lelia. You could not.

Julio. You are fo willing ?

Lelia. How !

Julio. Methinks this fhadow,
If you had fo much fhame as fits a woman,
(At leaft, of your way, miftrefs) long ere this
Had been laid off to me that underftand you.

Lelia. That underftand me ? Sir, you underftand,
Nor fhall, no more of me than Modefty
Will, without fear, deliver to a ftranger :
You underftand I'm honeft ; elfe, I tell you,
(Tho' you were better far than Julio)
You and your underftanding are two fools.
But, were we faints, thus we are ftill rewarded :
I fee that woman had a pretty catch on't,
That had made you the mafter of a kindnefs,
She durft not anfwer openly. Oh, me !
How eafily we women may be cozen'd !
I took this Julio, as I have a faith,
(This young diffembler, with the fober vizard)
For the moft modeft-temper'd gentleman,
The cooleft, quieteft, and beft companion,
For fuch an one I could have wifh'd a woman——

Julio. You've wifh'd me ill enough o' confcience ;
Make me no worfe, for fhame ! I fee, the more
I work by way of fervice to obtain you,
You work the more upon me. Tell me truly
(While I am able to believe a woman,

For,

For, if you use me thus, that faith will perish)
What is your end? and whither you will pull me?
Tell me; but tell me that I may not start at,
And have a cause to curse you.

Lelia. Bless me, goodness!
To curse me, did you say, Sir? Let it be
For too much loving you then; such a curse
Kill me withal, and I shall be a martyr.
You've found a new way to reward my doting,
And, I confess, a fit one for my folly;
For you yourself, if you have good within you,
And dare be master of it, know how dearly
This heart hath held you ever. Oh, good God,
That I had never seen that false man's eyes,
That dares reward me thus with fears [s] and curses!
Nor never heard the sweetness of that tongue,
That will, when this is known, yet cozen women!
Curse me, good Julio, curse me bitterly;
(I do deserve it for my confidence)
And I beseech thee, if thou hast a goodness
Of power yet in thee to confirm thy wishes,
Curse me to earth! for what should I do here,
Like a decaying flower, still withering
Under his bitter words, whose kindly heat
Should give my poor heart life? No; curse me, Julio!
Thou canst not do me such a benefit
As that, and well done, that the Heav'ns may hear it.

Julio. Oh, fair tears! were you but as chaste as subtle,
Like bones of saints, you would work miracles.
What were these women to a man that knew not
The thousand, thousand ways of their deceiving?
What riches had he found? Oh, he would think
Himself still dreaming of a blessedness,
That, like continual spring, should flourish ever:
For if she were as good as she is seeming,
Or, like an eagle, could renew her virtues,
Nature had made another world of sweetness.—
Be not so griev'd, sweet mistress; what I said,

---

[s] *Fears.*] i. e. Actions that *shock*, or *terrify* me.

You

You do, or fhould know, was but paffion:
Pray wipe your eyes, and kifs me. Take thefe trifles,
And wear them for me, which are only rich
When you will put them on. Indeed, I love you:
Befhrew my fick heart, if I grieve not for you!

Lelia. Will you diffemble ftill? I am a fool,
And you may eafily rule me. If you flatter,
The fin will be your own.

Julio. You know I do not.

Lelia. And fhall I be fo childifh once again,
After my late experience of your fpite,
To credit you? You do not know how deep
(Or, if you did, you would be kinder to me)
This bitternefs of yours has ftruck my heart.

Julio. I pray, no more.

Lelia. Thus you would do, I warrant,
If I were married to you.

Julio. Married to me?
Is that your end?

Lelia. Yes; is not that the beft end,
And, as all hold, the nobleft way of love?
Why do you look fo ftrange, Sir? Do not you
Defire it fhould be fo?

Julio. Stay!

Lelia. Anfwer me.

Julio. Farewell! [*Exit.*

Lelia. Ay! are you there? are all thefe tears loft then?
Am I fo overtaken by a fool,
In my beft days and tricks? My wife fellow,
I'll make you fmart for't, as I am a woman!
And, if thou be'ft not timber, yet I'll warm thee.
And is he gone?

Enter Woman.

Woman. Yes.

Lelia. He's not fo lightly ftruck,
To be recover'd with a bafe repentance;
I fhould be forry then. Fortune, I prithee
Give me this man but once more in my arms,
And, if I lofe him, women have no charms! [*Exeunt.*

A C T

Enter Jacomo and Fabritio.

Jac. SIGNIOR, what think you of this sound of
wars?

Fab. As only of a sound: They that intend
To do are like deep waters, that run quietly,
Leaving no trace[9] of what they were behind 'em.
This rumour is too common, and too loud,
To carry truth.

Jac. Shall we ne'er live to see
Men look like men again, upon a march?
This cold dull rusty peace makes us appear
Like empty pictures, only the faint shadows
Of what we should be. 'Would to God my mother
Had given but half her will to my begetting,
And made me woman, to sit still and sing,
Or be sick when I list, or any thing
That is too idle for a man to think of!
Would I had been a whore! 't had been a course
Certain, and (of my conscience) of more gain
Than two commands, as I would handle it.
'Faith, I could wish I had been any thing,
(Rather than what I am, a soldier)
A carrier, or a cobler, when I knew
What 'twas to wear a sword first! for their trades
Are, and shall be, a constant way of life,
While men send cheeses up, or wear out buskins.

Fab. Thou art a little too impatient,
And mak'st thy anger a far more vexation

---

[9] *Leaving no* face.] Mr. Seward substitutes *noise* for *face;* as the
latter word does not ' agree, says he, with the former or subsequent
' metaphors.' Mr. Sympson thinks ' that neither *face* or *noise* are
' at all proper in this place.' We think *trace* a much better word
than either of the others, if not the original.

Than

Than the not having wars. I am a foldier,
Which is my whole inheritance, yet I,
Tho' I could wifh a breach with all the world,
If not difhonourable, I am not fo malicious
To curfe the fair peace of my mother-country.
But thou want'ft money, and the firft fupply
Will bury thefe thoughts in thee.

   Jac. 'Pox o' peace!
It fills the kingdom full of holidays,
And only feeds the wants of whores and pipers,
And makes the idle drunken rogues get fpinfters.
'Tis true, I may want money, and no little,
And almoft cloaths too; of which if I'd both
In full abundance, yet againft all peace
(That brings up mifchiefs thicker than a fhower)
I would fpeak louder than a lawyer.
By Heav'n, it is the furfeit of all youth,
That makes the toughnefs and the ftrength of nations
Melt into women; it is an eafe that
Broods thieves and baftards only.

   Fab. This is more
(Tho' it be true) than we ought to lay open,
And feafons only of an indifcretion.
Believe me, Captain, fuch diftemper'd fpirits,
Once out of motion, tho' they be proof-valiant,
If they appear thus violent and fiery,
Breed but their own difgraces, and are nearer
Doubt and fufpect in princes, than rewards.

   Jac. 'Tis well they can be near 'em any way.
But call you thofe true fpirits ill-affected,
That, whilft the wars were, ferv'd like walls and ribs
To girdle in the kingdom, and now, fall'n
Thro' a faint peace into affliction,
Speak but their miferies? Come, come, Fabritio,
You may pretend what patience you pleafe,
And feem to yoke your wants like paffions [10];

---

   [10] *To yoke your wants* like *paffions.*] Mr. Seward, confidering
want as ' one of our paffions,' objects to this reading, and propofes
to fubftitute, *wants* AND *paffions.* Mr. Sympfon would read,

But, while I know thou art a foldier,
And a deferver, and no other harveft
But what thy fword reaps for thee to come in,
You fhall be pleas'd to give me leave to tell you,
You wifh a devil of this mufty peace:
To which prayer, as one that's bound in confcience,
And all " that love our trade, I cry, Amen!

Fab. Prithee no more; we fhall live well enough:
There's ways enough befides the wars, to men
That are not logs, and lie ftill for the hands
Of others to remove 'em.

Jac. You may thrive, Sir;
Thou'rt young and handfome yet, and well enough
To pleafe a widow; thou canft fing, and tell
Thefe foolifh love-tales, and indite a little,
And, if need be, compile a pretty matter,
And dedicate it to the Honourable;
Which may awaken his compaffion,
To make you clerk o' th' kitchen, and at length
Come to be married to my lady's woman,
After fhe's crack'd i' th' ring ".

Fab. 'Tis very well, Sir.

Jac. But what doft thou think fhalt become of me,
With all my imperfections? Let me die,
If I think I fhall ever reach above
A forlorn tapfter, or fome frothy fellow,
That ftinks of ftale beer!

------ *to* CLOAK *your wants like paffions.*
To yoke your wants like paffions may, for aught we fee, be the
right reading; and the whole paffage fignifies, that ' Fabritio might
' indeed pretend to patience, and endeavour to curb his neceffities
' and his appetites, yet he was in reality an enemy to peace.'

" And *all that love,* &c.] Seward reads, WITH *all,* &c. and fays,
' the old text is fcarcely grammar. The grammar is not more
licentious than that of many other paffages, and the meaning is
obvious.

" *After fhe's crack'd i' th' ring.*] This phrafe occurs in Hamlet,
act ii. fcene ii. ' Pray God your voice, like a piece of uncurrent
' gold, *be not crack'd within the ring.*' And again, as Mr. Steevens
obferves, in Ben Jonfon's Magnetic Lady; ' Light gold, and crack'd
' within the ring.' See alfo vol. ii. p. 297, of this Work.   R.

Fab.

Fab. Captain Jacomo,
Why fhould you think fo hardly of your virtues?

Jac. What virtues? By this light, I have no virtue
But down-right buffeting! What can my face,
(That is no better than a ragged map now,
Of where I've march'd and travell'd) profit me?
Unlefs it be for ladies to abufe,
And fay 'twas fpoil'd for want of a *bongrace*
When I was young, and now 'twill make a true
Prognoftication of what man muft be?
Tell me of a fellow that can mend nofes? and complain,
So tall a foldier fhould want teeth to his ftomach?
And how it was great pity, that it was,
That he that made my body was fo bufied
He could not ftay to make my legs too, but was driv'n
To clap a pair of cat-fticks to my knees,
For which I am indebted to two fchool-boys?
This muft follow neceffary.

Fab. There's no fuch matter.

Jac. Then for my morals, and thofe hidden pieces
That art beftows upon me, they are fuch,
That, when they come to light, I'm fure will fhame me;
For I can neither write, nor read, nor fpeak,
That any man fhall hope to profit by me;
And for my languages, they are fo many,
That, put them all together, they will fcarce
Serve to beg fingle beer in.   The plain truth is,
I love a foldier, and can lead him on,
And if he fight well, I dare make him drunk:
This is my virtue, and if this will do,
I'll fcramble yet amongft 'em.

Fab. 'Tis your way
To be thus pleafant ftill; but fear not, man,
For tho' the wars fail, we fhall fcrew ourfelves
Into fome courfe of life yet.

Jac. Good Fabritio,
Have a quick eye upon me, for I fear
This peace will make me fomething that I love not;
For, by my troth, tho' I am plain and dudgeon,

I would

I would not be an afs; and to fell parcels,
I can as foon be hang'd.   Prithee beſtow me,
And ſpeak ſome little good, tho' I deſerve not.

Enter Father.

Fab. Come, we'll confider more.   Stay ! this
Should be another windfall of the wars.

Jac. He looks indeed like an old tatter'd colours,
That every wind would borrow from the ſtaff :
Theſe are the hopes we have for all our hurts.
They have not caſt his tongue too ?

Father. They that ſay
Hope never leaves a wretched man that ſeeks her,
I think are either patient fools, or liars ;
I'm ſure I find it ſo ! for I am maſter'd
With ſuch a miſery and grief together,
That that ſtay'd anchor men lay hold upon
In all their needs, is to me lead that bows,
Or breaks, with every ſtrong ſea of my ſorrows.
I could now queſtion Heaven (were it well
To look into their juſtice) why thoſe faults,
Thoſe heavy ſins others provoke 'em with,
Should be rewarded on the heads of us
That hold the leaſt alliance to their vices :
But this would be too curious ; for I ſee
Our ſuffering, not diſputing, is the end
Reveal'd to us of all theſe miſeries.

Jac. Twenty ſuch holy hermits in a camp
Would make 'em all Carthuſians : I'll be hang'd
If he know what a whore is, or a health,
Or have a nature liable to learn,
Or ſo much honeſt nurture to be drunk.
I do not think he has the ſpleen to ſwear
A greater oath than ſempſters utter ſocks with [13].
Spur him a queſtion.

---

[13] UTTER *ſocks.*] i. e. *Sell* them. So in Shakeſpeare's Romeo,
    ' Such mortal drugs I have, but Mantua's law
    ' Is death to any he that *utters* them.'
Every *ſale,* which tends to render things common, is metaphorically
confidered as a kind of publication.

Father.

Father. They are ftrangers both
To me, as I to them, I hope. I would not have
Me and my fhame together known by any:
I'll rather lie myfelf unto another.

Fab. I need not afk you, Sir, your country;
I hear you fpeak this tongue: Pray what more are you?
Or have you been? if it be not offenfive
To urge you fo far. Mifery in your years
Gives every thing a tongue to queftion it.

Father. Sir, tho' I could be pleas'd to make my ills
Only mine own, for grieving other men,
Yet, to fo fair and courteous a demander,
That promifes compaffion, at worft pity[13],
I will relate a little of my ftory.
I am a gentleman, however thus
Poor and unhappy; which, believe me, Sir,
Was not born with me; for I well have tried
Both the extremes of fortune, and have found
Both dangerous. My younger years provok'd me,
(Feeling in what an eafe I flept at home,
Which to all ftirring fpirits is a ficknefs)
To fee far countries, and obferve their cuftoms:
I did fo, and I travell'd till that courfe
Stor'd me with language, and fome few flight manners,
Scarce worth my money; when an itch poffefs'd me
Of making arms my active end of travel.

· *Fab.* But did you fo?

  Father. I did; and twenty winters
· I wore the Chriftian caufe upon my fword,
Againft his enemies[14]. At Buda fiege,
Full many a cold night have I lodg'd in armour,
When all was frozen in me but mine honour;
And many a day, when both the fun and cannon

---

[13]. *That promifes* compaffion, *at worft* pity.] The Poets feem to
ufe *compaffion* in the fenfe of *relief* added to pity; *pity* as fimple
commiferation.

[14] *Againft* his *enemies.*] Mr. Seward would have us read *its* for
his, as neceffary to the grammar of the paffage: I fee no reafon for
this, becaufe it is ufual in the Saxon writers, and thofe who fucceeded
'em; Spenfer particularly abounds in it; our Authors too, as the learned
reader will obferve, have it more than once in their plays, and even
Milton himfelf has approv'd the practice.   *Sympfon.*

Strove

Strove who should most destroy us, have I stood
Mail'd up in steel, when my tough sinews shrunk,
And this parch'd body ready to consume
As soon to ashes, as the pike I bore.
Want has been to me as another nature;
Which makes me with this patience still profess it.
And if a soldier may, without vainglory,
Tell what h'has done, believe me, gentlemen,
I could turn over annals of my dangers!
With this poor weakness have I man'd a breach,
And made it firm with so much blood, that all
I had to bring me off alive was anger.
Thrice was I made a slave, and thrice redeem'd
At price of all I had; the miseries
Of which times, if I had a heart to tell,
Would make ye weep like children; but I'll spare ye.
   Jac. Fabritio, we two have been soldiers
Above these fourteen years, yet, o' my conscience,
All we have seen, compar'd to his experience,
Has been but cudgel-play, or cock-fighting [15]!
By all the faith I have in arms, I reverence
The very poverty of this brave fellow;
Which were enough itself, and his [16], to strengthen
The weakest town against half Christendom.
I was never so asham'd of service
In all my life before, now I consider
What I have done; and yet the rogues would swear
I was a valiant fellow: I do find
The greatest danger I have brought my life thro',
Now I have heard this worthy, was no more

---

[15] *Or* cock-fighting.] What *cock-fighting* has to do with gentleman of the sword, wou'd perhaps puzzle a grand council of war to
explain. But *mock-fighting*, as I read, carries on the sense of the
authors, and makes it consistent; cudgels being properly to be look'd
upon as no more than the *tela lusoria* of the ancients.   *Sympson.*
  Cock-fighting is much the best reading, and quite in Jacomo's character.

[16] And *his.*] The Editors of 1750 object to this reading, conjecture various others, and at last exhibit as *his.* The line is, to be
sure, rather hard; but as it may be understood, cannot warrantably
be altered.

Than

Than ftealing of a May-pole, or, at worft,
Fighting at fingle billet with a bargeman.

Fab. I do believe him, Jacomo.

Jac. Believe him?
I have no faith within me, if I do not.

Father. I fee they are foldiers,
And, if we may judge by affections,
Brave and deferving men. How they are ftirr'd
But with a mere relation of what may be!
Since I have won belief, and am not known,
Forgive me, Honour! I'll make ufe of thee.

Fab. Sir, 'would I were a man or great or able,
To look with liberal eyes upon your virtue.

Jac. Let's give him all we have, and leave off prating.
Here, foldier; there's even five months' pay; be merry,
And get thee handfome cloaths.

Fab. What mean you, Jacomo?

Jac. You are a fool!
The very ftory's worth a hundred pounds.
Give him more money.

Father. Gentlemen, I know not
How I am able to deferve this blefling;
But if I live to fee fair days again,
Something I'll do in honour of your goodnefs,
That fhall fhew thankfulnefs, if not defert.

Fab. If you pleafe, Sir, till we procure you place,
To eat with us, or wear fuch honeft garments
As our poor means can reach to, you fhall be
A welcome man: To fay more, were to feed you
Only with words. We honour what you've been,
For we are foldiers, tho' not near the worth
You fpake of lately.

Father. I do guefs ye fo;
And knew, unlefs ye were a foldier,
Ye could not find the way to know my wants.

Jac. But methinks all this while, you are too
temperate:
Do you not tell men fometimes of their dullnefs,
When you are grip'd, as now you are, with need?

I do;

I do; and let them know thofe filks they wear,
The war weaves for 'em; and the bread they eat
We fow, and reap again, to feed their hunger.
I tell them boldly, they are mafters of
Nothing but what we fight for; their fair women
Lie playing in their arms, whilft we, like Lares,
Defend their pleafures. I am angry too,
And often rail at thefe forgetful great men
That fuffer us to fue, for what we ought
To have flung on us, ere we afk.

   Father. I have
Too often told my griefs that way, when all
I reap'd was rudenefs of behaviour:
In their opinions, men of war that thrive,
Muft thank 'em when they rail, and wait to live.

   Fab. Come, Sir; I fee your wants need more relieving,
Than looking what they are: Pray go with us.

   Father. I thank you, gentlemen! Since you are
          pleas'd
To do a benefit, I dare not crofs it:
And what my fervice or endeavours may
Stand you in ftead, you fhall command, not pray.

   Jac. So you fhall us.
I'll to the taylor's with you bodily.   [*Exeunt.*

SCENE II.

Enter Frederick, Lodovico, and Pifo.

   Lod. Well, if this be true, I'll believe a woman
When I have nothing elfe to do.

   Pifo. 'Tis certain, if there be a way of truth
In blufhes, fmiles, and commendations;
For, by this light, I've heard her praife yon fellow
In fuch a pitch, as if fh' had ftudied
To crowd the worths of all men into him:
And I imagine thefe are feldom us'd
Without their fpecial ends, and by a maid
Of her defires and youth.

                         Fred.

Fred. It may be so.
She's free, as you, or I am, and may have,
By that prerogative, a liberal choice
In the bestowing of her love.

Lod. Bestowing?
If it be so, she has bestow'd herself
Upon a trim youth! Piso, what do you call him?

Piso. Why, captain Jacomo.

Lod. Oh, captain Jack-boy;
That is the gentleman.

Fred. I think he be
A gentleman at worst.

Lod. So think I too;
'Would he would mend, Sir!

Fred. And a tall one too.

Lod. Yes, of his teeth; for of my faith I think
They're sharper than his sword, and dare do more,
If the *beuffe* meet him fairly [17].

Fred. Very well!

Piso. Now do I wonder what she means to do
When she has married him.

Lod. Why, well enough;
Trail his pike under him, and be a gentlewoman
Of the brave Captain's company.

Fred. Do you hear me?
This woman is my sister, gentlemen.

Lod. I'm glad she's none of mine. But, Frederick,
Thou art not such a fool sure to be angry,
Unless it be with her: We are thy friends, man.

Fred. I think ye are.

Lod. Yes, faith! and do but tell thee
How she will utterly o'erthrow her credit,
If she continue gracing of this pot-gun.

Piso. I think she was bewitch'd, or mad, or blind;
She would ne'er have taken such a scare-crow else
Into protection. O' my life, he looks
Of a more rusty, swarth complexion,

---

[17] *If the beuffe meet him fairly.*] First folio. The two following editions say, *buff.* Seward, *beef.*

Than

Than an old arming doublet!

Lod. I would fend
His face to th' cutlers then, and have it fanguin'd;
'Twill look a great deal fweeter. Then his nofe
I would have fhorter; and my reafon is,
His face will be ill-mounted elfe.

Pifo. For his body,
I will not be my own judge, left I feem
A railer; but let others look upon't,
And if they find it any other thing
Than a trunk-cellar, to fend wines down in,
Or a long walking bottle, I'll be hang'd for't.
His hide (for fure he is a beaft) is ranker
Then the Mufcovy-leather, and grain'd like it;
And, by all likelihoods, he was begotten
Between a ftubborn pair of winter boots;
His body goes with ftraps, he is fo churlifh.

Lod. He's poor and beggarly, befides all this,
And of a nature far uncapable
Of any benefit; for his manners cannot
Shew him a way to thank a man that does one,
He's fo uncivil. You may do a part
Worthy a brother, to perfuade your fifter
From her undoing: If fhe prove fo foolifh
To marry this cait captain, look to find her,
Within a month, where you, or any good man,
Would blufh to know her; felling cheefe and prunes [18],
And retail'd bottle-ale. I grieve to think,
Becaufe I lov'd her, what a march this Captain
Will fet her into.

Fred. You are both, believe me,
Two arrant knaves; and, were it not for taking
So juft an execution from his hands
You have belied thus, I would fwaddle ye [19],
'Till I could draw off both your fkins like fcabbards.

---

[18] *Prunes.*] See note 66 on the Mad Lover.

[19] *Swaddle ye.*] He means *beat.* So Hudibras, b. i. c. i. 23, 24.
  ' Great on the bench, great in the faddle,
  ' That cou'd as well bind o'er as *fwaddle.*' *Sympfon.*

That man that you have wrong'd thus, tho' to me
He be a ftranger, yet I know fo worthy,
However low in fortune, that his worft parts,
The very wearing of his cloaths, would make
Two better gentlemen than you dare be;
For there is virtue in his outward things.

 Lod. Belike you love him then?

 Fred. Yes, marry do I.

 Lod. And will be angry for him?

 Fred. If you talk,
Or pull your face into a ftitch again²⁰,
As I love truth, I fhall be very angry!
Do not I know thee (tho' thou haft fome land,
To fet thee out thus among gentlemen)
To be a prating and vain-glorious afs?
I do not wrong thee now, for I fpeak truth.
Do not I know th' haft been a cudgel'd coward,
That has no cure for fhame but cloth of filver?
And think'ft the wearing of a gaudy fuit
Hides all difgraces?

 Lod. I underftand you not; you hurt not me,
Your anger flies fo wide.

 Pifo. Signior Frederick,
You much miftake this gentleman.

 Fred. No, Sir.

 Pifo. If you would pleafe to be lefs angry,
I'd tell you how——

 Fred. You had better ftudy, Sir,
How to excufe yourfelf, if you be able;
Or I fhall tell you once again——

 Pifo. Not me, Sir;

---

²⁰ *A* ftitch *again.*] 'Tis plain by *ftitch* here we muft underftand *fmile,* but how it is to be made out, perhaps may not be fo eafy to every capacity: I have not altered the text, though I fufpect it is corrupted, and as fuch propofe a conjecture which may ftand or fall according to its worth.
 Or draw *your face into a* fmirk *again.*
Smirk *comes from the A. S.* Smercian, *fubridere,* arridere, *to fmile.*
             Sympfon.
 Stitch *alludes to the face being, in laughter,* contracted, *or in a manner* convulfed.

For, I proteſt, what I have ſaid was only
To make you underſtand your ſiſter's danger.

Lod. He might, if it pleas'd him, conceive it ſo.

Fred. I might, if it pleas'd me, ſtand ſtill and hear
My ſiſter made a May-game, might I not?
And give allowance to your liberal jeſts
Upon his perſon, whoſe leaſt anger would
Conſume a legion of ſuch wretched people,
That have no more to juſtify their actions
But their tongues' ends? that dare lie every way,
As a mill grinds? From this hour, I renounce
All part of fellowſhip that may hereafter
Make me take knowledge of you, but for knaves;
And take heed, as ye love whole ſkins and coxcombs,
How, and to whom, ye prate thus. For this time,
I care not if I ſpare ye: Do not ſhake;
I will not beat ye, tho' ye do deſerve it
Richly.

Lod. This is a ſtrange courſe, Frederick!
But ſure you do not, or you would not, know us.
Beat us?

Piſo. 'Tis ſomewhat low, Sir, to a gentleman.

Fred. I'll ſpeak but few words, but I'll make 'em
      truths:
Get you gone both, and quickly, without murmuring,
Or looking big; and yet, before you go,
I will have this confeſs'd, and ſeriouſly.
That you two are two raſcals.

Lod. How!

Fred. Two raſcals.
Come, ſpeak it from your hearts; or, by this light,
My ſword ſhall fly among ye! Anſwer me,
And to the point, directly.

Piſo. You ſhall have
Your will for this time, ſince we ſee you're grown
So far untemperate: Let it be ſo, Sir,
In your opinion.

Fred. Do not mince the matter,
But ſpeak the words plain. And you, Lodovick,

That

That ſtand ſo tally [21] on your reputation,
You ſhall be he ſhall ſpeak it.

Lod. This is pretty!

Fred. Let me not ſtay upon't!

Lod. Well, we are raſcals;
Yes, Piſo, we are raſcals.

Fred. Get ye gone now!   [*Exeunt Lod. and Piſo.*
Not a word more! you're raſcals!

Enter Fabritio and Jacomo.

Fab. That ſhould be Frederick.

Jac. 'Tis he.   Frederick!

Fred. Who's that?

Jac. A friend, Sir.

Fred. It is ſo, by th' voice.
I've ſought you, gentlemen; and, ſince I've found you
So near our houſe, I'll force ye ſtay a while:
I pray let it be ſo.

Fab. It is too late;
We'll come and dine tomorrow with your ſiſter,
And do our ſervices.

Jac. Who were thoſe with you?

Fab. We met two came from hence.

Fred. Two idle fellows,
That you ſhall beat hereafter; and I'll tell you,
Some fitter time, a cauſe ſufficient for it.

Fab. But, Frederick, tell me truly; do you think
She can affect my friend?

Fred. No certainer [22]
Than when I ſpeak of him, or any other,
She entertains it with as much deſire
As others do their recreations.

Fab. Let not him have this light by any means:

---

[21] *So* tally.] From *tall,* i. e. *brave,* &c.
[22] *No certainer*
   Than when I ſpeak of him, or any other.] This line may eaſily
be miſunderſtood for want of attending to the conſtruction, as well as
one in Jonſon's Sejanus,
   ' Mean time give order that his books be burnt
   ' To th' Ædiles.'   *Sympſon.*

He

He will but think he's mock'd, and so grow angry,
Ev'n to a quarrel, he's so much distrustful
Of all that take occasion to commend him,
Women especially ; for which he shuns
All conversation with 'em, and believes
He can be but a mirth to all their sex.——
Whence is this musick ?

Fred. From my sister's chamber.

Fab. The touch is excellent ; let's be attentive.

Jac. Hark ! are the waits abroad ?

Fab. Be softer, prithee ;
'Tis private musick.

Jac. What a din it makes ?
I'd rather hear a Jew's trump than these lutes ;
They cry like school-boys.

Fab. Prithee, Jacomo !

Jac. Well, I will hear, or sleep, I care not whether.

Enter, at the window, Frank and Clora.

THE SONG.

1. Tell me, dearest, what is love ?
2. 'Tis a lightning from above ;
    'Tis an arrow, 'tis a fire,
    'Tis a boy they call Desire.
Both.   'Tis a grave,
        Gapes to have
Those poor fools that long to prove.

1. Tell me more, are women true ?
2. Yes, some are, and some as you.
    Some are willing, some are strange,
    Since you men first taught to change.
Both.   And till troth
        Be in both,
All shall love, to love anew.

1. Tell me more yet, can they grieve ?
2. Yes, and sicken sore, but live :

C 3   And

And be wife, and delay,
When you men are as wife as they.
Both.   Then I fee,
Faith will be,
Never 'till they both believe.

Frank. Clora! come hither! who are thefe below there?
Clora. Where?
Frank. There.
Clora. Ha! I fhould know their fhapes,
Tho' it be darkifh.   There are both our brothers:
What fhould they make thus late here?
Frank. What's the other?
Clora. What t'other?
Frank. He that lies along there.
Clora. Oh, I fee him,
As if he had a branch of fome great pedigree
Grew out on's belly.
Frank. Yes.
Clora. That fhould be,
If I have any knowledge in proportion——
Fab. They fee us.
Fred. 'Tis no matter.
Fab. What a log's this,
To fleep fuch mufick out?
Fred. No more; let's hear 'em.
Clora. [23] The Captain Jacomo; thofe are his legs,
Upon my confcience.
Frank. By my faith, and neat ones!
Clora. You mean, the boots; I think they're neat
by nature [24].
Frank. As thou art knavifh. 'Would I faw his face!
Clora. 'Twould fcare you in the dark.
Frank. A worfe than that
Has never fcar'd you, Clora, to my knowledge.
Clora. 'Tis true, for I have never feen a worfe;

[23] Clora. *If I have any knowledge in proportion——*] The
repetition of this line feems to be a miftake of the prefs or tranfcriber;
we have therefore omitted it.

[24] Neat *by nature.*] A pun upon NEAT's *leather.*

Nor,

Nor, while I say my prayers heartily,
I hope I shall not.

Frank. Well, I am no tell-tale:
But is it not great pity, tell me, Clora,
That such a brave deserving gentleman
As every one delivers this to be,
Should have no more respect and worth flung on him
By able men? Were I one of these great ones,
Such virtue should not sleep thus.

Clora. Were he greater,
He would sleep more, I think. I'll waken him.

Frank. Away, you fool!

Clora. Is he not dead already,
And they two taking order about his blacks?
Methinks they're very busy.
A fine clean corse he is! I'd have him buried
Ev'n as he lies, cross-leg'd, like one o'th' Templers,
(If his Westphalia gammons will hold crossing)
And on his breast a buckler, with a pike in't [15],
In which I would have some learned cutler
Compile an epitaph; and at his feet
A musquet, with this word [16] upon a label,
(Which from the cock's mouth thus should be
    deliver'd)
‘ I have discharg'd the office of a soldier.’

Frank. Well, if thy father were a soldier,
Thus thou wouldst use him.

Clora. Such a soldier
I would indeed.

Fab. If he hear this, not all
The power of man could keep him from the windows,
'Till they were down, and all the doors broke open.
For God's sake, make her cooler; I dare not venture

---

[15] *Pike* in't.] The pike and sword in funerals are laid upon the
shield, perhaps therefore the original might be *on't*; unless the term
in't be us'd in heraldry.   *Seward.*

In't, we apprehend, means *stuck in it*; and the whole design
makes a ludicrous picture.

[16] *Word* here means *sentence.* So Spenser in his Fairy Queen,
more than once.   *Sympson.*

C 4   To

To bring him elfe: I know he'll go to buffets
Within five words with her, if she holds this spirit.
Let's waken him, and away; we shall hear worse elfe.

Frank. Well, if I be not even with thee, Clora,
Let me be hang'd, for this! I know thou doft it
Only to anger me, and purge thy wit,
Which would break out elfe.

Clora. I have found ye; I'll
Be no more crofs. Bid 'em good night.

Frank. No, no;
They shall not know we've feen 'em. Shut the window.

                   [*Exeunt Frank and Clora.*

Fab. Will you get up, Sir?

Jac. Have you paid the fidlers?

Fab. You are not left to do it. Fy upon thee!
Haft thou forfworn manners?

Jac. Yes; unlefs they
Would let me eat my meat without long graces,
Or drink without a preface to the pledger [27],
Of ' Will it pleafe you?' ' Shall I be fo bold, Sir?'
' Let me remember your good bedfellow!'
And lie, and kifs my hand unto my miftrefs
As often as an ape does for an apple.
Thefe are mere fchifms in foldiers; (where's my friend?)
Thefe are to us as bitter as purgations:
We love that general freedom we are bred to;
Hang thefe faint fooleries! they fmell of peace.
Do they not, friend?

Fab. Faith, Sir, to me they are
As things indifferent; yet I ufe 'em not,
Or, if I did, they would not prick my confcience.

Fred. Come, fhall we go? 'Tis late.

Jac. Yes, any whither:
But no more mufick; it has made me dull.

Fab. Faith, any thing but drinking difturbs thee,
         Jacomo.
We'll ev'n to bed.

---

[27] ———— *to the pledger;*
  Oft will it pleafe, &c.] Corrected in 1750.

                            Jac.

Jac. Content.

Fab. Thou'lt dream of wenches.

Jac. I never think of any, (I thank God)
But when I'm drunk ; and then, 'tis but to caſt
A cheap way how they may be all deſtroy'd,
Like vermin. Let's away ; I'm very ſleepy.

Fab. Ay, thou art ever ſo, or angry. Come. [*Exe.*

ACT III. SCENE I.

Enter Julio and Angelo.

Julio. I WILL but ſee her once more, Angelo,
That I may hate her more, and then I am
Myſelf again.

Ang. I would not have thee tempt luſt ;
'Tis a way dangerous, and will deceive thee,
Hadſt thou the conſtancy of all men in thee.

Julio. Having her ſins before me, I dare ſee her,
Were ſhe as catching as the plague, and deadly,
And tell her ſhe is fouler than all thoſe,
And far more peſtilent, if not repentant ;
And, like a ſtrong man, chide her well, and leave her.

Ang. 'Tis eaſily ſaid. Of what complexion is ſhe ?

Julio. Make but a curious frame unto thyſelf,
As thou wouldſt ſhape an angel in thy thought ;
Such as the poets, when their fancies ſweat,
Imagine Juno is, or fair-ey'd Pallas ;
And one more excellent than all thoſe figures
Shalt thou find her. She's brown, but of a ſweetneſs,
(If ſuch a poor word may expreſs her beauty)
Believe me, Angelo, would do more miſchief
With a forc'd ſmile, than twenty thouſand Cupids,
With their love-quivers full of ladies' eyes,
And twice as many flames, could fling upon us.

Ang. Of what age is ſhe ?

Julio. As a roſe at faireſt,

Neither

Neither a bud, nor blown; but such a one,
Were there a Hercules to get again
With all his glory, or one more than he,
The god would chuse out 'mongst a race of women
To make a mother of[28]. She's outwardly
All that bewitches sense, all that entices;
Nor is it in our virtue to uncharm it.
And when she speaks, oh, Angelo, then musick
(Such as old Orpheus made, that gave a soul
To aged mountains, and made rugged beasts
Lay by their rages; and tall trees, that knew
No sound but tempests, to bow down their branches,
And hear, and wonder; and the sea, whose surges
Shook their white heads in Heav'n, to be as midnight
Still and attentive) steals into our souls
So suddenly, and strangely, that we are
From that time no more ours, but what she pleases!

   Ang. Why look, how far you've thrust yourself again
Into your old disease! Are you that man,
With such a resolution, that would venture
To take your leave of folly, and now melt
Ev'n in repeating her?

   Julio. I had forgot me.

   Ang. As you will still do.

   Julio. No; the strongest man
May have the grudging of an ague on him;

---

[28] *The God would chuse, &c.*] In Dryden's All for Love, or the World
Well Lost, act iv. is a beautiful passage, something similar to this of
our Authors:

    ' I pity Dolabella: but she's dangerous:
    ' Her eyes have pow'r, beyond Thessalian charms,
    ' To draw the moon from Heav'n; for eloquence,
    ' The sea green syrens taught her voice their flatt'ry;
    ' And, while she speaks, night steals upon the day,
    ' Unmark'd of those that hear: Then she's so charming,
    ' Age buds at sight of her, and swells to youth:
    ' The holy priests gaze on her when she smiles;
    ' And with heav'd hands, forgetting gravity,
    ' They bless her wanton eyes: Ev'n I who hate her,
    ' With a malignant joy behold such beauty;
    ' And, while I curse, desire it   *R.*

This

This is no more. Let's go; I'd fain be fit
To be thy friend again, for now I'm no man's!

Ang. Go you: I dare not go, I tell you truly;
Nor were it wise I should.

Julio. Why?

Ang. I am well,
And, if I can, will keep myself so.

Julio. Ha?
Thou mak'st me smile, tho' I have little cause,
To see how prettily thy fear becomes thee:
Art thou not strong enough to see a woman?

Ang. Yes, twenty thousand; but not such a one
As you have made her: I'll not lie for th' matter;
I know I'm frail, and may be cozen'd too,
By such a syren.

Julio. Faith, thou shalt go, Angelo!

Ang. Faith, but I will not! No; I know how far, Sir,
I'm able to hold out, and will not venture
Above my depth. I do not long to have
My sleep ta'en from me, and go pulingly,
Like a poor wench had lost her market-money;
And, when I see good meat, sit still and sigh,
And call for small beer, and consume my wit
In making anagrams, and faithful poesies:
I do not like that itch; I'm sure I had rather
Have the main pox, and safer.

Julio. Thou shalt go;
I must needs have thee as a witness with me
Of my repentance. As thou lov'st me, go!

Ang. Well, I will go, since you will have it so;
But if I prove a fool too, look to have me
Curse you continually, and fearfully.

Julio. And if thou seest me fall again, good Angelo,
Give me thy counsel quickly, lest I perish.

Ang. Pray God, I have enough to save myself!
For, as I have a soul, I'd rather venture
Upon a savage island than this woman! [*Exeunt.*

SCENE

S C E N E II.

Enter Father and Servant.

Father. From whom, Sir, comes this bounty ? for I
     think
You are miſtaken.

Serv. No, Sir ; 'tis to you,
I'm ſure, my miſtreſs ſent it.

Father. Who's your miſtreſs,
That I may give her thanks ?

Serv. The virtuous widow.

Father. The virtuous widow, Sir ? I know none
     ſuch.
Pray what's her name ?

Serv. Lelia.

Father. I knew you err'd ;
'Tis not to me, I warrant you. There, Sir ;
Carry't to thoſe ſhe feeds fat with ſuch favours ;
I am a ſtranger to her.

Serv. Good Sir, take it,
And, if you will, I'll ſwear ſhe ſent it to you ;
For I am ſure mine eye never went off you
Since you forſook the gentlemen you talk'd with
Juſt at her door.

Father. Indeed, I talk'd with two,
Within this half-hour, in the ſtreet.

Serv. 'Tis you, Sir,
And none but you, I'm ſent to. Wiſer men
Would have been thankful ſooner, and receiv'd it ;
'Tis not a fortune every man can brag of,
And from a woman of her excellence.

Father. Well, Sir, I'm catechiz'd. What more
     belongs to't ?

Serv. This only, Sir ; ſhe would entreat you come
This evening to her without fail.

Father. I will.

Serv. You gueſs where.

Father. Sir, I have a tongue elſe. [*Exit Servant.*
                              She

She is downright devil; or elfe my wants
And her difobedience have provok'd her
To look into her foul felf, and be forry.
I wonder how fhe knew me! I had thought
I'd been the fame to all I am to them
That chang'd me thus: God pardon me for lying!
For I have paid it home: Many a good man,
That had but found the profit of my way,
Would forfwear telling true again in hafte.

Enter Lodovico and Pifo.

Here are my praters: Now, if I did well,
I fhould belabour 'em; but I have found
A way to quiet 'em, worth a thoufand on't.
   Lod. If we could get a fellow that would do it!
   Father. What villainy is now in hand?
   Pifo. 'Twill be hard to be done, in my opinion,
Unlefs we light upon an Englifhman
With fevenfcore furfeits in him.
   Lod. Are the Englifhmen
Such ftubborn drinkers [29]?
   Pifo. Not a leak at fea
Can fuck more liquor: You fhall have their children
Chriften'd in mull'd fack, and, at five years old,
Able to knock a Dane down. Take an Englifhman,
And cry ' St. George!' and give him but a rafher,
And you fhall have him upon even terms
Defy a hogfhead. Such a one would do it
Home, boy, and like a workman.
   Lod. At what weapon [10]?

Pifo.

---

  [29] *Such ftubborn drinkers.*] This qualification in our countrymen is taken notice of by Iago in act ii. fcene iii. of Othello.   R.
  [10] *Lod. At what weapon?*] I have made a change in the perfons of the fpeakers *Lodovic* and *Pifo*, giving to *Lodovic* what was in the other edition fpoke by *Pifo* and *è contra*; as thinking the fpeeches fomething out of character. *Pifo*'s defign feems to be, by the whole tenor of the converfation, to make Jacomo foundly drunk: His hope of doing this is built upon one of our countrymen, whom he defcribes as capable of turning down an hogfhead with the fhoeing-horn of a
rafher.

Piſo. Sherry ſack ; I would have him drink ſtark
    dead,
If it were poſſible ; at worſt, paſt portage.
   Lod. What is the end then ?
   Piſo. Doſt thou not perceive it ?
If he be drunk dead, there's a fair end of him.
If not, this is my end, or by enticing,
Or by deceiving, to conduct him where
The fool is that admires him ; and if ſober
His nature be ſo rugged, what will't be
When he is hot with wine ? Come, let's about it :
If this be done but handſomely, I'll pawn
My head ſh' hath done with ſoldiers.
   Lod. This may do well.
   Father. Here's a new way to murder men alive !
I'll choak this train.—God ſave ye, gentlemen !
It is to you—ſtay !—yes, it is to you.
   Lod. What's to me ?
   Father. You're fortunate: I can't ſtand to tell you
    more now ;
Meet me here ſoon, and you'll be made a man. [*Exit.*
   Lod. What viſion's this ?
   Piſo. I know not.
   Lod. Well, I'll meet it ;
Think you o' th' other, and let me a while
Dream of this fellow.
   Piſo. For the drunkard, Lodovic,
Let me alone.
   Lod. Come, let's about it then.

                                 [*Exeunt.*

rather. But would the poet on this ſuppoſition put *At what weapon*
into the mouth of *Piſo*, make him aſk himſelf a queſtion and let *Lodovic* give the anſwer ? No ſurely. *Lod.* has certainly been dropt
upon us, who ſhould have interrupted *Piſo*'s narrative, both as to the
means and end of making the Captain drunk. What ſeems to confirm this, is the ſpeech of *Lodovic* at the cloſe of the ſcene, where he
bids *Piſo think of the other*, viz. making Jacomo fuddled ; to which
Piſo anſwers,
      For the drunkard Lodovic
      Let me alone.
                                 Sympſon.
                                 SCENE

SCENE III.

Enter Clora and Frank.

Clora. Ha, ha, ha! Pray let me laugh extremely.

Frank. Why? prithee why? haft thou fuch caufe?

Clora. Yes, faith;
My brother will be here ftraightway, and——

Frank. What?

Clora. The other party. Ha, ha, ha!

Frank. What party?
Wench, thou art not drunk?

Clora. No, faith.

Frank. Faith, thou haft been among the bottles,
Clora.

Clora. Faith, but I have not, Frank. Prithee be
handfome!
The Captain comes along too, wench.

Frank. Oh, is that it
That tickles ye?

Clora. Yes, and fhall tickle you too;
You underftand me!

Frank. By my troth, thou'rt grown
A ftrange lewd wench! I muft e'en leave thy company;
Thou wilt fpoil me elfe.

Clora. Nay, thou art fpoil'd to my hand.
Hadft thou been free, as a good wench ought to be,
When I went firft a-birding for thy love,
And roundly faid, that is the man muft do it,
I had done laughing many an hour ago.

Frank. And what doft thou fee in him, now thou
know'ft him,
To be thus laugh'd at?

Clora. Prithee be not angry,
And I'll fpeak freely to thee.

Frank. Do; I will not.

Clora. Then, as I hope to have a handfome hufband,
This fellow, in mine eye (and, Frank, I'm held
To have a fhrewd guefs at a pretty fellow)

Appears

Appears a ſtrange thing.

    Frank. Why? how ſtrange, for God's ſake?
He is a man, and one that may content
(For any thing I ſee) a right good woman:
And ſure I am not blind.

    Clora. There lies the queſtion;
For (but you ſay he is a man, and I
Will credit you) I ſhould as ſoon have thought him
Another of God's creatures: Out upon him!
His body, that can promiſe nothing
But lazineſs and long ſtrides.

    Frank. Theſe are your eyes!
Where were they, Clora, when you fell in love
With the old footman, for ſinging of Queen *Dido*?
And ſwore he look'd, in his old velvet trunks,
And his ſlic'd Spaniſh jerkin, like Don John?
You had a parlous judgment then, my Clora.

    Clora. Who told you that?

    Frank. I heard it.

    Clora. Come, be friends!
The ſoldier is a Mars. No more; we're all
Subject to ſlide away.

    Frank. Nay, laugh on ſtill.

    Clora. No, faith; thou art a good wench, and 'tis
        pity
Thou ſhouldſt not be well quarried at thy entering,
Thou art ſo high-flown for him. Look, who's there!

Enter *Fabritio and Jacomo.*

    Jac. Prithee, go ſingle; what ſhould I do there?
Thou know'ſt I hate theſe viſitations,
As I hate peace or perry.

    Fab. Wilt thou never
Make a right man?

    Jac. You make a right fool of me,
To lead me up and down to viſit women,
And be abus'd and laugh'd at. Let me ſtarve
If I know what to ſay, unleſs I aſk 'em
What their ſhoes coſt!

                                 Fab.

Fab. Fy upon thee, coward!
Canſt thou not ſing?

Jac. Thou know'ſt I can ſing nothing
But Plumpton-Park.

Fab. Thou wilt be bold enough,
When thou art enter'd once.

Jac. I'd rather enter
A breach: If I miſcarry, by this hand,
I'll have you by th' ears for't!

Fab. Save ye, ladies!

Clora. Sweet brother, I dare ſwear you're welcome
hither;
So is your friend.

Fab. Come, bluſh not, but ſalute 'em.

Frank. Good Sir, believe your ſiſter; you're moſt
welcome!
So is this worthy gentleman, whoſe virtues
I ſhall be proud to be acquainted with.

Jac. Sh' has found me out already, and has paid me.
Shall we be going?

Fab. Peace!—Your goodneſs, lady,
Will ever be afore us. For myſelf
I will not thank you ſingle, leſt I leave
My friend, this gentleman, out of acquaintance.

Jac. More of me yet?

Frank. 'Would I were able, Sir,
From either of your worths to merit thanks!

Clora. But, brother, is your friend thus ſad ſtill?
Methinks,
'Tis an unſeemly nature in a ſoldier.

Jac. What hath ſhe to do with me, or my behaviour?

Fab. He does but ſhew ſo: Prithee to him, ſiſter!

Jac. If I don't break thy head, I am no Chriſtian,
If I get off once!

Clora. Sir, we muſt entreat you
To think yourſelf more welcome, and be merry:
'Tis pity a fair man, of your proportion,
Should have a ſoul of ſorrow.

Jac. Very well!——

Pray,

Pray, gentlewoman, what would you have me fay?

Clora. Do not you know, Sir?

Jac. Not fo well as you,

That talk continually.

Frank. You've hit her, Sir.

Clora. I thank him, fo he has;

Fair fall his fweet face for it!

Jac. Let my face

Alone, I'd wifh you, left I take occafion

To bring a worfe in queftion.

Clora. Meaning mine?

Brother, where was your friend brought up? H'has fure

Been a great lover in his youth of pottage,

They lie fo dull upon his underftanding.

Fab. No more of that; thou'lt anger him at heart.

Clora. Then let him be more manly; for he looks

Like a great fchool-boy, that had been blown up

Laft night at Duft-Point.

Frank. You will never leave,

'Till you be told how rude you are. Fy, Clora!

Sir, will it pleafe you fit?

Clora. And I'll fit by you.

Jac. Woman, be quiet, and be rul'd, I'd wifh you.

Clora. I've done, Sir Captain.

Fab. Art thou not afham'd?

Jac. You are an afs! I'll tell you more anon;

Y'had better have been hang'd than brought me hither!

Fab. You're grown a fullen fool! Either be handfome,

Or, by this light, I will have wenches bait thee!

Go to the gentlewoman, and give her thanks,

And hold your head up! what?

Jac. By this light, I'll brain thee!

Frank. Now, o' my faith, this gentleman does nothing

But it becomes him rarely. Clora, look

How well this little anger, if it be one,

Shews in his face.

Clora. Yes, it fhews very fweetly.

Frank. Nay, do not blufh, Sir; o' my troth, it does!

I would be ever angry to be thus.

Fabritio,

Fabritio, o' my confcience, if I ever
Do fall in love, (as I will not forfwear it,
'Till I am fomething wifer) it muft be,
I will not fay directly with that face ;
But certainly fuch another as that is,
And thus difpos'd may chance to hamper me[11].

Fab. Doft thou hear this, and ftand ftill?

Jac. You will prate ftill!
I would you were not women ; I would take
A new courfe with ye.

Clora. Why, Courageous?

Jac. For making me a ftone to whet your tongues on.

Clora. Prithee, fweet Captain!

Jac. Go, go fpin, go hang!

Clora. Now could I kifs him.

Jac. If you long for kicking,
You'd beft come kifs me; do not tho', I'd wifh ye.
I'll fend my footman to thee ; he fhall leap thee,
An thou want'ft horfing. I will leave ye, ladies.

Frank. Befhrew my heart, you are unmannerly
To offer this unto a gentleman
Of his deferts, that comes fo worthily
To vifit me! I cannot take it well.

Jac. I come to vifit you, you foolifh woman?

Frank. I thought you did, Sir, and for that I thank
you ;
I would be loth to lofe thofe thanks. I know
This is but fome odd way you have, and, faith,
It does become you well, to make us merry :
I have heard often of your pleafant vein.

Fab. What wouldft thou afk more?

Jac. Pray, thou fcurvy fellow!
Thou haft not long to live. Adieu, dear damfels!
You filthy women, farewell, and be fober,

---

[11] Difpofe my *chance*.] Thus read the old copies, contrary both
to fenfe and grammar : The flight change in two words which I
have made, make the whole clear and confiftent ; Frank is praifing
Jacomo's anger, and fays naturally enough, *that a face thus difpos'd
may chance to captivate her affections.* *Seward.*

And

And keep your chambers!

Clora. Farewell, old don Diego!

Frank. Away, away!—You muſt not be ſo angry,
To part thus roughly from us: Yet to me
This does not ſhew as if 'twere yours; the wars
May breed men ſomething plain, I know; but not
Thus rude. Give me your hand, good Sir: I know
'Tis white, and——

Jac. If I were not patient,
What would become of you two prating houſewives?

Clora. For any thing I know, we would in to ſupper,
And there begin a health of luſty claret,
To keep care from our hearts; and it ſhould be——

Fab. I'faith to whom ?—Mark but this, Jacomo.

Clora. Ev'n to the handſom'ſt fellow now alive.

Fab. Do you know ſuch a one ?

Frank. He may be gueſs'd at,
Without much travel.

Fab. There's another item.

Clora. And he ſhould be a ſoldier.

Frank. 'Twould be better.

Clora. And yet not you, ſweet Captain.

Frank. Why not he ?

Jac. Well! I ſhall live to ſee your huſbands beat you,
And hiſs 'em on like bandogs.

Clora. Ha, ha, ha!

Jac. Green ſickneſſes and ſerving-man light on ye,
With greaſy codpieces, and woollen ſtockings!
The devil (if he dare deal with two women)
Be of your counſels! Farewell, plaiſterers! [*Exit.*

Clora. This fellow will be mad at Midſummer,
Without all doubt.

Fab. I think ſo too.

Frank. I'm ſorry,
He's gone in ſuch a rage. But ſure this holds him
Not every day.

Fab. Faith, every other day,
If he come near a woman.

Clora. I wonder how his mother could endure

Ta

To have him in her belly, he's so boisterous.

Frank. He's to be made more tractable, I doubt not.

Clora. Yes, if they taw him, as they do whit-leather,
Upon an iron, or beat him soft like stock-fish. [*Exe.*

SCENE IV.

Enter Lelia *and her Waiting-Woman, with a veil.*

Lelia. Art sure 'tis he?

Woman. Yes, and another with him.

Lelia. The more the merrier. Did you give that
    money,
And charg'd it be deliver'd where I shew'd you?

Woman. Yes, and what else you bad me.

Lelia. That brave fellow,
Tho' he be old, whate'er he be, shews toughness;
And such a one I long for, and must have
At any price; these young soft melting gristles
Are only for my safer ends.

Woman. They're here.

Lelia. Give me my veil; and bid the boy go sing
That song above, I gave him; the sad song.
Now if I miss him, I am curs'd. Go, wench,
And tell 'em I have utterly forsworn
All company of men; yet make a venture
At last to let 'em in: Thou know'st these things;
Do 'em to th' life.

Woman. I warrant you; I'm perfect.

Lelia. Some ill woman, for her use, would give
A million for this wench, she is so subtle.

Enter, to the door, Julio *and* Angelo.

Woman. Good Sir, desire it not; I dare not do it;
For since your last being here, Sir, believe me,
She has griev'd herself out of all company,
And, sweet soul, almost out of life too.

Julio. Prithee,
Let me but speak one word.

Woman. You will offend, Sir;

And

And yet your name is more familiar with her
Than any thing but sorrow. Good Sir, go.

Ang. This little varlet hath her lesson perfect;
These are the baits they bob with.

Jul. Faith, I will not.

Woman. I shall be chidden cruelly for this;
But you are such a gentleman——

Julio. No more.

Ang. There's a new tire, wench. Peace; thou'rt
    well enough.

Julio. What, has she musick?

Woman. Yes; for God's sake, stay;
'Tis all she feeds upon.

Julio. Alas, poor soul!

Ang. Now will I pray devoutly; for there's need
    on't.

THE SONG.

Away, delights; go seek some other dwelling,
    For I must die:
Farewell, false love; thy tongue is ever telling
    Lie after lie.
For ever let me rest now from thy smarts;
    Alas, for pity go,
    And fire their hearts
That have been hard to thee; mine was not so.

Never again deluding Love shall know me,
    For I will die;
And all those griefs that think to over-grow me,
    Shall be as I:
For ever will I sleep, while poor maids cry,
    Alas, for pity stay,
    And let us die
With thee; men cannot mock us in the clay [12].

---

[12] *Mock us in the* day.] Varied in 1750. In support of the alteration, Seward produces the following passage in Henry V.
    ' The dead with Charity inclos'd in *clay*.'
  The corruption is very easy; the *c* and *l* in the manuscript looking
like a *d*.

Julio.

Julio. Miſtreſs! not one word, miſtreſs? If I grieve
you,
I can depart again.

Ang. Let's go then quickly;
For if ſhe get from under this dark cloud,
We ſhall both ſweat, I fear, for't.

Julio. Do but ſpeak,
Tho' you turn from me, and ſpeak bitterly,
And I am gone; for that I think will pleaſe you.

Ang. Oh, that all women were thus ſilent ever,
What fine things were they!

Julio. You have look'd on me,
When, if there be belief in womens' words,
Spoken in tears, you ſwore you lov'd to do ſo.

Lelia. Oh, me, my heart!

Ang. Now, Julio, play the man,
Or ſuch another ' oh, me!' will undo thee.
'Would I had any thing to keep me buſy,
I might not hear her; think but what ſhe is,
Or I doubt mainly, I ſhall be i'th' meſh too.

Julio. Pray, ſpeak again.

Lelia. Where is my woman?

Woman. Here.

Ang. Mercy upon me! what a face ſhe has!
'Would it were veil'd again!

Lelia. Why did you let
This flattering man in to me? Did not I
Charge thee to keep me from his eyes again,
As carefully as thou wouldſt keep thine own?
Th'haſt brought me poiſon in a ſhape of Heav'n,
Whoſe violence will break the hearts of all,
Of all weak women, as it hath done mine,
That are ſuch fools to love, and look upon him.
Good Sir, be gone; you know not what an eaſe
Your abſence is.

Ang. By Heav'n, ſhe is a wonder!
I cannot tell what 'tis, but I am qualmiſh [11].

---

[11] *But I am ſqueamiſh.*] So firſt folio. The ſubſequent editions,
quamiſo.

Julio.

Julio. Tho' I defire to be here more than Heav'n,
As I am now, yet, if my fight offend you,
So much I love to be commanded by you,
That I will go. Farewell!

Lelia. I fhould fay fomething
Ere you depart, and I would have you hear me.
But why fhould I fpeak to a man that hates me,
And will but laugh at any thing I fuffer?

Julio. If this be hate——

Lelia. Away, away, deceiver!

Julio. Now help me, Angelo!

Ang. I'm worfe than thou art.

Lelia. Such tears as thofe might make another
woman
Believe thee honeft, Julio; almoft me,
That know their ends; for I confefs they ftir me.

Ang. What will become of me? I cannot go now,
If you would hang me, from her. Oh brave eye!
Steal me away, for God's fake, Julio.

Julio. Alas, poor man! I'm loft again too, ftrangely.

Lelia. No, I will fooner truft a crocodile
When he fheds tears, (for he kills fuddenly,
And ends our cares at once) or any thing
That's evil to our natures, than a man:
I find there is no end of his deceivings,
Nor no avoiding 'em, if we give way.
I was requefting you to come no more,
And mock me with your fervice; 'tis not well,
Nor honeft, to abufe us fo far: You may love too;
For tho', I muft confefs, I am unworthy
Of your love every way, yet I would have you
Think I am fomewhat too good to make fport of.

Julio. Will you believe me?

Lelia. For your vows and oaths,
And fuch deceiving tears as you fhed now,
I will, as you do, ftudy to forget 'em.

Julio. Let me be moft defpis'd of men——

Lelia. No more!
There is no new way left, by which your cunning
Shall

Shall once more hope to catch me. No, thou falfe man,
I will avoid thee, and, for thy fake, all
That bear thy ftamp, as counterfeit in love!
For I am open-ey'd again, and know thee.
Go, make fome other weep, as I have done,
That dare believe thee; go, and fwear to her
That is a ftranger to thy cruelty,
And knows not yet what man is, and his lyings,
How thou dieft daily for her; pour it out
In thy beft lamentations; put on forrow,
As thou canft, to deceive an angel, Julio,
And vow thyfelf into her heart, that when
I fhall leave off to curfe thee for thy falfhood,
Still a forfaken woman may be found
To call to Heav'n for vengeance!

   Ang. From this hour,
I heartily defpife all honeft women:
(I care not if the world took knowledge on't)
I fee there's nothing in them, but that folly
Of loving one man only. Give me henceforth,
(Before the greateft bleffing can be thought of,
If this be one) a whore; that's all I aim at.

   Julio. Miftrefs, the moft offending man is heard
Before his fentence: Why will you condemn me
Ere I produce the truth to witnefs with me,
How innocent I am of all your angers?

   Lelia. There is no trufting of that tongue; I know't,
And how far, if it be believ'd, it kills: No more, Sir!

   Julio. It never lied to you yet; if it did,
'Twas only when it call'd you mild and gentle.

   Lelia. Good Sir, no more! Make not my under-
       ftanding,
(After I've fuffer'd thus much evil by you)
So poor to think I have not reach'd the end
Of all your forc'd affections: Yet, becaufe
I once lov'd fuch a forrow, too, too dearly,
As that would ftrive to be, I do forgive you,
Ev'n heartily as I would be forgiven,
For all your wrongs to me (my charity

                     Yet

Yet loves you so far, tho' again I may not);
And wish, when that time [14] comes you will love truly,
(If you can ever do so) you may find
The worthy fruit of your affections,
True love again, not my unhappy harvest;
Which, like a fool, I sow'd in such a heart,
So dry and stony, that a thousand showers,
From these two eyes continually raining,
Could never ripen.

    Julio. You have conquer'd me!
I did not think to yield; but make me now
Ev'n what you will, my Lelia, so I may
Be but so truly happy to enjoy you.

    Lelia. No, no; those fond imaginations
Are dead and buried in me; let 'em rest!

    Julio. I'll marry you.

    Ang. The devil thou wilt, Julio?
How that word waken'd me! Come hither, friend!
Thou art a fool! Look stedfastly upon her:
Tho' she be all that I know excellent,
As she appears; tho' I could fight for her,
And run thro' fire; tho' I am stark mad too,
Never to be recover'd; tho' I would
Give all I had i' th' world to lie with her,
Ev'n to my naked soul (I'm so far gone);
Yet, methinks still, we should not dote away
That that is something more than ours, our honours.
I would not have thee marry her by no means
(Yet I should do so): Is she not a whore?

    Julio. She is; but such a one——

---

[14] *And wish when that time—*] Mr. Seward suspects something
left out here, necessary to complete the sense and grammar, or else
this line must be corrupted through the transposition of some particles;
and would read thus,

    I wish when the time comes, that you love truly,
    (If you can ever do so) you may find, &c.

I have not indeed altered the text, though I suspect it strongly to
be corrupt, and would propose reading thus,

    And wishes when th' time comes that you love, &c. *Sympson.*

    We confess ourselves unable to comprehend this note; but do not
perceive the least difficulty in the text.

                                 Ang.

Ang. 'Tis true, she's excellent;
And, when I well confider, Julio,
I fee no reafon we fhould be confin'd
In our affections; when all creatures elfe
Enjoy ftill where they like.

Julio. And fo will I then.

Lelia. He's faft enough I hope, now, if I hold him.

Ang. You muft not do fo tho', now I confider
Better what 'tis.

Julio. Do not confider, Angelo;
For I muft do it.

Ang. No; I'll kill thee firft:
I love thee fo well, that the worms fhall have thee
Before this woman, friend.

Julio. It was your counfel.

Ang. As I was a knave; not as I lov'd thee.

Julio. All this is loft upon me, Angelo;
For I muft have her.—I will marry you
When you pleafe: Pray look better on me.

Ang. Nay then, no more, friend; farewell, Julio!
I have fo much difcretion left me yet
To know, and tell thee, thou art miferable.

Julio. Stay; thou art more than fhe, and now I
find it.

Lelia. Is he fo?

Julio. Miftrefs!

Lelia. No; I'll fee thee ftarv'd firft!   [*Exit.*

Julio. Friend!

Ang. Fly her as I do, Julio; fhe's a witch.

Julio. Beat me away then; I fhall grow here ftill elfe.

Ang. That were the way to have me grow there
with thee.
Farewell, for ever!   [*Exit.*

Julio. Stay! I am uncharm'd.
Farewell, thou curfed houfe! from this hour be
More hated of me than a leprofy!   [*Exit.*

Enter Lelia.

Lelia. Both gone? A plague upon 'em both!

Am

Am I deceiv'd again? Oh, I would rail,
And follow 'em, but I fear the spite of people,
'Till I have emptied all my gall.
The next I seize upon shall pay their follies
To the last penny; this will work me worse;
He that comes next, by Heav'n, shall feel their curse!

　　　　　　　　　　　　　　　　　　　　[*Exeunt.*

SCENE V.

Enter Jacomo at one door, and Fabritio at another.

Fab. Oh, you're a sweet youth, so uncivilly
To rail, and run away?

Jac. Oh! are you there, Sir?
I'm glad I've found you? You've not now your ladies,
To shew your wit before.

Fab. Thou wou'lt not, wou'lt 'ou?

Jac. What a sweet youth I am, as you have made
　　　me,　　　　　　　　　　　　　　　　[*Draws.*
You shall know presently.

Fab. Put up your sword;
I've seen it often; 'tis a fox.

Jac. It is so;
And you shall feel it too. Will you dispatch, Sir,
And leave your mirth out? or I shall take occasion
To beat you, and disgrace you too.

Fab. Well; since
There is no other way to deal with you,
(Let's see your sword; I'm sure you scorn all odds)
I will fight with you.

　　　　　　[*They measure, and Fabritio gets his sword.*

Jac. How now?

Fab. Nay, stand out;
Or, by this light, I'll make you!

Jac. This is scurvy,
And out of fear done.

Fab. No, Sir; out of judgment;
For he that deals with thee (thou'rt grown so boisterous)

　　　　　　　　　　　　　　　　　　　　Must

Muft have more wits, or more lives than another,
Or always be in armour, or enchanted,
Or he is miferable.

Jac. Your end of this, Sir ?

Fab. My end is only mirth, to laugh at thee,
Which now I'll do in fafety : Ha, ha, ha !

Jac. 'Sheart ! then I'm grown ridiculous !

Fab. Thou art ;
And wilt be fhortly fport for little children,
If thou continueft this rude ftubbornnefs.

Jac. Oh, God, for any thing that had an edge !

Fab. Ha, ha, ha !

Jac. Fy, what a fhame it is,
To have a lubber fhew his teeth !

Fab. Ha, ha !

Jac. Why doft thou laugh at me, thou wretched
        fellow ?
Speak, with a pox ! and look you render me
Juft fuch a reafon——

Fab. I fhall die with laughing !

Jac. As no man can find fault with. I fhall have
Another fword, I fhall, you fleering puppy !

Fab. Does not this teftinefs fhew finely in thee ?
Once more, take heed of children ! If they find thee,
They'll break up fchool to bear thee company,
(Thou wilt be fuch a paftime) and hoot at thee,
And call thee Bloody-bones, and Spade[35], and Spit-fire,

---

[35] *And* Spade *and Spit fire.*] If one would compare thefe Authors
with themfelves, there feems to be reafon to fufpect this paffage as
corrupted : To put in *Spade*, which is a name that carries no terror
in it to children, between two which are ufually made ufe of for that
purpofe, feems to me not a little odd : What I conjecture we fhould
read is this,
    And call thee Bloody-bones, Raw-head, *and Spit fire,*
So in act iv. fcene iii. of this play, Clora fays of Jacomo,
    Here's Raw-head *come again.*
And in the Prophetefs, act iv. fcene v.
    —————— *Now I look*
    Like Bloody-bones and Raw-head *to fright children.*   *Sympfon.*
    It is common to this day, among the vulgar, to fay, when abufed,
' Call me any thing but *fpade.*'

And

And Gaffer Madman, and Go-by-Jeronimo [36],
And Will with a Whifp, and Come-Aloft, and Crack-
        Rope,
And old Saint Dennis with the dudgeon codpiece,
And twenty fuch names.

Jac. No, I think they will not.

Fab. Yes, but they will ; and nurfes ftill their chil-
        dren
Only with thee, and ' Here take him, Jacomo!'

Jac. God's precious, that I were but over thee
One fteeple height ! I'd fall and break thy neck.

Fab. This is the reafon I laugh at thee, and,
While thou art thus, will do. Tell me one thing.

Jac. I wonder how thou durft thus queftion me !
Prithee reftore my fword.

Fab. Tell me but one thing,
And it may be I will. Nay, Sir, keep out.

Jac. Well, I will be your fool now ; fpeak your mind,
        Sir.

Fab. Art thou not breeding teeth ?

Jac. How ! teeth ?

Fab. Yes, teeth ;
Thou wouldft not be fo froward elfe.

Jac. Teeth ?

Fab. Come ; 'twill make thee
A little rheumatic, but that's all one ;
We'll have a bib, for fpoiling of thy doublet,
And a fring'd muckender hang at thy girdle ;
I'll be thy nurfe, and get a coral for thee,
And a fine ring of bells.

Jac. Faith, this is fomewhat
Too much, Fabritio, to your friend that loves you:
Methinks, your goodnefs rather fhould invent
A way to make my follies lefs, than breed 'em.
I fhould have been more moderate to you ;
But I fee you defpife me.

Fab. Now I love you.

---

[36] *Go by, Jeronimo.*] An expreffion in the play of Jeronimo, which
was the but of ridicule for almoft every author of the times.   *R.*

There,

There, take your sword; continue so. I dare not
Stay now to try your patience; soon I'll meet you:
And, as you love your honours, and your state,
Redeem yourself well to the gentlewoman.
Farewell, 'till soon !   [*Exit.*

Jac. **Well,** I shall think of this.   [*Exit.*

SCENE VI.

Enter Host, Piso, and Boy with a glass of wine.

Piso. Nothing i' th' world but a dried tongue or two·
Host. Taste him, and tell me.
Piso. He's a valiant wine;
This must be he, mine Host.
  Host. This shall be *ipse.*
Oh, he's a devilish biting wine, a tyrant
Where he lays hold, Sir; this is he that scorns
Small beer should quench him, or a foolish caudle
Bring him to bed; no, if he flinch I'll shame him,
And draw him out to mull amongst old midwives.
  Piso. There is a soldier, I would have thee batter [17]
Above the rest, because he thinks there's no man
Can give him drink enough.
  Host. What kind of man ?
  Piso. That thou mayst know him perfectly, he's one
Of a left-handed making, a lank thing,
As if his belly were ta'en up with straw,
To hunt a match.
  Host. Has he no beard to shew him ?
  Piso. Faith, but a little; yet enough to note him,
Which grows in parcels, here and there a remnant :
And that thou mayst not miss him, he is one
That wears his forehead in a velvet scabbard.
  Host. That note's enough; he's mine; I'll fuddle
    . him,
Or lie i' th' suds. You will be here too ?
  Piso. Yes.

---

[17] *Have thee* **better.**] Amended in 1750.

'Till

'Till foon, farewell, and bear up.

Hoft. If I do not,

Say I am recreant; I'll get things ready.   [*Exeunt.*

ACT IV.   SCENE I.

Enter Julio and Angelo.

Julio. 'TIS ftrange thou fhouldft be thus, with thy
discretion.

Ang. I'm fure I am fo.

Julio. I am well, you fee.

Ang. Keep yourfelf warm then, and go home and fleep,
And pray to God thou mayft continue fo.
'Would I had gone to th'devil of an errand,
When I was made a fool to fee her! Leave me;
I am not fit for converfation.

Julio. Why, thou art worfe than I was.

Ang. Therefore leave me;
The nature of my ficknefs is not eas'd
By company or counfel: I am mad;
And, if you follow me with queftions,
Shall fhew myfelf fo.

Julio. This is more than error.

Ang. Pray be content that you have made me thus,
And do not wonder at me.

Julio. Let me know
But what you mean to do, and I am gone:
I would be loth to leave you thus elfe.

Ang. Nothing
That needs your fear; that is fufficient.
Farewell, and pray for me.

Julio. I would not leave you.

Ang. You muft and fhall.

Julio. I will then. 'Would yon woman
Had been ten fathom under ground, when firft
I faw her eyes!

                                            Ang.

Ang. Yet she had been dangerous;
For to some wealthy rock of precious stone,
Or mine of gold as tempting, her fair body
Might have been turn'd; which once found out by
      labour,
And brought to use, having her spells within it,
Might have corrupted states, and ruin'd kingdoms;
Which had been fearful, friend. Go; when I see thee
Next, I will be as thou art, or no more.
Pray do not follow me; you'll make me angry.
  Julio. Heav'n grant you may be right again!
  Ang. Amen!   [*Exeunt severally.*

SCENE II.

Enter Tavern-Boys, &c.

  Boy. Score a gallon of sack, and a pint of olives, to
      the Unicorn.
Above within. Why, drawer!
  Boy. Anon, anon!
Another Boy. Look into the Nag's-head there.
  2 Boy. Score a quart of claret to the Bar;
And a pound of sausages into the Flower-pot.

Enter First Servant, with wine.

  1 Serv. The devil's in their throats. Anon, anon!

Enter Second Servant.

  2 Serv. Mull a pint
Of sack there for the women in the Flower-de-luce,
And put in ginger enough; they belch like pot-
      guns:
And, Robin, fetch tobacco for the Peacock;
They will not be drunk till midnight else. How now!
How does my master?
  2 Boy. Faith, he lies, drawing on apace.
  1 Boy. That's an ill sign.

2 Boy. And fumbles with the pots too [18].

1 Boy. Then there's no way but one with him.

2 Boy. All the rest,

Except the Captain, are in *limbo patrûm*,

Where they lie fod in fack.

1 Boy. Does he bear up still?

2 Boy. Afore the wind still, with his lights up bravely:

All he takes in I think he turns to juleps,

Or h'has a world of stowage in his belly;

The rest look all like fire-drakes, and lie scatter'd

Like rushes round about the room. My master

Is now the loving'st man, I think, above ground——

1 Boy. 'Would he were always drunk then!

Within. Drawer!

2 Boy. Anon, anon, Sir!

1 Boy. And swears I shall be free tomorrow; and
       so weeps,

And calls upon my mistress!

2 Boy. Then he's right.

1 Boy. And swears the Captain must lie this night
       with her,

(And bad me break it to her with discretion)

That he may leave an issue after him,

Able to entertain a Dutch ambassador:

And tells him feelingly how sweet she is,

And how he stole her from her friends i'th' country,

And brought her up disguised with the carriers,

And was nine nights bereaving her her maidenhead,

And the tenth got a drawer.   Here they come.

Enter Jacomo, Hoft, Lodovico, and Pifo.

Within. Drawer!

1 Boy. Anon, anon! Speak to the Tiger, Peter.

Hoft. There's my bells, boys, my filver bell.

Pifo. 'Would he were hang'd

-----

[18] I wish our poets had been a little less satirical upon their master
Shakespear: This expression is a plain sneering parody upon the description of Falstaff's death, in Henry V. act ii. scene iii.
    ' For after I saw him *fumble* with the sheets, &c.'   *Sympson.*

As

As high as I could ring him!

Hoſt. Captain.

Jac. Ho, Boy?

Lod. Robin, ſufficient ſingle beer, as cold

As cryſtal; quench, Robin, quench.

1 *Boy.* I'm gone, Sir.

Hoſt. Shall we bear up ſtill? Captain, how I love
      thee!

Sweet Captain, let me kiſs thee! By this hand,

I love thee next to malmſey in a morning,

Of all things tranſitory.

Jac. I love thee too,

As far as I can love a fat man.

Hoſt. Doſt thou, Captain?

Sweetly? and heartily?

Jac. With all my heart, boy.

Hoſt. Then, welcome, Death!—Come, cloſe mine
      eyes, ſweet Captain;

Thou ſhalt have all.

Jac. What ſhall your wife have then?

Hoſt. Why, ſhe ſhall have

(Beſides my bleſſing, and a ſilver ſpoon)

Enough to keep her ſtirring in the world,

Three little children; one of them was mine,

Upon my conſcience; th' other two are Pagans [39]!

Jac. 'Twere good ſhe had a little fooliſh money,

To rub the time away with.

Hoſt. Not a rag [40],

Not a denier: No; let her ſpin, a God's name,

And raiſe her houſe again.

Jac. Thou ſhalt not die tho'.

Boy, ſee your maſter ſafe delivered;

He's ready to lie in.

---

19 *Th' other two are* Pagans.] In the Second part of Henry IV.
act ii. ſcene ii. Prince Henry, enquiring concerning Doll Tearſheet,
ſays, ' What *Pagan* may that be? upon which paſſage Mr. Steevens
remarks, that ' *Pagan* ſeems to have been a cant term implying
' irregularity, either of birth or manners;' and to prove it, cites
theſe two lines of our Author.   *R.*

40 A cant term this for a *farthing.*   *Sympſon.*

E 2   *Hoſt.*

Hoſt. Good night!

Jac. Good morrow!

Drink till the cow come home, 'tis all paid, boys.

Lod. A pox of ſack!

Hoſt. Marry, God bleſs my buts! Sack is a jewel;
'Tis comfortable, gentlemen.

Jac. More beer, boy;
Very ſufficient ſingle beer.

Boy. Here, Sir.
How is it, gentlemen?

Jac. But e'en ſo ſo.

Hoſt. Go before finely, Robin, and prepare
My wife; bid her be right and ſtraight; I come, boy.
And, ſirrah, if they quarrel, let 'em uſe
Their own diſcretions, by all means, and ſtir not;
And he that's kill'd ſhall be as ſweetly buried.
Captain, adieu! adieu, ſweet bully Captain!
One kiſs before I die, one kiſs!

Jac. Farewell, boy!

Hoſt. All my ſweet boys, farewell!   [*Exit.*

Lod. Go ſleep; you're drunk.

Jac. Come, gentlemen; I'll ſee you at your lodging.
You look not luſtily; a quart more?

Lod. No, boy.

Piſo. Get us a torch.

Boy. 'Tis day, Sir.

Jac. That's all one.

Piſo. Are not thoſe the ſtars, thou ſcurvy boy?

Lod. Is not Charle-wain there? tell me that! there?

Jac. Yes;
I've paid 'em truly. Do not vex him, ſirrah.

Piſo. Confeſs it, boy; or, as I live, I'll beat
Midnight into thy brains.

Boy. I do confeſs it.

Piſo. Then live; and draw more ſmall beer preſently.

Jac. Come, boys, let's hug together, and be loving,
And ſing, and do brave things. Cheerly, my hearts!
A pox o' being ſad! Now could I fly,
And turn the world about upon my finger.

                                        Come,

Come, ye ſhall love me; I'm an honeſt fellow:
Hang care and fortune! we are friends.

Lod. No, Captain.

Jac. Do not you love me? I love you two dearly.

Piſo. No, by no means; you are a fighting captain,
And kill up ſuch poor people as we are by th' dozens.

Lod. As they kill flies with fox-tails, Captain.

Jac. Well, Sir?

Lod. Methinks now, as I ſtand, the Captain ſhews
To be a very merciful young man.
And prithee, Piſo, let me have thy opinion.

Piſo. Then he ſhall have mercy that merciful is,
Or all the painters are Apocrypha.

Jac. I'm glad you have your wits yet. Will ye go?

Piſo. You had beſt ſay we're drunk.

Jac. Ye are.

Lod. You lie!

Jac. Ye're raſcals, drunken raſcals!

Piſo. 'Tis ſufficient.

Jac. And now I'll tell you why, before I beat ye:
You have been tampering any time theſe three days,
Thus to diſgrace me.

Piſo. That's a lie too.

Jac. Well, Sir!
Yet, I thank God, I've turn'd your points on you;
For which I'll ſpare ye ſomewhat, half a beating.

Piſo. I'll make you fart fire, Captain, by this hand,
An ye provoke—Do not provoke, I'd wiſh you.

Jac. How do you like this?   [*Beats them.*

Lod. Sure I am enchanted.

Piſo. Stay till I draw——

Jac. Diſpatch then; I am angry.

Piſo. And thou ſhalt ſee how ſuddenly I'll kill thee.

Jac. Thou dar'ſt not draw. Ye cold, tame, mangy
          cowards,
Ye drunken rogues, can nothing make ye valiant?
Not wine, nor beating?

Lod. If this way be ſuffer'd——
'Tis very well!

Jac. Go; there's your way; go and fleep!
I've pity on you; you fhall have the reft
Tomorrow when we meet.

Pifo. Come, Lodovic:
He's monftrous drunk now; there's no talking with
    him.

Jac. I am fo; when I'm fober, I'll do more.
Boy, where's mine Hoft?   [*Exeunt Lod. and Pifo.*

Boy. He's on his bed, afleep, Sir.   [*Exit.*

Jac. Let him alone then.   Now am I high proof
For any action; now could I fight bravely,
And charge into a wildfire; or I could love
Any man living now, or any woman,
Or indeed any creature that loves fack,
Extremely, monftroufly : I am fo loving,
Juft at this inftant, that I might be brought,
(I feel it) with a little labour, now to talk
With a juftice of peace, that to my Nature
I hate next an ill fword.   I will do
Some ftrange brave thing now ; and I have it here :
Pray God the air keep out! I feel it buzzing. [*Exit.*

SCENE III.

Enter Frederick, Frank, and Clora.

Clora. She loves him too much; that's the plain
    truth, Frederick;
For which, if I might be believ'd, I think her
A ftrange forgetter of herfelf: There's Julio,
Or twenty more——

Fred. In your eye, I believe you;
But, credit me, the Captain is a man,
Lay but his rough affections by, as worthy——

Clora. So is a refty jade a horfe of fervice,
If he would leave his nature. Give me one,
By your leave, Sir, to make a hufband of,
Not to be wean'd, when I fhould marry him :
Methinks, a man is mifery enough.

                             Fred.

Fred. You are too bitter. I'd not have him worſe;
Yet I ſhall ſee you hamper'd one day, lady,
I do not doubt it, for this hereſy.

Clora. I'll burn before! Come, prithee leave this
   ſadneſs,
This walking by thyſelf to ſee the devil,
This mumps, this *lachrimæ*, this love in ſippets;
It fits thee like a French hood.

Frank. Does it ſo?
I'm ſure it fits thee to be ever talking,
And nothing to the purpoſe: Take up quickly;
Thy wit will founder of all four elſe, wench,
If thou hold'ſt this pace; take up, when I bid thee.

Clora. Before your brother? fy!

Fred. I can endure it.

Enter Jacomo.

Clora. Here's Raw-head come again. Lord, how he
   looks!
Pray God we 'ſcape with broken pates!

Frank. Were I he,
Thou ſhouldſt not want thy wiſh. He has been
   drinking;
Has he not, Frederick?

Fred. Yes; but do not find it.

Clora. Peace, and let's hear his wiſdom.

Fred. You will mad him.

Jac. I'm ſomewhat bold, but that's all one.

Clora. A ſhort and pithy ſaying of a ſoldier.

Frank. As I live,
Thou art a ſtrange mad wench!

Clora. To make a parſon.

Jac. Ladies, I mean to kiſs you——

Clora. How he wipes
His mouth, like a young preacher! We ſhall have it.

Jac. In order as you lie before me: Firſt,
I will begin with you.

Frank. With me, Sir?

Jac. Yes.

E 4   *Frank.*

Frank. If you will promise me to kiss in ease,
I care not if I venture.

Jac. I'll kiss according to mine own inventions,
As I shall see cause; sweetly I would wish you.
I love you.

Frank. Do you, Sir?

Jac. Yes, indeed do I;
'Would I could tell you how!

Frank. I would you would, Sir!

Jac. I would to God I could; but 'tis sufficient,
I love you with my heart.

Frank. Alas, poor heart!

Jac. And I am sorry; but we'll talk of that
Hereafter, if't please God.

Frank. E'en when you will, Sir.

Clora. He's dismal drunk; would he were muzzled!

Jac. You,
I take it, are the next.

Frank. Go to him, fool.

Clora. Not I; he'll bite me.

Jac. When, wit? when?

Clora. Good Captain!

Jac. Nay, an you play bo-peep, I'll ha' no mercy,
But catch as catch may.

Fred. Nay, I'll not defend you.

Clora. Good Captain, do not hurt me! I am sorry
That e'er I anger'd you.

Jac. I'll tew you for't,
By this hand, wit, unless you kiss discreetly. [*Kisses her.*

Clora. No more, Sir.

Jac. Yes, a little more, sweet wit;
One taste more o' your office. Go thy ways,
With thy small kettle-drums; upon my conscience,
Thou art the best that e'er man laid his leg o'er.

Clora. He smells just like a cellar: Fy upon him!

Jac. Sweet lady, now to you. [*Going to Frederick.*

Clora. For love's sake, kiss him.

Fred. I shall not keep my countenance.

Frank. Try, prithee,

Jac.

Jac. Pray be not coy, sweet woman; for I'll kiss you.

I'm blunt; but you must pardon me.

Clora. Oh, God, my sides!

All. Ha, ha, ha, ha!

Jac. Why ha, ha, ha? why laugh?
Why all this noise, sweet ladies?

Clora. Lusty Laurence,
See what a gentlewoman you've saluted:
Pray God, she prove not quick!

Fred. Where were thine eyes,
To take me for a woman? ha, ha, ha!

Jac. Who art'a? art'a mortal?

Fred. I am Frederick.

Jac. Then Frederick is an ass, a scurvy Frederick,
To laugh at me.

Frank. Sweet Captain!

Jac. Away, woman!
Go stitch, and serve God; I despise thee, woman!
And Frederick shall be beaten. 'Sblood, you rogue,
Have you none else to make your puppies of
But me?

Fred. I prithee be more patient;
There's no hurt done.

Jac. 'Sblood, but there shall be, scab!

Clora. Help, help, for love's sake!

Frank. Who's within there?

Fred. So!
Now you have made a fair hand.

Jac. Why?

Fred. You've kill'd me. [*Falls as kill'd.*

Clora. Call in some officers, and stay the Captain!

Jac. You shall not need.

Clora. This is your drunkenness!

Frank. Oh, me! unhappy brother Frederick!
Look but upon me; do not part so from me!
Set him a little higher. He is dead!

Clora. Oh, villain, villain!

Enter

Enter Fabritio and Servants.

Fab. How now! what's the matter?

Frank. Oh, Sir, my brother! Oh, my deareſt brother!

Clora. This drunken trough has kill'd him.

Fab. Kill'd him?

Clora. Yes.

For God ſake, hang him quickly! he will do
Ev'ry day ſuch a murder elſe. There's nothing
But a ſtrong gallows that can make him quiet;
I find it in his nature too late.

Fab. Pray be quiet;

Let me come to him.

Clora. Some go for a ſurgeon!

Frank. Oh, what a wretched woman has he made me!

Let me alone, good Sir!

Fab. To what a fortune

Haſt thou reſerv'd thy life!

Jac. Fabritio.

Fab. Never entreat me; for I will not know thee,

Nor utter one word for thee, unleſs it be

To have thee hang'd.—For God ſake, be more
　　　　　temperate!

Jac. I have a ſword ſtill, and I am a villain!

Clora, &c. Hold, hold, hold!

Jac. Ha[41]!

Clora. Away with him, for Heaven's ſake!

He is too deſperate for our enduring.

Fab. Come, you ſhall ſleep; come, ſtrive not;

I'll have it ſo. Here, take him to his lodging;

And ſee him laid before you part.

Serv. We will, Sir. [*Exeunt Jacomo and Servants.*

Fred. Ne'er wonder; I am living yet, and well.

I thank you, ſiſter, for your grief; pray keep it

---

[41] *Jac. Ha?* Exit.] So, without authority, reads Sympſon; but it
is impoſſible the Author ſhould intend Jacomo to *depart* here, when
Fabritio's next ſpeech is partly addreſſed *to him*, and partly to the
Servants, directing them to ' take him to his lodging;' by which
ſpeech, alſo, we underſtand that *he ſtruggled* with them.

'Till I am fitter for it.

Fab. Do you live, Sir?

Fred. Yes; but 'twas time to counterfeit, he was
grown
To such a madness in his wine.

Fab. 'Twas well, Sir,
You had that good respect unto his temper,
That no worse followed.

Fred. If I had stood him,
Certain one of us must have perish'd. How now,
Frank?

Frank. Beshrew my heart, I tremble like an aspen!

Clora. Let him come here no more, for Heaven's sake,
Unless he be in chains.

Frank. I would fain see him
After he has slept, Fabritio, but to try
How he will be. Chide him, and bring him back.

Clora. You'll never leave, 'till you be worried with
him.

Frank. Come, brother; we'll walk in, and laugh a
little,
To get this fever off me.

Clora. Hang him, squib!
Now could I grind him into priming powder.

Frank. Pray will you leave your fooling?

Fab. Come, all friends [42].

Frank. Thou art enough to make an age of men sore,
Thou art so cross and peevish.

Fab. I will chide him;
And, if he be not graceless, make him cry for't.

---

[42] *Come, all friends.*
　　Frank. *Thou art enough to make an age of men* so,
　Thou art so cross and peevish.] ' This seems, says Mr. Sympson,
' to be as odd a reason as well could be given, to confirm the line
' above;' And he supposes that ' some line or lines have been dropt.'—
The first copy is much confused in this scene: It never mentions the
departure of Jacomo; but on Fabritio's saying ' Come, all friends,'
it says, *Exeunt*, as if all were to depart, though Fabritio and the two
ladies continue conversing.—The alteration of *so* to *sore* (which we
have made) destroys the absurdity which Sympson complains of,
and which every one must see.

Clora.

Clora. I'd go a mile (to fee him cry) in flippers,
He would look fo like a whey-cheefe.

Frank. 'Would we might fee him once more!

Fab. If you dare
Venture a fecond trial of his temper,
I make no doubt to bring him.

Clora. No, good Frank,
Let him alone : I fee his vein lies only
For falling out at wakes and bear-baitings,
That may exprefs him fturdy.

Fab. Now, indeed,
You are too fharp, fweet fifter ; for unlefs
It be this fin, which is enough to drown him,
I mean this fournefs, he's as brave a fellow,
As forward, and as underftanding elfe,
As any he that lives.

Frank. I do believe you ;
And, good Sir, when you fee him, if we have
Diftafted his opinion any way,
Make peace again.

Fab. I will. I'll leave ye, ladies.

Clora. Take heed! y' had beft; h' has fworn to pay
you elfe.

Fab. I warrant you; I have been often threaten'd.

Clora. When he comes next, I'll have the cough, or
tooth-ach,
Or fomething that fhall make me keep my chamber ;
I love him fo well.

Frank. 'Would you'd keep your tongue! [*Exeunt.*

SCENE IV.[43]

Enter Angelo.

Ang. I cannot keep from this ungodly woman,
This Lelia ; whom I know too, yet am caught ;

[43] *Scene IV.*] The meafure of this fcene (till the entrance of the
Father) is, in all editions prior to that of 1750, divided extremely
bad ; Mr. Sympfon then made a new divifion of the lines, which
feems to us far from fatisfactory. We have endeavoured to make
out a better and more natural one.

Her

Her looks are nothing like her : 'Would her faults
Were all in Paris print upon her face,
Cum privilegia to ufe 'em ftill ! I would write
An epiftle before it, on the infide of her mafk,
And dedicate it to the whore of Babylon ;
With a preface upon her nofe to the gentle reader :
And they fhould be to be fold
At the fign of the Whore's Head i' th' Pottage-pot,
In what ftreet you pleafe. But all this helps not me!
I'm made to be thus catch'd, paft any redrefs,
With a thing I contemn too. I've read Epictetus
Twice over 'gainft the defire of thefe outward things;
And ftill her face runs in my mind : I went
To fay my prayers, and they were fo laid out o' th' way,
That if I could find any prayers I had,
I am no Chriftian. This is the door, and the fhort is,
I muft fee her again.   [*He knocks.*

Enter Maid.

Maid. Who's there ?
Ang. 'Tis I :
I would fpeak with your miftrefs.
   Maid. Did fhe fend for you ?
   Ang. No; what then ? I would fee her. Prithee,
      by thy leave !
   Maid. Not by my leave ; for fhe will not fee you,
      but doth hate
You and your friend, and doth wifh you both hang'd ;
Which, being fo proper men, is great pity
That you are not.
   Ang. How is this ?
   Maid. For your fweet felf, in particular,
Who fhe refolves perfuaded your friend to neglect her,
She deemeth whipcord the moft convenient unction,
For your back and fhoulders.
   Ang. Let me in, I'll fatisfy her.
   Maid. And if 't fhall happen that you are in doubt
Of thefe my fpeeches, infomuch that you
Shall fpend more time in arguing at the door,

                        I am

I am fully perſuaded that my miſtreſs in perſon from
 above,
Will utter her mind more at large, by way
Of urine upon your head, that it may ſink
The more ſoundly into your underſtanding faculties.

 Ang. This is the ſtrangeſt thing! Good pretty ſoul,
Why doſt thou uſe me ſo? I pray thee
Let me in, Sweet-heart!

 Maid. Indeed I cannot, Sweet-heart!

 Ang. Thou art a handſome one, and this croſſneſs
Does not become thee.

 Maid. Alas, I cannot help it.

 Ang. Eſpecially to me: Thou know'ſt when I was
 here
I ſaid I lik'd thee of all thy miſtreſs' ſervants.

 Maid. So did I you; tho' it be not my fortune
To expreſs it at this preſent; for truly,
If you would cry, I cannot let you in.

 Ang. Pox on her! I muſt go the down-right way.——
  Look you,
Here is ten pound for you, let me ſpeak with her.

 Maid. I like your gold well, but it is a thing,
By Heav'n, I cannot do! She will not ſpeak with you,
Eſpecially at this time; ſh' has affairs.

 Ang. This makes her leave her jeſting yet.—But
  take it,
And let me ſee her; bring me to a place
Where, undiſcerned of herſelf, I may
Feed my deſiring eyes but half-an-hour.

 Maid. Why, faith, I think I can; and I will ſtretch
My wits and body too for gold. If you will ſwear,
As you are gentle, not to ſtir or ſpeak,
Whatever [45] you ſhall ſee or hear, now or hereafter—
Give me your gold: I'll plant you.

 Ang. Why, as I am a gentleman,
I will not.

 Maid. Enough. Quick! follow me. [*Exeunt.*

---

 45 *Where you ſhall.*] Varied by Sympſon.

Enter

Enter Servant.

Serv. Why, where's this maid ? She has much care
　　of her bufinefs !
Nell ! I think fhe be funk ! Why, Nell ! whiew !
　Maid [*within*]. What is the matter ?

Enter Maid.

Serv. I pray you heartily come away !
Oh, come, come. The gentleman my miftrefs invited
Is coming down the ftreet, and the banquet
Not yet brought out !　　[*They bring in the banquet.*
　Lelia [*within*]. Nell, firrah !
　Maid. I come, forfooth.
　Serv. Now muft I walk :
When there is any flefhly matters in hand,
My miftrefs fends me of a four hours' errand :
But if I go not about mine own bodily bufinefs
As well as fhe, I am a Turk.　　[*Exit.*

Enter Father.

　Father. What ! all wide open ? 'Tis the way to fin,
Doubtlefs ; but I muft on ; the gates of hell
Are not more paffable than thefe : How they
Will be to get out, God knows ; I muft try.
'Tis very ftrange ! If there be any life
Within this houfe, 'would it would fhew itfelf !
What's here ? a banquet ? and no mouth to eat,
Or bid me do it ? This is fomething like
The entertainment of adventurous knights
Ent'ring enchanted caftles ; for the manner,
Tho' there be nothing difmal to be feen,
Amazes me a little.　What is meant
By this ftrange invitation ? I will found
My daughter's meaning ere I fpeak to her,
If it be poffible ; for by my voice　　[*Mufick.*
She will difcover me.　Hark ! whence is this ?

T H E

THE SONG[46].

Come hither, you that love, and hear me sing
      Of joys still growing,
Green, fresh and lusty, as the pride of spring,
      And ever blowing.
Come hither, youths that blush, and dare not know
      What is desire,
And old men, worse than you, that cannot blow
      One spark of fire.
And with the power of my enchanting song,
Boys shall be able men, and old men young.

Enter Angelo above.

Come hither, you that hope, and you that cry;
      Leave off complaining;
Youth, strength, and beauty, that shall never die,
      Are here remaining.
Come hither, fools, and blush you stay so long
      From being blest,
And mad men worse than you, that suffer wrong,
      Yet seek no rest.
And in an hour, with my enchanting song,
You shall be ever pleas'd, and young maids long.

Enter Lelia and Woman, with night-gown and slippers.

Lelia. Sir, you are welcome hither! as this kiss,
Giv'n with a larger freedom than the use
Of strangers will admit, shall witness to you.—
Put the gown on him.—In this chair sit down.—
Give him his slippers.—Be not so amaz'd:
Here's to your health! and you shall feel this wine
Stir lively in me, in the dead of night.—
Give him some wine.—Fall to your banquet, Sir;
And let us grow in mirth. Tho' I am set
Now thus far off you, yet, four glasses hence,
I will sit here, and try, till both our bloods

---

[46] 'Tis a sufficient compliment to this Song, that Mr. Killigrew
has inserted it in his Thomaso, or Merry Wanderer. *Sympson.*

Shoot

Shoot up and down to find a paſſage out;
Then mouth to mouth will we walk up to bed,
And undreſs one another as we go;
Where both my treaſure, body, and my ſoul,
Are yours to be diſpos'd of.

    Father. Umh! umh!
                [*Makes ſigns of his white head and beard.*

    Lelia. You are old?
Is that your meaning? Why, you are to me
The greater novelty; all our freſh youth
Are daily offer'd me. Tho' you perform,
As you think, little, yet you ſatisfy
My appetite; from your experience
I may learn ſomething in the way of luſt
I may be better for. But I can teach
Theſe young ones: But this day I did refuſe
A pair of them; Julio and Angelo,
And told them they were, as they were, raw fools
And whelps.   [*Ang. makes diſcontented ſigns.*

    Maid. Pray God he ſpeak not!
        [*Maid lays her finger* croſs *her mouth to him.*

    Lelia. Why ſpeak you not,
Sweet Sir?

    Father. Umh!
      [*Stops his ears; ſhews he is troubled with the muſick.*

    Lelia. Peace there, that muſick! Now, Sir,
Speak to me.

    Father. Umh!   [*Points at the Maid.*

    Lelia. Why? would you have her gone?
You need not keep your freedom in for her;
She knows my life, that ſhe might write it; think
She is a ſtone: She is a kind of bawdy confeſſor,
And will not utter ſecrets.

    Father. Umh!   [*Points at her again.*

    Lelia. Be gone then,
Since he needs will have it ſo. 'Tis all one.
        [*Exit Maid. Father locks the door.*
Is all now as you would? Come, meet me then;
And bring a thouſand kiſſes on thy lips,

  Vol. VI.   F   And

And I will rob thee of 'em, and yet leave
Thy lips as wealthy as they were before.
   Father. Yes, all is as I would, but thou!
   Lelia. By Heaven,
It is my father!   [*Starts.*
   Father. And I do beseech thee
Leave these unheard-of lusts, which worse become thee
Than mocking of thy father. Let thine eyes
Reflect upon thy soul, and there behold
How loathed black it is ; and whereas now
Thy face is heav'nly fair, but thy mind foul,
Go but into thy closet, and there cry
'Till thou hast spoil'd that face, and thou shalt find
How excellent a change thou wilt have made,
For inward beauty.
   Lelia. Tho' I know him now
To be my father, never let me live
If my lust do abate ! I'll take upon me
To have known him all this while.
   Father. Look ! dost thou know me ?
   Lelia. I knew you, Sir, before.
   Father. What didst thou do ?
   Lelia. Knew you: And so unmov'dly have you borne
All the sad crosses that I laid upon you,
With such a noble temper, which indeed
I purposely cast on you, to discern
Your carriage in calamity, and you
Have undergone 'em with that brave contempt,
That I have turn'd the reverence of a child
Into the hot affection of a lover :
Nor can there on the earth be found, but yours,
A spirit fit to meet with mine.
   Father. A woman ?
Thou art not sure !
   Lelia. Look and believe.
   Father. Thou art
Something created to succeed the devil,
When he grows weary of his envious course,
And compassing the world. But I believe thee;
                      Thou

Thou didſt but mean to try my patience,
And doſt ſo ſtill : But better be advis'd,
And make thy trial with ſome other things
That ſafelier will admit a dalliance :
And if it ſhould be earneſt, underſtand
How curs'd thou art ! ſo far from Heaven, that thou
Believ'ſt it not enough to damn alone,
Or with a ſtranger, but wouldſt heap all ſins
Unnatural upon this aged head ;
And draw thy father to thy bed, and hell !

 Lelia. You are deceiv'd, Sir ; 'tis not againſt nature
For us to lie together : If you have
An arrow of the ſame tree with your bow,
Is't more unnatural to ſhoot it there
Than in another ? 'Tis our general nature
To procreate, as fire's is to conſume ;
And it will trouble you to find a ſtick
The fire will turn from. If 't be Nature's will
We ſhould not mix, ſhe will diſcover to us
Some moſt apparent croſſneſs, as our organs
Will not be fit ; which if we do perceive
We'll leave, and think it is her pleaſure
That we ſhould deal with others.

 Father. The doors are faſt ;
Thou ſhalt not ſay a prayer ! 'tis not God's will
Thou ſhouldſt. When this is done, I'll kill myſelf,
That never man may tell me I got thee.

  [*Father draws his ſword ; Angelo diſcovers himſelf.*
 Lelia. I pray you, Sir !—Help there !—for God's
  ſake, Sir !

 Ang. Hold, reverend Sir ! for honour of your age !
 Father. Who's that ?
 Ang. For ſafety of your ſoul, and of the ſoul
Of that too-wicked woman yet to die !
 Father. What art thou ? and how cam'ſt thou to that
  place ?
 Ang. I am a man ſo ſtrangely hither come,
That I have broke an oath in ſpeaking this ;
But I believe 'twas better broke than kept,
And I deſire your patience. Let me in,

And I proteſt I will not hinder you
In any act you wiſh, more than by word.
If ſo I can perſuade you, that I will not
Uſe violence, I'll throw my ſword down to you.
This houſe holds none but I, only a maid,
Whom I will lock faſt in, as I come down.
    Father. I do not know thee; but thy tongue doth ſeem
To be acquainted with the truth ſo well
That I will let thee in : Throw down thy ſword.
    Ang. There 'tis !
    Lelia. How came he there ? I am betray'd to ſhame !
The fear of ſudden death ſtruck me all over
So violently, that I ſcarce have breath
To ſpeak yet : But I have it in my head,
And out it ſhall, that, Father, may perhaps
O'er-reach you yet.   [*Father lets in Angelo.*
    Father. Come, Sir ; what is't you ſay ?
    Lelia. My Angelo ! By all the joys of love,
Thou art as welcome, as theſe pliant arms
Twin'd round, and faſt about thee, can perſuade thee !
    Ang. Away !
    Lelia. I was in ſuch a fright before thou cam'ſt !
Yon old mad fellow (it will make thee laugh,
Tho' it fear'd me) has talk'd ſo wildly here !
Sirrah, he ruſh'd in at my doors, and ſwore
He was my father, and, I think, believ'd it :
But that he had a ſword, and threaten'd me,
I'faith he was good ſport.   Good, thruſt him out,
That thou and I may kiſs together; wilt thou ?
    Father. Are you her champion ? and with theſe fair
            words,
Got in to reſcue her from me ?   [*Offers to run at him.*
    Ang. Hold, Sir !
I ſwear I do not harbour ſuch a thought :
I ſpeak it not for that you have two ſwords,
But for 'tis truth.
    Lelia. Two ſwords, my Angelo ?
Think this, that thou haſt two young brawny arms
And ne'er a ſword, and he has two good ſwords
And ne'er an arm to uſe 'em : Ruſh upon him !.
                         I could

I could have beaten him with this weak body,
If I had had the ſpirit of a man.

Ang. Stand from me, and leave talking, or by Heaven
I'll trample thy laſt damning word out of thee!

Father. Why do you hinder me then? ſtand away,
And I will rid her quickly.

Lelia. 'Would I were
Clear of this buſineſs! yet I cannot pray.

Ang. Oh, be advis'd! Why, you were better kill her,
If ſhe were good. Convey her from this place,
Where none but you, and ſuch as you appoint,
May viſit her; where let her hear of nought
But death and damning, (which ſhe hath deſerv'd)
'Till ſhe be truly, juſtly ſorrowful;
And then, lay mercy to her, who does know
But ſhe may mend?

Father. But whither ſhould I bear her?

Ang. To my houſe;
'Tis large and private; I will lend it you.

Father. I thank you, Sir; and happily it fits
With ſome deſign I have. But how ſhall we
Convey her——

Lelia. Will they carry me away?

Father. For ſhe will ſcratch and kick, and ſcream ſo
    loud
That people will be drawn to reſcue her.

Ang. Why, none can hear her here, but her own maid,
Who is as faſt as ſhe.

Father. But in the ſtreet?

Ang. Why, we will take 'em both into the kitchen,
There bind 'em, and then gag 'em, and then throw 'em
Into a coach I'll bring to the back-door,
And hurry 'em away.

Father. It ſhall be ſo.
I owe you much for this, and I may pay you:
There is your ſword. Lay hold upon her quickly.
This way with me, thou diſobedient child!
Why does thy ſtubborn heart beat at thy breaſt?
Let it be ſtill; for I will have it ſearch'd

'Till

'Till I have found a well of living tears
Within it, that shall spring out of thine eyes,
And flow all o'er thy body foul'd with sin,
'Till it have wash'd it quite without a stain.

 Lelia. Help! help! ah! ah! Murder! I shall be
   murder'd!   [*They drag her.*
I shall be murdered!

 Father. This helps thee not.

 Lelia. Basely murder'd, basely!

 Father. I warrant you.   [*Exeunt.*

A C T V. S C E N E I.

Enter Lodovico and Piso.

Lod. THIS roguy Captain has made fine work
     with us.

 Piso. I would the devil in a storm would carry him
Home to his garrison again. I ache all over,
That I am sure of! Certainly my body
Is of a wildfire [48], for my head rings backward,
Or else I have a morris in my brains.

 Lod. I'll deal no more with soldiers. Well re-
   member'd;
Did not the vision promise to appear
About this time again?

 Piso. Yes. Here he comes:
He's just on's word.

Enter Father.

 Father. Oh, they be here together.
She's penitent; and, by my troth, I stagger

---

 [48] *Is of a wildfire.*] So the old copies. The reading in the text
[*all* for *of*] is from Mr. Seward's conjecture, who thinks it much
more agreeable to the tenor of this speech.   *Sympson.*

 We believe the reading of the old copies right; meaning, *My
body is* [MADE] *of a wildfire.*

             Whether,

Whether, as now she is, either of these
Two fools be worthy of her : Yet, because
Her youth is prone to fall again, ungovern'd,
And marriage now may stay her, one of 'em
(And Piso, since I understand him abler)
Shall be the man; the other bear the charges,
And willingly, as I will handle it.
I have a ring here, which he shall believe
Is sent him from a woman I have thought of :
But e'er I leave it, I'll have one of his
In pawn worth two on't; for I will not lose
By such a mess of sugar-sops as this is;
I am too old.

    Lod. It moves again; let's meet it.

    Father. Now, if I be not out, we shall have fine sport.
I am glad I've met you, Sir, so happily;
You do remember me, I'm sure.

    Lod. I do, Sir.

    Piso. This is a short preludium to a challenge.

    Father. I have a message, Sir, that much concerns
           you,
And for your special good. Nay, you may hear too.

    Piso. What should this fellow mean ?

    Father. There is a lady—
How the poor thing begins to warm already—
Come to this town, (as yet a stranger here, Sir)
Fair, young, and rich, both in possessions,
And all the graces that make up a woman,
A widow, and a virtuous one.—It works;
He needs no broth upon't.

    Lod. What of her, Sir ?

    Father. No more but this; she loves you.

    Lod. Loves me ?

    Father. Yes;
And with a strong affection, but a fair one.
If you be wise and thankful, you are made:
There's the whole matter.

    Lod. I am sure I hear this.

    Father. Here is a ring, Sir, of no little value;

Which,

Which, after she had seen you at a window,
She bad me haste, and give it; when she blush'd
Like a blown rose.

Lod. But pray, Sir, by your leave—
Methinks your years should promise no ill meaning.

Father. I am no bawd, nor cheater, nor a courser [49]
Of broken-winded women: If you fear me,
I'll take my leave, and let my lady use
A fellow of more form; an honester
I'm sure she cannot.

Lod. Stay! you have confirm'd me:
Yet let me feel; you are in health?

Father. I hope so;
My water's well enough, and my pulse.

Lod. Then
All may be excellent. Pray pardon me;
For I am like a boy that had found money,
Afraid I dream still.

Piso. Sir, what kind of woman,
Of what proportion, is your lady?

Lod. Ay?

Father. I'll tell you presently her very picture:
D' you know a woman in this town they call—
Stay; yes; it is so—Lelia?

Piso. Not by sight.

Father. Nor you, Sir?

Lod. Neither.

---

49 *Nor a* coarser.] Though I have chang'd *coarser* to *courser*, as
we commonly pronounce it, yet I fancy we ought to make a farther
correction still, and for *courser* read *coser*, i. e. *mango*, a merchant or
dealer in, &c. The word *cose* in Scotch signifying to change or
barter. I am indebted to the ingenious and learned Mr. Lye, for this
sense of the word. *Vid. Junii Etymologicon Anglicanum ad verbum
cosed.* Sympson.

Though Mr. Sympson thus confidently says, ' I HAVE CHANGED,'
yet COURSER is the reading of the second folio; and is, as the context proves, evidently right; *a* COURSER *of* broken-winded *women*.
—In the same stile is his assertion, that, when Angelo (p. 78) is
persuading Lelia's Maid to admit him into the house, the other copies
make Angelo say, *This crossness does become thee*, and that ' he has
' inserted the particle NOT,' which, however, appears in the second
folio.

Father.

Father. Thefe are precious rogues,
To rail upon a woman they ne'er faw:
So they would ufe their kindred.   [*Afide.*

Pifo. We have heard tho'
She's very fair and goodly.

Father. Such another,
Juft of the fame complexion, making, fpeech,
(But a thought fweeter) is my lady.

Lod. Then
She muft be excellent indeed.

Father. Indeed fhe is,
And you will find it fo. You do believe me?

Lod. Yes, marry do I; and I am fo alter'd——

Father. Your happinefs will alter any man.
Do not delay the time, Sir: At a houfe
Where don Velafco lay, the Spanifh fignor,
Which now is fignor Angelo's, fhe is.

Lod. I know it.

Father. But before you fhew yourfelf,
Let it be night by all means; willingly
By day fhe would not have fuch gallants feen
Repair unto her; 'tis her modefty.

Lod. I'll go and fit myfelf.

Father. Do; and be fure
You fend provifion in, in full abundance,
Fit for the marriage; for this night, I know,
She will be yours. Sir, have you ne'er a token
Of worth to fend her back again? You muft;
She will expect it.

    Lod. Yes; pray give her this,   [*Gives a ring.*
And with it, all I have. I'm made for ever! [*Exit.*

    Pifo. Well, thou haft fools' luck. Should I live as
        long
As an old oak, and fay my prayers hourly,
I fhould not be the better of a penny.
I think the devil be my ghoftly father!
Upon my confcience, I am full as handfome;
I'm fure I have more wit, and more performance,
Which is a pretty matter.

                     Father.

Father. Do you think, Sir,
That your friend, fignor Pifo, will be conftant
Unto my lady? you fhould know him well.

Pifo. Who? fignor Pifo?

Father. Yes, the gentleman.

Pifo. Why, you are wide, Sir.

Father. Is not his name Pifo?

Pifo. No; mine is Pifo.

Father. How!

Pifo. It is indeed, Sir;
And his is Lodovic.

Father. Then I'm undone, Sir!
For I was fent at firft to Pifo. What a rafcal
Was I, fo ignorantly to miftake you!

Pifo. Peace;
There is no harm done yet.

Father. Now 'tis too late,
I know my error: At turning of a ftreet,
(For you were then upon the right-hand of him)
You chang'd your places fuddenly; where I
(Like a crofs blockhead [5]) loft my memory.
What fhall I do? My lady utterly
Will put me from her favour.

Pifo. Never fear it;
I'll be thy guard, I warrant thee. Oh, oh!
Am I at length reputed? For the ring,
I'll fetch it back with a light vengeance from him:
H' had better keep tame devils than that ring.
Art thou not fteward?

Father. No.

Pifo. Thou fhalt be fhortly.

Father. Lord, how he takes it!   [*Afide.*

Pifo. I'll go fhift me ftraight.
Art fure it was to Pifo?

Father. Oh, too fure, Sir.

---

[5] *A crofs blockhead.*] I have a ftrong fufpicion that *grofs* was the
original reading, *i. e.* what a great, ftupid, dull, &c. blockhead was I?
                                                        Sympfon.
Crofs may perhaps be ufed by the Poets in the fenfe of *blundering.*
                                                        Pifo.

Pifo. I'll mount thee, if I live, for't.—Give me
  patience,
Heaven, to bear this bleffing, I befeech thee !
I am but man ! I prithee break my head,
To make me underftand I'm fenfible.

Father. Lend me your dagger, and I will, Sir.

Pifo. No ;
I believe now, like a good Chriftian.

Father. Good Sir, make hafte ; I dare not go without
  you,
Since I have fo miftaken.

Pifo. 'Tis no matter :
Meet me within this half-hour at St. Margaret's.—
Well, go thy ways, old leg ! thou haft the trick on't.
          [*Exit.*

Enter Angelo and Julio.

Ang. How now ! the news ?

Father. Well, paffing well ; I have 'em
Both in a leafh, and made right for my purpofe.

Julio. I'm glad on't. I muft leave you.

Ang. Whither, man ?

Julio. If all go right, I may be faft enough too.

Ang. I cry you mercy, Sir ! I know your meaning :
Clora's the woman ; fhe's Frank's bedfellow,
Commend me to 'em ; and go, Julio,
Bring 'em to fupper all, to grace this matter :
They'll ferve for witneffes.

Julio. I will. Farewell !
  [*Ex. Julio at one door ; Ang. and Father at another.*

SCENE II.

Enter Clora, Frank, Frederick, and Maid.

Fred. Sifter, I brought you Jacomo to th' door :
He has forgot all that he faid laft night ;
And fhame of that makes him more loth to come.
I left Fabritio perfuading him ;
But 'tis in vain.

          Frank.

Frank. Alas, my fortune, Clora!

Clora. Now, Frank, fee what a kind of man you
     love,
That loves you when he's drunk.

Frank. If fo,
Faith I would marry him : My friends, I hope,
Would make him drink.

Clora. 'Tis well confider'd, Frank,
He has fuch pretty humours then.   Befides,
Being a foldier, 'tis better he fhould love you
When he's drunk, than when he's fober ; for then
He will be fure to love you the greateft part on's life.

Frank. And were not I a happy woman then ?

Clora. That ever was born, Frank, i'faith.

Fred. How now ! what fays he ?

Enter Fabritio.

Fab. Faith, you may as well 'tice a dog up
With a whip and bell, as him by telling him
Of love and women : He fwears they mock him.

Fred. Look how my fifter weeps.

Fab. Why, who can help it ?

Fred. Yes, you may fafely fwear fhe loves him.

Fab. Why, fo I did ; and may do all the oaths
Arithmetick can make, ere he believe me ;
And fince he was laft drunk, he is more jealous
They would abufe him.   If we could perfuade him
She lov'd, he would embrace it.

Fred. She herfelf
Shall bate fo much of her own modefty,
To fwear it to him, with fuch tears as now
You fee rain from her.

Fab. I believe 'twould work ;
But would you have her do't i' th' open ftreet ?
Or, if you would, he'll run away from her.
How fhall we get him hither ?

Fred. By entreaty.

Fab. 'Tis moft impoffible.   No ; if we could
Anger him hither, (as there is no way

But

But that to bring him) and then hold him faft,
Women and men, whilft fhe delivers to him
The truth feal'd with her tears, he would be pliant [51]
As a pleas'd child. He walks below for me,
Under the window.

Clora. We'll anger him, I warrant ye:
Let one o' th' maids take a good bowl of water,
Or fay it be a pifs-pot, and pour it
On's head.

Fab. Content! Hang me, if I like not
The caft on't rarely; for no queftion
'Tis an approv'd receipt to fetch fuch a fellow.
Take all the women-kind in this houfe, betwixt
The age of one and one hundred, and let them
Take unto them a pot or a bowl, containing
Seven quarts or upwards, and let them never leave
'Till the above-nam'd pot or bowl become full;
Then let one of them ftretch out her arm, and pour it
On his head, and, *probatum eft*, it will fetch him;
For in his anger he will run up, and then
Let us alone.

Clora. Go you and do it. [*Exit Maid.*
Frank. Good Clora, no.
Clora. Away, I fay, and do it. Never fear;
We have enough of that water ready diftill'd.
Frank. Why, this will make him mad, Fabritio;
He'll neither love me drunk, nor fober, now.
Fab. I warrant you. What, is the wench come up?

Enter Maid above.

Clora. Art thou there, wench?
Maid. Ay.
Fab. Look out then
If thou canft fee him.
Maid. Yes, I fee him; and by my troth

---

[51] *He would be plain.*] *Plain* being evidently corrupt, Mr. Seward
propofes to read *pliant*; and Mr. Sympfon, *fain*, i. e. (upon authority of Spenfer) *fond*. We think this very uncouth, and that Seward's
conjecture is much more plaufible.

He

He ſtands ſo fair, I could not hold, were he
My father. His hat's off too, and he's ſcratching
His head.

Fab. Oh, waſh that hand, I prithee.

Maid. God ſend thee good luck !
'Tis the ſecond time I have thrown thee out to-day.
Ha, ha, ha ! juſt on's head.

Frank. Alas !

Fab. What does he now ?

Maid. He gathers ſtones : God's light, he breaks
    all the ſtreet-windows ⁵² !

Jac. [*within.*] Whores ! bawds ! your windows, your
    windows !

Maid. Now he is breaking
All the low windows with his ſword : Excellent ſport !
Now he's beating a fellow that laugh'd at him ;
Truly the man takes it patiently : Now he goes
Down the ſtreet gravely, looking on each ſide ;
There's not one more dare laugh.

Frank. Does he go on ?

Maid. Yes.

Frank. Fabritio, you have undone a maid [*Kneels.*
By treachery ; know you ſome other better,

---

⁵² *The* ſtreet *windows*] This is a paſſage I can't at all reconcile
with the context ; as perhaps not being ſkill'd enough in Architecture ;
for what *windows* were the *ſtreet* ones ? High ones, no doubt ; becauſe
he breaks them with ſtones. But what were the low ones he is now
breaking with his ſword ? Were not theſe toward the ſtreet too ? If
they were not, why are they not diſtinguiſh'd, and if they be, then
there is a diſtinction without a difference. I ſuſpect the paſſage corrupted, and that to make our Poets talk ſenſe, and the whole paſſage
conſiſtent ; we ought to read,
      ——— *the* garret *windows.*
The Captain broke thoſe with ſtones, the garret being the place from
whence the jordan was diſcharg'd, but after his ammunition was
ſpent, like a brave officer he charges the lower windows ſword in
hand, and manfully makes a mighty breach in the innocent and in-
offenſive ground-room windows.   *Sympſon.*

  The *ſtreet*-windows mean ſimply the windows that look to the
ſtreet ; any of which he might throw ſtones at ; but he could reach
none but the *lower* ones with his ſword, which are therefore ne-
ceſſarily ſpecified.

You would prefer your friend to ? If you do not,
Bring him again ! I have no other hope
But you, that made me lose hope; if you fail me,
I ne'er shall see him, but shall languish out
A discontented life, and die contemn'd.

Fab. This vexes me ! I pray you be more patient.
If I have any truth, let what will happen, [*Lifts her up.*
I'll bring him presently. Do you all stand
At the street-door, the maids, and all, to watch
When I come back, and have some private place
To shuffle me into; for he shall follow
In fury, but I know I can out-run him:
As he comes in, clap all fast hold on him,
And use your own discretions.

Fred. We will do it.

Fab. But suddenly; for I will bring him hither,
With that unstopp'd speed, that he shall run over
All that's in's way: And tho' my life be ventur'd,
'Tis no great matter, I will do't.

Frank. I thank you, worthy Fabritio. [*Exeunt.*

SCENE III.

Enter Jacomo.

Jac. I ever knew no woman could abide me;
But am I grown so contemptible,
By being once drunk amongst 'em, that they begin
To throw piss on my head? for surely it was piss:
Huh, huh ! [*Seems to smell.*

Enter Fabritio.

Fab. Jacomo, how dost thou ?

Jac. Well; something troubled
With watrish humours.

Fab. Foh ! how thou stink'st !
Prithee stand further off me. Methinks these humours
Become thee better than thy dry cholerick humours,
Or thy wine-wet humours. Ha !

Jac. You're pleasant ;

But,

But, Fabritio, know I am not in the mood
Of suffering jests.

Fab. If you be not i'th' mood,
I hope you will not be moody. But truly
I cannot blame the gentlewomen; you stood eves-
        dropping
Under their window, and would not come up.

Jac. Sir, I suspect now, by your idle talk,
Your hand was in't; which, if I once believe,
Be sure you shall account to me.

Fab. The gentlewomen
And the maids have counted to you already;
The next turn I see is mine.

Jac. Let me die, but this
Is very strange! Good Fabritio, don't
Provoke me so.

Fab. Provoke you? You're grown
The strangest fellow! there's no keeping company with
        you.
Pish! take you that.
        [*Fab. gives him a box o'th' ear. Jac. draws his sword.*

Jac. Oh, all the devils! Stand, slave!

Fab. Follow me if thou dar'st.   [*Exit.*

Jac. Stay, coward, stay!   [*Exit running.*

SCENE IV.

Enter Frederick, Frank, Clora, Servant, and Maid.

Clora. Be ready; for I see Fabritio running,
And Jacomo behind him.

Enter Fabritio.

Fab. Where's the place?

Fred. That way, Fabritio.   [*Exit Fab.*

Enter Jacomo.

Jac. Where art thou, treacher? [*Fred. Clora, and
        Maid, lay hold on Jac.*] What's the matter, Sirs?
Why do you hold me? I am basely wrong'd!

        Torture

Torture and hell be with you! let me go!

[*They drag him to a chair, and hold him down in it.*

Fred. Good Jacomo, be patient; and but hear
What I can say: You know I am your friend;
If you yet doubt it, by my soul I am.

Jac. 'Sdeath, stand away! I would my breath were
     poison!

Fred. As I have life, that which was thrown on you,
And this now done, were but to draw you hither
For causes weighty, that concern yourself,
Void of all malice; which this maid, my sister,
Shall tell you.

Jac. Puh! a pox upon you all! you will not hold me
For ever here; and, till you let me go,
I'll talk no more.

Frank. As you're a gentleman,
Let not this boldness make me be believ'd
To be immodest! If there were a way
More silently to be acquainted with you,
God knows, that I would chuse; but as it is,
Take it in plainness: I do love you more
Than you do your content. If you refuse
To pity me, I'll never cease to weep;
And when mine eyes be out, I will be told
How fast the tears I shed for you do fall;
And if they do not flow abundantly,
I'll fetch a sigh shall make 'em start and leap,
As if the fire were under.

Jac. Fine mocking, fine mocking!

Fred. Mocking? Look how she weeps.

Jac. Does she counterfeit crying too?

Fred. Behold how the tears flow! Or pity her,
Or never more be call'd a man.

Jac. How's this?
Soft you, soft you, my masters! Is it possible, think
    you,
She should be in earnest?

Clora. Earnest? Ay, in earnest:
She is a fool to break so many sleeps,

That would have been found ones,
And venture such a face, and so much life,
For e'er an humorous afs i' th' world.

   Frank. Why, Clora,
I have known you cry as much for Julio,
That has not half his worth. All night you write
And weep, too much, I fear; I do but what
I should.

   Clora. If I do write, I'm anfwer'd, Frank.

   Frank. I would I might be fo!

   Jac. Good Frederick, let me go;
I would fain try if that thing do not counterfeit.

   Fred. Give me your fword then.

   Jac. No; but take my word,
As I am man, I will not hurt a creature
Under this roof, before I have deliver'd
Myfelf, as I am now, into your hands,
Or have your full confent.

   Fred. It is enough.

   Jac. Gentlewoman, I pray you let me feel your
        face:
I am an infidel, if she don't weep!
Stay; where's my handkerchief? I'll wipe
The old wet off: The fresh tears come! Pox on't, I am
A handfome gracious fellow amongft women,
And knew it not. Gentlewoman, how should I know
Thefe tears are for me? Is not your mother dead?

   Frank. By Heav'n, they are for you!

   Jac. 'Slight, I'll have my head curl'd and powder'd
Tomorrow by break of day. If you love me,
I pray you kifs me; for if I love you,
It shall be such love as I will not
Be afham'd of. If this be a mock,   [*Kiffes.*
It is the heartieft and the fweeteft mock
That e'er I tafted. Mock me fo again! [*Kiffes again.*

   Fred. Fy, Jacomo! why do you let her kneel
So long?

   Jac. It's true; I had forgot it, and should have
       done   [*Lifts her up.*
                        This

This twelvemonth: Pray you rife. Frederick,
If I could all this while have been perfuaded
She could have lov'd me, doft thou think I had
Not rather kifs her than another fhould?
And yet you may gull me, for aught I know;
But if you do, hell take me if I do not cut
All your throats fleeping!

Fred. Oh, do not think of fuch a thing.

Jac. Otherwise, if fhe be in earneft, the fhort is,
I am.

Frank. Alas, I am.

Jac. And I did not think it
Poffible any woman could have lik'd
This face: It's good for nothing, is it?

Clora. Yes,
It is worth forty fhillings to pawn, being lin'd [53]
Almoft quite thro' with velvet.

Frank. It is better
Than your Julio's.

Jac. Thou thinkeft fo;
But otherwife, in faith, it is not, Frank.

[*Whilft Jacomo is kiffing Frank,*

Enter Fabritio.

Fab. Hift, Jacomo! How doft thou, boy? ha?

Jac. Why, very well,
I thank you, Sir.

Fab. Doft thou perceive the reafon
Of matters and paffages yet, firrah, or no?

---

53 *Lined.*] In act iii. fcene vi. of this play, Pifo defcribes Jacomo as one that wore his forehead in a velvet fcabbard, and Clora here fays his face is worth forty fhillings to pawn upon account of its velvet lining. If *lin'd* be not a *Latinifm* here, we muft have the *lining* not on the *infide* as ufual, but on the *out.* What we may farther remark from hence is, the difference of patches in the Poet's days and in ours. The heroes of the blade then would have nothing lefs than velvet, whereas plain filk is thought good enough by thofe now. *Simpfon.*

Lined is, we believe, ufed in the fame fenfe to this day by artifans, *&c.* The actors, in particular, call marking their features for old characters *lining the face*; though that may, indeed, bear another fenfe.

Jac. 'Tis wondrous good, Sir.

Fab. I've done simply for you:
But now you're beaten to some understanding,
I pray you dally not with the gentlewoman,
But dispatch your matrimony with all convenient speed.

Fred. He gives good counsel.

Jac. And I'll follow it.

Fab. And I you[54]. Prithee do not take it unkindly;
For, trust me, I box'd thee for thy advancement:
A foolish desire I had to joggle thee
Into preferment.

Jac. I apprehend you, Sir;
And if I can study out a course how a bastinadoing
May any ways raise your fortunes in the state,
You shall be sure on't.

Fab. Oh, Sir, keep your way.
God send you much joy!

Clora. And me my Julio!   [*Julio speaks within.*
Oh, God, I hear his voice! Now he is true,
Have at a marriage, Frank, as soon as you!
                     [*Exeunt all but Frederick.*

Enter Messenger.

Mess. Sir, I would speak with you.

Fred. What is
Your hasty business, friend?

Mess. The duke commands
Your present attendance at court.

Fred. The cause?

Mess. I know not in particular:
But this; many are sent for more, about affairs
Foreign, I take it, Sir.

Fred. I will be there
Within this hour. Return my humble service.

Mess. I will, Sir.   [*Exit.*

Fred. Farewell, friend. What news with you?

---

[54] And *I you*.] The occasion should seem to require us to read,
AS *I you*.

Enter

Serv. My miſtreſs would deſire you, Sir, to follow
With all the haſte you can: She is gone to church,
To marry Captain Jacomo; and Julio,
To do as much for the young merry gentlewoman,
Fair miſtreſs Clora.

Fred. Julio marry Clora?
Thou art deceiv'd, I warrant thee.

Serv. No ſure, Sir;
I ſaw their lips as cloſe upon the bargain
As cockles.

Fred. Give 'em joy! I cannot now go;
The duke hath ſent for me in haſte.

Serv. This note, Sir,
When you are free, will bring you where they are.

[Exit.

Fred. [reading.] ' You ſhall find us all at ſignor
    ' Angelo's,
' Where Piſo, and the worthy Lelia
' Of famous memory, are to be married;
' And we not far behind.' 'Would I had time
To wonder at this laſt couple in hell [55].

---

[55] *Laſt couple in hell.*] This is alluding to a ruſtic diverſion, called,
I think, by another name in our Poets, Shakeſpear, and the play-
wrights of that time, *viz. barley-break.* Sir John Suckling has a
pretty poem wherein he deſcribes this diverſion, which, for the ſake
of my readers, I have here inſerted:

    ' Love, Reaſon, Hate, did once beſpeak
    ' Three mates to play at Barley break;
    ' Love, Folly took; and Reaſon, Fancy;
    ' And Hate conſorts with Pride; ſo dance they:
    ' Love coupled laſt, and ſo it fell
    ' That Love and Folly were in hell.

    ' They break, and Love would Reaſon meet,
    ' But Hate was nimbler on her feet;
    ' Fancy looks for Pride, and thither
    ' Hies, and they two hug together:
    ' Yet this new coupling ſtill doth tell
    ' That Love and Folly were in hell.

    ' The reſt do break again, and Pride
    ' Hath now got Reaſon on her ſide;

Enter Messenger again.

Mess. You are stay'd for, Sir.

Fred. I come. Pray God the business
Hold me not from this sport! I would not lose it.

[*Exeunt.*

SCENE V.

Enter Father, Piso, Angelo, and Lelia.

Ang. God give you joy, and make you live together
A happy pair!

Piso. I do not doubt we shall.   There was never
Poor gentleman had such a sudden fortune!
I could thrust my head betwixt two pales, and strip me
Out of my old skin like a snake. Will the guests come,
Thou saidst thou sentest for to solemnise
The nuptials?

Father. They will; I look'd for 'em
Ere this.

Enter Julio, Jacomo, Fabritio, Frank, and Clora.

Julio. By your leave all.

Father. They are here, Sir.

Julio. Especially, fair lady,
I ask your pardon; to whose marriage-bed
I wish all good success! I have here brought you
Such guests as can discern your happiness,
And best do know how to rejoice at it
(For such a fortune they themselves have run):
The worthy Jacomo, and his fair bride;
Noble Fabritio, (whom this age of peace
Has not yet taught to love aught but the wars)
And his true friend, this lady, who is but

' Hate and Fancy meet, and stand
' Untoucht by Love in Folly's hand;
' Folly was dull, but Love ran well,
' So Love and Folly were in hell.

But the reader may find a more exact and minute description of this
diversion in Sir Philip Sydney's Arcadia.   *Sympson.*

A piece

A piece of me.

Lelia. Sir, you are welcome all!
Are they not, Sir?   [*Exit Father.*

Piſo. Bring in ſome wine;
Some of the wine Lodovic the fool ſent hither.
Whoever thou bid'ſt welcome, ſhall find it.

Lelia. An unexpected honour
You have done to our too-haſty wedding.

Jac. Faith,
Madam, our weddings were as haſty as yours:
We're glad to run up and down any whither,
To ſee where we can get meat to our wedding.

Piſo. That Lodovic hath provided too, good aſs!

Ang. I thought you, Julio, would not thus have
            ſtolen
A marriage, without acquainting your friends.

Julio. Why, I did give thee inklings.

Ang. If a marriage
Should be thus ſlubber'd up in a play,
Ere almoſt any body had taken notice
You were in love, the ſpectators would take it
To be but ridiculous.

Julio. This was the firſt, and I
Will never hide another ſecret from you.

Enter Father.

Father. Sir, yonder's your friend Lodovic: Hide
            yourſelf,
And it will be the beſt ſport——

Piſo. Gentlemen,
I pray you take no notice I am here:
The coxcomb Lodovic is coming in.   [*Retires.*

Enter Lodovico.

Lod. Is that the lady?

Father. That is my lady.

Lod. As I live, ſhe's a fair one!
What make all theſe here?

Father. Oh, Lord, Sir, ſhe's ſo peſter'd——

Fab. Now will the sport be; it runs right as Julio
Told us.

Lod. Fair lady, health to you! Some words
I have, that require an utterance more private
Than this place can afford.

Lelia. I'll call my husband;
All business I hear with his ears now.

Lod. Good madam, no; (but I perceive your jest)
You have no husband; I'm the very man
That walk'd the streets so comely.

Lelia. Are you so?

Lod. Yes, faith; when Cupid first did prick your
heart.
I am not cruel, but the love begun
I' th' street I'll satisfy i' th' chamber fully.

Lelia. To ask a madman whether he be mad
Were but an idle question; if you be,
I do not speak to you; but if you be not,
Walk in the streets again, and there perhaps
I may dote on you; here I not endure you.

Lod. Good madam, stay; do not you know this ring?

Lelia. Yes, it was mine; I sent it by my man
To change, and so he did; it has a blemish,
And this he brought me for it: Did you change it?
Are you a goldsmith?

Lod. Sure the world is mad!
Sirrah, did you not bring me this ring from your lady?

Father. Yes, surely, Sir, did I; but your worship
Must e'en bear with me, for there was a mistaking in it;
And so, as I was saying to your worship,
My lady is now married.

Lod. Married? to whom?

Father. To your worship's friend Pifo.

Lod. 'Sdeath! to Pifo?

Pifo [*within*]. Ha, ha, ha!

Ang. Yes, Sir, I can assure you
She's married to him; I saw't with these grey eyes.

Lod. Why, what a rogue art thou then? Thou hast
——made me

Send

Send in provision too.

Father. Oh, a gentleman
Should not have such foul words in's mouth ;
But your worship's provision
Could not have come in at a fitter time.
Will it please you to taste any of your own wine ?
It may be the vintner has cozen'd you.

Lod. Pox, I am mad !

Ang. You have always plots, Sir ; and see how they
    fall out !

Jac. You had a plot upon me: How do you like
    this ?

Lod. I do not speak to you.

Fab. Because you dare not.

Lod. But I will have one of that old rogue's teeth
Set in this ring.

Father. Dost not thou know
That I can beat thee ?—Dost thou know it now ?
                    [*Discovers himself.*

Lod. He beat me once indeed.

Father. And if you have
Forgot it, I can call a witness. Come forth, Piso !
Remember you it ?

Piso. Faith, I do call to mind
Such a matter.

Father. And if I cannot still do't,
You are young, and will assist your father-in-law.

Piso. My father-in-law ?

Ang. Your father-in-law,
As sure as this is widow Lelia.

Piso. How ! widow Lelia ?

Father. I'faith, 'tis she, son.

Lod. Ha, ha, ha ! let my provision go !
I'm glad I have miss'd the woman.

Piso. Have you put
A whore upon me ?

Lelia. By Heav'n, you do me wrong !
I have a heart as pure as any woman's ;
And I mean to keep it so for ever.

                          Father.

Father. There is
No ſtarting now, ſon; if you offer it,
I can compel you; her eſtate is great,
But all made o'er to me, before this match:
Yet if you uſe her kindly, (as I ſwear
I think ſhe will deſerve) you ſhall enjoy it
During your life, all, ſave ſome ſlender piece
I will reſerve for my own maintenance;
And if God bleſs you with a child by her,
It ſhall have all.

Piſo. So I may have the means,
I do not much care what the woman is:
Come, my ſweetheart! as long as I ſhall find
Thy kiſſes ſweet, and thy means plentiful,
Let people talk their tongues out.

Lelia. They may talk
Of what is paſs'd; but all that is to come
Shall be without occaſions.

Julio. Shall we not make
Piſo and Lodovic friends?

Jac. Hang 'em, they dare not
Be enemies; or, if they be, the danger
Is not great. Welcome, Frederick!

Enter Frederick.

Fred. Firſt, joy unto you all! And next,
I think we ſhall have wars.

Jac. Give me ſome wine!
I'll drink to that.

Fab. I'll pledge.

Frank. But I
Shall loſe you then.

Jac. Not a whit, wench;
I'll teach thee preſently to be a ſoldier.

Fred. Fabritio's command, and yours,
Are both reſtor'd.

Jac. Bring me four glaſſes then!

Fab. Where are they?

Ang. You ſhall not drink 'em here. It is ſupper time;
And

And from my houſe no creature here ſhall ſtir
Theſe three days; mirth ſhall flow as well as wine.
   Father. Content. Within, I'll tell you more at large
How much I am bound to all, but moſt to you,
Whoſe undeſerved liberality
Muſt not eſcape thus unrequited.
   Jac. 'Tis happineſs to me, I did ſo well:
Of every noble action, the intent
Is to give Worth reward, Vice puniſhment. [*Exeunt.*

E P I L O G U E.

IF you miſlike (as you ſhall ever be
  Your own free judges) this play utterly,
For your own nobleneſs yet do not hiſs!
But, as you go by, ſay it was amiſs,
And we will mend: Chide us, but let it be
Never in cold blood! O' my honeſty,
(If I have any) this I'll ſay for all;
Our meaning was to pleaſe you ſtill, and ſhall.

my house no creature here shall thir,
e days, mirth shall flow as well as wine.
Continue. Whilst, I'll tell you more at large
h I am bound to all, but most to you.

elope thus unrequited.

is happiness in mind diff so well :
noble actions, the future

Worth reward, Vice punishment. [Exeunt.

_____

PROLOGUE.

midlike (as you shall ever be
wn free judg'd) this play uncivil,
own audience, yet do not hate him !
to go lay, say it was amain,
ll mend : at huts us, but let it be
cold blood ! O my country,
any) this kill, joy for all,
ing was to please you still, and shall.

THE

PROPHETESS.

A TRAGICAL HISTORY.

The Commendatory Verses by Gardiner and Hills ascribe this Play solely to Fletcher. It was first printed in the folio of 1647. Mr. Seward, on the authority of Langbaine, says, it was revived by Dryden: But in this particular, we apprehend, they are both mistaken; as Downes, the prompter, in his Roscius Anglicanus, positively assigns the revival of it, and the alterations and additions made to it, to Betterton. The piece, thus altered, after the manner of an Opera, was represented at the Queen's Theatre, and printed in quarto, 1690. Purcell composed the musick, and Priest the dances: It appears to have been revived at a considerable expence, and has within a few years been performed at Covent-Garden Theatre.

DRAMATIS

DRAMATIS PERSONÆ.

MEN.

Charinus, *emperor of Rome.*
Cofroe, *king of Perfia.*
Diocles, *of a private foldier elected co-emperor.*
Maximinian, *nephew to Diocles, and emperor by his donation.*
Volutius Aper, *murderer of Numerianus, the late emperor.*
Niger, *general of the Roman forces.*
Camurius, *a captain, and creature of Aper.*
Geta, *a jefter, fervant to Diocles, a merry knave.*
Perfian Lords.
Senators.
Soldiers.
Guard.
Suitors.
Ambaffadors.
Lictors.
Flamen.
Shepherd.
Countrymen.
Attendants.

WOMEN.

Aurelia, *fifter to Charinus.*
Caffana, *fifter to Cofroe, a captive, waiting on Aurelia.*
Delphia, *a* Prophetefs.
Drufilla, *niece to Delphia, in love with Diocles.*

SCENE, ROME.

THE

THE PROPHETESS.

Dio. ———————— *Upon my knees*
I thus receive you: and, so you vouchsafe it,
This day I'm doubly married, to the empire,
And your best self.
Delp. *False and perfidious villain!*   Act II.

M. A. Rooker delin.   J. Collyer sculp.

THE

PROPHETESS.

ACT I. SCENE I.

Enter Charinus, Aurelia, and Niger.

Charinus. YOU buz into my head ftrange like-
              lihoods,
        And fill me full of doubts: But
        what proofs, Niger,
What certainties, that my moft noble brother
Came to his end by murder? Tell me that;
Affure me by fome circumftance.

   Niger. I will, Sir;
And as I tell you truth, fo the gods profper me!
I've often nam'd this Aper.

   Char. True, you have done;
And in myfterious fenfes I have heard you
Break out o' th' fudden, and abruptly.

   Niger. True, Sir:
Fear of your unbelief, and the time's giddinefs,
Made me I durft not then go further. So your Grace
        pleafe,
Out of your wonted goodnefs, to give credit ˢ,
I fhall unfold the wonder.

   Aur. Do it boldly:
You fhall have both our hearty loves and hearings.

ˢ *Out of your wonted goodnefs to give* credit.] Sympfon thinks it
would be better to read,
             to give ear to't.

Niger.

Niger. This Aper then, this too-much-honour'd villain,
(For he deferves no mention of a good man)——
Great Sir, give ear—this moft ungrateful, fpiteful,
Above the memory of mankind mifchievous,
With his own bloody hands——
   Char. Take heed!
   Niger. I'm in, Sir;
And, if I make not good my ftory——
   Aur. Forward!
I fee a truth would break out: Be not fearful.
   Niger. I fay, this Aper, and his damn'd ambition,
Cut off your brother's hopes, his life, and fortunes:
The honour'd Numerianus fell by him,
Fell bafely, moft untimely, and moft treach'roufly;
For in his litter, as he bore him company,
Moft privately and cunningly he kill'd him.
Yet ftill he fills the faithful foldiers' ears
With ftories of his weaknefs; of his life;
That he dare not venture to appear in open,
And fhew his warlike face among the foldiers,
The tendernefs and weaknefs of his eyes,
Being not able to endure the fun yet:
Slave that he is, he gives out this infirmity
(Becaufe he would difpatch his honour too)
To arife from wantonnefs, and love of women;
And thus he juggles ftill.
   Aur. Oh, moft pernicious,
Moft bloody, and moft bafe! Alas, dear brother,
Art thou accus'd, and after death thy memory
Loaden with fhames and lies? thofe pious tears
Thou daily fhower'dft upon my father's monument,
(When in the Perfian expedition
He fell unfortunately by a ftroke of thunder)
Made thy defame and fins? thofe wept-out eyes,
The fair examples of a noble nature,
Thofe holy drops of love, turn'd by depravers
(Malicious poifon'd tongues) to thy abufes?
We muft not fuffer this.

                          Char.

Char. It fhews a truth now:
And fure this Aper is not right nor honeft,
He will not now come near me.

Niger. No; he dare not:
He has an inmate here, that's call'd a Confcience,
Bids him keep off.

Char. My brother honour'd him,
Made him firft captain of his guard, his next friend;
Then to my mother (to affure him nearer)
He made him hufband.

Niger. And withal ambitious;
For when he trod fo nigh, his falfe feet itch'd, Sir,
To ftep into the ftate.

Aur. If you believe, brother,
Aper a bloody knave, as 'tis apparent,
Let's leave difputing, and do fomething noble.

Char. Sifter, be rul'd. I am not yet fo pow'rful
To meet him in the field: H' has under him
The flower of all the empire, and the ftrength,
The Britain and the German cohorts; pray you be
            patient.
Niger, how ftands the foldier to him?

Niger. In fear more, Sir,
Than love or honour: He has loft their fair affections,
By his moft covetous and greedy griping.
Are you defirous to do fomething on him,
That all the world may know you lov'd your brother?
And do it fafely too, without an army?

Char. Moft willingly.

Niger. Then fend out a profcription,
Send fuddenly; and to that man that executes it,
(I mean that brings his head) add a fair payment,
No common fum: Then you fhall fee, I fear not,
Ev'n from his own camp, from thofe men that follow
            him,
Follow and flatter him, we fhall find one,
And, if he mifs, one hundred, that will venture it.

Aur. For his reward, (it fhall be fo, dear brother,
So far I'll honour him that kills the villain;
For fo far runs my love to my dead brother)

Let him be what he will, bafe, old, or crooked,
He fhall have me : Nay, which is more, I'll love him.
I will not be denied.

Char. You fhall not, fifter :
But you fhall know, my love fhall go along too.
See a profcription drawn ; and for his recompenfe,
My fifter, and half partner in the empire ;
And I will keep my word.

Aur. Now you do bravely.

Niger. And, tho' it coft my life, I'll fee it publifh'd.

Char. Away then, for the bufinefs.

Niger. I am gone, Sir :
You fhall have all difpatch'd to-night.

Char. Be profperous.

Aur. And let the villain fall.

Niger. Fear nothing, madam.   [*Exeunt.*

SCENE II.

Enter Delphia and Drufilla.

Druf. 'Tis true, that Diocles is courteous,
And of a pleafant nature, fweet and temperate ;
His coufin Maximinian, proud and bloody.

Delph. Yes, and miftruftful too, my girl : Take heed ;
Altho' he feem to love thee, and affect,
Like the more courtier, curious compliment,
Yet have a care.

Druf. You know all my affection,
And all my heart-defires, are fet on Diocles :
But, aunt, how coldly he requites this courtefy,
How dull and heavily he looks upon me !
Altho' I wooe him fometimes beyond modefty,
Beyond a virgin's care, how ftill he flights me !
And puts me ftill off with your prophecy,
And the performance of your late prediction,
That when he's emp'ror, then he'll marry me !
Alas, what hope of that ?

Delp. Peace, and be patient ;
For tho' he be now a man moft miferable,
Of no rank, nor no badge of honour on him,

                                                    Bred

Bred low and poor, no eye of favour shining;
And tho' my sure prediction of his rising,
Which can no more fail than the day or night does,
Nay, let him be asleep, will overtake him,
Hath found some rubs and stops, yet (hear me, niece,
And hear me with a faith) it shall come to him.
I'll tell thee the occasion.

Druf. Do, good aunt;
For yet I'm ignorant.

Delp. Chiding him one day,
For being too near and sparing for a soldier [2],
Too griping, and too greedy, he made answer,
' When I am Cæsar, then I will be liberal:'
I presently, inspir'd with holy fire,
And my prophetic spirit burning in me,
Gave answer from the gods; and this it was:
Imperator eris Romæ, cum Aprum grandem interfeceris [3]:
' Thou shalt be emperor, oh, Diocles,
' When thou hast kill'd a mighty boar.' From that time,
As giving credit to my words, he has employ'd
Much of his life in hunting: Many boars,
Hideous and fierce, with his own hands h' has kill'd too,
But yet not lighted on the fatal one,
Should raise him to the empire. Be not sad, niece;
Ere long he shall. Come; let's go entertain him:
For by this time, I guess, he comes from hunting:
And, by my art, I find this very instant
Some great design's o'foot.

Druf. The gods give good, aunt! 　　　　*[Exeunt.*

---

[2] This whole speech, is almost a translation from Vopiscus.
　　　　　　　　　　　　　　　　　Sympson.

[3] I could wish this *splendidus pannus*, this Latin piece of patch-work, was not to be found in the oldest edition: It might very well have been spared, and the Author's learning have suffered no detriment. 　　　　　　　　　　　*Sympson.*
　　Never was a more injudicious censure, than this of Mr. Sympson upon the above Latin line; it being absolutely necessary, to preserve the pun (for so it must be called) upon the name of *Aper*, for the prediction to be delivered in that language: But perhaps Mr. Sympson would have had the traitor's name Anglicised, and have called him *Volutius* BOAR.

SCENE III.

Enter Diocles, Maximinian, and Geta with a boar.

Dio. Lay down the boar.

Geta. With all my heart; I'm weary on't:
I shall turn Jew, if I carry many such burdens.
Do you think, master, to be emperor
With killing swine? You may be an honest butcher,
Or allied to a seemly family of souse-wives.
Can you be such an ass, my reverend master,
To think these springs of pork will shoot up Cæsars?

Maxi. The fool says true.

Dio. Come, leave your fooling, sirrah,
And think of what thou shalt be when I'm emperor.

Geta. 'Would it would come with thinking! for then
O' my conscience I should be at least a senator.

Maxi. A sowter;
For that's a place more fitted to thy nature,
If there could be such an expectation.
Or, say the devil could perform this wonder,
Can such a rascal as thou art hope for honour?
Such a log-carrying lout?

Geta. Yes; and bear it too,
And bear it swimmingly. I'm not the first ass, Sir,
Has borne good office, and perform'd it reverendly.

Dio. Thou being the son of a tiler, canst thou hope
        to be a senator?

Geta. Thou being the son of a tanner, canst thou hope
        to be an emperor?

Dio. Thou say'st true, Geta; there's a stop indeed:
But yet the bold and virtuous——

Geta. You're right, master,
Right as a gun! For we, the virtuous,
Tho' we be kennel-rakers, scabs, and scoundrels,
We, the discreet and bold—And yet, now I remem-
        ber it,
We tilers may deserve to be senators,
(And there we step before you thick-skin'd tanners)

For

For we are born three ftories high ; no bafe ones,
None of your groundlings, mafter.

Dio. I like thee well ;
Thou haft a good mind, as I have, to this honour [4].

Geta. As good a mind, Sir, of a fimple plaifterer :
And, when I come to execute my office,
Then you fhall fee——

Maxi. What ?

Geta. An officer in fury,
An officer as he ought to be. Do you laugh at it ?
Is a fenator, in hope, worth no more reverence ?
By thefe hands, I'll clap you by th' heels the firft hour
of it !

Maxi. O' my confcience, the fellow believes !

Dio. Ay, do, do, Geta ;
For if I once be emperor——

Geta. Then will I
(For wife men muft be had to prop the republick)
Not bate you a fingle ace of a found fenator.

Dio. But what fhall we do the whilft ?

Geta. Kill fwine, and foufe 'em,
And eat 'em when we've bread.

Maxi. Why didft thou run away
When the boar made toward thee ? art thou not valiant ?

Geta. No, indeed am I not ; and 'tis for mine honour
too :
I took a tree, 'tis true, gave way to th' monfter ;
Hark what Difcretion fays : ' Let fury pafs ;
' From the tooth of a mad beaft, and the tongue of
a flanderer [5],
' Preferve thine honour.'

---

[4] *Thou haft a good mind.*] Betterton, in his alteration of this play,
reads,

    Thou haft as good a *mind as I have,* &c.
Sympfon follows him, but claims the merit of the variation.

[5] *Thine honour.*] *To preferve thy* honour *from the tooth of a mad
beaft,* is fcarcely fenfe. The deficiency of the verfe gives room to
fufpect that fomething is dropt. I read,

    —— *of a mad beaft, and the tongue of*
  A flanderer preferve thee (or thyfelf) and honour.   *Seward.*

                                           Dio.

Dio. He talks like a full senator.
Go, take it up, and carry't in. 'Tis a huge one;
We never kill'd so large a swine; so fierce too,
I never met with yet.

Maxi. Take heed! it stirs again.
How nimbly the rogue runs up! he climbs like a
        squirrel.

Dio. Come down, you dunce! Is it not dead?

Geta. I know not.

Dio. His throat is cut, and his bowels out.

Geta. That's all one.
I'm sure his teeth are in; and, for any thing I know,
He may have pigs of his own nature in's belly.

Dio. Come, take him up, I say, and see him dress'd;
He's fat, and will be lusty meat; away with him,
And get some of him ready for our dinner.

Geta. Shall he be roasted whole,
And serv'd up in a souce-tub? a portly service!
I'll run i' th' wheel myself.

Maxi. Sirrah, leave your prating,
And get some piece of him ready presently;
We're weary both, and hungry.

Geta. I'll about it.
What an inundation of brewis shall I swim in! [*Exit.*

Dio. Thou'rt ever dull and melancholy, cousin,
Distrustful of my hopes.

Maxi. Why, can you blame me?
Do men give credit to a juggler?

Dio. Thou know'st she is a Prophetess.

Maxi. A small one,
And as small profit to be hop'd for by her.

Dio. Thou art the strangest man! How does thy hurt?
The boar came near you, Sir.

Maxi. A scratch, a scratch.

Dio. It aches and troubles thee, and that makes thee
        angry,

Maxi. Not at the pain, but at the practice, uncle,
The butcherly base custom of our lives now:
Had a brave enemy's sword drawn so much from me,
                                                    Or

Or danger met me in the head o'th' army,
T''have blush'd thus in my blood had been mine honour;
But to live bafe, like fwine-herds, and believe too!
To be fool'd out with tales, and old wives' dreams,
Dreams when they're drunk!

   Dio. Certain, you much miftake her.

   Maxi. Miftake her? hang her! To be made her
         purveyors,
To feed her old chaps, to provide her daily,
And bring in feafts, whilft fhe fits farting at us,
And blowing out her Prophecies at both ends!

   Dio. Prithee be wife: Doft thou think, Maximinian,
So great a rev'rence, and fo ftaid a knowledge——

   Maxi. Sur-rev'rence, you would fay! What truth?
         what knowledge?
What any thing, but eating, is good in her?
'Twould make a fool prophefy, to be fed continually.
What do you get? Your labour and your danger,
Whilft fhe fits bathing in her larded fury.
Infpir'd with full deep cups, who cannot prophefy?
A tinker, out of ale, will give predictions;
But who believes?

   Dio. She is a holy druid,
A woman noted for that faith, that piety,
Belov'd of Heav'n.

   Maxi. Heav'n knows, I don't believe it.
Indeed, I muft confefs, they're excellent jugglers;
Their age upon fome fools too flings a confidence:
But what grounds have they, what elements to work on?
Shew me but that! the fieve and fheers; a learn'd one.
I have no patience to difpute this queftion,
'Tis fo ridiculous! I think the devil does help 'em;
Or rather, mark me well, abufe 'em, uncle:
For they're as fit to deal with him, thefe old women,
They are as jump and fquar'd out to his nature——

   Dio. Thou haft a perfect malice.

   Maxi. So I would have
Againft thefe purblind prophets; for, look ye, Sir,
Old women will lie monftroufly, fo will the devil,

(Or elfe h'has had much wrong, upon my knowledge);
Old women are malicious, fo is he;
They're proud, and covetous, revengeful, lech'rous,
All which are excellent attributes o'th' devil:
They would at leaft feem holy, fo would he;
And, to veil o'er thefe villainies, they'd prophefy;
He gives them leave now and then to ufe their cunnings,
Which is to kill a cow, or blaft a harveft,
Make young pigs pipe themfelves to death, choke
    poultry,
And chafe a dairy-wench into a fever
With pumping for her butter:
But when he makes thefe agents to raife emperors,
When he difpofes Fortune as his fervant,
And ties her to old wives' tales——

  Dio. Go thy ways;
Thou art a learned fcholar, againft credit.
You hear the prophecy.

  Maxi. Yes; and I laugh at it,
And fo will any man can tell but twenty,
That is not blind, as you are blind, and ignorant.
D' you think fhe knows your fortune?

  Dio. I do think it.

  Maxi. I know fhe has the name of a rare foothfayer;
But do you in your confcience believe her holy?
Infpir'd with fuch prophetic fire?

  Dio. Yes, in my confcience.

  Maxi. And that you muft, upon neceffity,
From her words, be a Cæfar?

  Dio. If I live——

  Maxi. There's one ftop yet.

  Dio. And follow her directions.

  Maxi. But do not juggle with me.

  Dio. In faith, coufin,
So full a truth hangs ever on her prophecies,
That how I fhould think otherwife——

  Maxi. Very well, Sir;
You then believe (for methinks 'tis moft neceffary)
She knows her own fate?

                              Dio.

Dio. I believe it certain.

Maxi. Dare you but be so wise to let me try it?
For I stand doubtful.

Dio. How?

Maxi. Come nearer to me,
Because her cunning devil shall not prevent me;
Close, close, and hear.—If she can turn this destiny,
I'll be of your faith too.   [*Whispers Diocles.*

Dio. Forward; I fear not;
For if she knows not this, sure she knows nothing.

Enter Delphia.

I am so confident——

Maxi. Faith, so am I too,
That I shall make her devil's sides hum.

Dio. She comes here;
Go take your stand.

Maxi. Now holy[6], or you howl for't!   [*Retires.*

Dio. 'Tis pity this young man should be so stubborn:
Valiant he is, and to his valour temperate,
Only distrustful of delays in fortune;
I love him dearly well.

Delp. Now, my son Diocles,
Are you not weary of your game to-day?
And are you well?

Dio. Yes, mother, well and lusty;
Only you make me hunt for empty shadows.

Delp. You must have patience: Rome was not
        built in one day;

---

[6] *Now* holly, &c.] I read *hallow ye.*—Maximinian did not believe
Delphia had any divinity about her, and therefore when designing
to shoot at her, should seem to say, *now hallow you,* i. e. render
yourself *holy,* or, *you howl for it.* As to the old reading, I have no
idea of it at all; and what I purpose will read in the verse as two
syllables only.   *Seward.*

  The whole conversation respecting Delphia turns upon the question,
Whether she is really *holy,* or only pretends to be so: Maximinian's
meaning, therefore, seems to us to be, ' Now [YOU MUST BE]
holy, or you howl for't;' and then presents an arrow,
  Betterton's alteration gives the line thus:
   ' *Now* shew your holiness, *or you howl for't,* beldame!

                     And

And he that hopes, muſt give his hopes their currents.
You've kill'd a mighty boar.

Dio. But I'm no emperor.
Why do you fool me thus, and make me follow
Your flattering expectation hour by hour?
Riſe early, and ſleep late? to feed your appetites,
Forget my trade, my arms? forſake mine honour?
Labour and ſweat to arrive at a baſe memory?
Oppoſe myſelf to hazards of all ſorts,
Only to win the barb'rous name of Butcher?

Delp. Son, you are wiſe.

Dio. But you are cunning, mother;
And with that cunning[7], and the faith I give you,
You lead me blindly to no end, no honour.
You find you're daily fed, you take no labour,
Your family at eaſe, they know no market;
And therefore, to maintain this, you ſpeak darkly,
As darkly ſtill you nouriſh it; whilſt I
(Being a credulous and obſequious coxcomb)
Hunt daily, and ſweat hourly; to find out
To clear your myſtery, kill boar on boar,
And make your ſpits and pots bow with my bounties:
Yet I ſtill poorer, further ſtill——

Delp. Be provident,
And tempt not the gods' dooms; ſtop not the glory.
They're ready to fix on you; you're a fool then:
Chearful and grateful takers the gods love,
And ſuch as wait their pleaſures with full hopes;
The doubtful and diſtruſtful man Heav'n frowns at.
What I have told you by my inſpiration,
I tell you once again, muſt and ſhall find you.

Dio. But when? or how?

Delp. Cum Aprum interfeceris.

Dio. I have kill'd many.

Delp. Not the Boar they point you;
Nor muſt I reveal further, 'till you clear it:
The lots of glorious men are wrapt in myſteries,

---

[7] *And with that* cannon] The amendment in the text was made by Betterton, but is claimed by Sympſon.

And

And fo deliver'd; common and flight creatures,
That have their ends as open as their actions,
Eafy and open fortunes follow.

   Maxi. [*coming forward.*] I fhall try
How deep your infpiration lies hid in you,
And whether your brave fpirit have a buckler
To keep this arrow off; I'll make you fmoke elfe.

   Dio. Knowing my fortune fo precifely, punctually,
And that it muft fall without contradiction,
Being a ftranger, of no tie unto you,
Methinks you fhould be ftudied in your own;
In your own deftiny, methinks, moft perfect:
And every hour, and every minute, mother,
(So great a care fhould Heav'n have of her minifters)
Methinks your fortunes both ways fhould appear to you,
Both to avoid, and take. Can the ftars now,
And all thofe influences you receive into you,
Or fecret infpirations you make fhow of,
If an hard fortune hung, and were now ready
To pour itfelf upon your life, deliver you?
Can they now fay, ' Take heed?'

   Delp. Ha? Pray you come hither.

   Maxi. I would know that: I fear your devil will
           cozen you;
And, ftand as clofe as you can, I fhall be with you.

   Delp. I find a prefent ill.

   Dio. How?

   Delp. But I fcorn it.

   Maxi. Do you fo? do you fo?

   Delp. Yes, and laugh at it, Diocles.
Is it not ftrange, thefe wild and foolifh men
Should dare to oppofe the power of deftiny?
That power the gods fhake at? Look yonder, fon.

   Maxi. Have you fpied me? then have at you!

   Delp. Do; fhoot boldly!
Hit me, and fpare not, if thou canft.

   Dio. Shoot, coufin.

   Maxi. I cannot; mine arm's dead; I have no feeling!
Or, if I could fhoot, fo ftrong is her arm'd virtue,
                     She'd

She'd catch the arrow flying.

Delp. Poor doubtful people!
I pity your weak faiths.

Dio. Your mercy, mother!
And, from this hour, a deity I crown you.

Delp. No more of that.

Maxi. Oh, let my prayers prevail too!
Here like a tree I dwell elſe: Free me, mother,
And, greater than great fortune, I'll adore thee!

Delp. Be free again, and have more pure thoughts
in you.

Dio. Now I believe your words moſt conſtantly;
And when I have that power you've promis'd to me—

Delp. Remember then your vow: My niece Druſilla,
I mean, to marry her, and then you proſper.

Dio. I ſhall forget my life elſe.

Delp. I am a poor weak woman; to me no worſhip.

Enter Niger, Geta, and ſoldiers.

Geta. And ſhall he have as you ſay, that kills this
Aper?

Delp. Now mark, and underſtand.

Niger. The proſcription's up,
I' th' market-place 'tis up; there you may read it:
He ſhall have half the empire.

Geta. A pretty farm, i'faith.

Niger. And th' emperor's ſiſter, bright Aurelia,
Her to his wife.

Geta. You ſay well, friend: But, hark you;
Who ſhall do this?

Niger. You, if you dare.

Geta. I think ſo:
Yet, I could poiſon him in a pot of perry;
He loves that veng'ancely. But when I have done this,
May I lie with the gentlewoman?

Niger. Lie with her? what elſe, man?

Geta. Yes, man;
I have known a man married that never lay with his
wife:

Thoſe

Those dancing-days are done.

Niger. These are old soldiers,
And poor, it seems. I'll try their appetites.
'Save ye, brave soldiers!

Maxi. Sir, you talk'd of proscriptions?

Niger. 'Tis true; there is one set up from the emperor,
Against Volutius Aper.

Dio. Aper?

Delp. Now!
Now have you found the Boar?

Dio. I have the meaning;
And, blessed mother——

Niger. He has scorn'd his master,
And bloodily cut off by treachery
The noble brother to him.

Dio. He lives here, Sir,
Sickly and weak.

Niger. Did you see him?

Maxi. No.

Niger. He's murder'd;
So you shall find it mention'd from the emperor,
And, honest faithful soldiers, but believe it;
For, by the Gods, you'll find it so; he's murder'd!
The manner how, read in the large proscription.

Delp. It is most true, son, and he cozens you;
Aper's a villain false.

Dio. I thank you, mother,
And dare believe you. Hark you, Sir! the recompense
As you related——

Niger. Is as firm as faith, Sir,
Bring him alive or dead.

Maxi. You took a fit time,
The general being out o' th' town; for tho' we love him
    not,
Yet, had he known this first, you had paid for't dearly.

Dio. 'Tis Niger; now I know him; honest Niger,
A true sound man; and I believe him constantly.
Your business may be done, make no great hurry
For your own safety.

Niger.

Niger. No; I'm gone, I thank you. [*Exit.*

Dio. Pray, Maximinian, pray.

Maxi. I'll pray and work too.

Dio. I'll to the market-place, and read the offer;
And, now I've found the Boar——

Delp. Find your own faith too,
And remember what you have vow'd.

Dio. Oh, mother!——

Delp. Prosper.

Geta. If my master and I do this, there's two emperors,
And what a show will that make! how we shall bounce
      it! [*Exeunt.*

ACT II. SCENE I.

Enter Drusilla and Delphia.

Druf. LEAVE us, and not vouchsafe a parting kiss
      To her, that in his hopes of greatness lives,
And goes along with him in all his dangers?

Delph. I grant 'twas most inhuman.

Druf. Oh, you give it
Too mild a name! 'twas more than barbarous!
And you a partner in it.

Delp. I, Drusilla?

Druf. Yes; you have blown his swoln pride to that
      vastness,
As he believes the earth is in his fathom;
This makes him quite forget his humble being:
And can I hope that he, that only fed
With the imagin'd food of future empire,
Disdains ev'n those that gave him means, and life,
To nourish such desires, when he's possess'd
Of his ambitious ends (which must fall on him,
Or your predictions are false) will ever
Descend to look on me?

Delp. Were his intents

                              Perfidious

Perfidious as the seas or winds; his heart
Compos'd of falshood; yet the benefit,
The greatness of the good he has from you,
(For what I have conferr'd is thine, Drusilla)
Must make him firm and thankful : But if all
Remembrance of the debts he stands engag'd for,
Find a quick grave in his ingratitude,
My powerful art, that guides him to this height,
Shall make him curse the hour he e'er was rais'd,
Or sink him to the centre.

Druf. I had rather
Your art could force him to return that ardour
To me, I bear to him; or give me power
To moderate my passions : Yet I know not;
I should repent your grant, tho' you had sign'd it
(So well I find he's worthy of all service).
But to believe that any check to him
In his main hopes, could yield content to me,
Were treason to true love, that knows no pleasure,
The object that it doats on ill affected !

Delp. Pretty simplicity ! I love thee for't,
And will not sit an idle looker-on,
And see it cozen'd. Dry thy innocent eyes,
And cast off jealous fears, (yet promises
Are but lip-comforts) and but fancy aught
That's possible in nature, or in art,
That may advance thy comfort, and be bold
To tell thy soul 'tis thine; therefore speak freely.

Druf. You new-create me ! To conceal from you
My virgin fondness, were to hide my sickness
From my physician. Oh, dear aunt, I languish
For want of Diocles' sight: He is the sun
That keeps my blood in a perpetual spring;
But, in his absence, cold benumbing winter
Seizes on all my faculties. Would you bind me
(That am your slave already) in more fetters,
And, in the place of service, to adore you ?
Oh, bear me then (but 'tis impossible,
I fear, to be effected) where I may

See

See how my Diocles breaks thro' his dangers,
And in what heaps his honours flow upon him,
That I may meet him in the height and pride
Of all his glories, and there (as your gift)
Challenge him as mine own.

   Delp. Enjoy thy wishes:
This is an easy boon, which, at thy years,
I could have giv'n to any ; but now grown
Perfect in all the hidden mysteries
Of that inimitable art, which makes us
Equal ev'n to the gods, and nature's wonders,
It shall be done as fits my skill and glory :
To break thro' bolts and locks, a scholar's prize
For thieves and pick-locks ! to pass thro' an army,
Cover'd with night, or some disguise, the practice
Of poor and needy spies ! No, my Drusilla,
From Ceres I will force her winged dragons,
And in the air hang over the tribunal,
The music of the spheres attending on us.
There, as his good star, thou shalt shine upon him,
If he prove true, and as his angel guard him :
But if he dare be false, I, in a moment,
Will put that glorious light out, with such horror
As if th' eternal night had seiz'd the sun,
Or all things were return'd to the first chaos,
And then appear like furies.

   Druf. I will do
Whate'er you shall command.

   Delp. Rest then assur'd,
I am the mistress of my art, and fear not.
                        [*Soft musick. Exeunt.*

SCENE II.

Enter Aper, Camurius, Guard, a litter covered.

   Aper. Your care of your sick emp'ror, fellow-soldiers,
In colours to the life doth shew your love,
And zealous duty : Oh, continue in it !
And tho' I know you long to see and hear him,
                            Impute

Impute it not to pride, or melancholy,
That keeps you from your wishes; such state-vices
(Too, too familiar with great princes) are
Strangers to all the actions of the life
Of good Numerianus.   Let your patience
Be the physician to his wounded eyes,
(Wounded with pious sorrow for his father)
Which time and your strong patience will recover,
Provided it prove constant.   [*Goes to the litter.*

   1 *Guard.* If he counterfeit,
I will hereafter trust a prodigal heir,
When he weeps at his father's funeral.

   2 *Guard.* Or a young widow, following a bed-rid
        husband
(After a three-years' groaning) to the fire.

   3 *Guard.* Note his humility, and with what soft
        murmurs
He does enquire his pleasures.

   1 *Guard.* And how soon
He is instructed.

   2 *Guard.* How he bows again too.

   Aper. All your commands, dread Cæsar, I'll impart
To your most ready soldier, to obey them;
So, take your rest in peace.—It is the pleasure
            [*Turning from the litter to the Guards.*
Of mighty Cæsar (his thanks still remember'd
For your long patience, which a donative,
Fitting his state to give, shall quickly follow)
That you continue a strict guard upon
His sacred person, and admit no stranger
Of any other legion to come near him;
You being most trusted by him.   I receive
Your answer in your silence.—Now, Camurius,
Speak without flatt'ry: Hath thy Aper acted
This passion to the life?

   Cam. I would applaud him,
Were he saluted Cæsar: But I fear
These long-protracted counsels will undo us;
And 'tis beyond my reason, he being dead,

You should conceal yourself, or hope it can
Continue undiscover'd.

Aper. That I've kill'd him,
Yet feed these ignorant fools with hopes he lives,
Has a main end in't. The Pannonian cohorts
(That are my own, and sure) are not come up;
The German legions waver; and Charinus,
Brother to this dead dog, (hell's plagues on Niger!)
Is jealous of the murder, and, I hear,
Is marching up against me. 'Tis not safe,
'Till I have power to justify the act,
To shew myself the author: Be therefore careful
For an hour or two (till I have fully sounded
How the tribunes and centurions stand affected)
That none come near the litter. If I find them
Firm on my part, I dare profess myself;
And then, live Aper's equal!

Cam. Does not the body
Begin to putrify?

Aper. That exacts my haste:
When, but ev'n now, I feign'd obedience to it,
As I had some great business to impart,
The scent had almost choak'd me; be therefore
    curious [7],
All keep at distance.   [*Exit.*

Cam. I am taught my parts;
Haste you, to perfect yours.

1 *Guard.* I'd rather meet
An enemy i' th' field, than stand thus nodding
Like to a rug-gown'd watchman.

   Enter Diocles, Maximinian, and Geta.

Maxi. The watch at noon [8]?
This is a new device.

Cam. Stand!

---

[7] *Curious.*] *i. e.* Cautious.   *Sympson.*
[8] *Geta. The watch at noon?*] The old books give this speech to
Geta, whom we thought the most unlikely person on the stage to
make the remark, before we consulted Betterton's edition, which we
have followed, in giving it to *Maximinian.*

              Dio.

Dio. I am arm'd
Againſt all danger.

Maxi. If I fear to follow,
A coward's name purſue me!

Dio. Now, my fate,
Guide and direct me!

Cam. You are rude and ſaucy,
With your forbidden feet to touch this ground,
Sacred to Cæſar only, and to theſe
That do attend his perſon! Speak, what are you?

Dio. What thou, nor any of thy faction are,
Nor ever were; ſoldiers, and honeſt men.

Cam. So blunt?

Geta. Nay, you ſhall find he's good at the ſharp too.

Dio. No inſtruments of craft, engines of murder,
That ſerve the emperor only with oil'd tongues,
Sooth and applaud his vices, play the bawds
To all his appetites; and when you've wrought
So far upon his weakneſs, that he's grown
Odious to the ſubject and himſelf,
And can no further help your wicked ends,
You rid him out o' th' way.

Cam. Treaſon!

Dio. 'Tis truth,
And I will make it good.

Cam. Lay hands upon 'em;
Or kill them ſuddenly!

Geta. I am out at that;
I do not like the ſport.

Dio. What's he that is
Owner of any virtue worth a Roman,
Or does retain the mem'ry of the oath
He made to Cæſar, that dares lift his ſword
Againſt the man that (careleſs of his life)
Comes to diſcover ſuch a horrid treaſon,
As, when you hear't, and underſtand how long
You've been abus'd, will run you mad with fury?
I am no ſtranger, but (like you) a ſoldier,
Train'd up one from my youth: And there are ſome

With

With whom I've serv'd, and (not to praise myself)
Must needs confess they have seen Diocles,
In the late Britain wars, both dare and do
Beyond a common man.

    1 Guard. Diocles?

    2 Guard. I know him;
The bravest soldier of the empire.

    Cam. Stand!
If thou advance an inch, thou'rt dead.

    Dio. Die thou,   [*Kills Camurius.*
That durst oppose thyself against a truth
That will break out, tho' mountains cover it!

    Geta. I fear this is a sucking pig, no boar,
He falls so easy.

    Dio. Hear me, fellow soldiers;
And if I make it not apparent to you
This is an act of justice, and no murder,
Cut me in pieces. I'll disperse the cloud
That hath so long obscur'd a bloody act
Ne'er equal'd yet. You all know with what favours
The good Numerianus ever grac'd
The provost Aper?

    Guard. True.

    Dio. And that those bounties
Should have contain'd him (if he e'er had learn'd
The elements of honesty and truth)
In loyal duty: But Ambition never
Looks backward on Desert, but with blind haste
Boldly runs on: But I lose time. You're here
Commanded by this Aper to attend
The emp'ror's person, to admit no stranger
To have access to him, or come near his litter,
Under pretence, forsooth, his eyes are sore,
And his mind troubled: No, my friends, you're cozen'd;
The good Numerianus now is past
The sense of wrong or injury.

    Guard. How! dead?

    Dio. Let your own eyes inform you. [*Opens the litter.*

    Geta. An emperor's cabinet?

                                     Fough!

Fough! I have known a charnel-house smell sweeter.
If emperor's flesh have this favour, what will mine do,
When I am rotten?

   1 *Guard.* Most unheard-of villainy!
   2 *Guard.* And with all cruelty to be reveng'd.
   3 *Guard.* Who is the murderer? Name him, that
       we may
Punish it in his family.

   Dio. Who but Aper?
The barbarous and most ingrateful Aper?
His desperate poniard printed on his breast
This deadly wound. Hate to vow'd enemies
Finds a full satisfaction in death,
And tyrants seek no further: He, a subject,
And bound by all the ties of love and duty,
Ended not so; but does deny his prince
(Whose ghost, forbad a passage to his rest,
Mourns by the Stygian shore) his funeral-rites.
Nay, weep not; let your loves speak in your anger,
And, to confirm you gave no suffrage to
The damned plot, lend me your helping hands
To wreak the parricide; and if you find
That there is worth in Diocles to deserve it,
Make him your leader.

   Guard. A Diocles, a Diocles!
   Dio. We'll force him from his guards.—And now,
       my stars,
If you have any good for me in store,
Shew it, when I have slain this fatal Boar! [*Exeunt.*

SCENE III.

Enter Delphia and Drusilla, in a throne drawn by dragons.

   Delp. Fix here, and rest awhile your sail-stretch'd
      wings [9],

---

9 *Sail stretched wings.*] I can't forbear transcribing a stanza out
of our inimitable Spenser, which whether our poets had in their eye
or no here, the reader must judge. B. i. C. xi. Stan. 10.

   ' His flaggy wings when forth he did display,
   ' Were like two sails, in which the hollow wind

         ' L

That have out-ftript the winds.   The eye of Heav'n
Durft not behold your fpeed, but hid itfelf
Behind the grofieft clouds ; and the pale moon
Pluck'd in her filver horns, trembling for fear
That my ftrong fpells fhould force her from her fphere:
Such is the power of art.

   Druf. Good aunt, where are we ?

   Delp. Look down, Drufilla, on thefe lofty towers,
Thefe fpacious ftreets, where every private houfe
Appears a palace to receive a king :
The fite, the wealth, the beauty of the place,
Will foon inform thee 'tis imperious Rome,
Rome, the great miftrefs of the conquer'd world.

   Druf. But, without Diocles, it is to me
Like any wildernefs we have pafs'd o'er :
Shall I not fee him ?

   Delp. Yes, and in full glory,
And glut thy greedy eyes with looking on
His profperous fuccefs.   Contain thyfelf ;
For tho' all things beneath us are tranfparent,
The fharpeft-fighted (were he eagle-ey'd)
Cannot difcover us.   Nor will we hang
Idle fpectators to behold his triumph ;

*Enter Diocles, Maximinian, Geta, Guard, Aper, Senators,
      Officers, with litter.*

But, when occafion fhall prefent itfelf,
Do fomething to add to it.   See, he comes.

   Druf. How god-like he appears ! With fuch a grace,
The giants that attempted to fcale Heaven,
When they lay dead on the Phlegrean plain,
 - Mars did appear to Jove.

   Delp. Forbear.

  ' Is gathered full, and worketh fpeedy way:
  ' And eke the pens that did his pinions bind,
  ' Were like main-yards, with flying canvas lin'd ;
  ' With which, when as him lift the air to beat,
  ' And there by force unwonted paffage find,
  ' The clouds before him fled for terror great,
 ' And all the heavens ftood full amazed with his threat.' *Sympfon.*
                                          Dio.

Dio. Look on this,
And when with horror thou haſt view'd thy deed,
Thy moſt accurſed deed, be thine own judge,
And ſee (thy guilt conſider'd) if thou canſt
Perſuade thyſelf, whom thou ſtandſt bound to hate,
To hope or plead for mercy.

Aper. I confeſs
My life's a burden to me.

Dio. Thou art like thy name,
A cruel Boar, whoſe ſnout hath rooted up
The fruitful vineyard of the commonwealth.
I long have hunted for thee; and ſince now
Thou'rt in the toil, it is in vain to hope
Thou ever ſhalt break out. Thou doſt deſerve
The hangman's hook, or to be puniſhed
More majorum, whipt with rods to death,
Or any way that were more terrible:
Yet, ſince my future fate depends upon thee,
Thus to fulfil great Delphia's prophecy,
Aper (thou fatal Boar) receive the honour [*Kills Aper.*
To fall by Diocles' hand!—Shine clear, my ſtars,
That uſher'd me to taſte this common air,
In my entrance to the world, and give applauſe
To this great work!

Delp. Strike muſick from the ſpheres! [*Muſick.*

Druſ. Oh, now you honour me!

Dio. Ha! in the air?

All. Miraculous!

Maxi. This ſhews the gods approve
The perſon, and the act. Then if the ſenate
(For in their eyes I read the ſoldiers' love)
Think Diocles worthy to ſupply the place
Of dead Numerianus, as he ſtands
His heir in his revenge, with one conſent
Salute him emperor.

Sen. Long live Diocles!
Auguſtus, *Pater Patriæ,* and all titles
That are peculiar only to the Cæſars,
We gladly throw upon him.

I 4

Guard.

Guard. We confirm it,
And will defend his honour with our swords
Against the world.   Raise him to the tribunal.

   1 *Sen.* Fetch the imperial robes; and, as a sign
We give him absolute power of life and death,
Bind this sword to his side.

   2 *Sen.* Omit no ceremony
That may be for his honour.   [*Song.*

   Maxi. Still the gods
Express that they are pleas'd with this election.

   Geta. My master is an emperor, and I feel
A senator's itch upon me : 'Would I could hire
These fine invisible fidlers to play to me
At my instalment.

   Dio. I embrace your loves,
And hope the honours that you heap upon me
Shall be with strength supported : It shall be
My study to appear another Atlas,
To stand firm underneath this heav'n of empire,
And bear it boldly.   I desire no titles,
But as I shall deserve 'em.   I will keep
The name I had, being a private man,
Only with some small difference; I will add
To Diocles but two short syllables [10],
And be call'd Dioclesianus.

   Geta. That is fine !
I'll follow the fashion; and, when I'm a senator,
I will be no more plain Geta, but be call'd
Lord Getianus.

----

   [10] —— *but two short syllables,*
   And be call'd Dioclesianus.] Thus run all the copies ancient and
modern : It was doubtless for want of attention in our Authors, or
their editors, that this passage has come down to us so incorrect : For
if we must read *two short syllables,* what must we do with *Dioclesia-*
nus, which is certainly an addition of three ? And if we read *Dio-*
clesian, which is much more agreeable to the measure, we shall be
embarrassed with that unlucky addition of *Geta,* to be called *Getianus.*
I am, however, upon the whole, for reading *Dioclesian,* because the
verse will run better, and because he is called so through the rest of
the play.   *Sympson.*

                                                     Drus.

Druf. He ne'er thinks of me,
Nor of your favour.

Enter Niger.

Delp. If he dares prove false,
These glories shall be to him as a dream,
Or an enchanted banquet.
  Niger. From Charinus,
From great Charinus, who with joy hath heard
Of your proceedings, and confirms your honours:
He, with his beauteous sister, fair Aurelia,
Are come in person, like themselves attended,
To gratulate your fortune.   [*Loud musick.*

Enter Charinus, Aurelia, and attendants.

  Dio. For thy news,
Be thou in France pro-consul.—Let us meet
The emperor with all honour, and embrace him.
  Druf. Oh, aunt, I fear this princess doth eclipse
The opinion of my beauty, tho' I were
Myself to be the judge!
  Delp. Rely on me.
  Char. 'Tis virtue, and not birth, that makes us noble:
Great actions speak great minds, and such should govern;
And you are grac'd with both. Thus, as a brother,
A fellow, and co-partner in the empire,
I do embrace you. May we live so far
From difference, or emulous competition,
That all the world may say, altho' two bodies,
We have one mind!
  Aur. When I look on the trunk
Of dear Numerianus, I should wash
His wounds with tears, and pay a sister's sorrow
To his sad fate; but since he lives again
In your most brave revenge, I bow to you,
As to a power that gave him second life,
And will make good my promise. If you find
That there is worth in me that may deserve you,
And that in being your wife, I shall not bring
                              Disquiet

Difquiet and difhonour to your bed,
(Altho' my youth and fortune fhould require
Both to be fued and fought to) here I yield
Myfelf at your devotion.

   Dio. Oh, you gods,
Teach me how to be thankful ! You have pour'd
All bleffings on me, that ambitious man
Could ever fancy : 'Till this happy minute
I ne'er faw beauty, or believ'd there could be
Perfection in a woman ! I fhall live
To ferve and honour you.   Upon my knees
I thus receive you ; and, fo you vouchfafe it,
This day I'm doubly married, to the empire,
And your beft felf.

   Delp. Falfe and perfidious villain !

   Druf. Let me fall headlong on him ! Oh, my ftars !
This I forefaw and fear'd.

   Char. Call forth a Flamen.
This knot fhall now be tied.

   Delp. But I will loofe it,
If art or hell have any ftrength. [*Thunder and lightning.*

Enter a Flamen.

   Char. Prodigious !

   Mani. How foon the day's o'ercaft !

   Flamen. The figns are fatal ;
Juno fmiles not upon this match, and fhews too
She has her thunder.

   Dio. Can there be a ftop
In my full fortune ?

   Char. We're too violent,
And I repent the hafte : We firft fhould pay
Our lateft duty to the dead, and then
Proceed difcreetly.   Let's take up the body ;
And when we've plac'd his afhes in his urn,
We'll try the gods again ; for, wife men fay,
Marriage and obfequies don't fuit one day. [*Sen. Ex.*

   Delp. So ; 'tis deferr'd yet, in defpite of falfhood.
Comfort, Drufilla ; for he fhall be thine,

                                  Or

Or wish, in vain, he were not[11].   I will punish
His perjury to the height.   Mount up, my birds[12],
Some rites I'm to perform to Hecate,
To perfect my designs; which once perform'd,
He shall be made obedient to thy call,
Or in his ruin I will bury all.   [*Ascend in the throne.*

ACT III. SCENE I.

Enter Maximinian.

Maxi. WHAT powerful star shin'd at this man's
                          nativity,
And bless'd his homely cradle with full glory?
What throngs of people press and buz about him,
And with their humming flatteries sing him Cæsar?
Sing him aloud, and grow hoarse with saluting him?
How the fierce-minded soldier steals in to him,
Adores and courts his honour? at his devotion
Their lives, their virtues, and their fortunes laying?

---

[11] *Or wish in vain he were* not. *I will punish*] To talk thus was
not talking like a Prophetess, or like a person of common sense. *He
shall be yours,* says she to Drusilla, *or wish in vain, he were not.*
Why so? What occasion for Diocles to wish in vain that he was not
here? Since 'twas fact that he was not: The alteration I have made,
depends only upon the change of a point, and the addition of a
single letter, one of which might be easily overlook'd, and the
other dropt.

   Mr. Seward, upon my laying my finger on this passage, agreed
it was corrupt, and offer'd to read *now* for *not:* The Reader is
left to his choice, seeing both are at his service.   *Sympson.*

   Sympson reads, *Or wish in vain he were.* NOTE, *I will punish, &c.*
The meaning of the text obviously is, ' He shall be thine, or wish
' he had no *existence;* which I will prevent his putting a period to.'

[12] *Mount up, my birds.*] She means *dragons.* Thus what has,
or is supposed to have, wings, as the dragons here, is by our poets
called a *bird.* Shakespear takes much the same kind of liberty in his
Antony and Cleopatra, when he calls his aspics *worms of Nile;* and
Milton, in imitation of his great master, gives the serpent in Para-
dise Lost the same name, as coming I suppose under the denomination
of reptiles.   *Sympson.*

Charinus

Charinus sues, the emperor entreats him,
And, as a brighter flame, takes his beams from him;
The bless'd and bright Aurelia, she dotes on him,
And, as the god of love, burns incense to him;
All eyes live on him: Yet I'm still Maximinian,
Still the same poor and wretched thing, his servant.
What have I got by this? where lies my glory?
How am I rais'd and honour'd? I have gone as far
To wooe this purblind honour, and have pass'd
As many dangerous expeditions,
As noble, and as high; nay, in his destiny,
Whilst 'twas unknown, have run as many hazards,
And done as much, sweat thro' as many perils;
Only the hangman of Volutius Aper,
Which I mistook, has made him emperor,
And me his slave.

Enter Delphia and Drusilla.

Delp. Stand still! he cannot see us,
'Till I please. Mark him well; this discontentment
I've forc'd into him, for thy cause, Drusilla.

Maxi. Can the gods see this,
See it with justice, and confer their blessings
On him, that never flung one grain of incense
Upon their altars? never bow'd his knee yet?
And I that have march'd foot by foot, struck equally,
And, whilst he was a-gleaning, have been praying,
Contemning his base, covetous———

Delp. Now we'll be open.

Maxi. Bless me! and with all reverence———

Delp. Stand up, son,
And wonder not at thy ungrateful uncle:
I know thy thoughts, and I appear to ease 'em.

Maxi. Oh, mother, did I stand the tenth part to you
Engag'd and fetter'd, as mine uncle does,
How would I serve, how would I fall before you!
The poorer powers we worship———

Delp. Peace, and flatter not;
Necessity and anger draws this from you,
Of both which I will quit you. For your uncle

I spoke

I spoke this honour, and it fell upon him,
Fell to his full content: He has forgot me,
For all my care, forgot me, and his vow too;
As if a dream had vanish'd, so h' has lost me,
And I him; let him now stand fast! Come hither;
My care is now on you.

Maxi. Oh, blessed mother!

Delp. Stand still, and let me work.—So!—Now,
                 Maximinian,
Go, and appear in court, and eye Aurelia;
Believe what I have done concerns you highly.
Stand in her view, make your addresses to her;
She is the stair of honour. I'll say no more,
But Fortune is your servant: Go.

Maxi. With reverence,
All this as holy truths——   [*Exit.*

Delp. Believe, and prosper.

Druf. Yet all this cures not me! But as much credit,
As much belief from Dioclesian——

Enter Geta, Lictors, and Suitors with petitions.

Delp. Be not dejected; I have warn'd you often,
The proudest thoughts he has I'll humble.—Who's this?
Oh, 'tis the fool and knave grown a grave officer.
Here's hot and high preferment.

Geta. What's your bill?
For gravel for the Appian way, and pills?
Is the way rheumatick?

1 Suit. 'Tis piles, an't please you.

Geta. Remove me those piles to Port Esquiline";

---

[13] *Port Esquiline.*] So our great Spenser, from whom this passage
seems to have been taken. B. ii. C. ix. Stan. 32.

          ' But all the liquor, which was foul and waste,
          ' Not good nor serviceable else for ought,
          ' They in another great round vessel plac'd,
          ' 'Till by a conduit-pipe it thence were brought:
          ' And all the rest, that noyous was and nought,
          ' By secret ways that none might it espy,
          ' Was close convey'd, and to the back gate brought,
          ' That cleped was *Port Esquiline*, whereby
          ' It was avoided quite, and thrown out privily.' *Sympson.*

Fitter the place, my friend : You fhall be paid.

  1 Suit. I thank your worfhip.

  Geta. Thank me when you have it,

Thank me another way, you are an afs elfe :

I know my office. You are for the ftreets, Sir.

Lord, how ye throng! That knave has eaten garlick;

Whip him, and bring him back.

  3 Suit. I befeech your worfhip;

Here's an old reckoning for the dung and dirt, Sir.

  Geta. It ftinks like thee ; away ! Yet let him tarry;

His bill fhall quit his breath. Give your petitions

In feemly fort, and keep your hats off, decently.

' For fcouring the water-courfes thro' the cities ;'

A fine periphrafis of a kennel-raker !

Did you fcour all, my friend ? You had fome bufinefs;

Who fhall fcour you ? You're to be paid, I take it,

When furgeons fwear you have perform'd your office.

  4 Suit. Your worfhip's merry.

  Geta. We muft be fometimes witty,

To nick a knave ; 'tis as ufeful as our gravity.

I'll take no more petitions ; I am pefter'd !

Give me fome reft.

  4 Suit. I've brought the gold, an't pleafe you,

About the place you promis'd.

  Geta. See him enter'd.

How does your daughter ?

  4 Suit. Better your worfhip thinks of her.

  Geta. This is with the leaft. But let me fee your
      daughter ;

'Tis a good forward maid; I'll join her with you.—

I do befeech ye leave me !

  Lict. Ye fee the edile's bufy.

  Geta. And look t' your places, or I'll make ye fmoke
      elfe !—

Sirrah, I drank a cup of wine at your houfe yefterday,

A good fmart wine.

  Lict. Send him the piece ; he likes it.

  Geta. And eat the beft wild boar at that fame farmer's.

  2 Suit. I've half left yet; your worfhip fhall
      command it.

                                 Geta.

Geta. A bit will ferve.   Give me fome reft! Gods
　　help me,
How fhall I labour when I am a fenator!

Delp. 'Tis a fit place indeed.—'Save your maftership!
Do you know us, Sir?

Geta. Thefe women are ftill troublefome.
There be houfes providing for fuch wretched women,
And fome fmall rents, to fet ye a-fpinning.

Druf. Sir,
We are no fpinfters; nor, if you look upon us,
So wretched as you take us.

Delp. Does your mightinefs,
That is a great deftroyer of your memory,
Yet underftand our faces?

Geta. Prithee keep off, woman!
Is it not fit I fhould know every creature.
Altho' I've been familiar with thee heretofore,
I muft not know thee now; my place neglects thee.
Yet, 'caufe I deign a glimpfe of your remembrances,
Give me your fuits, and wait me a month hence.

Delp. Our fuits are, Sir, to fee the emperor,
The emperor Dioclefian, to fpeak to him,
And not to wait on you.   We've told you all, Sir.

Geta. I laugh at your fimplicity, poor women.
See the emperor? Why, you are deceiv'd; now
The emperor appears but once in feven years,
And then he fhines not on fuch weeds as you are.—
Forward, and keep your ftate; and keep beggars
　　from me.

Druf. Here is a pretty youth.   [*Exeunt Geta, &c.*

Enter Diocles.

Delp. He fhall be pretty,
Or I will want my will.   Since you're fo high, Sir,
I'll raife you higher, or my art fhall fail me.
Stand clofe; he comes.

Dio. How am I crofs'd and tortur'd!
My moft-wifh'd happinefs, my lovely miftrefs,
That muft make good my hopes, and link my greatnefs,
　　　　　　　　　　　　　　　　　　　　　Yet

Yet fever'd from mine arms ! Tell me, high Heav'n,
How have I fin'd, that you fhould fpeak in thunder,
In horrid thunder, when my heart was ready
To leap into her breaft ? the prieft was ready ?
The joyful virgins and the young men ready ?
When Hymen ftood, with all his flames about him,
Bleffing the bed ? the houfe with full joy fweating ?
And Expectation, like the Roman eagle,
Took ftand, and call'd all eyes ? It was your honour;
And, ere you give it full, do you deftroy it ?
Or was there fome dire ftar, fome devil, that did it ?
Some fad malignant angel to mine honour ?
With you I dare not rage.

   Delp. With me thou canft not,
Tho' it was I. Nay, look not pale and frighted ;
I'll fright thee more : With me thou canft not quarrel.
I rais'd the thunder to rebuke thy falfhood,
(Look here) to her thy falfhood. Now be angry,
And be as great in evil as in empire.

   Dio. Blefs me, ye powers !

   Delp. Thou haft full need of bleffing.
'Twas I that, at thy great inauguration,
Hung in the air unfeen ; 'twas I that honour'd thee
With various muficks, and fweet-founding airs ;
'Twas I infpir'd the foldier's heart with wonder,
And made him throw himfelf with love and duty,
Low at thy feet ; 'twas I that fix'd him to thee.
But why did I all this ? To keep thy honefty,
Thy vow, and faith : That once forgot and flighted,
Aurelia in regard, the marriage ready,
The prieft and all the ceremonies prefent,
'Twas I that thunder'd loud, 'twas I that threaten'd,
'Twas I that caft a dark face over Heaven,
And fmote ye all with terror.

   Druf. Yet confider,
As you are noble, as I have deferv'd you ;
For yet you're free : If neither faith nor promife,
The deeds of elder times, may be remember'd,
Let thefe new-dropping tears, (for I ftill love you)

               Thefe

These hands held up to Heaven———

Dio. I must not pity you ;

'Tis not wise in me.

Delp. How! not wise?

Dio. Nor honourable.

A princess is my love, and dotes upon me ;
A fair and lovely princess is my mistress :
I am an emperor.   Consider, Prophetess,
Now my embraces are for queens and princesses,
For ladies of high mark, for divine beauties :
To look so low as this cheap common sweetness
Would speak me base, my names and glories nothing.
I grant I made a vow ; what was I then ?
As she is now, of no sort, (hope made me promise)
But now I am [15], to keep this vow were monstrous,
A madness, and a low inglorious fondness.

Delp. Take heed, proud man !

Drus. Princes may love with titles,
But I with truth.

Delp. Take heed ! Here stands thy destiny,
Thy fate here follows.

Dio. Thou doting sorceress,
Wouldst have me love this thing, that is not worthy
To kneel unto my saint, to kiss her shadow?
Great princes are her slaves ; selected beauties
Bow at her beck ; the mighty Persian's daughter
(Bright as the breaking East, as mid-day glorious)
Waits her commands, and grows proud in her pleasures.
I'll see her honour'd ; some match I shall think of,
That shall advance ye both ; mean time, I'll favour ye.

                                              [*Exit.*

---

[15] *But now I am.*] Now I am what? of no sort, &c. to be sure.
But this is not what he meant to say, but, as it seems, quite the contrary.   And accordingly I have reform'd the text.

Mr. Seward offer'd the same conjecture.   *Sympson.*

The meaning, we think, is, ' I was then of no rank, *but now I*
' am of high condition.' This is rather inaccurately expressed ; but
may be fairly deduced from the old text.

Betterton reads, *But* AS *I am* ; Sympson and Seward, *But* AS *I'm*
now.

Delp. Mean time, I'll haunt thee!—Cry not, wench;
      be confident,
Ere long, thou shalt more pity him (observe me)
And pity him in truth, than now thou seek'st him:
My art and I are yet companions. Come, girl. [*Exe.*

SCENE II.

Enter Geta and Lictors.

Geta. I am too merciful, I find it, friends,
Of too soft a nature, to be an officer;
I bear too much remorse.

    1 *Lict.* 'Tis your own fault, Sir;
For, look you, one so newly warm in office
Should lay about him blindfold, like true justice:
Hit where it will, the more you whip and hang, Sir,
(Tho' without cause; let that declare itself afterward)
The more you are admir'd.

    Geta. I think I shall be.

    2 *Lict.* Your worship is a man of a spare body,
And prone to anger.

    Geta. Nay, I will be angry;
And the best is, I need not shew my reason.

    2 *Lict.* You need not, Sir; your place is without
      reason;
And what you want in growth and full proportion,
Make up in rule and rigour.

    Geta. A rare counsellor!
Instruct me further. Is it fit, my friends,
The emperor, my master Dioclesian,
Should now remember or the times or manners
That call'd him plain down Diocles?

    1 *Lict.* He must not;
It stands not with his royalty.

    Geta. I grant ye.
I being then the edile Getianus,
A man of place, and judge, is it held requisite
I should commit to my consideration
Those rascals of remov'd and ragged hours,

That

That with unrev'rend mouths call'd me flave Geta?

  2 Lict. You muft forget their names; your honour
      bids you.

  Geta. I do forget; but I will hang their natures.
I will afcend my place, which is of juftice;
And, Mercy, I forget thee.

  Suit. A rare magiftrate!
Another Solon fure.

  Geta. Bring out the offenders.

  1 Lict. There are none yet, Sir; but no doubt there
      will be.
But if you pleafe touch fome things of thofe natures—

  Geta. And am I ready, and mine anger too,
The melancholy of a magiftrate upon me,
And no offenders to execute my fury?
Ha! no offenders, knaves?

  1 Lict. There are knaves indeed, Sir;
But we hope fhortly to have 'em for your worfhip.

  Geta. No men to hang or whip? Are ye good officers,
That provide no fuel for a judge's fury?
In this place fomething muft be done; this chair, I tell ye,
When I fit down, muft favour of feverity:
Therefore, I warn ye all, bring me lewd people,
Or likely to be lewd (twigs muft be cropt too);
Let me have evil perfons in abundance,
Or make 'em evil; 'tis all one, do but fay fo,
That I may have fit matter for a magiftrate,
And let me work. If I fit empty once more,
And lofe my longing, as I am true Edile,
And as I hope to rectify my country,
You are thofe fcabs I'll fcratch off from the common-
      wealth,
You are thofe rafcals of the ftate I treat of [16];
And you fhall find and feel——

  2 Lict. You fhall have many,
Many notorious people.

---

[16] *I treat of.*] Seward thinks this reading flat, and therefore fub-
ftitutes, *I'll tread on.* We cannot think any change neceffary.
Fetterton reads, *You are thofe rafcals of the ftate I'll punifh.*

              Geta.

Geta. Let 'em be people,
And take ye notorious to yourfelves. Mark me, my
        Lictors,
And you the reft of my officials ;
If I be angry, (as my place will afk it)
And want fit matter to difpofe my authority,
I'll hang a hundred of ye : I'll not ftay longer,
Nor enquire no further into your offences ;
It is fufficient that I find no criminals,
And therefore I muft make fome ; if I cannot,
Suffer myfelf ; for fo runs my commiffion.
    Suit. An admirable, zealous, and true juftice !
    1 *Lict.* I cannot hold ! If there be any people,
Of what degree foever, or what quality,
That would behold the wonderful works of juftice
In a new officer, a man conceal'd yet,
Let him repair, and fee, and hear, and wonder
At the moft wife and gracious Getianus !

       Enter Delphia and Drufilla.

    Geta. This qualifies a little.—What are thefe ?
    Delp. You fhall not mourn ftill : Times of recreation,
To allay this fadnefs, muft be fought.—What's here ?
A fuperftitious flock of fenfelefs people
Worfhipping a fign in office ?
    Geta. Lay hold on her,   [*Guards feize her.*
And hold her faft,
She will flip thro' your fingers like an eel elfe ;
I know her tricks. Hold her, I fay, and bind her ;
Or, hang her firft, and then I'll tell her wherefore.
    Delp. What have I done ?
    Geta. Th'haft done enough to undo thee ;
Thou haft preffed to the emperor's prefence without
        my warrant,
I being his key and image.
    Delp. You are an image indeed,
And of the coarfeft ftuff, and the worft making,
That e'er I look'd on yet : I'll make as good
An image of an afs.

                      Geta.

Geta. Befides, thou art a woman of a lewd life.

Delp. I am no whore, Sir; nor no common fame
Has yet proclaim'd me to the people vicious.

Geta. Thou art to me a damnable lewd woman,
Which is as much as all the people fwore it.
I know thou art a keeper of tame devils:
And whereas great and grave men of my place
Can by the laws be allow'd but one a-piece,
For their own fervices and recreations,
Thou, like a traiterous quean, keep'ft twenty devils,
Twenty in ordinary!

Delp. Pray you, Sir, be pacified:
If that be all, and if you want a fervant,
You fhall have one of mine fhall ferve for nothing,
Faithful, and diligent, and a wife devil too;
Think for what end.

Geta. Let her alone: 'Tis ufeful; [*Guards releafe her.*
We men of bufinefs muft ufe fpeedy fervants.
Let me fee your family.

Delp. Think but one, he's ready.

Geta. A devil for intelligence? No, no,
He'll lie beyond all travellers.   A ftate-devil?
Neither; he will undo me at mine own weapon.
For execution? He will hang me too.
I'd have a handfome, pleafant, and a fine She-devil,
To entertain the ladies that come to me;
A travell'd devil too, that fpeaks the tongues,
And a neat carving devil.   [*Mufick.*

Enter a She-devil.

Delp. Be not fearful.

Geta. A pretty brown devil, i'faith. May I not kifs
       her?

Delp. Yes, and embrace her too; fhe is your fervant.
Fear not, her lips are cool enough.

Geta. She is marvellous well mounted. What's her
       name?

Delp. Lucifera.

Geta. Come hither, Lucifera, and kifs me.

Delp.

Delp. Let her set on your knee.

Geta. The chair turns! Hey, boys!
Pleasant, i'faith! and a fine facetious devil. [*Dance.*

Delp. She would whisper in your ear, and tell you
  wonders.

Geta. Come!—What's her name?

Delp. Lucifera.

Geta. Come, Lucie;
Come, speak thy mind.—I am certain burnt to ashes!
      [*Exeunt omnes præter Geta.*
I have a kind of glass-house in my codpiece!
Are these the flames of state? I'm roasted over,
Over, and over-roasted. Is this office?
The pleasure of authority? I'll no more on't;
'Till I can punish devils too, I'll quit it.
Some other trade now, and some course less dangerous,
Or certainly I'll tile again for two-pence. [*Exit.*

S C E N E   III.

*Enter Charinus, Aurelia, Cassana, Ambassadors, and
Attendants.*

Aur. Never dispute with me; you cannot have her.
Nor name the greatness of your king; I scorn him.
Your knees to me are nothing; should he bow too,
It were his duty, and my power to slight him [17].

Char. She is her woman, (never sue to me)
And in her power to render her or keep her;
And she, my sister, not to be compell'd,
Nor have her own snatch'd from her.

Amb. We desire not,
But for what ransom she shall please to think of;
Jewels, or towns, or provinces.

Aur. No ransom;

---

[17] *My power to slight him.*] Sympson would read,
  —— *my part to slight him;*
but the text is much better than the proposed variation, and seems
confirmed, and explained, by the next speech,
  And in her power to render her or keep her.

No,

THE PROPHETESS.

No, not your king's own head, his crown upon it,
And all the low subjections of his people.

Amb. Fair princes should have tender thoughts.

Aur. Is she too good
To wait upon the mighty emperor's sister?
What princess of that sweetness, or that excellence,
Sprung from the proudest and the mightiest monarchs,
But may be highly blest to be my servant?

Cas. 'Tis most true, mighty lady.

Aur. Has my fair usage
Made you so much despise me and your fortune,
That you grow weary of my entertainments?
Henceforward, as you are, I will command you,
And as you were ordain'd, my prisoner,
My slave, and one I may dispose of any way;
No more my fair companion. Tell your king so;
And if he had more sisters, I would have 'em,
And use 'em as I please. You have your answer.

Amb. We must take some other way: Force must
    compel it.   [*Exeunt Ambassadors.*

Enter Maximinian.

Maxi. Now, if thou be'st a Prophetess, and canst do
Things of that wonder that thy tongue delivers,
Canst raise me too, I shall be bound to speak thee:
I half believe; confirm the other to me,
And monuments to all succeeding ages,
Of thee, and of thy piety——Now she eyes me.
Now work, great power of art! She moves unto me:
How sweet, how fair, and lovely her aspects are!
Her eyes, like bright Eoan flames, shoot thro' me.

Aur. Oh, my fair friend, where have you been?

Maxi. What am I?
What does she take me for? Work still, work strongly!

Aur. Where have you fled my loves and my em-
    braces?

Maxi. I am beyond my wits!

Aur. Can one poor thunder,
Whose causes are as common as his noises,

K 4   Make

Make you defer your lawful and free pleasures?
Strike terror to a soldier's heart, a monarch's?
Thro' all the fires of angry Heav'n, thro' tempests
That sing of nothing but destruction,
Ev'n underneath the bolt of Jove, then ready,
And aiming dreadfully, I would seek you,
And fly into your arms.

  Maxi. I shall be mighty,
And (which I never knew yet) I am goodly;
For certain, a most handsome man.

    Char. Fy, sister!
What a forgetful weakness is this in you!
What a light presence! These are words and offers
Due only to your husband, Dioclesian;
This free behaviour only his.

    Aur. 'Tis strange,
That only empty names compel affections:
This man you see, give him what name or title,
Let it be ne'er so poor, ne'er so despised, brother,
This lovely man——

    Maxi. Tho' I be hang'd, I'll forward!
For, certain, I am excellent, and knew not.

    Aur. This rare and sweet young man—See how he
        looks, Sir.

    Maxi. I'll justle hard, dear uncle.

    Aur. This thing, I say,
Let him be what he will, or bear what fortune,
This most unequall'd man, this spring of beauty,
Deserves the bed of Juno.

    Char. You're not mad?

    Maxi. I hope she be; I'm sure I'm little better.

    Aur. Oh, fair, sweet man!

    Char. For shame, refrain this impudence!

    Maxi. 'Would I had her alone, that I might seal this
        blessing!
Sure, sure she should not beg. If this continue,
As I hope Heav'n it will, uncle, I'll nick you,
I'll nick you, by this life! Some would fear killing
In the pursuit now of so rare a venture;

                                    Enter

Enter Diocles.

I'm covetous to die for such a beauty.
Mine uncle comes; now if she stand, I'm happy.

Char. Be right again, for honour's sake!

Dio. Fair mistress——

Aur. What man is this? Away! what saucy fellow?
Dare any such base groom press to salute me?

Dio. Have you forgot me, fair? or do you jest with
   me?
I'll tell you what I am. Come, pray you look lovely.
Nothing but frowns and scorns?

Aur. Who is this fellow?

Dio. I'll tell you who I am; I am your husband.

Aur. Husband to me?

Dio. To you. I'm Dioclesian.

Maxi. More of this sport, and I am made, old
   mother!
Effect but this thou hast begun——

Dio. I am he, lady,
Reveng'd your brother's death, slew cruel Aper;
I'm he the soldier courts, the empire honours,
Your brother loves; am he, my lovely mistress,
Will make you empress of the world.

Maxi. Still excellent!
Now I see too, mine uncle may be cozen'd;
An emperor may suffer like another.
Well said, old mother! hold but up this miracle——

Aur. Thou liest! thou art not he; thou a brave
   fellow?

Char. Is there no shame, no modesty, in women?

Aur. Thou one of high and full mark?

Dio. Gods, what ails she?

Aur. Generous and noble? Fy! thou liest most
   basely.
Thy face, and all aspect upon thee, tells me
Thou art a poor Dalmatian slave, a low thing,
Not worth the name of Roman: Stand off further!

Dio. What may this mean?

          Aur.

Aur. Come hither, my Endymion ;
Come, fhew thyfelf, and all eyes be blefs'd in thee !
  Dio. Ha ! what is this ?
  Aur. Thou, fair ftar that I live by,
Look lovely on me, break into full brightnefs !
Look ; here's a face now of another making,
Another mould ; here's a divine proportion ;
Eyes fit for Phœbus 'felf, to gild the world with;
And there's a brow arch'd like the ftate of Heaven :
Look how it bends, and with what radiance,
As if the fynod of the gods fat under :
Look there, and wonder ! Now behold that fellow,
That admirable thing, cut with an axe out.
  Maxi. Old woman, tho' I cannot give thee re-
      compenfe,
Yet, certainly, I'll make thy name as glorious——
  Dio. Is this in truth ?
  Char. She's mad, and you muft pardon her.
  Dio. She hangs upon him ; fee !
  Char. Her fit is ftrong now.
Be not you paffionate.
  Dio. She kiffes !
  Char. Let her ;
'Tis but the fondnefs of her fit.
  Dio. I'm fool'd !
And if I fuffer this——
  Char. Pray you, friend, be pacified ;
This will be off anon. She goes in.   [*Exit Aurelia.*
  Dio. Sirrah !
  Maxi. What fay you, Sir ?
  Dio. How dare thy lips, thy bafe lips——
  Maxi. I am your kinfman, Sir, and no fuch bafe one.
I fought no kiffes, nor I had no reafon
To kick the princefs from me ; 'twas no manners :
I never yet compell'd her ; of her courtefy
What fhe beftows, Sir, I am thankful for.
  Dio. Be gone, villain !
  Maxi. I will, and I will go off with that glory,
And magnify my fate.   [*Exit.*
                                          Dio.

Dio. Good brother, leave me:
I'm to myfelf a trouble now.
  Char. I'm forry for't.
You'll find it but a woman-fit to try you.
  Dio. It may be fo; I hope fo.
  Char. I am afham'd, and what I think I blufh at.
                                            [*Exit.*

  Dio. What mifery hath my great fortune bred me!
And how far muft I fuffer! Poor and low ftates,
'Tho' they know wants and hungers, know not thefe,
Know not thefe killing fates: Little contents them,
And with that little they live kings, commanding
And ordering both their ends and loves. Oh, Honour!
How greedily men feek thee, and, once purchas'd,
How many enemies to man's peace bring'ft thou!
How many griefs and forrows, that like fheers,
Like fatal fheers, are fheering off our lives ftill!
How many fad eclipfes do we fhine thro'!

             Enter Delphia and Drufilla, veiled.

When I prefum'd I was blefs'd in this fair woman—
  Delp. Behold him now, and tell me how thou lik'ft
       him.
  Dio. When all my hopes were up, and Fortune dealt
       me
Ev'n for the greateft and the happieft monarch,
Then to be cozen'd, to be cheated bafely!
By mine own kinfman crofs'd! Oh, villain kinfman!
Curfe of my blood! becaufe a little younger,
A little fmoother-fac'd! Oh, falfe, falfe woman,
Falfe and forgetful of thy faith! I'll kill him.
But can I kill her hate too? No. He wooes not,
Nor worthy is of death; becaufe fhe follows him,
Becaufe fhe courts him, fhall I kill an innocent?
Oh, Diocles! 'Would thou hadft never known this,
Nor furfeited upon this fweet ambition,
That now lies bitter at thy heart! Oh, Fortune,
'That thou haft none to fool and blow like bubbles,
But kings, and their contents!
                                            Delp.

Delp. What think you now, girl?

Druf. Upon my life, I pity his misfortune.
See how he weeps! I cannot hold.

Delp. Away, fool!
He muſt weep bloody tears before thou haſt him.—
How fare you now, brave Dioclefian?
What! lazy in your loves? Has too much pleaſure
Dull'd your moſt mighty faculties?

Dio. Art thou there,
More to torment me? Doſt thou come to mock me?

Delp. I do; and I do laugh at all thy ſufferings:
I that have wrought 'em, come to ſcorn thy wailings.
I told thee once, ' This is thy fate, this woman;
' And as thou uſeſt her, ſo thou ſhalt proſper.'
It is not in thy power to turn this deſtiny,
Nor ſtop the torrent of thoſe miſeries
(If thou negleсt'ſt her ſtill) ſhall fall upon thee.
Sigh that thou art diſhoneſt, falſe of faith,
Proud, and doſt think no power can croſs thy pleaſures;
Thou'lt find a fate above thee.

Druf. Good aunt, ſpeak mildly:
See how he looks and ſuffers.

Dio. I find and feel, woman,
That I am miſerable.

Delp. Thou art moſt miſerable.

Dio. That as I am the moſt, I am moſt miſerable.
But didſt thou work this?

Delp. Yes, and will purſue it.

Dio. Stay there, and have ſome pity. Fair Druſilla,
Let me perſuade thy mercy, (thou haſt lov'd me)
Altho' I know my ſuit will ſound unjuſtly,
To make thy love the means to loſe itſelf,
Have pity on me!

Druf. I will do.

Delp. Peace, niece!
Altho' this ſoftneſs may become your love,
Your care muſt ſcorn it. Let him ſtill contemn thee,
And ſtill I'll work; the ſame affection
He ever ſhews to thee, be't ſweet or bitter,

The

The same Aurelia shall shew him; no further:
Nor shall the wealth of all his empire free this.

Dio. I must speak fair.—Lovely young maid, forgive
me,
Look gently on my sorrows! You that grieve too[18],
I see it in your eyes, and thus I meet it.

Druf. Oh, aunt, I'm blefs'd!

Dio. Be not both young and cruel;
Again I beg it, thus.

Enter Aurelia.

Druf. Thus, Sir, I grant it.
He's mine own now, aunt.

Delp. Not yet, girl; thou'rt cozen'd.

Aur. Oh, my dear lord, how have I wrong'd your
patience!
How wander'd from the truth of my affections!
How, like a wanton fool, shun'd that I lov'd most!
But you are full of goodnefs to forgive, Sir,
As I of grief to beg, and shame to take it:
Sure I was not myfelf! some strange illufion,
Or what you pleafe to pardon——

Dio. All, my deareft;
All, my delight! and with more pleafure take thee,
Than if there had been no fuch dream; for, certain,
It was no more.

Aur. Now you have feal'd forgivenefs,
I take my leave; and the Gods keep your goodnefs!
[*Exit.*

Delp. You fee how kindnefs profpers: Be but fo kind
To marry her, and fee then what new fortunes,

---

[18] *You* that *grieve too.*] The particle *that*, feems to have no
right of place here: If we muft have a monofyllable to fill up, it
feems, as if *thofe* was a more fignificant one than the prefent *that*,
and ought to agree with *forrows* as the antecedent. However, as no
great matter depends upon it, I leave it to every one's judgment,
which way he will read. *Sympfon.*

That ftands for *who*;—and the paffage means, ' Pity me! pity me,
' you that grieve! I fee your grief in your eyes, and meet it with a
' kifs.'

New

New joys, and pleasures, far beyond this lady,
Beyond her greatness too——
    Dio. I'll die a dog first!
Now I am reconcil'd, I will enjoy her
In spite of all thy spirits, and thy witchcrafts.
    Delp. Thou shalt not, fool!
    Dio. I will, old doting devil!
And wert thou any thing but air and spirit,
My sword should tell thee——
    Delp. I contemn thy threatnings;
And thou shalt know I hold a power above thee.——
We must remove Aurelia. Come.—Farewell, fool!
When thou shalt see me next, thou shalt bow to me.
    Dio. Look thou appear no more to cross my
          pleasures!   [*Exeunt.*

ACT IV. SCENE I.

Enter Chorus.

SO full of matter is our history,
  Yet mix'd, I hope, with sweet variety,
The accidents not vulgar too, but rare,
And fit to be presented, that there wants
Room in this narrow stage, and time, to express,
In action to the life, our Dioclesian
In his full lustre: Yet (as the statuary,
That by the large size of Alcides' Foot,
Guess'd at his whole proportion) so we hope
Your apprehensive judgments will conceive
Out of the shadow we can only shew,
How fair the body was; and will be pleas'd,
Out of your wonted goodness, to behold,
As in a silent mirror, what we cannot,
With fit conveniency of time allow'd
For such presentments, cloath in vocal sounds.
Yet with such art the subject is convey'd,

                              That

That every scene and paffage fhall be clear
Ev'n to the groffeft underftander here. [*Loud mufick.*]

Dumb Show.

*Enter, at one door, Delphia and Ambaffadors; they
whifper together; they take an oath upon her hand;
fhe circles them, kneeling, with her magick rod; they
rife and draw their fwords. Enter, at the other
door, Dioclefian, Charinus, Maximinian, Niger,
Aurelia, Caffana, and Guard; Charinus and Niger
perfuading Aurelia; fhe offers to embrace Maximinian;
Diocles draws his fword, keeps off Maximinian, turns
to Aurelia, kneels to her, lays his fword at her feet;
fhe fcornfully turns away: Delphia gives a fign; the
Ambaffadors and foldiers rufh upon them, feize on
Aurelia, Caffana, Charinus, and Maximinian; Dioclefian and others offer to refcue them; Delphia raifes
a mift. Exeunt Ambaffadors and prifoners, and
the reft difcontented.*

The fkilful Delphia finding, by fure proof,
The prefence of Aurelia dim'd the beauty
Of her Drufilla; and, in fpite of charms,
The emperor her brother, great Charinus,
Still urg'd her to the love of Dioclefian,
Deals with the Perfian Legates, that were bound
For the ranfom of Caffana, to remove
Aurelia, Maximinian, and Charinus,
Out of the fight of Rome; but takes their oaths
(In lieu of her affiftance) that they fhall not,
On any terms, when they were in their power,
Prefume to touch their lives: This yielded to,
They lie in ambufh for 'em. Dioclefian,
Still mad for fair Aurelia, that doted
As much on Maximinian, twice had kill'd him,
But that her frown reftrain'd him: He purfues her
With all humility, but fhe continues
Proud and difdainful. The fign given by Delphia,
The Perfians break thro', and feize upon

Charinus

Charinus and his fister, with Maximinian,
And free Caffana. For their fpeedy refcue,
Enraged Dioclefian draws his fword,
And bids his Guard affift him : Then too weak
Had been all oppofition and refiftance
The Perfians could have made againft their fury,
If Delphia by her cunning had not rais'd
A foggy mift, which as a cloud conceal'd them,
Deceiving their purfuers. Now be pleas'd,
That your imaginations may help you
To think them fafe in Perfia, and Dioclefian
For this difafter circled round with forrow,
Yet mindful of the wrong. Their future fortunes
We will prefent in action ; and are bold,
In that which follows, that the moft fhall fay,
'Twas well begun, but the end crown'd the play
                                        [*Exit.*

SCENE II.

Enter Diocles, Niger, Senators, and Guard.

Dio. Talk not of comfort! I have broke my faith,
And the gods fight againft me : And proud man,
However magnified, is but as duft
Before the raging whirlwind of their juftice.
What is it to be great, ador'd on earth,
When the immortal powers that are above us
Turn all our bleffings into horrid curfes,
And laugh at our refiftance, or prevention,
Of what they purpofe ! Oh, the furies that
I feel within me ! whipp'd on, by their angers,
For my tormentors ! Could it elfe have been
In nature, that a few poor fugitive Perfians,
Unfriended, and unarm'd too, could have robb'd me
(In Rome, the world's metropolis, and her glory ;
In Rome, where I command, environ'd round
With fuch invincible troops that know no fear,
But want of noble enemies) of thofe jewels
I priz'd above my life, and I want power

                                        To

To free them, if thofe gods I have provok'd
Had not giv'n fpirit to the undertakers,
And in their deed protected 'em ?
 Niger. Great Cæfar,
Your fafety does confirm you are their care ;
And that, howe'er their practices reach others,
You ftand above their malice.
 1 *Sen.* Rome in us
Offers (as means to further your revenge)
The lives of her beft citizens, and all
They ftand poffefs'd of.
 1 *Guard.* Do but lead us on
With that invincible and undaunted courage
Which waited bravely on you, when you appear'd
The minion of Conqueft, married rather
To glorious Victory, and we will drag
(Tho' all the enemies of life confpire
Againft our undertakings) the proud Perfian
Out of his ftrongeft hold.
 2 *Guard.* Be but yourfelf,
And do not talk, but do.
 3 *Guard.* You've hands and fwords,
Limbs to make up a well-proportion'd army,
That only want in you an head to lead us.
 Dio. The gods reward your goodnefs ! and believe,
Howe'er (for fome great fin) I am mark'd out
The object of their hate, tho' Jove ftood ready
To dart his three-fold thunder on this head,
It could not fright me from a fierce purfuit
Of my revenge. I will redeem my friends,
And, with my friends, mine honour ; at leaft, fall
Like to myfelf, a foldier.
 Niger. Now we hear
Great Dioclefian fpeak.
 Dio. Draw up our legions :
And let it be your care, my much-lov'd Niger,
To haften the remove. And, fellow-foldiers,
Your love to me will teach you to endure
Both long and tedious marches.

1 *Guard.* Die he accurs'd
That thinks of reft or fleep before he fets
His foot on Perfian earth !
  Niger. We know our glory,
The dignity of Rome, and, what's above
All can be urg'd, the quiet of your mind,
Depends upon our hafte.
  Dio. Remove to-night ;
Five days fhall bring me to you.
  All. Happinefs
To Cæfar, and glorious victory !   [*Exeunt.*
  Dio. The chearfulnefs of my foldiers gives affurance
Of good fuccefs abroad, if firft I make
My peace at home here. There is fomething chides me,
And fharply tells me, that my breach of faith
To Delphia and Drufilla is the ground
Of my misfortunes : And I muft remember,
While I was lov'd, and in great Delphia's grace,
She was as my good angel, and bound Fortune
To profper my defigns: I muft appeafe her.
Let others pay their knees, their vows, their prayers,
To weak imagin'd powers ; fhe's my all,
And thus I do invoke her.——Knowing Delphia,
Thou more than woman ! and, tho' thou vouchfafeft
To grace the earth with thy celeftial fteps,
And tafte this groffer air, thy heav'nly fpirit
Hath free accefs to all the fecret counfels
Which a full fenate of the gods determine
When they confider man ; the brafs-leav'd book
Of fate lies open to thee, where thou read'ft,
And fafhioneft the deftinies of men
At thy wifh'd pleafure ; look upon thy creature,
And, as thou twice haft pleafed to appear
To reprehend my fafhood, now vouchfafe
To fee my low fubmiffion !

       Delphia and Drufilla appear.
  Delp. What's thy will ?
Falfe, and unthankful, (and in that deferving
                            All

All human sorrows) dar'st thou hope from me
Relief or comfort?

Dio. Penitence does appease
Th' incensed powers, and sacrifice takes off
Their heavy angers: Thus I tender both;
The master of great Rome, and, in that, lord
Of all the sun gives heat and being to,
Thus sues for mercy. Be but as thou wert,
The pilot to the bark of my good fortunes,
And once more steer my actions to the port
Of glorious Honour, and if I fall off
Hereafter from my faith to this sweet virgin,
Join with those powers that punish perjury
To make me an example, to deter
Others from being false!

Druf. Upon my soul,
You may believe him! Nor did he e'er purpose
To me but nobly; he made trial how
I could endure unkindness; I see truth
Triumphant in his sorrow. Dearest aunt,
Both credit him, and help him! and, on assurance
That what I plead for you cannot deny,
I raise him thus, and with this willing kiss
I seal his pardon.

Dio. Oh, that I e'er look'd
Beyond this abstract of all woman's goodness!

Delp. I'm thine again; thus I confirm our league,
I know thy wishes, and how much thou suffer'st
In honour for thy friends; thou shalt repair all,
For to thy fleet I'll give a fore-right wind
To pass the Persian Gulf; remove all lets
That may molest thy soldiers in their march
That pass by land; and Destiny is false,
If thou prove not victorious. Yet remember,
When thou art rais'd up to the highest point
Of human happiness, such as move beyond it
Must of necessity descend. Think on't;
And use those blessings that the gods pour on you
With moderation!

Dio.

Dio. As their oracle,
I hear you and obey you, and will follow
Your grave directions.

Delp. You will not repent it. [*Exeunt.*

SCENE III.

Enter Niger, Geta, Guard, and Soldiers, with ensigns.

Niger. How do you like your entrance to the war?
When the whole body of the army moves,
Shews it not gloriously?

Geta. 'Tis a fine May-game;
But eating and drinking I think are forbad in't;
(I mean, with leisure) we walk on, and feed
Like hungry boys that haste to school; or, as
We carried fish to the city, dare stay no where,
For fear our ware should stink.

1 Guard. That's the necessity
Of our speedy march.

Geta. Sir, I do love my ease,
And tho' I hate all feats of judicature,
I mean i' th' city, for conveniency,
I still will be a justice in the war,
And ride upon my foot-cloth. I hope a captain
(And a gown'd captain too) may be dispens'd with.
I tell you, (and don't mock me) when I was poor,
I could endure, like others, cold and hunger;
But since I grew rich, let but my finger ache,
Or feel but the least pain in my great toe,
Unless I have a doctor, mine own doctor,
That may assure me, I am gone.

Niger. Come, fear not;
You shall want nothing.

1 Guard. We will make you fight
As you were mad.

Geta. Not too much of fighting, friend;
It is thy trade, that art a common soldier;
We officers, by our place, may share the spoil,
And never sweat for't.

2 Guard.

2 Guard. You shall kill, for practice,
But your dozen or two a-day.

Geta. Thou talk'st as if
Thou wert lousing thyself; but yet I will make danger;
If I prove one o' th' worthies, so: However,
I'll have the fear of the gods before my eyes,
And do no hurt, I warrant you.

Niger. Come, march on,
And humour him for our mirth.

1 Guard. 'Tis a fine pea-goose²⁰.

Niger. But one that fools to the emperor, and, in that,
A wife man, and a soldier.

1 Guard. True morality!   [*Exeunt.*

SCENE IV.

*Enter Cofroe, Caffana, Perfians; and Charinus, Maxi-
minian, Aurelia, bound, with foldiers.*

Cofroe. Now, by the Perfian gods, moft truly welcome!
Encompafs'd thus with tributary kings,
I entertain you. Lend your helping hands
To feat her by me; and, thus rais'd, bow all,
To do her honour. Oh, my beft Caffana,
Sifter, and partner of my life and empire,
We'll teach thee to forget, with prefent pleafures,
Thy late captivity; and this proud Roman,
That us'd thee as a flave, and did difdain
A princely ranfom, fhall, if fhe repine,
Be forc'd by various tortures to adore
What fhe of late contemn'd.

Caf. All greatnefs ever
Attend Cofroe! Tho' Perfia be ftil'd
The nurfe of pomp and pride, we'll leave to Rome
Her native cruelty. For know, Aurelia,
(A Roman princefs, and a Cæfar's fifter)
Tho' late (like thee) captiv'd²¹, I can forget

---

²⁰ *Pea-goofe.*] *i. e.* A filly creature.   *Sympfon.*

²¹ *Tho' now, like thee captiv'd.*] So firft folio; the fecond fays,
tho' LATE, which is clearly right. Sympfon and Seward feeing the

Thy barb'rous ufage; and tho' thou to me,
When I was in thy power, didft fhew thyfelf
A moft infulting tyrannefs, I to thee
May prove a gentle miftrefs.

Aur. Oh, my ftars!
A miftrefs? Can I live, and owe that name
To flefh and blood? I was born to command,
Train'd up in fovereignty; and I, in death,
Can quit the name of flave: She that fcorns life,
May mock captivity.

Char. Rome will be Rome
When we are nothing; and her power's the fame,
Which you once quak'd at.

Maxi. Dioclefian lives;
(Hear it, and tremble!) lives, thou king of Perfia,
The mafter of his fortune, and his honour:
And tho' by devilifh arts we were furpriz'd,
And made the prey of magick and of theft,
And not won nobly, we fhall be redeem'd,
And by a Roman war; and every wrong
We fuffer here, with intereft be return'd
On the infulting doer!

1 *Perf.* Sure thefe Romans
Are more than men.

2 *Perf.* Their great hearts will not yield,
They cannot bend to any adverfe fate,
Such is their confidence.

Cofroe. They then fhall break!
Why, you rebellious wretches, dare you ftill
Contend, when the leaft breath or nod of mine
Marks you out for the fire[22], or to be made
The prey of wolves or vultures? The vain name
Of Roman legions I flight thus, and fcorn;
And for that boafted bugbear, Dioclefian,
Which you prefume on, 'would he were the mafter

corruption of the firft book, and overlooking the fecond (tho' infinitely the beft) edition, exhibit this nonfenfe:
　　Though NOW, *like me captiv'd.*
　22 *Marks you* out *for.*] Seward, unwarrantably, as we think,
varies the text to, *Marks you* OR *for,* &c.

But of the spirit to meet me in the field !
He soon should find, that our Immortal Squadrons[21],
That with full numbers ever are supplied,
(Could it be possible they should decay)
Dare front his boldest troops, and scatter 'em,
As an high-tow'ring falcon on her stretches,
Severs the fearful fowl. And, by the sun,
The moon, the winds, the nourishers of life,
And by this sword, the instrument of death,
Since that you fly not humbly to our mercy,
But yet dare hope your liberty by force,
If Dioclesian dare not attempt
To free you with his sword, all slavery
That cruelty can find out to make you wretched,
Falls heavy on you !
    Maxi. If the sun keeps his course,
And the earth can bear his soldiers' march, I fear not.
    Aur. Or liberty, or revenge !
    Char. On that I build too.   [*A trumpet.*
    Aur. A Roman trumpet ?
    Maxi. 'Tis : Comes it not like
A pardon to a man condemn'd ?

Enter Niger.

    Cosroe. Admit him.
The purpose of thy coming ?
    Niger. My great master,
The lord of Rome, (in that all power is spoken)
Hoping that thou wilt prove a noble enemy,
And (in thy bold resistance) worth his conquest,
Defies thee, Cosroe.
    Maxi. There is fire in this.
    Niger. And to encourage thy laborious powers
To tug for empire, dares thee to the field,
With this assurance; if thy sword can win him,

---

    [21] *Immortal squadrons.*] These were a body of Persian soldiers,
whose number, Herodotus says, was never more or less than ten
thousand. The reason of the name our authors give themselves.
    That with full numbers ever are supply'd.   *Sympson.*

Or force his legions with thy barbed horse
But to forsake their ground, that not alone
Wing'd Victory shall take stand on thy tent,
But all the provinces and kingdoms held
By the Roman garrisons in this eastern world,
Shall be deliver'd up, and he himself
Acknowledge thee his sovereign. In return
Of this large offer, he asks only this,
That 'till the doubtful die of war determine
Who has most power, and should command the other,
Thou wouldst entreat thy prisoners like their births,
And not their present fortune; and to bring 'em
Guarded, into thy tent, with thy best strengths,
Thy ablest men of war, and thou thyself
Sworn to make good the place. And if he fail
(Maugre all opposition can be made)
In his own person to compel his way,
And fetch them safely off, the day is thine,
And he, like these, thy prisoner.

   Cosroe. Tho' I receive this
But as a Roman brave, I do embrace it,
And love the sender. Tell him, I will bring
My prisoners to the field, and, without odds,
Against his single force, alone defend 'em;
Or else with equal numbers.—Courage, noble princes!
And let posterity record, that we
This memorable day restor'd to Persia
That empire of the world great Philip's son
Ravish'd from us, and Greece gave up to Rome.
This our strong comfort [24], that we cannot fall
Ingloriously, since we contend for all.   [*Exeunt.*
                              [*Flourish, alarms.*

---

[24] *This our strong comfort.*] This slight alteration restores the
verb here, without which the sentence would be harsh and elliptical.
                                       Sympson.

   The alteration is *'tis* for *this*; but the old reading is much, much
best, and most elegant.

SCENE

SCENE V.

Enter Geta, Guard, and Soldiers.

Geta. I'll swear the peace against 'em ! I am hurt :
Run for a surgeon, or I faint !

1 *Guard.* Bear up, man ;
'Tis but a scratch.

Geta. Scoring a man o'er the coxcomb
Is but a scratch with you.   Pox o'your occupation,
Your scurvy scuffling trade ! I was told before,
My face was bad enough ; but now I look
Like Bloody-Bone, and Raw-Head, to fright children :
I am for no use else.

2 *Guard.* Thou shalt fright men.

1 *Guard.* You look so terrible now ! But see your
             face
I' th' pummel of my sword.

Geta. I die ! I'm gone !
Oh, my sweet physiognomy !

Enter three Persians.

2 *Guard.* They come ;
Now fight, or die indeed.

Geta. I will 'scape this way.
I cannot hold my sword : What would you have
Of a maim'd man ?

1 *Guard.* Nay, then I have a goad
To prick you forward, ox.

2 *Guard.* Fight like a man,
Or die like a dog.

Geta. Shall I, like Cæsar, fall
Among my friends ? no mercy ? *Et tu Brute ?*
You shall not have the honour of my death ;
I'll fall by the enemy first.

1 *Guard.* Oh, brave, brave Geta ! [*Persians driven off.*
He plays the devil now.

Enter

Enter Niger.

Niger. Make up for honour!
The Perfians fhrink ; the paffage is laid open ;
Great Dioclefian, like a fecond Mars,
(His ftrong arm govern'd by the fierce Bellona)
Performs more than a man : His fhield ftuck full [25]
Of Perfian darts, which now are his defence
Againft the enemies' fwords, ftill leads the way.
Of all the Perfian forces, one ftrong fquadron,
          [*Alarms continued.*
In which Cofroe in his own perfon fights,
Stands firm, and yet unrouted : Break thro' that,
The day and all is ours.   [*Retreat.*
 All. Victory, victory!   [*Exeunt. Flourifh.*

SCENE VI.

*Enter (in triumph, with Roman enfigns) Guard, Diocle-
fian, Charinus, Aurelia, Maximinian, Niger, Geta ;
Cofroe, Caffana, Perfians, as prifoners ; Delphia and
Drufilla privately.*

 Dio. I am rewarded in the act ; your freedom
To me's ten thoufand triumphs : You, Sir, fhare
In all my glories. And, unkind Aurelia,
From being a captive, ftill command the victor.
Nephew, remember by whofe gift you're free.
You I afford my pity ; bafer minds
Infult on the afflicted : You fhall know,
Virtue and courage are admir'd and lov'd
In enemies ; but more of that hereafter.
Thanks to your valour ; to your fwords I owe
This wreath triumphant. Nor be thou forgot,
My firft poor bondman ! Geta, I am glad
Thou'rt turn'd a fighter.
 Geta. 'Twas againft my will ;
But now I am content with't.

---

[25] Struck *full.*] So the former editions.

             Char.

Char. But imagine
What honours can be done to you beyond these,
Transcending all example; 'tis in you
To will, in us to serve it.

Niger. We will have
His statue of pure gold set in the capitol,
And he that bows not to it as a god,
Makes forfeit of his head.

Maxi. I burst with envy!
And yet these honours, which, conferr'd on me,
Would make me pace on air, seem not to move him.

Dio. Suppose this done, or were it possible
I could rise higher still, I am a man;
And all these glories, empires heap'd upon me,
Confirm'd by constant friends and faithful guards,
Cannot defend me from a shaking fever,
Or bribe the uncorrupted dart of Death
To spare me one short minute. Thus adorn'd
In these triumphant robes, my body yields not
A greater shadow than it did when I
Liv'd both poor and obscure; a sword's sharp point
Enters my flesh as far; dreams break my sleep,
As when I was a private man; my passions
Are stronger tyrants on me; nor is greatness
A saving antidote [26] to keep me from
A traitor's poison. Shall I praise my fortune,
Or raise the building of my happiness
On her uncertain favour? or presume
She is my own, and sure, that yet was never
Constant to any? Should my reason fail me,
(As flatt'ry oft corrupts it) here is an example
To speak, how far her smiles are to be trusted:
The rising sun, this morning, saw this man
The Persian monarch, and those subjects proud

---

[26] *A* saving *antidote to keep me, &c.*] *A* saving antidote, *to save or keep me, &c.* seems to be too inaccurate (not to say tautological) an expression, for such correct authors as ours; I with submission would read thus,
  A sovereign *antidote, &c.*   *Sympson.*
SAVING *antidote* very properly defines *a* PRESERVATIVE.

         That

That had the honour but to kifs his feet;
And yet, ere his diurnal progrefs ends,
He is the fcorn of Fortune. But you'll fay,
That fhe forfook him for his want of courage,
But never leaves the bold: Now, by my hopes
Of peace and quiet here, I never met
A braver enemy! And, to make it good,
Cofroe, Caffana, and the reft, be free,
And ranfomlefs return!

  Cofroe. To fee this virtue
Is more to me than empire; and to be
O'ercome by you, a glorious victory.

  Maxi. What a devil means he next!

  Dio. I know that glory
Is like Alcides' fhirt, if it ftay on us
'Till pride hath mix'd it with our blood; nor can we
Part with it at pleafure; when we would uncafe,
It brings along with it both flefh and finews,
And leaves us living monfters.

  Maxi. 'Would 'twere come
To my turn to put it on! I'd run the hazard.

  Dio. No; I will not be pluck'd out by the ears
Out of this glorious caftle; uncompell'd,
I will furrender rather: Let it fuffice,
I've touch'd the height of human happinefs,
And here I fix *nil ultra*. Hitherto
I've liv'd a fervant to ambitious thoughts,
And fading glories; what remains of life,
I dedicate to Virtue; and, to keep
My faith untainted, farewell, pride and pomp!
And circumftance of glorious majefty,
Farewell for ever!—Nephew, I have noted,
That you have long with fore eyes look'd upon
My flourifhing fortune; you fhall have poffeffion
Of my felicity: I deliver up
My empire, and this gem I priz'd above it,
And all things elfe that made me worth your envy,
Freely unto you.—Gentle Sir, your fuffrage,
To ftrengthen this. The foldiers' love I doubt not:

                                                His

His valour, gentlemen, will deferve your favours,
Which let my prayers further. All is yours.——
But I have been too liberal, and given that
I muft beg back again.

   Maxi. What am I fall'n from!

   Dio. Nay, ftart not: It is only the poor Grange,
The patrimony which my father left me,
I would be tenant to.

   Maxi. Sir, I am yours:
I will attend you there.

   Dio. No; keep the court;
Seek you in Rome for honour: I will labour
To find content elfewhere. Diffuade me not;
By Heaven, I am refolv'd!——And now, Drufilla,
Being as poor as when I vow'd to make thee
My wife, if thy love fince hath felt no change,
I'm ready to perform it.

   Druf. I ftill lov'd
Your perfon, not your fortunes; in a cottage,
Being yours, I am an emprefs.

   Delp. And I'll make
The change moft happy.

   Dio. Do me then the honour,
To fee my vow perform'd. You but attend
My glories to the urn; where be it afhes,
Welcome my mean eftate! and, as a due,
Wifh reft to me, I honour unto you.   [*Exeunt.*

ACT V. SCENE I.

Enter Chorus.

Chorus. THE war with glory ended, and Cofroe,
       Acknowledging his fealty to Charinus,
Difmifs'd in peace, returns to Perfia:
The reft, arriving fafely unto Rome,
Are entertain'd with triumphs: Maximinian,

By

By the grace and interceſſion of his uncle,
Saluted Cæſar: But good Diocleſian,
Weary of pomp and ſtate, retires himſelf,
With a ſmall train, to a moſt private Grange
In Lombardy [27] ; where the glad country ſtrives
With rural ſports to give him entertainment :
With which delighted, he with eaſe forgets
All ſpecious trifles, and ſecurely taſtes
The certain pleaſures of a private life.
But oh, Ambition, that eats into,
With venom'd teeth, true thankfulneſs and honour,
And, to ſupport her greatneſs, faſhions fears,
Doubts, and preventions to decline all dangers,
Which, in the place of ſafety, prove her ruin!
All which be pleas'd to ſee in Maximinian,
To whom his conferr'd ſov'reignty was like
A large ſail fill'd full with a fore-right wind,
That drowns a ſmaller bark: And he once fall'n
Into ingratitude, makes no ſtop in miſchief,
But violently runs on. Allow Maximinian all,
Honour, and empire, abſolute command;
Yet being ill, long great he cannot ſtand.   [*Exit.*

SCENE II.

Enter Maximinian and Aurelia.

Aur. Why droops my lord, my love, my life, my
     Cæſar?
How ill this dullneſs doth comport with greatneſs!
Does not, with open arms, your fortune court you?
Rome know you for her maſter? I myſelf
Confeſs you for my huſband? love and ſerve you?
If you contemn not theſe, and think them curſes,
I know no bleſſings that ambitious fleſh
Could wiſh to feel beyond 'em.

---

[27] *In* Lombardy.] *Dalmatia* was the real country, to which Diocleſian retired: But *Lombardy* being a finer climate for a farmer, was,
I ſuppoſe, the reaſon why our Poets have choſe to fix him there.

Symphon.

Maxi.

Maxi. Beſt Aurelia,
The parent and the nurſe to all my glories,
'Tis not that, thus embracing you, I think
There is a heaven beyond it, that begets
Theſe ſad retirements ; but the fear to loſe
What it is hell to part with.   Better to have liv'd
Poor and obſcure, and never ſcal'd the top
Of hilly empire, than to die with fear
To be thrown headlong down, almoſt as ſoon
As we have reach'd it !
 Aur. Theſe are panick terrors
You faſhion to yourſelf.   Is not my brother
(Your equal and co-partner in the empire)
Vow'd and confirm'd your friend ? the ſoldier conſtant ?
Hath not your uncle Diocleſian taken
His laſt farewell o' th' world ?   What then can ſhake
  you ?
 Maxi. The thought I may be ſhaken, and aſſurance
That what we do poſſeſs is not our own,
But has depending on another's favour :
For nothing's more uncertain, my Aurelia,
Than power that ſtands not on his proper baſis,
But borrows his foundation.   I'll make plain
My cauſe of doubts and fears ; for what ſhould I
Conceal from you, that are to be familiar
With my moſt private thoughts ?   Is not the empire
My uncle's gift ? and may he not reſume it
Upon the leaſt diſtaſte ? Does not Charinus
Croſs me in my deſigns ? and what is majeſty
When 'tis divided ? Does not the inſolent ſoldier
Call my command his donative ? and what can take
More from our honour ? No, my wife Aurelia,
If I to you am more than all the world,
As ſure you are to me ; as we deſire
To be ſecure, we muſt be abſolute,
And know no equal ; when your brother borrows
The little ſplendor that he has from us,
And we are ſerv'd for fear, not at entreaty,
We may live ſafe ; but 'till then, we but walk
         With

With heavy burdens on a sea of glass,
And our own weight will sink us.

    Aur. Your mother brought you
Into the world an emperor; you persuade
But what I would have counsel'd. Nearness of blood,
Respect of piety, and thankfulness,
And all the holy dreams of virtuous fools,
Must vanish into nothing, when Ambition
(The maker of great minds, and nurse of honour)
Puts in for empire. On then, and forget
Your simple uncle; think he was the master
(In being once an emperor) of a jewel,
Whose worth and use he knew not. For Charinus,
(No more my brother) if he be a stop
To what you purpose, he to me's a stranger,
And so to be remov'd.

    Maxi. Thou more than woman!
Thou masculine greatness, to whose soaring spirit
To touch the stars seems but an easy flight,
Oh, how I glory in thee! Those great women
Antiquity is proud of, thou but nam'd,
Shall be no more remember'd. But persevere,
And thou shalt shine among those lesser lights,

    Enter Charinus, Niger, and Guard.

To all posterity, like another Phœbe,
And so ador'd as she is.

    Aur. Here's Charinus,
His brow furrow'd with anger.

    Maxi. Let him storm!
And you shall hear me thunder.

    Char. He dispose of
My provinces at his pleasure? and confer
Those honours, that are only mine to give,
Upon his creatures?

    Niger. Mighty Sir, ascribe it
To his assurance of your love and favour,
And not to pride or malice.

    Char. No, good Niger;

Courtesy

Courtefy fhall not fool me; he fhall know
I lent a hand to raife him, and defend him,
While he continues good; but the fame ftrength,
If pride make him ufurp upon my right,
Shall ftrike him to the centre.—You're well met, Sir.

Maxi. As you make the encounter. Sir, I hear
That you repine, and hold yourfelf much griev'd,
In that, without your good leave, I beftow'd
The Gallian proconfulfhip upon
A follower of mine.

Char. 'Tis true; and wonder
You durft attempt it.

Maxi. Durft, Charinus?

Char. Durft;
Again I fpeak it. Think you me fo tame,
So leaden and unactive, to fit down
With fuch difhonour? But, recall your grant,
And fpeedily; or, by the Roman gods,
Thou trip'ft thine own heels up, and haft no part
In Rome, or in the empire.

Maxi. Thou haft none,
But by permiffion. Alas, poor Charinus,
Thou fhadow of an emperor, I fcorn thee,
Thee, and thy foolifh threats! The gods appoint him
The abfolute difpofer of the earth,
That has the fharpeft fword: I'm fure, Charinus,
Thou wear'ft one without edge. When cruel Aper
Had kill'd Numerianus, thy brother,
(An act that would have made a trembling coward
More daring than Alcides) thy bafe fear
Made thee wink at it; then rofe up my uncle,
For the honour of the empire, and of Rome,
Againft the traitor, and, among his guards,
Punifh'd the treafon. This bold daring act
Got him the foldiers' fuffrages to be Cæfar.
And howfoever his too-gentle nature
Allow'd thee the name only, as his gift,
I challenge the fucceffion.

Char. Thou art cozen'd.

When

When the receiver of a courtesy
Cannot sustain the weight it carries with it,
'Tis but a trial[23], not a present act.
Thou hast in a few days of thy short reign,
In over-weening pride, riot, and lusts,
Sham'd noble Dioclesian, and his gift;
Nor doubt I, when it shall arrive unto
His certain knowledge, how the empire groans
Under thy tyranny, but he will forsake
His private life, and once again resume
His laid-by majesty; or, at least, make choice
Of such an Atlas as may bear this burden,
Too heavy for thy shoulders. To effect this,
Lend your assistance, gentlemen; and then doubt not
But that this mushroom, sprung up in a night,
Shall as soon wither. And for you, Aurelia,
If you esteem your honour more than tribute
Paid to your loathsome appetite, as a fury
Fly from his loose embraces. So, farewell!
Ere long you shall hear more.   [*Exeunt.*

  Aur. Are you struck dumb,
That you make no reply?
  Maxi. Sweet, I will do,
And after talk: I will prevent their plots,
And turn them on their own accursed heads.
My uncle? good! I must not know the names
Of piety or pity. Steel my heart,
Desire of empire, and instruct me, that
The prince that over others would bear sway,
Checks at no let that stops him in his way! [*Exeunt.*

---

[23] *'Tis but a tryal.*] The sense designed is certainly, *not at present,*
or *as yet an irrevocable act or deed.* If the words do not seem to
the reader to convey this sense, a slight change will: He may read
          —— *not a perfect act,*
But I would not have the text disturbed.   *Seward.*
  Betterton reads,
          ' 'Tis but a trial, not a *confirm'd* act.'
The word *present,* in the text, bears the same sense as *confirm'd* or
perfect, in the variations of Seward and Betterton.

SCENE.

SCENE III.

Enter three Shepherds and two Countrymen.

1 *Shep.* Do you think this great man will continue
     here?

2 *Shep.* Continue here? what elfe? h' has bought
     the great farm;
A great man, with a great inheritance,
And all the ground about it, all the woods too,
And ftock'd it like an emperor.   Now, all our fports
     again,
And all our merry gambols, our May-ladies,
Our evening dances on the green, our fongs,
Our holiday good cheer, our bagpipes now, boys,
Shall make the wanton laffes fkip again,
Our fheep-fhearings, and all our knacks.

3 *Shep.* But hark you,
We muft not call him emperor.

1 *Countr.* That's all one;
He's the king of good fellows, that's no treafon;
And fo I'll call him ftill, tho' I be hang'd for't.
I grant you h' has giv'n his honour to another man,
He cannot give his humour; he's a brave fellow,
And will love us, and we'll love him.   Come hither,
     Ladon;
What new fongs, and what geers?

3 *Shep.* Enough.   I'll tell ye;
He comes abroad anon to view his grounds,
And, with the help of Thirfis, and old Egon,
(If his whorfon cold be gone) and Amaryllis,
And fome few more o' th' wenches, we will meet him,
And ftrike him fuch new fprings [29], and fuch free
     welcomes,

---

[29] *Springs* here means tunes. So bifhop Douglafs in his Tranfla-
tion of Virgil. Book vi. page 167.
    ' Gif Orpheus mycht reduce agane I gefs
    ' From Hell his fpoufe's goift, with his fueit ftringeis,
    ' Playand on his harp of Trace fa pleafand *fpringis.*

Shall make him scorn an empire, forget majesty,
And make him bless the hour he liv'd here happy.

2 *Countr.* And we will second ye, we honest carters,
We lads o'th' lash, with some blunt entertainment;
Our teams to two-pence, we'll give him some content,
Or we'll bawl fearfully!

3 *Shep.* He can't expect now
His courtly entertainments, and his rare musicks,
And ladies to delight him with their voices;
Honest and cheerful toys from honest meanings,
And the best hearts they have. We must be neat all;
On goes my russet jerkin with blue buttons.

1 *Shep.* And my green slops I was married in; my
       bonnet,
With my carnation point with silver tags, boys;
You know where I won it.

1 *Countr.* Thou wilt ne'er be old, Alexis.

1 *Shep.* And I shall find some toys that have been
      favours,
And nosegays, and such knacks; for there be wenches.

3 *Shep.* My mantle goes on too I play'd young
      Paris in,
And the new garters Amaryllis sent me.

1 *Countr.* Yes, yes; we'll all be handsome, and wash
      our faces.
Neighbour, I see a remnant of March dust
That's hatch'd into your chaps: I pray you be careful,
And mundify your muzzle[30].

Enter Geta.

2 *Countr.* I'll to the barbers;
It shall cost me I know what.—Who's this?

3 *Shep.* Give room, neighbours!

So Chaucer in his House of Fame. Book iii. line 143, &c.
    ' There saw I famous old and young
    ' Piperis all of the Duche tong,
    ' To lerning love dauncis and *springis*,
    ' Reyis and the straungè thingis.'   *Sympson.*
  30 *Mundify your muzzle.*] i. e. Clean your mouth, your chaps.

A great.

A great man in our ſtate. Gods bleſs your worſhip!

2 Countr. Encreaſe your maſterſhip!

Geta. Thanks, my good people.

Stand off, and know your duties!—As I take it,

You are the labouring people of this village,

And you that keep the ſheep. Stand further off yet,

And mingle not with my authority;

I am too mighty for your company.

3 Shep. We know it, Sir; and we deſire your worſhip

To reckon us amongſt your humble ſervants;

And that our country ſports, Sir——

Geta. For your ſports, Sir,

They may be ſeen, when I ſhall think convenient,

When, out of my diſcretion, I ſhall view 'em,

And hold 'em fit for licence.—Ye look upon me,

And look upon me ſeriouſly, as you knew me:

'Tis true, I've been a raſcal, as you are,

A fellow of no mention, nor no mark,

Juſt ſuch another piece of dirt, ſo faſhion'd;

But time, that purifies all things of merit,

Has ſet another ſtamp. Come nearer now,

And be not fearful (I take off my auſterity);

And know me for the great and mighty ſteward

Under this man of honour; know ye for my vaſſals,

And at my pleaſure I can diſpeople ye,

Can blow you and your cattle out o'th' country:

But fear me, and have favour. Come, go along with me,

And I will hear your ſongs, and perhaps like 'em.

3 Shep. I hope you will, Sir.

Geta. 'Tis not a thing impoſſible.

Perhaps I'll ſing myſelf, the more to grace ye;

And if I like your women——

3 Shep. We'll have the beſt, Sir,

Handſome young girls.

Geta. The handſomer the better.

Enter Delphia.

'May bring your wives too; 'twill be all one charge

to ye;

For

For I muſt know your families.

Delp. 'Tis well ſaid,
'Tis well ſaid, honeſt friends. I know ye're hatching
Some pleaſurable ſports for your great landlord;
Fill him with joy, and win him a friend to ye,
And make this little Grange ſeem a large empire,
Let out ³⁰ with home contents: I'll work his favour,
Which daily ſhall be on ye.

3 Shep. Then we'll ſing daily,
And make him the beſt ſports——

Delp. Inſtruct 'em, Geta,
And be a merry man again.

Geta. Will you lend me a devil,
That we may dance a while?

Delp. I'll lend thee two;
And bag-pipes that ſhall blow alone.

Geta. I thank you;
But I'll know your devils of a cooler complexion firſt.
Come, follow, follow; I'll go ſit and ſee ye.

Delp. Do; and be ready an hour hence, and bring'em;
For in the grove you'll find him.   [*Exeunt.*

Enter Diocles ³¹ *and Druſilla.*

Dio. Come, Druſilla,
The partner of my beſt contents! I hope now
You dare believe me.

Druſ. Yes, and dare ſay to you,
I think you now moſt happy.

---

³⁰ Let *out.*] Probably we ſhould read, SET *out.*

³¹ *Enter* Diocles *and Druſilla.*] Though the emperor had quitted
his imperial dignity, and retired to his farm, it does not appear by
any accounts, that he ever reduced his name, as our editors have
done for him here, to pure plain *Diocles.* I ſay the editors, not the
poets, becauſe in the concluſion of this act the ſoldiers give him his
imperial addition,
  Long live the good and gracious Dioclefian.   *Sympſon.*
  Theſe cavils at the ſtage-directions are not only idle, but ridiculous;
and, beſides this, Sympſon ſuffers him, in the Dumb Show (at the
beginning of the fourth act) to be called both *Diocles* and *Dioclefian:*
This probably proceeded from overſight in him; in us it proceeds
from our thinking it too inſignificant for attention.

                                                  Dio.

Dio. You say true, sweet;
For, by my soul, I find now by experience,
Content was never courtier.

Druf. I pray you walk on, Sir;
The cool shades of the grove invite you.

Dio. Oh, my dearest!
When man has cast off his ambitious greatness,
And sunk into the sweetness of himself;
Built his foundation upon honest thoughts;
Not great, but good, desires his daily servants,
How quietly he sleeps! How joyfully
He wakes again, and looks on his possessions,
And from his willing labours feeds with pleasure!
Here hang no comets in the shapes of crowns
To shake our sweet contents; nor here, Drusilla,
Cares, like eclipses, darken our endeavours:
We love here without rivals, kiss with innocence:
Our thoughts as gentle as our lips, our children
The double heirs both of our forms and faiths.

Druf. I'm glad ye make this right use of this sweetness,
This sweet retiredness.

Dio. 'Tis sweet indeed, love,
And every circumstance about it shews it.
How liberal is the spring in every place here!
The artificial court shews but a shadow,
A painted imitation of this glory.
Smell to this flower; here Nature has her excellence;
Let all the perfumes of the empire pass this,
The carefull'st lady's cheek shew such a colour;
They're gilded and adulterate vanities.
And here in poverty dwells noble nature.
What pains we take to cool our wines, to allay us,
And bury quick the fuming God to quench us.

                                    [*Musick below.*

Methinks this chrystal well——Ha! what strange
                musick?
'Tis underneath, sure!—How it stirs and joys me!
How all the birds set on! the fields redouble
Their odoriferous sweets! Hark how the echoes——

                    M 4   *Enter*

Enter a Spirit from the well.

Druſ. See, Sir, thoſe flowers
From out the well, ſpring to your entertainment.

Enter Delphia.

Dio. Bleſs me !
Druſ. Be not afraid ; 'tis ſome good angel
That's come to welcome you.

    Delp. Go near, and hear, ſon.   [*Song.*
    Dio. Oh, mother, thank you, thank you ! this was
        your will.
    Delp. You ſhall not want delights to bleſs your
        preſence.
Now you are honeſt, all the ſtars ſhall honour you.

Enter Shepherds and Dancers.

Stay ; here are country ſhepherds ; here's ſome ſport
    too,
And you muſt grace it, Sir ; 'twas meant to welcome
    you.
A king ſhall never feel your joy : Sit down, ſon.

*A dance of Shepherds and Shepherdeſſes ; Pan leading
the men, Ceres the maids.*

Hold, hold ! my meſſenger appears. Leave off, friends,
Leave off a while, and breathe.

    Dio. What news ? You're pale, mother.
    Delp. No ; I am careful of thy ſafety, ſon.
Be not affrighted, but ſit ſtill ; I'm with thee.

Enter Maximinian, Aurelia, and Soldiers.

And now, dance out your dance.—D' you know that
    perſon ?
Be not amaz'd, but let him ſhew his dreadfulleſt.

    Maxi. How confident he ſits amongſt his pleaſures,
And what a cheerful colour ſhews in's face !
And yet he ſees me too, the ſoldiers with me.

    Aur. Be ſpeedy in your work, (you will be ſtopt elſe)
                            And

And then you are an emperor!

Maxi. I'll about it.

Dio. My royal coufin, how I joy to fee you,
You and your royal emprefs!

Maxi. You're too kind, Sir.
I come not to eat with you, and to furfeit
In thefe poor clownifh pleafures ; but to tell you,
I look upon you like my winding-fheet,
The coffin of my greatnefs, nay, my grave :
For whilft you are alive——

Dio. Alive, my coufin?

Maxi. I fay, alive.—I am no emperor;
I'm nothing but mine own difquiet.

Dio. Stay, Sir!

Maxi. I cannot ftay. The foldiers dote upon you.
I would fain fpare you ; but mine own fecurity
Compels me to forget you are my uncle,
Compels me to forget you made me Cæfar ;
For, whilft you are remember'd, I am buried.

Dio. Did not I make you emperor, dear coufin?
The free gift from my fpecial grace?

Delp. Fear nothing.

Dio. Did not I chufe this poverty, to raife you?
That royal woman gave into your arms too?
Blefs'd you with her bright beauty? Gave the foldier,
The foldier that hung to me, fix'd him on you?
Gave you the world's command?

Maxi. This cannot help you.

Dio. Yet this fhall eafe me. Can you be fo bafe,
          coufin,
So far from noblenefs, fo far from nature,
As to forget all this? to tread this tie out?
Raife to yourfelf fo foul a monument
That every common foot fhall kick afunder?
Muft my blood glue you to your peace?

Maxi. It muft, uncle ;
I ftand too loofe elfe, and my foot too feeble :
You gone once, and their love retir'd, I'm rooted.

Dio. And cannot this remov'd poor ftate obicure me?

                                              I do

I do not feek for yours, nor enquire ambitioufly
After your growing fortunes. Take heed, my kinfman!
Ungratefulnefs and blood mingled together,
Will, like two furious tides——

   Maxi. I muft fail thro' 'em;
Let 'em be tides of death, Sir, I muft ftem up.

   Dio. Hear but this laft, and wifely yet confider!
Place round about my Grange a garrifon,
That if I offer to exceed my limits,
Or ever in my common talk name emperor,
Ever converfe with any greedy foldier,
Or look for adoration, nay, for courtefy,
Above the day's falute——Think who has fed you,
Think, coufin, who I am. D'you flight my mifery?
Nay, then I charge thee! Nay, I meet thy cruelty.

   Maxi. This cannot ferve; prepare. Now fall on,
       foldiers,
And all the treafure that I have——

                 [Thunder and lightning.

   1 *Sold.* The earth fhakes;
We totter up and down; we cannot ftand, Sir;
Methinks the mountains tremble too.

   2 *Sold.* The flafhes,
How thick and hot they come! We fhall be burnt all!

   Delp. Fall on, foldiers!
You that fell innocent blood, fall on full bravely!

   1 *Sold.* We cannot ftir.

   Delp. You have your liberty;
So have you, lady: One of you come do it.

            [A hand with a bolt appears above.

D'ye ftand amaz'd? Look o'er thy head, Maximinian,
Look, to thy terror, what over hangs thee;
Nay, it will nail thee dead: Look how it threatens thee!
' The bolt for vengeance on ungrateful wretches;
' The bolt of innocent blood:' Read thofe hot cha-
     racters,
And fpell the will of Heav'n. Nay, lovely lady,
You muft take part too, as fpur to Ambition.
Are you humble? Now fpeak; my part is ended.

                       Does

Does all your glory shake?

Maxi. Hear us, great uncle,
Good and great Sir, be pitiful unto us!
Below your feet we lay our lives; be merciful!
Begin you, Heaven will follow.

Aur. Oh, it shakes still!

Maxi. And dreadfully it threatens. We acknowledge
Our base and foul intentions: Stand between us!
For faults confess'd, they say, are half forgiven:
We're sorry for our sins. Take from us, Sir,
That glorious weight that made us swell, that poison'd
    us;
That mass of majesty I labour'd under,
(Too heavy and too mighty for my manage)
That my poor innocent days may turn again,
And my mind, pure, may purge me of these curses.
By your old love, the blood that runs between us——

        [*The hand taken in.*

Aur. By that love once you bare to me! by that, Sir,
That blessed maid enjoys——

Dio. Rise up, dear cousin,
And be your words your judges! I forgive you.
Great as you are, enjoy that greatness ever,
Whilst I mine own content make mine own empire.
Once more I give you all; learn to deserve it,
And live to love your good more than your greatness.——
Now shew your loves to entertain this emperor,
My honest neighbours! Geta, see all handsome.
Your Grace must pardon us; our house is little;
But such an ample welcome as a poor man
And his true love can make you and your empress——
Madam, we have no dainties.

Aur. 'Tis enough, Sir;
We shall enjoy the riches of your goodness.

Sold. Long live the good and gracious Dioclesian!

Dio. I thank you, soldiers; I forgive your rashness.
And, royal Sir, long may they love and honour you!

       [*Drums beat a march afar off.*

What drums are those?

           Delp.

Delp. Meet 'em, my honeſt ſon ;
They are thy friends, Charinus and the old ſoldiers,
That come to reſcue thee from thy hot couſin.
But all is well; and turn all into welcomes !
Two emperors you muſt entertain now.

Dio. Oh, dear mother,
I've will enough, but I want room and glory.

Delp. That ſhall be my care. Sound your pipes
        now merrily,
And all your handſome ſports: Sing 'em full welcomes !

Dio. And let 'em know, our true love breeds more
       ſtories,
And perfect joys, than kings do, and their glories.

                                    [*Exeunt.*

THE

QUEEN OF CORINTH.

A TRAGI-COMEDY.

---

*The Commendatory Verses by Hills assign this Play wholly to Fletcher.
It was first printed in the folio of 1647. We do not know of any
alteration that has been made to it, nor has it been acted these
many years.*

DRAMATIS

DRAMATIS PERSONÆ.

MEN.

Agenor, *prince of Argos.*
Theanor, *son of the Queen of Corinth, a vicious prince.*
Leonidas, *the Corinthian general, brother to Merione.*
Euphanes, *a noble young gentleman, favourite to the Queen.*
Crates, *elder brother to Euphanes, a malicious beautefeu¹.*
Conon, *Euphanes's confidant, and fellow-traveller.*
Neanthes, ⎫
Sosicles, ⎬ *Courtiers.*
Eraton, ⎭
Onos, *or* Lamprias, *a very foolish traveller.*
Tutor, ⎫ *to Onos, two foolish knaves.*
Uncle, ⎬
Gentlemen, *servants to Agenor.*
A page to lord Euphanes.

Marshal, Vintner, and Drawers.

WOMEN.

Queen of Corinth, *a wise and virtuous widow.*
Merione, *a virtuous lady, honourably solicited by prince Agenor.*
Beliza, *a noble lady, mistress to Euphanes.*

SCENE, CORINTH.

¹ *Boutefeu.*] An incendiary.

THE

THE QUEEN OF CORINTH.

Oh, Heaven!
Is this the happy time? my hope to this come? *Act II*

J.J. Barralet delin.t   C. Grignion sculp.t

QUEEN OF CORINTH.

ACT I. SCENE I.

Enter Neanthes, Sosicles, and Eraton.

Eraton. THE general is return'd then?

Nean. With much honour.

Sof. And peace concluded with the prince of Argos?

Nean. To the Queen's wishes: The conditions
    sign'd
So far beyond her hopes, to the advantage
Of Corinth, and the good of all her subjects,
That tho' Leonidas, our brave general,
Ever came home a fair and great example,
He never yet return'd or with less loss
Or more deserved honour.

Era. Have you not heard
The motives to this general good?

Nean. The main one
Was admiration first in young Agenor
(For by that name we know the prince of Argos)
Of our Leonidas' wisdom and his valour;
Which, tho' an enemy, first in him bred wonder,
That liking, love succeeded that, which was
Follow'd by a desire to be a friend,
Upon what terms soever, to such goodness.
They had an interview; and, that their friendship
Might with our peace be ratified, it was concluded,

Agenor,

Agenor, yielding up all such strong places
As he held in our territories, should receive
(With a sufficient dower paid by the Queen)
The fair Merione for his wife.

   Era. But how
Approves the Queen of this? since we well know,
Nor was her highness ignorant, that her son
The prince Theanor made love to this lady,
And in the noblest way.

   Nean. Which she allow'd of,
And I have heard from some familiar with
Her nearest secrets, she so deeply priz'd her,
Being from an infant train'd up in her service,
(Or, to speak better, rather her own creature)
She once did say, that if the prince should steal
A marriage without her leave, or knowledge,
With this Merione, with a little suit
She should grant both their pardons; whereas now,
To shew herself forsooth a Spartan lady,
And that 'tis in her power, now it concerns
The common good, not alone to subdue
Her own affections, but command her son's,
She has not only forc'd him with rough threats
To leave his mistress, but compell'd him, when
Agenor made his entrance into Corinth,
To wait upon his rival.

   Sof. Can it be
The prince should sit down with this wrong?

   Nean. I know not;
I am sure I should not.

   Era. Trust me, nor I:
A mother is a name; but, put in balance
With a young wench, 'tis nothing. Where did you
      leave him?

   Nean. Near Vesta's temple (for there he dismiss'd
      me)
And full of troubled thoughts, calling for Crates:
He went with him, but whither, or to what purpose,
I am a stranger.

Enter

Enter Theanor and Crates.

Era. They're come back, Neanthes.

The. I like the place well.

Cra. Well, Sir? it is built
As if the architect had been a prophet,
And fashion'd it alone for this night's action;
The vaults so hollow, and the walls so strong,
As Dian there might suffer violence,
And with loud shrieks in vain call Jove to help her;
Or should he hear, his thunder could not find
An entrance to it.

The. I give up myself
Wholly to thy direction, worthiest Crates:
And yet the desp'rate cure that we must practise
Is in itself so foul, and full of danger,
That I stand doubtful whether 'twere more manly
To die not seeking help, or that help being
So deadly, to pursue it.

Cra. To those reasons
I have already urg'd, I will add these:
For, but consider, Sir——   [*They talk apart.*

Era. It is of weight
Whate'er it be, that with such vehement action
Of eye, hand, foot, nay, all his body's motion,
Crates incites the prince to.

Nean. Then observe,
With what variety of passions he
Receives his reasons: Now he's pale, and shakes
For fear or anger; now his natural red
Comes back again, and with a pleasing smile
He seems to entertain it. 'Tis resolv'd on,
Be it what 'twill: To his ends may it prosper,
Tho' the state sink for't!

Cra. Now you are a prince
Fit to rule others, and, in shaking off
The bonds in which your mother fetters you,
Discharge your debt to Nature: She's your guide;
Follow her boldly, Sir.

Vol. VI.   N   *The.*

The. I am confirm'd,
Fall what may fall.

Cra. Yet still difguife your malice
In your humility.

The. I am inftructed.

Cra. Tho' in your heart there rage a thoufand
      tempefts,
All calmnefs in your looks.

The. I fhall remember.

Cra. And at no hand, tho' thefe are us'd as agents,
Acquaint them with your purpofe, 'till the inftant
That we employ them; 'tis not fit they have
Time to confider: When 'tis done, reward
Or fear will keep them filent. Yet you may
Grace them as you pafs by; 'twill make them furer,
And greedier to deferve you[a].

The. I'll move only
As you would have me. Good day, gentlemen!
Nay, fpare this ceremonious form of duty
To him that brings love to you, equal love,
And is in nothing happier than in knowing
It is return'd by you; we are as one.

Sof. I am o'erjoyed! I know not
How to reply; but——

Era. Hang all *buts!*—My lord,
For this your bounteous favour——

Nean. Let me fpeak.
If to feed vultures here, after the halter
Has done his part, or if there be a hell
To take a fwinge or two there, may deferve this—

Sof. We're ready.

Era. Try us any way.

Nean. Put us to it.

The. What jewels I have in you!

Cra. Have thefe fouls,
That for a good look, and a few kind words,

---

[a] *To deferve you.*] Sympfon and Seward chufe to read, *ferve* inftead
of *deferve*: We think the latter word genuine, if not preferable. *To
deferve you* fignifies *to merit your favour.*

Part with their essence?

The. Since you will compel me
To put that to the trial which I doubt not,
Crates, may be suddenly, will instruct you
How, and in what, to shew your loves: Obey him
As you would bind me to you.

Cra. 'Tis well grounded;
Leave me to rear the building.

Nean. We will do——

Cra. I know it.

Era. Any thing you'll put us to.   [*Exeunt.*

SCENE II.

Enter Leonidas, Merione, and Beliza.

Leo. Sister, I reap the harvest of my labours
In your preferment; be you worthy of it,
And with an open bosom entertain
A greater fortune than my love durst hope for!
Be wise, and welcome it: Play not the coy
And foolish wanton, with the offer'd bounties
Of him that is a prince. I was woo'd for you,
And won, Merione; then, if you dare
Believe the object that took me was worthy,
Or trust my judgment, in me think you were
Courted, sued to, and conquer'd.

Mer. Noble brother,
I have and still esteem you as a father,
And will as far obey you; my heart speaks it:
And yet, without your anger, give me leave
To say, that in the choice of that on which
All my life's joys or sorrows have dependance,
It had been fit, ere you had made a full
And absolute grant of me to any other,
I should have us'd mine own eyes, or at least
Made you to understand, whether it were
Within my power to make a second gift
Of my poor self.

Leo. I know what 'tis you point at,

The

The prince Theanor's love ; let not that cheat you ;
His vows were but mere courtship ; all his service
But practice how to entrap a credulous lady.
Or, grant it serious, yet you must remember,
He's not to love, but where the Queen his mother
Must give allowance, which to you is barr'd up ;
And therefore study to forget that ever
You cherish'd such a hope.

   Mer. I would I could!

   Leo. But brave Agenor, who is come in person
To celebrate this marriage, for your love
Forgives the forfeit of ten thousand lives,
That must have fallen under the sword of war
Had not this peace been made ; which general good
Both countries owe to his affection to you.
Oh, happy sister, ask this noble lady,
Your bosom friend (since I fail in my credit)
What palm Agenor's name, above all princes
That Greece is proud of, carries, and with lustre.

   Bel. Indeed, fame gives him out for excellent ;
And, friend, I doubt not but when you shall see him,

     Enter a Servant, who whispers Beliza [3].

He'll so appear to you.—Art sure 'tis he ?

   Ser. As I live, madam——

   Bel. Virtue enable me to contain my joy !
'Tis my Euphanes ?

   Ser. Yes.

   Bel. And he's in health ?

   Ser. Most certainly, madam.

   Bel. I'll see him instantly.
So, prithee, tell him.   *[Exit Servant.*

   Mer. I yield myself too weak
In argument to oppose you ; you may lead me
Whither you please.

   Leo. 'Tis answer'd like my sister ;

---

   [3] *Enter a Servant.*] Without the addition I have made to this
direction, every reader perhaps would not take the abrupt question,
Art sure 'tis he ? in a proper light.   *Sympson.*

                              And

And if in him you find not ample caufe
To pray for me, and daily, on your knees,
Conclude I have no judgment.

Mer. May it prove fo!
Friend, fhall we have your company?

Bel. Two hours hence
I will not fail you.

Leo. At your pleafure, madam. [*Exe. Leo. and Mer.*

Enter Euphanes.

Bel. Could I in one word fpeak a thoufand wel-
  comes,
And hearty ones, you have 'em. Fy! my hand?
We ftand at no fuch diftance : By my life,
The parting kifs you took before your travel
Is yet a virgin on my lips, preferv'd
With as much care as I would do my fame,
To entertain your wifh'd return.

Euph. Beft lady,
That I do honour you, and with as much reafon
As ever man did Virtue; that I love you,
Yet look upon you with that reverence
As holy men behold the fun, the ftars,
The temples, and their gods, they all can witnefs;
And that you have deferv'd this duty from me,
The life, and means of life, for which I owe you,
Commands me to profefs it, fince my fortune
Affords no other payment.

Bel. I had thought,
That for the trifling courtefies, as I call them,
(Tho' you give them another name) you had
Made ample fatisfaction in th' acceptance;
And therefore did prefume you had brought home
Some other language.

Euph. No one I have learn'd
Yields words fufficient to exprefs your goodnefs;
Nor can I ever chufe another theme,
And not be thought unthankful.

Bel. Pray you no more,

N 3
As

As you refpect me.

Euph. That charm is too powerful
For me to difobey it. 'Tis your pleafure,
And not my boldnefs, madam.

Bel. Good Euphanes,
Believe I am not one of thofe weak ladies,
That (barren of all inward worth) are proud
Of what they cannot truly call their own,
Their birth or fortune, which are things without
               them:
Nor in this will I imitate the world,
Whofe greater part of men think when they give
They purchafe bondmen, not make worthy friends:
By all that's good I fwear, I never thought
My great eftate was an addition to me,
Or that your wants took from you.

Euph. There are few
So truly underftanding or themfelves or what
They do poffefs.

Bel. Good Euphanes, where benefits
Are ill conferr'd, as on unworthy men [4],
That turn them to bad ufes, the beftower,
For wanting judgment how and on whom to place them,
Is partly guilty: But when we do favours
To fuch as make them grounds on which they build
Their noble actions, there we improve our fortunes
To the moft fair advantage. If I fpeak
Too much, tho' I confefs I fpeak not well [5],
Prithee remember 'tis a woman's weaknefs,
And then thou wilt forgive it.

Euph. You fpeak nothing
But what would well become the wifeft man:
And that by you deliver'd is fo pleafing
That I could hear you ever.

Bel. Fly not from

---

[4] *As to unworthy men.*] Amended by Sympfon.
[5] *I fpeak well.*] The infertion of the word *not* is recommmended by Sympfon. The anfwer of Euphanes, and all that follows, proves it to be the original reading.

Your

THE QUEEN OF CORINTH. 199

Your word, for I arreſt it: And will now
Expreſs myſelf a little more, and prove
That whereas you profeſs yourſelf my debtor,
That I am yours.

Euph. Your ladyſhip then muſt uſe
Some ſophiſtry I never heard of.

Bel. By plain reaſons;
For, look you, had you never ſunk beneath
Your wants, or if thoſe wants had found ſupply
From Crates, your unkind and covetous brother,
Or any other man, I then had miſs'd
A ſubject upon which I worthily
Might exerciſe my bounty: Whereas now,
By having happy opportunity
To furniſh you before, and in your travels,
With all conveniencies that you thought uſeful,
That gold which would have ruſted in my coffers,
Being thus employ'd, has render'd me a partner
In all your glorious actions. And whereas,
Had you not been, I ſhould have died a thing
Scarce known, or ſoon forgotten; there's no trophy
In which Euphanes for his worth is mention'd,
But there you have been careful to remember,
That all the good you did came from Beliza.

Euph. That was but thankfulneſs.

Bel. 'Twas ſuch an honour,
And ſuch a large return for the poor traſh
I ventur'd with you, that, if I ſhould part
With all that I poſſeſs, and myſelf too,
In ſatisfaction for it, 'twere ſtill ſhort
Of your deſervings.

Euph. You o'er-prize them, madam.

Bel. The Queen herſelf hath given me gracious
      thanks
In your behalf; for ſhe hath heard, Euphanes,
How gallantly you have maintain'd her honour
In all the courts of Greece: And reſt aſſur'd
(Tho' yet unknown) when I preſent you to her,
Which I will do this evening, you ſhall find

N 4   That

That she intends good to you.

Euph. Worthiest lady,
Since all you labour for is the advancement
Of him that will live ever your poor servant,
He must not contradict it.

Bel. Here's your brother;
'Tis strange to see him here.

Enter Crates.

Cra. You're welcome home, Sir!
(Your pardon, madam.) I had thought my house,
Considering who I am, might have been worthy
Of your first visit.

Euph. 'Twas not open to me
When last I saw you; and to me 'tis wonder
That absence, which still renders men forgotten,
Should make my presence wish'd for.

Bel. That's not it;
Your too-kind brother, understanding that
You stand in no need of him, is bold to offer
His entertainment.

Cra. He had never wanted
Or yours, or your assistance, had he practis'd
The way he might have took, to have commanded
Whatever I call mine.

Euph. I studied many,
But could find none.

Cra. You would not find yourself, Sir,
Or in yourself, what was due to me from you;
The privilege my birth bestow'd upon me
Might challenge some regard.

Euph. You had all the land, Sir;
What else did you expect? And I am certain
You kept such strong guards to preserve it yours,
I could force nothing from you.

Cra. Did you ever
Demand help from me?

Euph. My wants have, and often,
With open mouths, but you nor heard nor saw them.

May-be,

May-be, you look'd I should petition to you,
As you went to your horse; flatter your servants,
To play the brokers for my furtherance;
Sooth your worst humours, act the parasite
On all occasions; write my name with theirs
That are but one degree remov'd from slaves;
Be drunk when you would have me, then wench with
       you,
Or play the pandar; enter into quarrels,
Altho' unjustly grounded, and defend them,
'Cause they were yours: These are the tyrannies
Most younger brothers groan beneath; yet bear them
From the insulting heir, selling their freedoms
At a less rate than what the state allows
The salary of base and common strumpets:
For my part, ere on such low terms I feed
Upon a brother's trencher, let me die
The beggar's death, and starve!
  Cra. 'Tis bravely spoken,
Did what you do rank with it.
  Bel. Why, what does he
You would not wish were yours?
  Cra. I'll tell you, lady,
Since you rise up his advocate, and boldly
(For now I find, and plainly, in whose favour
My love and service to you was neglected).
For all your wealth, nay, add to that your beauty,
And put your virtues in, (if you have any)
I would not yet be pointed at, as he is,
For the fine courtier, the woman's man,
That tells my lady stories, dissolves riddles,
Ushers her to her coach, lies at her feet
At solemn masques, applauding what she laughs at;
Reads her asleep a-nights, and takes his oath
Upon her pantofles, that all excellence
In other madams does but zany hers:
These you are perfect in, and yet these take not
Or from your birth or freedom.
  Euph. Should another

Say this, my deeds, not looks fhould fhew——
  Bel. Contemn it:
His envy fains this, and he's but reporter,
Without a fecond, of his own dry fancies.
  Cra. Yes, madam, the whole city fpeaks it with me;
And tho' it may diftafte, 'tis certain you
Are brought into the fcene, and with him cenfur'd;
For you are given out for the provident lady,
That, not to be unfurnifh'd for her pleafures,
(As, without them, to what vain ufe is greatnefs!)
Have made choice of an able man, a young man,
Of an Herculean back, to do you fervice;
And one you may command too, that is active,
And does what you would have him.
  Bel. You are foul-mouth'd!
  Cra. That can fpeak well, write verfes too, and good
    ones,
Sharp and conceited, whofe wit you may lie with
When his performance fails him; one you have
Maintain'd abroad to learn new ways to pleafe you;
And, by the gods, you well reward him for it,
No night in which, while you lie fick and panting,
He watches by you, but is worth a talent;
No conference in your coach, which is not paid with
A fcarlet fuit: This the poor people[6] mutter,
Tho' I believe, for I am bound to do fo,
A lady of your youth, that feeds high too,
And a moft exact lady, may do all this
Out of a virtuous love, the laft-bought vizard
That lechery purchas'd.
  Euph. Not a word beyond this!
The reverence I owe to that one womb
In which we both were embrions, makes me fuffer
What's paft, but if continued——
  Bel. Stay your hand!

---

[6] *Poor people.*] I have a ftrong fufpicion that *moft* is the reading
we ought to follow, but I have not ventured to difturb the text.
                    Sympfon.

The text is beft.

The

The Queen shall right my honour.

Cra. Let him do it;
It is but marrying him. And, for your anger,
Know that I slight it! When your goddess here
Is weary of your sacrifice, as she will be,
You know my house, and there amongst my servants
Perhaps you'll find a livery.   [*Exit.*

Bel. Be not mov'd;
I know the rancor of his disposition,
And turn it on himself by laughing at it;
And in that let me teach you.

Euph. I learn gladly.   [*Exeunt.*

SCENE III.

Enter Neanthes, Sosicles, and Eraton, severally.

Nean. You're met unto my wishes; if you ever
Desir'd true mirth so far as to adventure
To die with the extremity of laughter,
I come before the object that will do it,
Or let me live your fool.

Sos. Who is't, Neanthes?

Nean. Lamprias the usurer's son.

Era. Lamprias? the youth
Of six and fifty?

Sos. That was sent to travel
By rich Beliza, 'till he came to age
And was fit for a wife?

Nean. The very same.
This gallant, with his Guardian and his Tutor,
(And, of the three, who is most fool I know not)
Are newly come to Corinth: I'll not stale them
By giving up their characters [7]; but leave you
To make your own discoveries. Here they are, Sir.

---

[7] *By giving up their, &c.*] The particle *up* I have left out of the
present text, though it stands in all the other copies, because it con-
founds the sense: *Giving up a character* is a phrase of a quite different import to what he would say here, as the least attention will
make evident enough.   *Sympson.*

To give up is right. It does not here signify *to renounce*, in the
modern acceptation, but to *describe*.

Enter

Enter Onos, Uncle, and Tutor.

Tutor. That leg a little higher; very well.
Now put your face into the traveller's posture;
Exceeding good.

Uncle. Do you mark how they admire him?

Tutor. They will be all my scholars, when they know
And understand him truly.

Era. Phœbus guard me
From this new Python!

Sof. How they have trim'd him up
Like an old reveller!

Nean. Curl'd him and perfum'd him;
But that was done with judgment, for he looks
Like one that purg'd perpetually. Trust me,
That witch's face of his is painted too,
And every ditch upon it buries more
Than would set off ten bawds and all their tenants!

Sof. See how it moves towards us.

Nean. There's a salutation!—
'Troth, gentlemen, you have bestow'd much travel
In training up your pupil.

Tutor. Sir, great buildings
Require great labours; which yet we repent not,
Since for the country's good we have brought home
An absolute man.

Uncle. As any of his years,
Corinth can shew you.

Era. He's exceeding meagre.

Tutor. His contemplation——

Uncle. Besides, 'tis fit
Learners should be kept hungry.

Nean. You all contemplate;
For three such wretched pictures of lean famine
I never saw together.

Uncle. We have fat minds, Sir,
And travell'd to save charges. Do you think
'Twas fit a young and hopeful gentleman
Should be brought up a glutton? He's my ward;

Nor

Nor was there ever, where I bore the bag,
Any fuperfluous wafte.

Era. Pray you can it fpeak?

Tutor. He knows all languages, but will ufe none,
They're all too big for's mouth, or elfe too little
To exprefs his great conceits. And yet of late,
With fome impulfion, he hath fet down,
In a ftrange method, by the way of queftion,
And briefly too⁸, all bufinefs whatfoever,
That may concern a gentleman.

Nean. Good Sir, let's hear him.

Tutor. Come on, Sir.

Nean. They have taught him, like an ape,
To do his tricks by figns. Now he begins.

Onos. When fhall we be drunk together?

Tutor. That's the firft.

Onos. Where fhall we whore to-night?

Uncle. That ever follows.

Era. 'Ods me, he now looks angry.

Onos. Shall we quarrel?

Nean. With me at no hand, Sir.

Onos. Then let's proteft.

Era. Is this all?

Tutor. Thefe are, Sir, the four new virtues
That are in fafhion; many a mile we meafur'd
Before we could arrive unto this knowledge.

Nean. You might have fpar'd that labour, for at
    home here
There's little elfe in practice. Ha! the Queen?
Good friends, for half an hour remove your motion⁹;
Tomorrow willingly, when we've more leifure,
We'll look on him again.

Onos. Did I not rarely?

Uncle. Excellent well.

Tutor. He fhall have fix plumbs for it.

                             [*Exeunt Onos, &c.*

---

⁸ *And briefly, to all.*] Corrected by Mr. Sympfon.

⁹ *Motion.*] *i. e.* Puppet. See note 13 on Rule a Wife and Have
a Wife.

                                         Enter

Enter Agenor, Leonidas, Theanor, Queen, Merione,
Beliza, Euphanes, Crates, ladies and attendants,
with lights.

Queen. How much my court is honour'd, princely
       brother,
In your vouchfafing it your long'd-for prefence,
Were tedious to repeat, fince 'tis already
(And heartily) acknowledg'd. May the gods,
That look into kings' actions, fmile upon
The league we have concluded ; and their juftice
Find me out to revenge it, if I break
One article!

Age. Great miracle of queens,
How happy I efteem myfelf, in being
Thought worthy to be number'd in the rank
Of your confed'rates, my love and beft fervice
Shall teach the world hereafter ; but this gift
With which you have confirm'd it, is fo far
Beyond my hopes and means e'er to return,
That of neceffity I muft die oblig'd
To your unanfwer'd bounty.

The. The fweet lady
In blufhes gives your highnefs thanks.

Queen. Believe it,
On the Queen's word, fhe is a worthy one ;
And I am fo acquainted with her goodnefs,
That but for this peace that hath chang'd my purpofe,
And to her more advancement, I fhould gladly
Have call'd her daughter.

The. Tho' I am depriv'd of
A bleffing, 'tis not in the fates to equal,
To fhew myfelf a fubject as a fon,
Here I give up my claim, and willingly
With mine own hand deliver you what once
I lov'd above myfelf ; and from this hour,
(For my affection yields now to my duty)
Vow never to folicit her.

Cra. 'Tis well cover'd.
Neanthes, and the reft ! [*Exe. Cra. Nean. Sof. Era.*
                               Queen.

Queen. Nay, for this night
You muſt (for 'tis our country faſhion, Sir)
Leave her to her devotions; in the morning
We'll bring you to the temple.

Leo. How in this
Your highneſs honours me!

Mer. Sweet reſt to all!

Age. This kiſs, and I obey you.

Bel. Pleaſe it your highneſs,
This is the gentleman.

Queen. You're welcome home, Sir.—
Now, as I live, one of a promiſing preſence.—
I've heard of you before, and you ſhall find
I'll know you better; find out ſomething that
May do you good, and reſt aſſur'd to have it.
Were you at Sparta lately?

Euph. Three days ſince, madam,
I came from thence.

Queen. 'Tis very late.
Good night, my lord! Do you, Sir, follow me;
I muſt talk further with you.

Age. All reſt with you!   [*Exeunt.*

Enter Crates, Neanthes, Eraton, and Soſicles, diſguiſed.

Cra. She muſt paſs thro' this cloiſter; ſuddenly
And boldly ſeize upon her.

Nean. Where's the prince?

Cra. He does expect us at the place I ſhew'd you.

Enter Merione and Servant.

I hear one's footing; peace, 'tis ſhe.

Mer. Now leave me;   [*Exit Servant.*
I know the way; tho', Veſta witneſs with me,
I never trod it with ſuch fear.—Help, help!

Cra. Stop her mouth cloſe; out with the light;
I'll guide you.   [*Exeunt.*

ACT

ACT II. SCENE I.

Enter Merione, as newly ravish'd.

Mer. TO whom now shall I cry? What pow'r
        thus kneel to,
And beg my ravish'd honour back upon me?
Deaf, deaf, you gods of goodnefs, deaf to me,
Deaf Heav'n to all my cries ; deaf hope, deaf juftice!
I am abus'd, and you, that fee all, faw it,
Saw it, and fmil'd upon the villain did it ;
Saw it, and gave him ftrength : Why have I pray'd
    to ye,
When all the world's eyes have been funk in flumbers?
Why have I then pour'd out my tears? kneel'd to ye?
And from the altar of a pure heart fent ye
Thoughts like yourfelves, white, innocent, vows purer
And of a fweeter flame [10] than all earth's odours?
Why have I fung your praifes, ftrew'd your temples,
And crown'd your holy priefts with virgin rofes?
Is it we hold ye powerful, to deftroy us?
Believe and honour ye, to fee us ruin'd?
Thefe tears of anger thus I fprinkle toward ye,
You that dare fleep fecure whilft virgins fuffer ;
Thefe ftick like comets [11], blaze eternally,
'Till, with the wonder, they have wak'd your juftice,
And forc'd ye fear our curfes, as we yours. .

Enter Theanor and Crates, with vizards.
My fhame ftill follows me, and ftill proclaims me.

---

[10] *Sweeter* flame.] Though I have not difturbed the text, I fufpect we fhould read *fame.*   *Sympfon.*

[11] *Thefe ftick like comets.*] To compare *tears* to *comets*, *fire* to *water*, is fo ftrange an allufion, that we cannot help thinking a line has been dropt here ; and the two following lines almoft prove that the *curfes* and *execrations* of the fuffering innocent (not the *tears* which fhe *fprinkles*) are what fhe means by faying,
    THESE *ftick like* COMETS, BLAZE *eternally.*

He

He turns away in fcorn! I am contemn'd too;
A more unmanly violence than the other:
Bitten, and flung away? Whate'er you are,
Sir, you that have abus'd me, and now moft bafely
And facrilegioufly robb'd this fair temple,
I fling all thefe behind me, but look upon me,
But one kind loving look, be what you will,
So from this hour you will be mine, my hufband.
And you, his hand in mifchief, I fpeak to you too,
Counfel him nobly now; you know the mifchief,
The moft unrighteous act he has done; perfuade him,
Perfuade him like a friend, knock at his confcience
'Till fair Repentance follow. Yet be worthy of me,
And fhew yourfelf, if ever good thought guided you:
You've had your foul will; make't yet fair with
       marriage;
Open yourfelf and take me, wed me now.
                    [*Draws his dagger.*
More fruits of villainy? Your dagger? Come;
You're merciful; I thank you for your medicine.

Enter the reft difguifed.

Is that too worthy too? Devil! thou with him!
Thou penny bawd to his luft! Will not that ftir thee?
Do you work by tokens now? Be fure I live not,
For your own fafeties, knaves. I will fit patiently:
But, as you are true villains, the devil's own fervants,
And thofe he loves and trufts, make it as bloody
An act, of fuch true horror, Heav'n would fhake at;
'Twill fhew the braver. Goodnefs, hold my hope
      faft,
And in thy mercies look upon my ruins,

*Enter fix difguifed, finging and dancing to a horrid
   mufick, and fprinkling water on her face.*

And then I'm right!—My eyes grow dead and heavy.
Wrong me no more, as ye are men.
  The. She's faft.
  Cra. Away with her.   [*Exeunt.*

SCENE II.

Enter Agenor and Gentlemen, with torches.

Age. Now, Gentlemen, the time's come now t'enjoy
That fruitful happiness my heart has long'd for.
This day be happy call'd[12]; and when old Time
Brings it about each year, crown'd with that sweetness
It gives me now, see every man observe it,
And, laying all aside bears show of business,
Give this to joy and triumph. How fit my cloaths?

1 Gent. Handsome, and wondrous well, Sir.

Age. Do they shew richly?
For to those curious eyes even Beauty envies,
I must not now appear poor, or low-fashion'd.
Methinks I am younger than I was, far younger;
And such a promise in my blood I feel now,
That, if there may be a perpetual youth
Bestow'd on man, I am that soul shall win it.
Does my hair stand well? Lord, how ill-favour'dly
You have dress'd me to-day! how baldly! Why
      this cloak?

2 Gent. Why, 'tis the richest, Sir.

Age. And here you have put me on
A pair of breeches look like a pair of bagpipes.

1 Gent. Believe, Sir, they shew bravely.

Age. Why these stockings?

2 Gent. Your leg appears——

Age. Poh! I would have had 'em peach-colour;
All young and new about me. And this scarf here,
A goodly thing! you have trick'd me like a puppet.

1 Gent. I'll undertake to rig forth a whole navy,
And with less labour, than one man in love:
They're never pleas'd.

2 Gent. Methinks he looks well.

1 Gent. Well
As man can look, as handsome. Now do I wonder

---

[12] *This day be happy call'd,* &c.] Rowe has closely copied this
speech, in the beginning of the Fair Penitent.

He

He found not fault his nofe was put on ugly,
Or his eyes look'd too grey, and rail at us :
They are the wayward'ft things, thefe lovers.

  2 Gent. All will be right
When once it comes to th' puſh.

  1 Gent. I would they were at it,
For our own quiet ſake.

  Age. Come, wait upon me ;
And bear yourſelves like mine, my friends, and
        nobly.   [*Exeunt.*

SCENE III.

Enter Theanor, Crates, and Eraton, bringing Merione.

  Erat. This is her brother's door.

  Cra. There lay her down then ;
Lay her along. She's faſt ſtill ?

  Erat. As forgetfulneſs [13].

  Cra. Be not you ſtirr'd now, but away to your
      mother,
Give all attendance, let no ſtain appear
Of fear, or doubt in your face; carry yourſelf con-
      fidently.

  The. But whither runs your drift now ?

  Cra. When ſhe wakes,
Either what's done will ſhew a mere dream to her,
And carry no more credit; or, ſay ſhe find it,
Say ſhe remember all the circumſtances,
Twenty to one the ſhapes in which they were acted,
The horrors, and the ſtill affrights we ſhew'd her,
Riſing in wilder figures to her memory,
Will run her mad, and no man gueſs the reaſon :
If all theſe fail, and that ſhe riſe up perfect,
And ſo collect herſelf, believe this, Sir,
Not knowing who it was that did this to her,
Nor having any power to gueſs; the thing done too

---

[13] *Ser. As forgetfulneſs.*] As there is no *Servant* preſent, nor
any perſon whoſe name begins in this manner, we have given the
ſpeech to *Eraton.*

Being the utter undoing of her honour
If it be known, and to the world's eye publiſh'd,
Eſpecially at this time when Fortune courts her,
She muſt and will conceal it, nay, forget it:
The woman is no Lucrece. Get you gone, Sir;
And, as you would have more of this ſport, fear not.

   The. I am confirm'd. Farewell!

   Cra. Farewell! Away, Sir.
Diſperſe yourſelves; and, as you love his favour,
And that that crowns it, gold, no tongues amongſt ye!
You know your charge; this way goes no ſuſpicion[14].

                           [*Exeunt.*

Enter Agenor, and Leonidas, with two Gentlemen, with
lights.

   Age. You are ſtirring early, Sir.

   Leo. It was my duty
To wait upon your Grace.

   Age. How fares your ſiſter,
My beauteous miſtreſs? What, is ſhe ready yet?

   Leo. No doubt ſhe'll loſe no time, Sir: Young
            maids in her way
Tread upon thorns, and think an hour an age,
'Till the prieſt has done his part, that theirs may
        follow.
I ſaw her not ſince yeſterday i'th' evening;
But, Sir, I'm ſure ſhe is not ſlack: Believe me,
Your Grace will find a loving ſoul.

   Age. A ſweet one;
And ſo much joy I carry in the thought of it,
So great a happineſs to know ſhe is mine,
(Believe me, noble brother) that to expreſs it
Methinks a tongue's a poor thing, can do nothing,

---

[14] *Goes no ſuſpicion.*] Though this may be underſtood, it is ſuch
a low and ſtiff expreſſion, that I can ſcarce think it genuine. The
word *gives*, inſtead of *goes*, makes clearer Engliſh, but I believe the
original might be
      ———*this way go*———*no ſuſpicion*; *i. e.* Be ſure ye take care,
not to give the leaſt ſuſpicion by your conduct.   *Seward.*
We think the text needs no change.

                                 Imagination

Imagination lefs [15].   Who's that that lies there?

Leo. Where, Sir?

Age. Before the door; it looks like a woman.

Leo. This way I came abroad, but then there was
  nothing.

One of the maids o'erwatch'd belike.

Age. It may be.

Leo. But methinks this is no fit place to fleep in.

1 *Gent.* 'Tis fure a woman, Sir; fhe has jewels on
  too:

She fears no foul play fure.

Leo. Bring a torch hither;

Yet 'tis not perfect day. I fhould know thofe garments.

Age. How found fhe fleeps!

Leo. I'm forry to fee this!

Age. Do you know her?

Leo. And you now, I am fure, Sir.

Age. My miftrefs? How comes this?

*Enter Queen, Theanor, Beliza, Euphanes, Neanthes,
  and attendants.*

Leo. The Queen and her train?

Queen. You know my pleafure.

Euph. And will be moft careful.

Queen. Be not long abfent;

The fuit you preferr'd is granted.

Nean. This fellow mounts

Apace, and will tower o'er us like a falcon.

Queen. Good morrow to ye all! Why ftand ye
  wondring?

Enter the houfe, Sir, and bring out your miftrefs;

You muft obferve our ceremonies. What's the matter?

What's that ye ftand at? How! Merione?

Afleep i' th' ftreet? Belike fome fudden palfy,

---

[15] *Imagination* lefs.] Sympfon propofes to read,
    Imagination —— Blefs us, *who's that,* &c.
  Seward, *Imagination* SCARCE; and they jointly have another reading, *imaginationlefs,* one word. We think the text unexceptionable,
  and their objections futile and trifling.

As

As she stept out last night upon devotion,
To take her farewell of her virgin state,
The air being sharp and piercing, struck her suddenly.
See if she breathe.

 Leo. A little.

 Queen. Wake her then;
'Tis sure a fit.

 Age. She wakes herself: Give room to her.

 Queen. See how the spirits struggle to recover,
And strongly reinforce their strengths; for certain,
This was no natural sleep.

 The. I'm of your mind, madam.

 § *Queen.* No, son, it cannot be.

 The. Pray Heav'n, no trick in't!
Good soul, she little merits such a mischief.

 Queen. She's broad awake now, and her sense clears
   up;
'Twas sure a fit. Stand off.

 Mer. The Queen, my love here,
And all my noble friends? Why, where am I?
How am I tranc'd, and mop'd! I' th' street? Heav'n
  bless me!
Shame to my sex! o'th' ground too?--Oh, I remember--

 Leo. How wild she looks!

 Age. Oh, my cold heart, how she trembles!

 Mer. Oh, I remember, I remember!

 Queen. What's that?

 Mer. My shame, my shame, my shame! Oh, I
  remember,
My never-dying shame!

 The. Here has been villainy.

 Queen. I fear so too.

 Mer. You are no furies, are ye?
No horrid shapes sent to affright me?

 Age. No, sweet;
We are your friends. Look up; I am Agenor,
(Oh, my Merione!) that loves you dearly,
And come to marry you.

 Leo. Sister, what ail you?

Speak out your griefs, and boldly.

Age. Something fticks here
Will choak you elfe.

Mer. I hope it will.

Queen. Be free, lady;
You have your loving friends about you.

Age. Dear Merione,
By the unfpotted love I ever bore you,
By thine own goodnefs———

Mer. Oh, 'tis gone, 'tis gone, Sir;
I'm now I know not what; pray ye look not on me;
No name is left me, nothing to inherit,
But that detefted, bafe, and branded——

Age. Speak it,
And how: Difeafes of moft danger,
Their caufes once difcover'd, are eafily cur'd.
My fair Merione———

Mer. I thank your love, Sir:
When I was fair Merione, unfpotted,
Pure, and unblafted in the bud you honour'd [16],
White as the heart of truth, then, prince Agenor,
Even then I was not worthy of your favour.
Wretch that I am, lefs worthy now of pity!
Let no good thing come near me; Virtue fly me;
You that have honeft noble names, defpife me;
For I am nothing now but a main peftilence,
Able to poifon all! Send thofe unto me
That have forgot their names, ruin'd their fortunes,
Defpis'd their honours; thofe that have been virgins
Ravifh'd and wrong'd, and yet dare live to tell it.

The. Now it appears too plain.

Mer. Send thofe fad people
That hate the light, and curfe fociety;
Whofe thoughts are graves, and from whofe eyes
   continually
Their melting fouls drop out, fend thofe to me;
And when their forrows are moft excellent,
So full that one grief more cannot be added,

---

[16] *You honour'd,*] Seward reads, *You honour'd* ME.

My

My ſtory like a torrent ſhall devour 'em.
Hark! it muſt out: But pray ſtand cloſe together,
And let not all the world hear.

    Leo. Speak it boldly.

    Mer. And, royal lady, think but charitably!
Your Grace has known my breeding.

    Queen. Prithee, ſpeak it.

    Mer. Is there no ſtranger here? Send off your
      ſervants.
And yet it muſt be known.—I ſhake.

    Age. Sweet miſtreſs!

    Mer. I am abus'd, baſely abus'd! do you gueſs yet?
Come cloſe; I'll tell ye plainer; I am whor'd,
Raviſh'd, and robb'd of honour!

    Leo. Oh, the devil!

    Age. What helliſh ſlave was this?

    The. A wretch, a wretch,
A damned wretch! Do you know the villain, lady?

    Mer. No.

    The. Not by gueſs?

    Mer. Oh, no.

    The. It muſt be known.

    Queen. Where was the place?

    Mer. I know not neither.

    Age. Oh, Heaven!
Is this the happy time? my hope to this come?

    Leo. Neither the man nor circumſtances?

    The. His tongue,
Did you not hear his tongue? no voice?

    Mer. None, none, Sir:
All I know of him was his violence.

    Age. How came you hither, ſweet?

    Mer. I know not neither.

    The. A cunning piece of villainy.

    Mer. All I remember
Is only this: Going to Veſta's temple,
To give the goddeſs my laſt virgin prayers,
Near to that place I was ſuddenly ſurpriz'd,
By five or ſix diſguis'd, and from thence violently

                            To

To my dishonour hal'd : That act perform'd,
Brought back ; but how, or whither, 'till I wak'd
   here——

The. This is so monstrous, the gods cannot suffer it;
I have not read, in all the villainies
Committed by the most obdurate rascals,
An act so truly impious.

Leo. 'Would I knew him !

The. He must be known ; the devil cannot hide him.

Queen. If all the art I have, or power, can do it,
He shall be found ; and such a way[17] of justice
Inflicted on him——A lady wrong'd in my court?
And this way robb'd, and ruin'd?

The. Be contented, madam ;
If he be above ground, I will have him.

Age. Fair virtuous maid, take comfort yet, and
   flourish,
In my love flourish ; the stain was forc'd upon you,
None of your will's, nor yours. Rise, and rise mine still,
And rise the same white, sweet, fair soul, I lov'd ye ;
Take me the same.

Mer. I kneel and thank you, Sir ;
And I must say you are truly honourable,
And dare confess my will yet still a virgin :
But so unfit and weak a cabinet
To keep your love and virtue in am I now,
That have been forc'd and broken, lost my lustre ;
I mean this body, so corrupt a volume,
For you to study goodness in, and honour,
I shall entreat your Grace, confer that happiness
Upon a beauty Sorrow never saw yet.
And when this grief shall kill me, (as it must do)
Only remember yet you had such a mistress[18] ;
And if you then dare shed a tear, yet honour me.

---

[17] *A way of justice.*] Probably we should read, *weight* ; *way* is
very flat.

[18] Yet *you had such a mistress* ;
  ——— yet *honour me.*] Sympson substitutes *that* for *yet* in
these places ; but the old reading is much best.

Good

Good gentlemen, exprefs your pities to me,
In feeking out this villainy. And my laft fuit
Is to your Grace, that I may have your favour
To live a poor recluse nun with this lady,
From court and company, 'till Heaven fhall hear me,
And fend me comfort, or death end my mifery.

   Queen. Take your own will; my very heart bleeds
       for thee.

   Age. Farewell, Merione! fince I have not thee,
I'll wed thy goodnefs, and thy memory.

   Leo. And I her fair revenge.

   The. Away; let's follow it;
For he's fo rank i' th' wind we cannot mifs him.

                       [*Exeunt.*

S C E N E IV.

Enter Crates and Conon.

   Cra. Conon? You're welcome home! you're
       wondrous welcome!
Is this your firft arrival?

   Con. Sir, but now
I reach'd the town.

   Cra. You're once more welcome then.

   Con. I thank you, noble Sir.

   Cra. Pray you do me the honour
To make my poor houfe firft——

   Con. Pray, Sir, excufe me;
I have not feen mine own yet; nor made happy
Thefe longing eyes with thofe I love there.—What is
       this? a tavern?

   Cra. It feems fo by the outfide.

   Con. Step in here then;
And fince it offers itfelf fo freely to us,
A place made only for liberal entertainment,
Let's feek no further, but make ufe of this,
And, after the Greek fafhion, to our friends
Crown a round cup or two.

                       Enter

Enter Vintner and Drawer.

Cra. Your pleasure, Sir.
Drawers! who waits within?

Draw. Anon, anon, Sir.

Vint. Look into the Lilly-pot. Why, Mark, there!
You're welcome, gentlemen! heartily welcome,
My noble friend!

Cra. Let's have good wine, mine host,
And a fine private room.

Vint. Will you be there, Sir?
What is't you'll drink? I'll draw your wine myself.
Cushions, ye knaves! Why, when?

Re-enter Drawer.

Draw. Anon, anon, Sir.

Vint. Chios, or Lesbos, Greek?

Cra. Your best and neatest.

Vint. I'll draw ye that shall dance.

Cra. Away; be quick then.   [*Exit Vintner.*

Con. How does your brother, Sir, my noble friend,
The good Euphanes? In all my course of travel,
I met not with a gentleman so furnish'd
In gentleness and courtesy; believe, Sir,
So many friendly offices I receiv'd from him,
So great and timely, and enjoy'd his company
In such an open and a liberal sweetness,
That when I dare forget him——

Cra. He is in good health, Sir;
But you will find him a much-alter'd man;
Grown a great courtier, Sir.

Con. He is worthy of it.

Cra. A man drawn up, that leaves no print behind
        him
Of what he was. Those goodnesses you speak of
That have been in him, those that you call freedoms,
Societies, and sweetness, look for now, Sir,
You'll find no shadows of them left, no found;
The very air he has liv'd in alter'd. Now behold him,
                                                    And

And you shall see a thing walk by, look big upon you,
And cry for place: ' I am the Queen's; give room there!'
If you bow low, may-be he'll touch the bonnet,
Or fling a forc'd smile at you, for a favour.

 Con. He is your brother, Sir.

 Cra. These forms put off,
Which travel and court holy-water sprinkle on him,
I dare accept and know him. You'll think it strange, Sir,
That ev'n to me, to me, his natural brother,
And one by birth he owes a little honour too——

Enter Vintner with wine.

But that's all one. Come, give me some wine, mine host.
Here's to your fair return !

 Con. I wonder at it !
But sure h' has found a nature not worth owning
In this way [19]; else I know he is tender carried.—
I thank you, Sir. And now durst I presume,
For all you tell me of these alterations
And stops in his sweet nature (which 'till I find so,
I have known him now so long, and look'd so thro' him,
You must give me leave to be a little faithless)
I say, for all these, if you please to venture,
I'll lay the wine we drink, let me send for him
(Ev'n I, that am the poorest of his fellowship)
But by a boy o' th' house too, let him have business,
Let him attend the Queen, nay, let his mistress
Hold him betwixt her arms, he shall come to me,
And shall drink with me too, love me, and heartily ;
Like a true honest man, bid me welcome home :
I'm confident.

 Cra. You'll lose.

 Con. You'll stand to th' wager?

 Cra. With all my heart.

 Con. Go, Boy, and tell Euphanes——

 Boy. He's now gone up the street, Sir, with a great
   train of gallants.

 Cra. What think you now, Sir?

---

[19] *In this* way.] Seward, we think injudiciously, reads *man* for *way*.

Con.

Con. Go, and overtake him:
Commend my love unto him, (my name's Conon)
Tell him I'm new arriv'd, and where I am,
And would requeſt to ſee him preſently.
You ſee I uſe old dudgeon phraſe to draw him.

    Cra. I'll hang and quarter when you draw him
        hither.

    Con. Away, Boy.

    Boy. I am gone, Sir.   *[Exit.*

    Con. Here's to you now !
And you ſhall find his travel has not ſtopt him,
As you ſuppoſe, nor alter'd any freedom;
But made him far more clear and excellent.
It draws the groſſneſs off the underſtanding,
And renders active and induſtrious ſpirits :
He that knows moſt mens' manners, muſt of neceſſity
Beſt know his own, and mend thoſe by example.
'Tis a dull thing to travel like a mill-horſe,
Still in the place he was born in, lam'd and blinded;
Living at home is like it. Pure and ſtrong ſpirits,
That, like the fire, ſtill covet to fly upward,
And to give fire, as well as take it, cas'd up and mew'd
        here,
I mean at home, like luſty mettled horſes,
Only tied up in ſtables [20], to pleaſe their maſters,
Beat out their fiery lives in their own litters.
Why don't you travel, Sir?

    Cra. I've no belief in't,
I ſee ſo many ſtrange things, half unhatch'd too [19],
Return, thoſe that went out men, and good men,
They look like poach'd eggs, with the ſoul ſuck'd out,

---

    [20] *Up in* ſtables.] Mr. Seward joined with me in reading *ſtalls* for
ſtables, which, though no great improvement to the ſenſe, is to that
of the meaſure.   *Sympſon.*

    Variations for the ſake of meaſure *only,* are inadmiſſible. Our
Authors, and all others of their time, were very licentious in that
reſpect.

    [19] *Strange things half unhatch'd,* to

    Return, thoſe that went, &c.] There is probably ſome omiſſion
here; however, the variation we have made affords a more plauſible
reading than the former editions.

                                               Empty

Empty and full of wind: All their affections
Are bak'd in rye-cruft, to hold carriage
From this good town to t'other; and when they are
   open'd,
They're so ill-cook'd and mouldy——

Con. You are pleasant.

Cra. I'll shew you a pack of these: I have 'em for you,
That have been long in travel too.

Con. Please you, Sir.

Cra. You know the Merchants' Walk, Boy?

2 *Boy.* Very well.

Cra. And you remember those gentlemen were here
The other day with me?

2 *Boy.* Yes.

Cra. Then go thither,
For there I am sure they are; pray 'em come hither,
(And use my name) I would be glad to see 'em.

Enter First Boy.

1 *Boy.* Your brother's coming in, Sir.

Vint. Odds my passion!
Out with the plate, ye knaves; bring the new cushions,
And wash those glasses I set by for high-days;
Perfume the rooms along. Why, sirrah!

1 *Boy.* Here, Sir.

Vint. Bid my wife make herself ready handsomely,
And put on her best apron; it may be,
The noble gentleman will look upon her.

Enter Euphanes and two Gentlemen.

Euph. Where is he, Boy?

Vint. Your worship's heartily welcome!
It joys my very heart to see you here, Sir.
The gentleman that sent for your honour——

Euph. Oh, good mine host!

Vint. To my poor homely house, an't like your
   honour——

Euph. I thank thine honour, good mine host. Where
  is he?

               Con.

Con. What think you now?—My beſt Euphanes!

Euph. Conon!

Welcome, my friend! my noble friend, how is it?

Are you in ſafety come, in health?

Con. All health, all ſafety,

Riches, and all that makes content and happineſs,

Now I am here, I have. How have you far'd, Sir?

Euph. Well, I thank Heaven; and never nearer,
   friend,

To catch at great occaſion.

Con. Indeed I joy in't.

Euph. Nor am I for myſelf born in theſe fortunes;

In truth I love my friends.

Con. You were noble ever.   [*Euph. ſalutes Cra.*

Cra. I thought you had not known me.

Euph. Yes; you are my brother,

My elder brother too: 'Would your affections

Were able but to aſk that love I owe to you,

And as I give, preſerve it!—Here, friend Conon,

To your fair welcome home!

Con. Dear Sir, I thank you.

Fill it to th' brim, boy. Crates!

Cra. I will pledge you;

But for that glorious comet, lately fir'd——

Con. Fy, fy, Sir, fy!

Euph. Nay, let him take his freedoms;

He ſtirs not me, I vow to you; much leſs ſtains me.

Cra. Sir, I can't talk with that neat travelling tongue.

Con. As I live, he has the worſt belief in men abroad!

Enter Second Boy.

I'm glad I am come home.

 2 *Boy.* Here are the gentlemen.

 Cra. Oh, let 'em enter. Now you that truſt in travel,

And make ſharp beards and little breeches deities,

You that enhance the daily price of toothpicks,

And hold there is no home-bred happineſs,

Behold a model of your minds and actions.

 Euph. Tho' this be envious, yet, done i' th' way of
  mirth,

            I am

I am content to thank you for't.

Con. 'Tis well yet.

Cra. Let the masque enter.

Enter Onos, Uncle, and Tutor.

Onos. A pretty tavern 'faith, of a fine structure!

* *Uncle.* Bear yourself like a gentleman; here's six-
    pence,
And be sure you break no glasses.

Tutor. Hark ye, pupil;
Go as I taught you, hang more upon your hams,
And put your knees out bent; there; yet a little.
Now I beseech ye, be not so improvident
To forget your travelling pace, 'tis a main posture,
And to all unair'd gentlemen will betray you:
Play with your Pisa beard. Why, where's your brush,
    pupil?
He must have a brush, Sir.

Uncle. More charge yet?

Tutor. Here, take mine;
These elements of travel he must not want, Sir.

Uncle. Ma'foy, he has had some nineteen-pence in
    elements;
What would you more?

Tutor. Durus mehercle pater!

Con. What, monsieur Onos, the very pump of travel²¹!
Sir, as I live, you've done me the greatest kindness—
Oh, my fair Sir, Lampree, the careful Uncle
To this young hopeful issue! Monsieur Tutor too,
The father to his mind! Come, come; let's hug, boys.
Why, what a bunch of travel do I embrace now!
Methinks I put a girdle about Europe.
How has the boy profited?

Uncle. He has enough, Sir,
If his too-fiery mettle do not mar it.

Con. Is he not thrifty yet?

Tutor. That's all his fault;

---

²¹ Pump *of travel?*] I suspect that for *pump* here we should read
pink. The *pink of courtesy* is a well known phrase.   *Sympson.*

Too

Too bounteous minded, being under age too ;
A great confumer of his ftock in pippins :
H' had ever a hot ftomach.

Con. Come hither, Onos.
Will you love me for this fine apple ?

Onos. Ouy.

Con. And will you be rul'd by me fometimes ?

Onos. 'Faith, I will.

Con. That's a good boy.

Uncle. Pray give not the child fo much fruit ;
He's of a raw complexion.

Euph. You, monfieur Hard-Egg !
Do you remember me ? Do you remember
When you and your confort travell'd thro' Hungary ?

Con. He's in that circuit ftill.

Euph. Do you remember
The cantle of immortal cheefe you carried with you,
The half-cold cabbage in a leather fachel,
And thofe invincible eggs that would lie in your bowels
A fortnight together, and then turn to bedftaves ;
Your four milk that would choak an Irifhman,
And bread was bak'd in Cæfar's time for the army ?

Con. Providence, providence.

Tutor. The foul of travel.

Euph. Can the boy fpeak yet ?

Tutor. Yes ; and as fine a gentleman,
I thank my able knowledge, h' has arriv'd at,
Only a little fparing of his language,
Which every man of obfervation——

Uncle. And of as many tongues——

Tutor. Pray be content, Sir ;
You know you are for the bodily part, the purfe,
I for the magazine, the mind.

Euph. Come hither, fpringal.

Onos. That in the Almain tongue fignifies a gentleman.

Euph. What think you of the forms of Italy or Spain?

Onos. I love mine own country pippin.

Tutor. Nobly anfwer'd ;

Born for his country first.

Euph. A great philosopher!
What horses do you prefer?

Onos. The white horse, Sir;
There where I lie; honest, and a just beast.

Tutor. O caput lepidum! A child to say this!
Are these figures[22] for the mouths of infants?

Con. Onos, what wenches?
Come, tell me true.

Onos. I cannot speak without book.

Con. When shall we have one? ha?

Onos. Steal me from mine Uncle;
For, look you, I am broke out horribly
For want of fleshly physick; they say I am too young,
And that 'twill spoil my growth; but, could you
        help me——

Con. Meet me tomorrow, man; no more.

Euph. You think now
You've open'd such a shame to me of travel,
By shewing these thin cubs! You've honour'd us
Against your will, proclaim'd us excellent:
Three frails of sprats, carried from mart to mart,
Are as much meat as these, to more use travell'd;
A bunch of bloated fools! Methinks your judgment
Should look abroad sometimes, without your envy.

Cra. Such are most of you. So I take my leave,
And when you find your womens' favour fail,
'Tis ten to one you'll know yourself, and seek me,
Upon a better muster of your manners.

Con. This is not handsome, Sir.

Euph. Pray take your pleasure:
You wound the wind us much.

Cra. Come you with me;
I've business for you presently. There's for your
        wine;
I must confess I lost it.

Onos. Shall I steal to you?
And shall we see the wench?

---

22 *Are these figures.*] Sympson reads, *Are these* FIT *figures.*

Con. A dainty one.

Onos. And have a difh of pippins?

Con. What? a peck, man.

Tutor. Will you wait, Sir?

Con. Pray let's meet oftner, gentlemen;
I would not lofe ye.

Tutor. Oh, fweet Sir!

Con. Do you think I would?
Such noted men as you?

Onos, Uncle, Tutor. We are your fervants! [*Exeunt.*

Euph. That thing they would keep in everlafting
            nonage,
My brother, for his own ends, has thruft on
Upon my miftrefs: 'Tis true, he fhall be rich,
If ever he can get that rogue his Uncle
To let him be of years to come to inherit it.
Now, what the main drift is——

Con. Say you fo? no more words:
I'll keep him company 'till he be of years,
(Tho' it be a hundred years) but I'll difcover it;
And ten to one I'll crofs it too.

Euph. You are honeft,
And I fhall ftudy ftill your love. Farewell, Sir!
For thefe few hours I muft defire your pardon;
I've bufinefs of importance. Once a-day,
At leaft, I hope you'll fee me; I muft fee you elfe:
So, once more, you are welcome!

Con. All my thanks, Sir;
And when I leave to love you, life go from me!
                                    [*Exeunt.*

ACT

ACT III. SCENE I.

Enter Theanor and Crates.

Cra. WHY, Sir, the kingdom's his; and no
                    man now
Can come to Corinth, or from Corinth go,
Without his licence; he puts up the tithes
Of every office thro' Achaia;
From courtier to the carter hold of him;
Our lands, our liberties, nay, very lives,
Are shut up in his closet, and let loose
But at his pleasure; books, and all discourse,
Have now no patron, nor direction,
But glorified Euphanes; our cups are guilty
That quench our thirsts, if not unto his health.
Oh, I could eat my heart, and fling away
My very soul, for anguish! Gods, nor men,
Should tolerate such disproportion.

    The. And yet is he belov'd; whether it be virtue,
Or seeming virtue, which he makes the cloak
To his ambition.

    Cra. Be it which it will,
Your highness is too tame, your eyes too film'd,
To see this, and sit still: The lion should not
Tremble to hear the bellowing of the bull.
Nature, excuse me! tho' he be my brother,
You are my country's father, therefore mine:
One parallel line of love I bend on him,
All lines of love and duty meet in you,
As in their centre; therefore hear, and weigh,
What I shall speak. You know the Queen your
                    mother
Did, from a private state, your father raise;
So all your royalty you hold from her:
She is older than she was, therefore more doting;

                    And

And what know we but blindnefs of her love,
(That hath, from underneath the foot of Fortune,
Set even Euphanes' foot on Fortune's head)
Will take him by the hand, and cry, ' Leap now
' Into my bed?' 'tis but a trick of age;
Nothing impoffible.

    The. What d'ye infer on this?

    Cra. Your pardon, Sir,
With reverence to the Queen: Yet why fhould I
Fear to fpeak plain what pointeth to your good?
A good old widow is a hungry thing
(I fpeak of other widows, not of queens).

    The. Speak to thy purpofe.

    Cra. I approach it. Sir,
Should young Euphanes clafp the kingdom thus,
And pleafe the good old lady fome one night,
What might not fhe be wrought to put on you,
Quite to fupplant your birth? neither is fhe
Paft children, as I take it.

    The. Crates, thou fhak'ft me!
Thou, that doft hate thy brother for my love,
In my love find one; henceforth be my brother.
This giant I will fell beneath the earth;
I will fhine out, and melt his artful wings:
Euphanes, from my mother's fea of favours,
Spreads like a river, and runs calmly on,
Secure yet from my ftorms; like a young pine
He grows up planted under a fair oak,
Whofe ftrong large branches yet do fhelter him,
And every traveller admires his beauty:
But, like a wind, I'll work into his cranks,
Trouble his ftream, and drown all veffels that
Ride on his greatnefs. Under my mother's arms,
Like to a ftealing tempeft will I fearch,
And rend his root from her protection.

    Cra. Ay; now Theanor fpeaks like prince
        Theanor.

    The. But how fhall we provoke him to our fnares?
He has a temper malice cannot move

To

To exceed the bounds of judgment; he's so wise,
That we can pick no cause to affront him.

   Cra. No?
What better than his crossing your intent?
The suit I'd to you? Conon's forfeit state
(Before he travell'd) for a riot, he
Hath from your mother got restor'd to him.

   The. Durst he? What is this Conon?

   Cra. One that hath,
As people say, in foreign countries pleasur'd him.

Enter Onos, Uncle, Tutor, Neanthes, Sosicles, and Eraton.

But now no more;
They have brought the travellers I told you of.
That's the sweet youth that is my brother's rival,
That curls his head, for he has little hair,
And paints his vizor, for it is no face,
That so desires to follow you, my lord:
Shew 'em some countenance, and 'twill beget
Our sport at least.

   The. What villainous crab-tree legs
He makes[21]! His shins are full of true-love knots.

   Cra. His legs were ever villainous, since I knew
      him.

   Era. Faith his Uncle's shanks are somewhat the
      better.

   Nean. But is it possible he should believe
He's not of age? Why, he is fifty, man;
In's jubilee, I warrant! 'Slight, he looks
Older than a groat; the very stamp on's face
Is worn out with handling.

---

  [21] *Crab-tree legs*

He makes?] Sympson dislikes this reading, and would substitute
has for *makes*; which is clearly for the worse, as in all probability
Onos enters making ridiculous congees.—To MAKE *a leg* is a common
manner of speaking of a bow or congee: It occurs frequently in our
Authors. See Wild-Goose Chace, vol. v. p. 254,

    I'll make *my three* legs,
     Kiss my hand twice, and, if I smell no danger,
      If the interview be clear, may be I'll speak to her.

                                 Sos.

Sof. Why, I tell you,

All men believe it when they hear him speak,

He utters such single matter in so infantly a voice.

Nean. He looks as like a fellow that I have seen

Accommodate gentlemen with tobacco in our theatres.

Onos. Most illustrious prince!

Era. A pox on him, he is gelt! how he trebles!

Onos. I am a gentleman o' both sides.

Tutor. He means (so't please your highness) both

       by father and mother.

Sof. Thou a gentleman? thou an ass.

Nean. He is ne'er the further from being a gen-

       tleman, I assure you.

Tutor. May it please your Grace, I am another.

Nean. He is another ass, he says; I believe him.

Uncle. We be three, heroical prince.

Nean. Nay then, we must have the picture of 'em,

       and the word *nos sumus*.

Tutor. That have travell'd all parts of the globe

       together.

Uncle. For my part, I have seen the vicissitude of

       Fortune before.

Onos. Peace, Uncle; for tho' you speak a little

       better than I——

Nean. 'Tis a very little, in truth.

Onos. Yet we must both give place, as they say,

To the best speaker, the Tutor.

Tutor. Yet since it hath pleased your radiance to

decline so low, as on us poor and unworthy dung-

hills——

Nean. What a stinking knave's this!

Tutor. Our peregrination was ne'er so felicitated,

as since we enter'd the line of your gracious favour,

under whose beamy aspect, and by which infallible

mathematical compass, may we but hereafter presume

to sail, our industries have reach'd their desir'd termi-

nation and period; and we shall voluntarily sacrifice

our lives to your resplendent eyes, both the altars

and fires of our devoted offerings.

Onos.

Onos. Oh, divine Tutor!

Cra. Can you hold, Sir?

Era. He has spoken this very speech to some whore
in Corinth.

Nean. A plague on him for a fustian dictionary!
On my conscience, this is the Ulyssean Traveller [14]
that sent home his image riding upon elephants to
the great Mogol.

Sos. The same; his wit is so huge, nought but an
elephant could carry him.

Era. So heavy, you mean.

Nean. These three are ev'n the finest one fool
tripartite that was e'er discover'd.

Sos. Or a treatise of Famine, divided into three
branches.

Era. The prince speaks.

The. I thank ye for your loves; but, as I told you,
I have so little means to do for those
Few followers I have already, that
I would have none shipwreck themselves and fortune
Upon my barren shelf. Sue to Euphanes,

---

[14] *The* Ulyssean *Traveller that sent home,* &c.] The *Ulyssean
Traveller* here mentioned was the celebrated Thomas Coryate, who
is supposed to have travelled more miles on foot than any person of
that age, or in any period since. He was undoubtedly not in his
perfect senses; but was a man of considerable learning, and appears
to have related faithfully what he saw; for he became ridiculous
chiefly by dwelling with too much attention on the trifling accidents
which happened to him during his journey. In the year 1608, he
set out from England, and went on foot as far as Venice, and back
again; a journey which he completed in five months. He published
an account of it in the year 1611, in a large quarto volume, containing
655 pages, beside more than 100 filled with Commendatory Verses by
Ben Jonson, and most of the wits of the age, who both laughed at
him and flattered his vanity at the same time. An extract from this
singular performance is given p. 246. He afterwards travelled into
Persia, and from thence into the East-Indies, still on foot, and died
at Surat in the year 1617. The piece alluded to by our Author was
entitled, ‘ Thomas Coriate, Traveller for the English Wits, greeting.
‘ From the Court of the Great Mogul, resident at the Towne of
‘ Asmere in Easterne India. Printed by W. Jaggard and Henry
‘ Featherston, 1616.’ quarto. It has, in the frontispiece, a representation of the Author riding on an elephant.   *R.*

For

For he is prince, and queen; I would have no man
Curfe me in his old age.

Cra. Alas, Sir, they defire to follow you
But afar off; the further off the better.

Tutor. Ay, Sir; an't be feven mile off, fo we may
but follow you, only to countenance us in the con-
fronts and affronts, which (according to your highnefs' will) we mean on all occafions to put upon the
lord Euphanes.

Onos. He fhall not want gibing nor jeering, I warrant him; if he do, I'll forfwear wit.

Nean. It has forfworn thee, I'll fwear; it is the
ancient enemy to thy houfe.

The. Well, be it fo; I here receive ye, for my followers a great way off.

Nean. Seven miles, my lord; no further.

Onos. By what time, Sir, (by this meafure) may I
come to follow him in his chamber?

Nean. Why, when his chamber, Sir, is feven miles
long.

Enter Euphanes, Conon, Page, Gentlemen and attendants.

Gent. Make way there for my lord Euphanes!

Cra. Look, Sir! Jove appears,
The peacock of our ftate, that fpreads a train
Brighter than Iris' blufhes after rain.

Euph. You need not thank me, Conon: In your love
You antedated what I can do for you,
And I in gratitude was bound to this,
And am to much more; and whate'er he be
Can with unthankfulnefs affoil me, let him
Dig out mine eyes, and fing my name in verfe,
In ballad verfe, at every drinking houfe,
And no man be fo charitable to lend me
A dog to guide my fteps.

Nean. Hail to Euphanes!

Sof. Mighty Euphanes!

Era. The great prince Euphanes!

Tutor. Key of the court, and jewel of the Queen!

Uncle.

Uncle. Sol in our firmament!

Onos. Pearl in the ftate's eye!

Nean. Being a black man.

Era. Miftrefs of the land!

Nean. Our humble, humble, poor petitions are,
That we may hold our places.

All. May we?

Euph. Yes;
Be you malicious knaves ftill; and you fools.

Con. This is the prince's and your brother's fpite.

Euph. I know't, but will not know it.

Con. Yonder they are.
Whofe fine child's this?

Uncle. Sir!

Onos. Uncle, le'be,
Let him alone, he is a mighty prince.

Euph. I afk your highnefs' pardon! I proteft
By Jupiter I faw you not.

The. Humph! it may be fo.
You've rais'd fuch mountains 'twixt your eyes and me,
That I am hidden quite. What do you mean, Sir?
You much forget yourfelf.

Euph. I fhould much more,
Not to remember my due duty to your Grace.
I know not wherein I have fo tranfgrefs'd
My fervice to your highnefs, to deferve
This rigour and contempt, not from you only,
But from your followers, with the beft of whom
I was an equal in my loweft ebb:
Befeech you, Sir, refpect me as a **gentleman**;
I will be never more in heart to you.
Five fair defcents I can derive myfelf,
From fathers worthy both in arts and arms.
I know your goodnefs companies your greatnefs,
But that you are perverted: Royal Sir,
I am your humbleft fubject; ufe your pleafure,
But do not give protection to the wrongs
Of thefe fubordinate flaves, whom I could crufh
By that great deftin'd favour which my miftrefs

And

And your majeſtic mother deigns to me,
But in reſpect of you. I know lean envy
Waits ever on the ſteps of virtue advanc'd;
But why your mother's grace gets me diſgrace,
Or renders me a ſlave to bear theſe wrongs,
I do not know. Oh, mediocrity,
Thou prizeleſs jewel, only mean men have,
But cannot value; like the precious gem
Found in the muckhill by the ignorant cock!

  The. Your creamy words but cozen; how durſt you
Intercept me ſo lately to my mother?
And what I meant your brother, you obtain'd
Unto the forfeiter again.

  Cra. Your anſwer
To that, my lord my brother.

  Euph. May I periſh
If e'er I heard you intended ſuch a ſuit!
Tho' 'twould have ſtuck an ignominious brand
Upon your highneſs, to have given your ſervant
A gentleman's whole ſtate of worth and quality,
Confiſcate only for a youthful brawl.

  The. Your rudiments are too ſaucy; teach your page.

  Con. Ay, ſo are all things but your flatterers.

  Onos. Hold you your prating!

  Con. You know where you are, you fleeten face!

  Euph. Yet,
Sir, to appeaſe and ſatisfy your anger,
Take what you pleaſe from me, and give it him,
In lieu of this. You ſhall not take it neither,
I freely will impart it, half my ſtate;
Which, brother, if you pleaſe——

  Cra. I'll ſtarve in chains firſt,
Eat my own arms!

  Euph. Oh, that you ſaw yourſelf!
You ne'er made me ſuch offer in my poorneſs;
And 'cauſe, to do you eaſe, I ſought not to you,
You thus malign me; yet your nature muſt not
Corrupt mine, nor your rude examples lead me:
If mine can mend you, I ſhall joy. You know

I fear

I fear you not; you've feen me prov'd a man
In every way of fortune; 'tis my comfort
I know no more fuch brothers in the world
As Crates is.

   Con. Nor I fuch as Euphanes:
The temper of an angel reigns in thee!

   Euph. Your royal mother, Sir, (I had forgot)
Entreats your prefence.

   The. You have done her errand;
I may do yours.   *[Exit.*

   Euph. Let it be truth, my lord.

   Con. Crates, I'll queftion you for this.

   Cra. Pifh, your worft!   *[Exit.*

   Con. Away, you hounds, after your fcent!

   Onos. Come, we'll fcorn to talk to 'em: Now
       they're gone,
We'll away too.   *[Exeunt.*

   Con. Why bear you this, my lord?

   Euph. To fhew the paffive fortitude the beft;
Virtue's a folid rock, whereat being aim'd
The keeneft darts of envy, yet unhurt
Her marble heroes ftand, built of fuch bafes,
Whilft they recoil, and wound the fhooters' faces.

         Enter Queen and Ladies.

   Con. My lord, the Queen.

   Queen. Gentle Euphanes, how,
How doft thou, honeft lord? Oh, how I joy
To fee what I have made! like a choice workman,
That having fram'd a mafter-piece, doth reap
An univerfal commendation!
Princes are gods in this. I'll build thee yet,
The good foundation fo pleafes me,
A ftory or two higher; let dogs bark:
They're fools that hold them dignified by blood,
They fhould be only made great that are good.

   Euph. Oraculous madam!

   Queen. Sirrah, I was thinking,
If I fhould marry thee, what merry tales

                        Our

Our neighbour iſlands would make of us :
But let that paſs; you have a miſtreſs
That would forbid our bans. Troth, I have wiſh'd
A thouſand times that I had been a man ;
Then I might fit a day with thee alone, and talk ;
But as I am, I muſt not. There's no ſkill
In being good, but in not being thought ill.
Sirrah, who's that ?

 Euph. So't pleaſe your majeſty,
Conon, the friend I ſued for.

 Queen. 'Tis diſpatch'd.

 Con. Gracious madam,
I owe the gods and you my life.

 Queen. I thank you,
I thank you heartily ; and I do think you
A very honeſt man ; he ſays you are.   I
But now I'll chide thee : What's the cauſe my ſon
(For my eye's every where, and I have heard)
So inſolently does thee contumelies
Paſt ſufferance (I am told), yet you complain not ?
As if my juſtice were ſo partial
As not to right the meaneſt : Credit me,
I'll call him to a ſtrict account, and fright,
By his example, all that dare curb me
In any thing that's juſt. I ſent you for him.

 Euph. Humbly he did return, he would wait on you.
But let me implore your majeſty, not to give
His highneſs any check, for worthleſs me ;
They are court-cankers, and not counſellors,
That thus inform you ; they do but hate the prince,
And would ſubvert me. I ſhould curſe my fortune,
Even at the higheſt, to be made the gin [25]
To unſcrew a mother's love unto her ſon :
Better had my pale flame in humble ſhades
Been ſpent unſeen, than to be rais'd thus high,
Now to be thought a meteor to the ſtate,
Portending ruin and contagion.

---

[25] *Gin*] Here only means *inſtrument*, or *means*, &c. not as we
take it now, for a trap or ſnare.   *Sympſon.*

               Beſeech

Beseech you then rest satisfied, the prince
Is a most noble-natur'd gentleman,
And never did to me but what I took
As favours from him; my blown billows must not
Strive 'gainst my shore, that should confine me, nor
Justle with rocks to break themselves to pieces.

Queen. Well, thou'rt the composition of a god:
My lion, lamb, my eaglet, and my dove,
Whose soul runs clearer than Diana's fount!
Nature pick'd several flowers from her choice banks,
And bound them up in thee, sending thee forth
A posy for the bosom of a queen.

Lady. The prince attends you.

Queen. Farewell, my good lord,
My honest man. Stay; hast no other suit?
I prithee tell me; sirrah, thine eye speaks
As if thou hadst; out with it, modest fool!

Euph. With favour, madam, I would crave your
leave
To marry, where I'm bound in gratitude;
The immediate means she was to all my being,
Nor do I think your wisdom, sacred Queen,
Fetters in favours, taking from me so
The liberty that meanest men enjoy.

Queen. To marry? you're a fool! thou'st anger'd me.
Leave me; I'll think on't. [*Exe. Euph. and Con.*
Only to try thee this, for tho' I love thee,

Enter Theanor.

I can subdue myself, but she that can
Enjoy thee, doth enjoy more than a man.—
Nay, rise without a blessing, or kneel still!
What's, Sir, the reason you oppose me thus,
And seek to darken what I would have shine?
Eclipse a fire much brighter than thyself,
Making your mother not a competent judge
Of her own actions?

The. Gracious madam, I
Have done no more than what in royalty,

And

And to preferve your fame, was fit to do:
Heard you the peoples' talk of you, and him
You favour fo, his greatnefs, and your love,
The pity given to me, you would excufe me.
They prate as if he did difhonour you;
And what know I, but his own lavifh tongue
Has utter'd fome fuch fpeeches? he is call'd
The king of Corinth.

   Queen. They are traitors all:
I wear a cryftal cafement 'fore my heart,
Thro' which each honeft eye may look into't;
Let it be profpect unto all the world,
I care not this.

   The. This muft not be my way.   [*Afide.*
Your pardon, gracious madam! Thefe incitements
Made me not fhew fo clear a countenance
Upon the lord Euphanes as I would;
Which fince your majefty affects fo grievoufly,
I'll clear the black cloud off it, and henceforth
Vow on this knee all love and grace to him.

   Queen. Rife, with my bleffing; and to prove this
       true,
Bear him from me this cabinet of jewels
In your own perfon; tell him, for his marrying,
He may difpofe him how and when he pleafe. [*Exit.*

   The. I fhall difcharge my duty and your will.
Crates!

Enter Crates.

   Cra. I have heard all, my lord: How luckily
Fate pops her very fpindle in our hands!
This marriage with Beliza you fhall crofs;
Then have I one attempt for Lamprias more
Upon this Phaeton: Where's Merione's ring,
That in the rape you took from her?

   The. 'Tis here.

   Cra. In, and effect our purpofe. You, my lord,
Shall difobey your mother's charge, and fend
This cabinet by fome fervant of her own,

                  That

That what succeeds may have no reference
Unto your highnefs.

The. On, my engine, on !

Cra. Now, if we be not ftruck by Heaven's own
hand,
We'll ruin him, and on his ruins ftand.   [*Exeunt.*

SCENE II.

Enter Agenor, Leonidas, Merione, and Beliza.
                                        [*A fad fong* [26].

Age. Thefe heavy airs feed forrow in her, lady,
And nourifh it too ftrongly ; like a mother
That fpoils her child with giving on't the will.

Bel. Some lighter note.   [*A lighter fong* [27].

Leo. How like a hill of fnow fhe fits, and melts,
Before the unchafte fire of others' luft !
What heart can fee her paffion, and not break ?

---

[26] *A fad fong.*] The following *fong* not being in the firft folio, we
have remov'd it from the text :

> Weep no more, nor figh nor groan,
> Sorrow calls * no time that's gone :
> Violets pluck'd, the fweeteft rain
> Makes not frefh nor grow again ;
> Trim thy locks, look chearfully,
> Fate's hidden ends eyes cannot fee.
> Joys as winged dreams fly faft,
> Why fhould fadnefs longer laft ?
> Grief is but a wound to woe ;
> Gentleft fair, mourn, mourn no moe.

[27] *A lighter fong.*] For the reafon urged in the laft note, we have
removed this *fong* alfo :

> Court-ladies, laugh and wonder. Here is one
> That weeps becaufe her maidenhead is gone ;
> Whilft you do never fret, nor chafe, nor cry,
> But when too long it keeps you company.
> Too well you know, maids are like towns on fire,
> Wafting themfelves, if no man quench defire.
> Weep then no more, fool : A new maidenhead
> Thou fuffer'ft lofs of, in each chafte tear fhed.

* *Sorrow calls.*] Sympfon reads RE*calls*, and prefcribes the pro-
nouncing *forrow* as one fyllable, *f'row* ; but who can fo pronounce it ?

Age.

Age. Take comfort, gentle madam ! You know well
Even actual sins, committed without will,
Are neither sins nor shame, much more compell'd ;
Your honour's no whit less, your chastity
No whit impair'd, for fair Merione
Is more a virgin yet than all her sex.

Mer. Alas, 'tis done[28] !

Age. Why burn these tapers now ?
Wicked and frantic creatures joy in night.

Leo. Imagine fair Merione had dream'd
She had been ravish'd, would she sit thus then
Excruciate ?

Mer. Oh !

Bel. Fy, fy ! how fond is this !
What reason for this surfeit of remorse ?
How many that have done ill, and proceed,
Women that take degrees in wantonness,
Commence, and rise in rudiments of lust,
That feel no scruple of this tenderness ?

Mer. Pish !

Bel. Nor are you matchless in mishap ; ev'n I
Do bear an equal part of misery ;
That love, belov'd, a man the crown of men,
Whom how I've friended[29], and how rais'd, 'tis better
That all do know and speak it than myself.
When he sail'd low, I might have made him mine,
Now, at his full gale, it is questionable
If ever I o'er-take him.

Age. Wherefore sits
My Phœbe shadow'd in a sable cloud ?
Those pearly drops which thou let'st fall like beads,
Numb'ring on them thy vestal orisons,
Alas, are spent in vain ! I love thee still ;
In midst of all these showers thou sweetlier scent'st,

---

[28] *Alas, 'tis done.*] Mr. Seward concurred with me in taking this passage out of the mouth of *Agenor*, and putting it into that of *Merione*, to whom it undoubtedly belongs : For she breaks out into this passionate sentence, and interrupts the prince, before he could conclude his consolatory address. *Sympson.*

[29] *Whom I have friended.*] Amended by Sympson.

Like a green meadow on an April-day,
In which the fun and Weft-wind play together,
Striving to catch and drink the balmy drops.

Enter Euphanes and Servant.

Serv. The lord Euphanes, madam.   [*Exit Mer.*
Age. Poor Merione!
She loaths the light, and men.   [*Exit with Leo.*
  Euph. The virtuous gods preferve my miftrefs!
  Bel. Oh, my moft-honour'd lord, thofe times are
      chang'd.
  Euph. Let times and men change! Could Heav'n
      change, Euphanes
Should never change to be devoted ever
To fair Beliza. Should my load of honours,
Or any grace which you were author of,
Detract mine honour, and diminifh grace?
The gods forbid! You here behold your fervant,
Your creature, gentle lady, whofe found fleeps
You purchas'd for him, whofe food you paid for,
Whofe garments were your charge, whofe firft prefer-
      ment
You founded; then, what fince the gracious Queen
Hath, or can rear, is upon your free land,
And you are miftrefs of.
  Bel. Mock me not, gentle lord;
You fhine now in too high a fphere for me:
We're planets now disjoin'd for ever! Yet,
Poor fuperftitious innocent that I am,
Give leave that I may lift my hands, and love,
Not in idolatry, but perfect zeal:
For, credit me, I repent nothing I have done,
But, were it to begin, would do the fame.
  Euph. There are two feas in Corinth, and two
      Queens,
And but there, not two fuch i' th' fpacious univerfe.
I came to tender you the man you've made,
And like a thankful ftream to retribute
All you, my ocean, have enrich'd me with.

                                        You

You told me once you'd marry me.

Bel. Another mock? You were wont to play fair play.
You scorn poor helps; he that is sure to win,
May slight mean hearts, whose hand commands the
     Queen.

Euph. Let me be held the knave thro' all the stock
When I do slight my mistress! You know well
The gracious inclination of the Queen,
Who sent me leave this morning to proceed
To marry as I saw convenience,
And a great gift of jewels: Three days hence
The general sacrifice is done to Vesta,
And can you by then be accommodated,
Your servant shall wait on you to the temple.

Bel. 'Till now I never felt a real joy indeed.

Euph. Here then I seal my duty, here my love,
'Till which, vouchsafe to wear this ring, dear mistress;
'Twas the Queen's token, and shall celebrate
Our nuptials.

Bel. Honour still raise, and preserve
My honour'd lord, as he preserves all honour!

          [*Exit Euph.*

Enter Agenor, Leonidas, and Merione.

Age. Why shift you places thus, Merione,
And will not lend a word? Couldst thou so soon
Leave sorrow as the place, how blest were I!
But 'twill not be; grief is an impudent guest,
A follower every where, a hanger-on,
That words nor blows can drive away.

Leo. Dear sister!

Bel. Who can be sad? Out with these tragic lights,
And let day repossess her natural hours;
Tear down these blacks, cast ope the casements wide,
That we may jocundly behold the sun.
I did partake with sad Merione
In all her mourning; let her now rejoice
With glad Beliza, for Euphanes is
As full of love, full of humility,

      Q 2   As

As when he wanted.

Mer. Oh! that——

Leo. Help! she faints!

Her grief has broke her heart.

Mer. No: That——that——

Age. Miſtreſs, what point you at?

Her lamps are out, yet ſtill ſhe extends her hand

As if ſhe ſaw ſomething antipathous

Unto her virtuous life.

Leo. Still, ſtill ſhe points,

And her lips move, but no articulate ſound

Breathes from 'em. Siſter, ſpeak, what moves you thus?

Bel. Her ſpirits return.

Mer. Oh, hide that fatal ring!

Where had it you, Beliza?

Bel. What hid fate

Depends on it?—Euphanes gave it me,

As holy pledge of future marriage.

Mer. Then is Euphanes the foul raviſher!

Let me ſpeak this, and die. That diſmal night

Which ſeal'd my ſhame upon me, was that ring

The partner of my robb'd virginity.

Leo. Euphanes?

Age. Strange!

Bel. Impoſſible!

Mer. Impoſſible to have redreſs on him,

Chief ſervant of the Queen. Ha! I have read

Somewhere, I'm ſure, of ſuch an injury

Done to a lady, and how ſhe durſt die!   [*Exit.*

Age. Oh, follow her, Beliza.

Bel. To aſſure her

The unlikelihood of this.   [*Exit.*

Age. Love hides all ſins.

What's to be done, Leonidas?

Leo. Why, this——

Amazement takes up all my faculties!

The plagues of gods and men will muſter all

To avenge this tyranny. Oh, frontleſs man,

To dare do ill, and hope to bear it thus!

Firſt let's implore, then cure.

Age. Who, who can truſt
The gentle looks and words of two-fac'd man?
Like Corinth's double torrent, you and I
Will ruſh upon the land; nor ſhall the Queen
Defend this villain in his villainy:
Luſt's violent flames can never be withſtood,
Nor quench'd, but with as violent ſtreams of blood.

[*Exeunt.*

ACT IV. SCENE I.

Enter Crates, Uncle, Tutor, and Onos.

Onos. THINKS he to carry her, and live?
    Cra. It ſeems ſo.
And ſhe will carry him, the ſtory ſays.

Onos. Well; hum!
Have I for this, thou fair, but falſeſt fair,
Stretch'd this ſame ſimple leg over the ſea?
What tho' my baſhfulneſs, and tender years,
Durſt ne'er reveal my affection to thy teeth?
Deep Love ne'er tattles, and, ſay they, Love's bit
The deeper dipp'd, the ſweeter ſtill is it.

Tutor. Oh, ſee the power of love! he ſpeaks in rhime.

Cra. Oh, love will make a dog howl in rhime.
Of all the lovers yet I have heard or read,
This is the ſtrangeſt: But his Guardian,
And you his Tutor, ſhould inform him better;
Thinks he that love is anſwer'd by inſtinct?

Tutor. He ſhould make means;
For certain, Sir, his baſhfulneſs undoes him,
For from his cradle, h' had a ſhameful face,
Thus walks he night and day, eats not a bit,
Nor ſleeps one jot, but's grown ſo humorous,
Drinks ale, and takes tobacco as you ſee,
Wears a ſteeletto at his codpiece cloſe,

Q 3

Stabs

Stabs on the leaft occafion ; ftrokes his beard,
Which now he puts i' th' pofture of a T,
The Roman T ; your T beard is the fafhion,
And twifold doth exprefs the enamour'd courtier,
As full as your fork-carving traveller [30].

[30] Fork-*carving traveller.*] As every new cuftom is a good fund
for fatire, to your wits of all forts ; fo I imagine here, could we
know the precife time when this play was wrote, we might fix the
æra of the introduction of *forks*, the ufe of which it fo agreeably
bantered. Nor are our Authors the only fatirifts upon this occafion.
Ben Jonfon has joined the laugh with 'em againft this cuftom, in his
Devil's an Afs, act v. fcene iv. Meercraft fays to Gilt-head and Sledge.

   ' Have I deferv'd this from you two ? for all
   ' My pains at court, to get you each a patent.
     ' *Gilt.* For what ?
     ' *Meer.* Upo' my project o' the *forks.*
     ' *Sle.* Forks ? what be they ?   [*The project of* forks.
     ' *Meer.* The laudable ufe of *forks,*
   ' Brought into cuftom here as they are in Italy,
   ' To th' fparing o' *napkins.*'   *Sympfon.*

The ' precife time' when the ufe of *forks* was introduced into this
kingdom will appear with certainty, from the following extract from
' Coryat's Crudities, haftily gobled up in five Moneths Travells in
' France, Savoy, Italy, Rhetia, commonly called the Grifons Coun-
' try, Helvetia, alias Switzerland, fome parts of High-Germany,
' and the Netherlands, &c. 1611,' 4to, p. 90. As the paffage is
curious, on account of its defcribing one of the cuftoms of the times,
we fhall make no apology for the length of it. ' Here I wil men-
' tion a thing that might have been fpoken of before, in difcourfe of
' the firft Italian towne. I obferved a cuftome in all thofe Italian
' cities and townes through the which I paffed, that is not ufed in any
' other country that I faw in my travels, neither do I thinke that any
' other nation of Chriftendome doth ufe it, but only Italy. The
' Italian, and alfo moft ftrangers that are commorant in Italy, doe al-
' waies at their meales ufe a little *forke,* when they cut their meate.
' For while with their knife, which they hold in one hand, they cut
' the meate out of the difh, they faften their *forke,* which they hold
' in their other hand, upon the fame difh. So that whatfoever he be
' that fitting in the company of any others at meale, fhould unad-
' vifedly touch the difh of meate with his fingers from which all at
' the table doe cut, he will give occafion of offence unto the com-
' pany, as having tranfgreffed the lawes of good manners, infomuch
' that for his error he fhall be at leaft brow-beaten, if not repre-
' hended in wordes. This forme of feeding I underftand is gene-
' rally ufed in all places of Italy, their *forkes* being for the moft part
' made of yron or fteele, and fome of filver, but thofe are ufed only
' by gentlemen. The reafon of this their curiofity is, becaufe the
' Italian cannot by any meanes indure to have his difh touched with
                                ' fingers,

Onos. Oh, black clouds of discontent, invelop me;
Garters, fly off; go, hatband, bind the brows
Of some dull citizen that fears to ake;
And, leg, appear now in simplicity,
Without the trappings of a courtier;
Burst, buttons, burst, your bachelor is worm'd!

Cra. A worm-eaten bachelor thou art indeed.

Onos. And, devil Melancholy, possess me now[10]!

Uncle. Cross him not in this fit I advise you, Sir.

Onos. Die, crimson rose, that didst adorn these
    cheeks,
For itch of love is now broke forth on me!

Uncle. Poor boy, 'tis true; his wrists and hands
    are scabby.

Onos. Burn, eyes, out in your sockets, sink and stink;
Teeth, I will pick you to the very bones;
Hang, hair, like hemp, or like the Isling cur's[11],
For never powder, nor the crisping-iron,
Shall touch these dangling locks; oh, ruby lips,
Love hath to you been like wine vinegar,
Now you look wan and pale, lips, ghosts ye are,
And my disgrace sharper than mustard-seed!

Cra. How like a chandler he does vent his passions!
Risum teneatis?

Onos. Well sung the poet,
Love is a golden *bubo,* full of dreams;

' fingers, seeing all mens fingers are not alike cleane. Hereupon, I
' myself thought good to imitate the Italian fashion, by this *forked*
' cutting of meate, not only while I was in Italy, but also in Ger-
' many, and oftentimes in England since I came home; being once
' quipped for that frequent using of my *forke,* by a certaine learned
' gentleman, a familiar friend of mine, one M. Laurence Whitaker,
' who in his merry humour doubted not to call me at table *Furcifer,*
' only for using a *forke* at feeding, but for no other cause.'   R.

10 Possesses *me now.*] So all former editions.

11 Isling *curs.*] Probably ISLAND *curs,* as in the following passage
from Massinger's Picture, act v. scene i.

   ' ——would I might lie
   ' Like a dog under her table, and serve for a footstool,
   ' So I might have my belly full of that
   ' Her *Island* cur refuses.'   R.

That

That ripen'd breaks, and fills us with extremes.

Tutor. A golden *bubble*, pupil; oh, grofs folecifm
To chafter ears that underftand the Latin.

Onos. I will not be corrected now;
I am in love! Revenge is now the cud
That I do chew: I'll challenge him.

Cra. Ay, marry, Sir.

Uncle. Your honour bids you, nephew; on and
      profper.

Onos. But none will bear it from me; times are
      dangerous.

Cra. Carry it yourfelf, man.

Onos. Tutor, your counfel. I'll do nothing, Sir,
Without him.

Uncle. This may rid thee, valiant coz,
Whom I have kept this forty year my ward;
Fain would I have his ftate, and now of late
He did enquire at Ephefus for his age[32],
But the church-book being burnt with Dian's temple,
He loft his aim. I've tried to famifh him,
Marry he'll live o' th' ftones; and then for poifons,
He is an antidote 'gainft all of 'em;
He fprung from Mithridates; he's fo dry and hot,
He will eat fpiders fafter than a monkey;
His maw, unhurt, keeps quickfilver like a bladder;
The largeft dofe of camphire, opium,
Harms not his brain; I think his fkull's as empty
As a fuck'd egg; vitriol and oil of tartar
He will eat toafts of; henbane, I am fure,
And hemlock, I have made his pot-herbs often.

Cra. If he refufe you, yours is then the honour;
If he accept, he being fo great, you may
Crave both to chufe the weapon, time, and place,
Which may be ten years hence, and Calicut,
Or underneath the line, to avoid advantage.

Onos. I am refolv'd.

Tutor. By your favour, pupil,

---

[32] *For his age,*] 'Tis to be wifhed our Authors had not been guilty of this and the like anachronifms. *Symfom.*

Whence

Whence shall this challenge rise? for you must ground it
On some such fundamental base, or matter,
As now the gentry set their lives upon.
Did you e'er cheat him at some ordinary,
And durst he say so, and be angry? if thus,
Then you must challenge him. Hath he call'd your
     whore
Whore? tho' she be, beside yours, twenty mens',
Your honour, reputation, is touch'd then,
And you must challenge him. Has he denied
On thirty *damme's* to accommodate money?
Tho' you have broke threescore before to him [11],
Here you must challenge him. Durst he ever shun
To drink two pots of ale wi'ye? or to wench,
Tho' weighty business otherwise importun'd?
He is a proud lord,
And you may challenge him. Has he familiarly
Dislik'd your yellow starch [14], or said your doublet
Was not exactly frenchified? or that, that report
In fair terms was untrue? or drawn your sword,
Cried 'twas ill mounted? has he given the lie
In circle, or oblique, or semi-circle,

---

[11] *Though he have broke threescore before to you.*] Amended in 1750.

[14] Yellow *starch.*] This was invented by one Turner, a tire-woman, a court bawd; who, afterwards, was amongst the miscreants concerned in the murder of Sir Thomas Overbury, for which she was hanged at Tyburn, and would die in a *yellow* ruff of her own invention: Which made *yellow* starch so odious, that it immediately went out of fashion.   *Warburton.*

Stubbs, in his Anatomie of Abuses, published in 1595, speaks of starch of various colours.

———' The one arch or pillar wherewith the devil's kingdome of great ruffes is underpropped, is a certain kinde of liquid matter, which they call *starch*, wherein the devill hath learned them to wash and die their ruffes, which, being drie, will stand stiff and in-flexible about their neckes. And this starch they make of divers substances, sometimes of wheate flower, of branne, and other graines: Sometimes of rootes, and sometimes of other thinges: Of all collours and hues, as white, redde, blewe, purple, and the like.'

In The World toss'd at Tennis, a masque by Middleton, 1620, *the five starches* are personified, and introduced contesting for superiority.   *Steevens.*

Or

Or direct parallel ? you muſt challenge him.

   Onos. He never gave my direct apparel [15] the lie
    in's life.

   Tutor. But, for the crown of all, has he refus'd
To pledge your miſtreſs' health ? tho' he were ſick,

Enter Neanthes and Page.

And crav'd your pardon, you muſt challenge him,
There's no avoiding ; one or both muſt drop.

   Onos. Exquiſite Tutor !

   Nean. Crates, I've ſought you long ; what make
    you here
Fooling with theſe three-farthings, while the town
Is all in uproar, and the prince our maſter,
Seiz'd by Leonidas and Agenor, carried
And priſoner kept i'th' caſtle flanks
The Weſt part of the city, where they vow
To hold him 'till your brother, lord Euphanes,
Be render'd to 'em, with his life to ſatiſfy
The rape, by him ſuſpected to Merione ?
The Queen refuſes to deliver him,
Pawning her knowledge for his innocency,
And dares 'em do their worſt on prince Theanor ;
The whole ſtate's in combuſtion.

   Cra. Fatal ring !

   Uncle. What will become of us ?

   Nean. And ſhe hath given commiſſion to Euphanes
And Conon, who have levied men already,
With violence to ſurprize the tower, and take 'em.
What will you do ?

   Cra. Along wi'ye, and prevent
A further miſchief. Gentlemen, our intents
We muſt defer ; you are the prince's followers.

   Nean. Will ye walk with us ?

   Uncle. You ſhall pardon us.

   Tutor. We are his followers afar off, you know,

---

[15] *My direct apparel.*] Sympſon, not thinking this blunder of
Onos was intended by the Poets, reads,
   He never gave me th' direct parallel lie in's life.

                       And

And are contented to continue so. [*Exe. Cra. and Nean.*

Onos. Sir boy!

Page. Sir fool! a challenge to my lord?
How dar'st thou, or thy ambs-ace here, think of him?
Ye crow-pick'd heads, which your thin shoulders bear
As do the poles on Corinth bridge the traitors';
Why, you three nine-pins, you talk of my lord,
And challenges? you shall not need: Come, draw;
His Page is able to swinge three such whelps.
Uncle, why stand ye off? Long-man, advance.

Onos. 'Slight, what have we done, Tutor?

Tutor. He is a boy,
And we may run away with honour.

Page. That ye shall not;
And being a boy, I am fitter to encounter
A child in law as you are, under twenty.
Thou sot, thou three-score sot! and that's a child
Again, I grant you.

Uncle. Nephew, here's an age:
Boys are turn'd men, and men are children.

Page. Away, ye peasants with your bought gentry!
Are not you he, when your fellow passengers,
Your last transportment, being assail'd by a galley,
Hid yourself i'th' cabbin; and the fight done
Peep'd above hatches, and cried, ' Have we taken,
' Or are we ta'en?' Come, I do want a slipper,
But this shall serve: Swear all as I would have you,
Or I will call some dozen brother pages,
(They're not far off, I'm sure) and we will blanket you
Until you piss again.

All. Nay, we will swear, Sir.

Page. 'Tis your best course.
First, you shall swear never to name my lord,
Or hear him nam'd hereafter, but bare-headed;
Next, to begin his health in every place,
And never to refuse to pledge it, tho'
You surfeit to the death; lastly, to hold
The poorest, littlest page in reverence,
To think him valianter, and a better gentleman,

Than

Than you three stamp'd together, and to give him
Wine and tobacco wheresoe'er you meet,
And the best meat, if he can stay.

All. We swear it loyally.

Page. Then I dismiss you,
True liegemen to the pantofle;
I had more articles, but I have business
And cannot stay now: So adieu, dear monsieur,
Tres noble & tres puissant!

Uncle. Adieu, monsieur!

Onos. *A vostre service & commandement.*

Tutor. I told you, pupil, you'd repent this foollery.

Onos. Who? I repent? you are mistaken, Tutor,
I ne'er repented any thing yet in my life,
And scorn to begin now. Come, let's be melancholy [36].

[*Exeunt.*

SCENE II.

Enter Queen, Euphanes, Conon, and Lords.

Lord. 'Twere better treat with 'em.

Queen. I will no treaties
With a league-breaker and a rebel; shall I
Article with a traitor? be compell'd
To yield an innocent unto their fury,
Whom I have prov'd so to you?

Euph. Gracious Queen,
Tho' your own godlike disposition
Would succour virtue, and protect the right;
Yet, for the publick good, for the dear safety
Of your most royal only son, consent
To give me up the sacrifice to their malice:
My life is aim'd at, and 'twere better far
The blood of twenty thousand such as I
Purpled our seas, than that your princely son
Should be endanger'd.

Queen. Still well said, honest fool!

---

[36] *Come, let's be melancholy.*] See note 58, on the Mad Lover.

Were

Were their demand but one hair from thy head,
By all the gods, I'd fcorn 'em! Were they here,
The majefty that dwells upon this brow
Should ftrike 'em on their knees. As for my fon,
Let 'em no more dare than they'll anfwer: I
An equal mother to my country am,
And every virtuous fon of it is fon
Unto my bofom, tender as mine own.

Con. Oh, you are heav'nly, madam, and the gods
Can fuffer nothing pafs to injure you!
The life that Conon promis'd, he ftands now
Ready to pay with joy.

Queen. Farewell both;
Succefs attend you! you have foldiers been,
Tam Marti quam Mercurio; if you bring not peace,
Bring me their heads.

Con. I will put fair for one. [*Exe. Queen and Lords.*

Euph. Double the guard upon her highnefs' perfon.
Conon, you muft perform a friendly part,
Which I fhall counfel you.

Con. I am your fervant. [*Exeunt.*

SCENE III.

Enter Theanor, Agenor, and Leonidas, above.

Leo. Make good that fortification, and the watch
Keep ftill upon the battlements. Royal Sir,
Weigh but our injuries; we have told you fully
The manner and the matter hales us thus;
Nor fhall this upftart mufhroom, bred i' th' night,
Sit brooding underneath your mother's wings
His damn'd impieties.

Age. For yourfelf, brave prince,
Fear nothing that this face of arms prefents;
We afk the ravifher, and have no means
To win him from your moft indulgent mother
But by this practice.

The. Stout Leonidas,
Princely Agenor, your wrongs cry fo loud,

That

That whoso would condemn you is not heard;
I blame you not; who but Euphanes durst
Make stories like to this? My wrongs, as strong,
Ask my revengeful arm to strengthen yours;
As for my fear, know you, and Greece throughout,

Enter Euphanes and Conon.

Our mother was a Spartan princess born,
That never taught me to spell such a word.
   Con. Sir, you do tempt your life.
   Euph. Conon, no more.
Do thus, as thou wouldst save it. [*Sound trumpet within.*
   Age. What trumpet's this?
   Leo. Beneath I do perceive
Two arm'd men single, that give us summons
As they would treat.
   Age. Let us descend.
   Con. My lord,
I would you would excuse me, and proceed
According to the Queen's directions.
   Euph. Friend,
As thou wouldst wear that title after death,

Enter below Theanor, Agenor, Leonidas, and soldiers.

Perform my charge. No soldier, on his life,
Approach us nearer.
   Con. Safety to both the princes; loyalty
To you, lord general. The Queen, your mistress
As well as ours, tho' not thro' fear [17], to cut
Civil dissention from her land, and save
Much guiltless blood, that uproar ever thirsts,
And for the safeguard of her son, by me
(As you demand) hath sent the lord Euphanes
To plead his own cause, or to suffer death,
As you shall find him worthy; so, delivering
The prince back, I shall leave him to your guard.
   Leo. The Queen is good and gracious: Kiss her hand.
   Age. And seal our duties. Sir, depart in peace.

---

17 *Though not to fear.*] Amended by Sympson.

The.

The. Oh, Sir, you now perceive, when in the scales
Nature and fond affection weigh together,
One poizes like a feather; and you know, my lords,
What's to be done.

Euph. Your highness is unarm'd;
Please you to use mine, and to lead the army
Back to your mother. Conon, march you with 'em.

Con. I will, my lord.—But not so far as not
To bring you help, if danger look upon you. [*Exit.*

Euph. Why do you look so strangely, fearfully,
Or stay your deathful hand? Be not so wise
To stop your rage. Look how unmov'dly here
I give myself my country's sacrifice,
An innocent sacrifice: Truth laughs at death,
And terrifies the killer more than kill'd;
Integrity thus armless seeks her foes,
And never needs the target nor the sword,
Bow, nor envenom'd shafts.

Leo. We are amaz'd,
Not at your eloquence, but impudence,
That dare thus front us.

Age. Kill him! Who knows not
The iron forehead that bold Mischief wears?

Leo. Forbear awhile, Agenor; I do tremble,
And something sits like virtue in his face,
Which the gods keep.

Euph. Agenor, strike; Leonidas,
You that have purchas'd fame on certain grounds,
Lose it on supposition: Smear your hands
In guiltless blood, laugh at my martyrdom;
But yet remember, when posterity
Shall read your volumes fill'd with virtuous acts,
And shall arrive at this black bloody leaf,
Noting your foolish barbarism, and my wrong,
(As time shall make it plain) what follows this
Decyphering any noble deed of yours
Shall be quite lost, for men will read no more.

Leo. Why, dare you say you're innocent?

Euph. By all the gods, as they, of this foul crime.

Why,

Why, gentlemen, pry clean thro' my life,
Then weigh these circumstances. Think you that he
Which made day night, and men to furies turn'd,
Durst not trust silence, vizors, nor her sense
That suffer'd; but with charms and potions
Cast her asleep, (for all this I've enquir'd)
Acted the fable of Proserpine's rape,
The place (by all description) like to hell;
And all to perpetrate unknown his lust;
Would fondly in his person bring a ring,
And give it a betrothed wife, i' th' same house
Where the poor injur'd lady liv'd and groan'd?

Age. Hell gives us art to reach the depth of sin,
But leaves us wretched fools, when we are in.

Euph. Had it giv'n me that art, and left me so,
I would not thus into the lion's jaws
Have thrust myself defenceless, for your good,
The prince's safety, or the commonweal's.
You know the Queen denied me, and sent us
Commanders to surprize you, and to raze
This tower down; we had power enough to do it,
Or starve you, as you saw, and not to tender
My person to your wrath, which I have done,
Knowing my heart as pure as infants' sleep.

Leo. What think you, Sir?

Age. No harm, I'm sure; I weep.

Euph. The gods are just, and mighty. But to give
you
Further assurance, and to make yourselves
Judges and witnesses of my innocence,
Let me demand this question; on what night
Was this foul deed committed?

Age. On the eve
Before our marriage meant.

Euph. Leonidas,
(Your rage being off, that still drowns memory)
Where was yourself and I that very night,
And what our conference?

Leo. By the gods, 'tis true:

Both

Both in her highnefs' chamber, conferring
Even of this match until an hour of day,
And then came I to call you. We are fham'd!

Age. Utterly loft, and fham'd!

Euph. Neither; be chear'd;
He that could find this out, can pardon it.
And know, this ring was fent me from the Queen;
How fhe came by it, yet is not enquir'd:
Deeper occurrents hang on't, and pray Heav'n
That my fufpicions prove as falfe as yours!
Which for the world ('till I have greater proof)
I dare not utter what, nor whom they touch:
Only this build upon, with all my nerves
I'll labour with ye, 'till Time waken Truth.

Age. There are our fwords, Sir; turn the points on us.

Leo. Punifh rebellion, and revenge your wrong.

Euph. Sir, my revenge fhall be to make your peace:
Neither was this rebellion, but rafh love.

Enter Conon.

Con. How's this? Unarm'd left, now found doubly
   arm'd?
And thofe, that would have flain him, at his feet?
Oh, Truth, thou art a mighty conquerefs.—
The Queen, my lord, perplex'd in care of you,
That, crofs to her command, hazard yourfelf,
In perfon here is come into the field,
And, like a leader, marches in the head
Of all her troops; vows that fhe will demolifh
Each ftone of this proud tower, be you not fafe;
She chafes like ftorms in groves, now fighs, now weeps,
And both fometimes, like rain and wine commix'd;
Abjures her fon for ever, 'lefs himfelf
Do fetch you off in perfon, that did give
Yourfelf to fave him of your own free will,
And fwears he muft not, nor is fit to live.

Euph. Oh, fhe's a miftrefs for the gods!

Age. And thou
A godlike fervant, fit for her.

Leo. Wide Greece
May boaſt, becauſe ſhe cannot boaſt thy like.
　Euph. Thus, Conon, tell her highneſs.
　Con. My joy flies!
　Euph. Let's tow'rd her march.　Stern drum, ſpeak
　　　gentle peace.
　Leo. We are priſoners; lead us.　Ne'er was known
A precedent like this; one unarm'd man,
Suſpected, to captive with golden words
(Truth being his ſhield) ſo many arm'd with ſwords.
[*Exeunt.*

*Enter, at one door, Queen, Theanor, Crates, Conon,
lords, and ſoldiers; at another, Euphanes (with two
ſwords), Agenor, Leonidas, and ſoldiers.　Euphanes
preſents Leonidas on his knees to the Queen; Agenor,
bare-headed, makes ſhow of ſorrow to the Queen; ſhe
ſtamps, and ſeems to be angry at the firſt.　Euphanes
perſuades her, lays their ſwords at her feet; ſhe kiſſes
him, gives them their ſwords again, they kiſs her hand
and embrace; the ſoldiers lift up Euphanes, and ſhout.
Theanor and Crates diſcovered; Conon whiſpers with
Crates, Euphanes with Agenor, and Leonidas obſerves
it, who ſeem to promiſe ſomething; Euphanes directs
his Page ſomewhat.　Exeunt all but Theanor and
Crates.*

　The. We are not lucky, Crates; this great torrent
Bears all before him.
　Cra. Such an age as this
Shall ne'er be ſeen again.　Virtue grows fat,
And Villainy pines; the furies are aſleep;
Miſchief, 'gainſt goodneſs aim'd, is like a ſtone,
Unnat'rally forc'd up an eminent hill,
Whoſe weight falls on our heads and buries us;
We ſpringe ourſelves, we ſink in our own bogs.
　The. What's to be done?
　Cra. Repent, and grow good.
　The. Piſh!
'Tis not the faſhion, fool, 'till we grow old.

The

The peoples' love to him now scares me more
Than my fond mother's; both which, like two floods,
Bearing Euphanes up, will o'erflow me;
And he is worthy : 'Would he were in Heav'n !
But that hereafter. Crates, help me now,
And henceforth be at ease.

Cra. Your will, my lord ?

The. Beliza is to marry him forthwith ;
I long to have the first touch of her too ;
That will a little quiet me.

Cra. Fy, Sir !
You'll be the tyrant to Virginity ;
To fall but once is manly, to persevere
Beastly, and desp'rate.

The. Cross me not, but do't :
Are not the means, the place, the instruments,
The very same ? I must expect you suddenly. [*Exit.*

Cra. I must obey you.
Who is in evil once a companion,
Can hardly shake him off, but must run on.
Here I appointed Conon to attend,
Him, and his sword ; he promis'd to come single,

Enter Conon and Page.

To avoid prevention : He's a man on's word.

Con. You're well met, Crates.

Cra. If we part so, Conon.

Con. Come, we must do these mutual offices ;
We must be our own seconds, our own surgeons,
And fairly fight, like men, not on advantage.

Cra. You have an honest bosom.

Con. Your's seems so.

Cra. Let's pair our swords : You are a just gentleman.

Con. You might be so. Now shake hands, if you
         please ;
Tho' it be the cudgel fashion, 'tis a friendly one.

Cra. So , stand off.

Page. That's my cue to beckon 'em. [*Exit.*

Con.

Con. Crates, to expostulate your wrongs to me
Were to doubt of 'em, or wish your excuse
In words, and so return like maiden knights;
Yet freely thus much I profess; your spleen
And rugged carriage toward your honour'd brother
Hath much more stirr'd me up, than mine own
      cause;
For I did ne'er affect these bloody men,
But hold 'em fitter be made public hangmen,
Or butchers call'd than valiant gentlemen.
'Tis true, stamp'd valour does upon just grounds;
Yet for whom justlier should I expose my life
Than him, unto whose virtue I owe all.
    Cra. Conon, you think by this great deed of yours
To insinuate yourself a lodging nearer
Unto my brother's heart: Such men as you
Live on their undertakings for their lords,
And more disable them by answering for 'em,
Than if they sat still; make 'em but their whores,
For which end gallants now-a-days do fight.
But here we come not to upbraid; what men
Seem the rash world will judge; but what they are,
Heav'n knows: And this—Horses? we are descried [39]:
One stroke, for fear of laughter.

Enter Euphanes, Agenor, Leonidas, and Page.

Con. Half a score.
    Euph. Hold, hold! on your allegiance, hold!
    Age. He that strikes next——
    Leo. Falls like a traitor on our swords.
    Euph. Oh, Heav'n, my brother bleeds! Conon, thou
      art
A villain, an unthankful man, and shalt
Pay me thy blood for his, for his is mine!
Thou wert my friend, but he is still my brother;
And tho' a friend sometimes be nearer said,

---

[39] Horses, *we are descry'd.*] Sympson would read,
    CURSE ON'T, *we are descry'd.*

In

In fome gradation, it can never be,
Where that fame brother can be made a friend;
Which, deareft Crates, thus low I implore:
What in my poverty I would not feek,
Becaufe I would not burden you, now here
In all my height of blifs I beg of you,
Your friendfhip; my advancement, Sir, is yours;
I never held it ftrange; pray ufe it fo.
We are but two, which number Nature fram'd
In the moft ufeful faculties of man,
To ftrengthen mutually and relieve each other:
Two eyes, two ears, two arms, two legs and feet,
That where one fail'd, the other might fupply;
And I, your other eye, ear, your arm and leg,
Tender my fervice, help, and fuccour to you.

   Age. Leo. A moft divine example!
   Euph. For, dear brother,
You have been blind, and lame, and deaf, to me;
Now be no more fo: In humility
I give you the duty of a younger brother,
Which take you as a brother, not a father,
And then you'll pay a duty back to me.

   Cra. 'Till now I have not wept thefe thirty years.

   Euph. Difcording brothers are like mutual legs,
Supplanting one another; he that feeks
Aid from a ftranger, and forfakes his brother,
Does but like him that madly lops his arm,
And to his body joins a wooden one;
Cuts off his natural leg, and trufts a crutch;
Plucks out his eye to fee with fpectacles.

   Cra. Moft dear Euphanes, in this crimfon flood
Wafh my unkindnefs out; you have o'ercome me,
Taught me humanity and brotherhood:
Full well knew Nature thou wert fitter far
To be a ruler o'er me than a brother,
Which henceforth be! Jove furely did defcend,
When thou wert gotten, in fome heav'nly fhape,
And greet my mother, as the poets tell
Of other women.

Age.

Age. Be this holiday!

Leo. And noted ever with the whiteſt ſtone!

Con. And pardon me, my lord! Look you, I bleed
Faſter than Crates. What I've done I did
To reconcile your loves, to both a friend;
Which my blood cement, never to part or end!

Age. Moſt worthy Conon!

Leo. Happy riſe; this day
Contracts more good than a whole age hath done.

Euph. Royal Agenor, brave Leonidas,
You are main cauſes, and muſt ſhare the fame.

Cra. Which, in ſome part, this hour ſhall requite,
For I have aim'd my black ſhafts at white marks,
And now I'll put the clue into your hands,
Shall guide you moſt perſpicuouſly to the depth
Of this dark labyrinth, where ſo long you were loſt,
Touching this old rape, and a new intent,
Wherein your counſel, and your active wit,
My deareſt brother, will be neceſſary.

Euph. My prophecy is come; prove my hopes true,
Agenor ſhall have right, and you no wrong.
Time now will pluck her daughter from her cave[40].
Let's hence, to prevent rumour. My dear brother,
Nature's divided ſtreams the higheſt ſhelf
Will over-run at laſt, and flow to itſelf. [*Exeunt.*

---

[40] *Time now will pluck,* &c.] ' In the title-page of this laſt,' (viz.
the edition of The Poeſies of George Gaſcoigne, Eſq. 1575) ' by
' way of printer's or bookſeller's device, is an ornamental wooden
' cut, tolerably well executed, wherein Time is repreſented drawing
' the figure of Truth out of a pit or cavern, with this legend,
' *Occulta veritas tempore patet.*' Percy's Reliques of Antient Poetry,
vol. iii. This ſeems to have ſuggeſted the idea in the above line.
Dr. Percy adds, that ' it was not improbable but the accidental ſight
' of this, or ſome other title-page containing the ſame device, ſug-
' geſted to Rubens that well known deſign of a ſimilar kind, which
' he has introduced into the Luxemburg-gallery, and which has been
' ſo juſtly cenſured for the unnatural manner of its execution.' R.

ACT

ACT V. SCENE I.

Enter Crates, Euphanes, Neanthes, Soficles, and Eraton.

Euph. I'VE won the lady to it, and that good
 Which is intended to her, your faith only
And secresy must make perfect; think not, Sir,
I speak as doubting it, for I dare hazard
My soul upon the trial.
 Cra. You may safely;
But are Agenor and Leonidas ready
To rush upon him in the act, and seize him
I' th' height of his security?
 Euph. At all parts
As you could wish them.
 Cra. Where's the lady?
 Euph. There
Where you appointed her to stay.
 Cra. 'Tis wisely order'd.
 Euph. Last, when you have him sure, compel him
  this way;
For, as by accident, here I'll bring the Queen
To meet you; 'twill strike greater terror to him,
To be ta'en unprovided of excuse,
And make more for our purposes. [*Exit.*
 Cra. Come, Neanthes;
Our fames and all are at the stake.
 Nean. 'Tis fit,
That since relying on your skill, we venture
So much upon one game, you play with cunning,

Enter Theanor.

Or we shall rise such losers as——
 Sof. The prince!
 Cra. The plot is laid, Sir; howsoe'er I seem'd
A little scrupulous, upon better judgment
  R 4 I have

I have effected it.

The. 'Tis the laft fervice
Of this foul kind I will employ you in.

Cra. We hope fo, Sir.

The. And I will fo reward it——

Nean. You are bound to that ; in every family
That does write luftful, your fine bawd gains more
(For, like your broker, he takes fees on both fides)
Than all the officers o' th' houfe.

Sof. For us then
To be a great man's pandars, and live poor,
That were a double fault.

Cra. Come, you lofe time, Sir ;
We will be with you inftantly : The deed done,
We have a mafque that you expect not.

The. Thou
Art ever careful; for Jove's Mercury
I would not change thee.   [*Exit.*

Era. There's an honour for you.

Nean. To be compar'd with the celeftial pimp,
Jove's fmock-fworn fquire, don Hermes.

Cra. I'll deferve it ;
And, gentlemen, be affur'd, tho' what we do now
Will to the prince Theanor look like treafon
And bafe difloyalty, yet the end fhall prove,
(When he's firft taught to know himfelf, then you)
In what he judg'd us falfe, we were moft true. [*Exeunt.*

SCENE II.

Enter Euphanes, Agenor, Leonidas, and Conon.

Euph. Only make hafte, my lords ; in all things elfe
You are inftructed : You may draw your fwords
For fhow, if you think good, but on my life
You will find no refiftance in his fervants,
And he's himfelf unarm'd.

Age. I would he were not ;
My juft rage fhould not then be loft.

                                             Euph.

Euph. Good Sir,
Have you a care no injury be done
Unto the perfon of the prince; but, Conon,
Have you an eye on both; it is your truft
That I rely on.

Con. Which I will difcharge,
Affure yourfelf, moft faithfully.

Euph. For the lady,
I know your beft refpect will not be wanting:
Then, to avoid fufpicion and difcovery,
I hold it requifite, that as foon as ever
The Queen hath feen her, fhe forfake the place,
And fit herfelf for that which is projected
For her good, and your honour.

Leo. If this profper,
Believe it you have made a purchafe of
My fervice and my life.

Euph. Your love I aim at.

Leo. Here I fhall find you?

Euph. With the Queen.

Con. Enough, Sir.   [*Exit.*

Enter Page.

Page. The Queen enquires for you, my lord; I've
          met
A dozen meffengers in fearch of you.

Enter Queen, ladies and attendants.

Euph. I knew I fhould be fought for. As I wifh'd,
She's come herfelf in perfon.

Queen. Are you found, Sir?
I wonder where you fpend your hours; methinks
Since I fo love your company, and profefs
'Tis the beft comfort this life yields me, mine
Should not be tedious to you.

Euph. Gracious madam,
To have the happinefs to fee and hear you,
Which by your bounty is conferr'd upon me,
I hold fo great a bleffing, that my honours

                                        And

And wealth, compar'd to that, are but as cyphers
To make that number greater; yet your pardon
For borrowing from my duty fo much time,
As the provifion for my fudden marriage
Exacted from me.

Queen. I perceive this marriage
Will keep you often from me; but I'll bear it.
She's a good lady, and a fair, Euphanes:
Yet, by her leave, I will fhare with her in you;
I am pleas'd that in the night fhe fhall enjoy you,
And that's fufficient for a wife; the day-time
I will divorce you from her.

Leo. [*within.*] We will force you,
If you refift.

Queen. What noife is that?

The. [*within.*] Bafe traitors!

Euph. It moves this way.

*Enter Agenor, Leonidas with Theanor, Merione like
Beliza, Conon, Crates, Neanthes, Soficles, Eraton,
and guard.*

Queen. Whate'er it be, I'll meet it;
I was not born to fear. Who's that? Beliza?

Euph. My worthieft, nobleft miftrefs! [*Exit Mer.*

Queen. Stay her! ha?
All of you look as you were rooted here,
And wanted motion: What new Gorgon's head
Have you beheld, that you are all turn'd ftatues?
This is prodigious! has none a tongue
To fpeak the caufe?

Leo. Could every hair, great Queen,
Upon my head yield an articulate found,
And all together fpeak, they could not yet
Exprefs the villainy we have difcover'd:
And yet, when with a few unwilling words
I have deliver'd what muft needs be known,
You'll fay I am too eloquent, and wifh
I had been born without a tongue.

Queen. Speak boldly;

For

For I, unmov'd with any lofs, will hear.

Leo. Then know, we have found out the ravifher
Of my poor filter, and the place and means
By which th' unfortunate, tho' fair Beliza,
Hath met a fecond violence.

Euph. This confirms
What but before I doubted to my ruin.
My lady ravifh'd?

Queen. Point me out the villain,
That guilty wretched monfter, that hath done this,
That I may look on him; and in mine eye
He reads his fentence.

Leo. That I truly could
Name any other but the prince! that heard,
You have it all.

Queen. Wonder not that I fhake;
The miracle is greater that I live,
Having endur'd the thunder that thy words
Have thrown upon me!—Dar'ft thou kneel, with
       hope   [*Theanor kneels.*
Of any favour, but a fpeedy death,
And that too in the dreadfull'ft fhape that can
Appear to a defpairing leprous foul,
If thou haft any? No, libidinous beaft,
Thy luft hath alter'd fo thy former being,
By Heav'n I know thee not!

The. Altho' unworthy,
Yet ftill I am your fon.

Queen. Thou lieft, lieft falfly!
My whole life never knew but one chafte bed,
Nor e'er defir'd warmth but from lawful fires;
Can I be then the mother to a goat,
Whofe luft is more infatiate than the grave,
And like infectious air engenders plagues,
To murder all that's chafte or good in woman?
The gods I from my youth have ferv'd and fear'd,
Whofe holy temples thou haft made thy brothels;
Could a religious mother then bring forth
So damn'd an atheift? Read but o'er my life,

                                  My

My actions, manners; and, made perfect in them,
But look into the story of thyself
As thou art now, (not as thou wert, Theanor)
And reason will compel thee to confess,
Thou art a stranger to me.

   Age. Note but how heavy [41]
The weight of guilt is! it so low hath sunk him,
That he wants power to rise up in defence
Of his bad cause.

   Queen. Persuade me not, Euphanes!
This is no prince, nor can claim part in me:
My son was born a freeman; this, a slave
To beastly passions, a fugitive
And runaway from Virtue [42]. Bring bonds for him!
By all the honour that I owe to justice,
He loses me for ever that seeks to save him!
Bind him, I say; and like a wretch that knows
He stands condemn'd before he hears the sentence,
With his base agents, from my sight remove him,
And lodge them in the dungeon! as a Queen
And patroness to justice I command it.
Thy tears are like unseasonable showers,
And in my heart now steel'd can make no entrance;
Thou'rt cruel to thyself, fool, 'tis not want
In me of soft compassion; when thou left'st

---

[41] *Agen. Note but—*] The giving this speech to *Agenor*, as all the copies do, makes strange work with the following one of the Queen. For she bids *Euphanes* persuade her not, &c. But how could he persuade her, when, by the old edition, not he but *Agenor* had been pleading for the prince? But if we put *Euphanes* for *Agenor*, as I have done, the business is concluded, and all is right.   *Sympson.*

   Mr. Sympson, not the old copies, makes ' strange work' here; for surely the disputed speech does not ' plead for the prince;' nor does that speech at all suit the benignant character of *Euphanes*, though it does the enraged *Agenor*. The *persuasion* to which the Queen replies must be delivered in dumb-show.

[42] *And run away from Virtue.*] The change of the verb into a substantive, by the help of a poor hyphen, gives a different and elegant sense to this passage, which was not one of the clearest before.

                                       Sympson.

   We see no necessity for the POOR *hyphen: Runaway* should be one word.

                                                    To

To be a fon, I ceas'd to be a mother.
Away with them! The children I will leave
To keep my name, to all pofterities,
Shall be the great examples of my juftice,
The government of my country, which fhall witnefs
How well I rul'd myfelf. Bid the wrong'd ladies
Appear in court tomorrow; we will hear them;
And by one act of our feverity,
For fear of punifhment, or love to virtue,
Teach others to be honeft: All will fhun
To tempt her laws, that would not fpare her fon. [*Ex.*

SCENE III.

Enter Onos, Uncle, and Tutor.

Uncle. Nay, nephew!
Tutor. Pupil, hear but reafon!
Onos. No;
I have none, and will hear none. Oh, my honour!
My honour blafted in the bud! my youth,
My hopeful youth, and all my expectation
Ever to be a man, are loft for ever!
Uncle. Why, nephew, we as well as you are dubb'd
Knights o' th' pantofle.
Tutor. And are fhouted at,
Kick'd, fcorn'd, and laugh'd at, by each page and
          groom;
Yet with erected heads we bear it.
Onos. Alas,
You have years, and ftrength to do it; but were you,
As I, a tender griftle, apt to bow,
You would like me, with cloaks enveloped,
Walk thus, then ftamp, then ftare.
Uncle. He will run mad,
I hope, and then all's mine.
Tutor. Why, look you, pupil,
There are for the recovery of your honour
Degrees of medicines: For a tweak by the nofe
A man's to travel but fix months, then blow it,

And

And all is well again; the baftinado
Requires a longer time, a year or two,
And then 'tis buried. I grant you have been baffled;
'Tis but a journey of fome thirty years,
And it will be forgotten.

 Onos. Think you fo?

 Tutor. Affuredly.

 Uncle. He may make a fhorter cut,
But hang or drown himfelf, and, on my life,
'Twill no more trouble him.

 Onos. I could ne'er endure
Or hemp or water, they are dangerous **tools**
For youth to deal with; I will rather follow
My Tutor's counfel.

 Tutor. Do fo.

 Onos. And put in
For my fecurity, that I'll not return
In thirty years, my whole 'ftate to my uncle.

 Uncle. That I like well of.

 Onos. Still provided, Uncle,
That at my coming home you will allow me
To be of age, that I may call to account
This Page that hath abus'd me.

 Uncle. 'Tis a match.

 Onos. Then, Corinth, thus the bafhful Lamprias
Takes leave of thee; and for this little time
Of thirty years, will labour all he can,
Tho' he goes young forth, to come home a man. [*Ex.*

S C E N E IV.

Enter Euphanes and Marfhal.

 Euph. Are your prifoners ready?

 Mar. When it fhall pleafe the Queen
To call them forth, my lord.

 Euph. Pray you do me the favour
To tell me how they have borne themfelves this night
Of their imprifonment?

 Mar. Gladly, Sir: Your brother,

With

With the other courtiers, willingly receiv'd
All courtesies I could offer; eat, and drank,
And were exceeding merry, so dissembling
Their guilt, or confident in their innocence,
That I much wonder'd at it. But the prince,
That, as born highest, should have grac'd his fall
With greatest courage, is so sunk with sorrow,
That to a common judgment he would seem
To suffer like a woman; but to me,
That from the experience I have had of many,
Look further in him, I do find the deep
Consideration of what's past, more frights him
Than any other punishment.

 Euph. That is indeed
True magnanimity; the other but
A desp'rate bastard valour.

 Mar. I press'd to him,
And, notwithstanding the Queen's strict command,
(Having your lordship's promise to secure me)
Offer'd to free him from his bonds, which he
Refus'd, with such a sorrow, mix'd with scorn,
That it amaz'd me; yet I urg'd his highness
To give one reason for't: He briefly answer'd,
That he had sat in judgment on himself,
And found that he deserv'd them; that he was
A ravisher, and so to suffer like one;
Which is the reason of my tears, he addeth,
For wer't not I again should break the laws
By scorning all their rigour can inflict,
I should die smiling.

 Euph. I forbear to wonder
That you were mov'd that saw this, I am struck
With the relation so. 'Tis very well;
See all things ready. I do wish I could
Send comfort to the prince; (be ready with him)
'Tis in the Queen's breast only, which for us
To search into were sauciness, to determine
What she thinks fit.   [*Bar brought in.*

             Enter

Enter Leonidas, with Merione in white; Euphanes, with Beliza in black; Queen, Agenor, Conon; Marshal, with Theanor, Crates, Sosicles, Eraton; lords, ladies and guard.

Lord. Make way there for the Queen!

Queen. Read first the law, and what our anceftors
Have in this cafe provided, to deter
Such-like offenders. To you, gentle ladies,
This only: 'Would I could as well give comfort,
As bid you be fecure from fear or doubt
Of our difpleafure! be as confident
As if your plea were 'gainft a common man,
To have all right from us; I will not grieve
For what's not worth my pity. Read the law.

Clerk [*reading*]. Lycurgus the nineteenth againft
rapes[41]: It is provided, and publickly enacted and
confirmed, That any man of what degree foever, offering violence to the chaftity of a virgin, fhall, *ipfo
facto*, be liable to her accufation, and according to the
faid law be cenfur'd; ever provided, that it fhall be
in the choice of the faid virgin fo abufed, either to
compel the offender to marry her without a dowry,
if fo fhe will be fatisfied, or demanding his head for
the offence, to have that accordingly performed.

Queen. You hear this: What do you demand?

Mer. The benefit
The law allows me.

Bel. For the injury
Done to mine honour, I require his head.

Mer. I likewife have an eye upon mine honour;
But knowing that his death cannot reftore it,
I afk him for my hufband.

Bel. I was ravifh'd,
And will have juftice.

Mer. I was ravifh'd too;

---

[41] Lycurgus *the nineteenth*.] What bufinefs had *Lycurgus*' laws at Corinth? This is an odd proceeding, to commit a rape in one country, and be try'd and condemn'd for it by the laws of another.

Sympfon.

I kneel

I kneel for mercy.

Bel. I demand but what
The law allows me.

Mer. That which I defire
Is by the fame law warranted.

Bel. The rape
On me hath made a forfeit of his life,
Which in revenge of my difgrace I plead for.

Mer. The rape on me gives me the privilege
To be his wife, and that is all I fue for.

Age. A doubtful cafe.

Leo. Such pretty lawyers, yet
I never faw nor read of.

Euph. May the Queen
Favour your fweet plea, madam!

Bel. Is that juftice?
Shall one that is to fuffer for a rape
Be by a rape defended? Look upon
The publick enemy of chaftity,
This luftful fatyr, whofe enrag'd defires
The ruin of one wretched virgin's honour
Would not fuffice; and fhall the wreck of two
Be his protection? May-be I was ravifh'd
For his luft only, thou for his defence;
Oh, fine evafion! fhall with fuch a flight
Your juftice be deluded? your laws cheated?
And he that for one fact deferv'd to die,
For finning often, find impunity?
But that I know thee, I would fwear thou wert
A falfe impoftor, and fuborn'd to this:
And it may be thou art, Merione;
For hadft thou fuffer'd truly what I have done,
Thou wouldft like me complain, and call for vengeance,
And, our wrongs being equal, I alone
Should not defire revenge: But be it fo!
If thou prevail, even he will punifh it,
And foolifh mercy fhew'd to him undo thee.
Confider, fool, before it be too late,
What joys thou canft expect from fuch a hufband,

To whom thy firſt, and what's more, forc'd embraces,
Which men ſay heighten pleaſure, were diſtaſteful.

Mer. 'Twas in reſpect that then they were unlawful,
Unbleſs'd by Hymen, and left ſtings behind them,
Which from the marriage-bed are ever baniſh'd.
Let this court be then the image of Jove's throne,
Upon which grace and mercy ſtill attend,
To intercede between him and his juſtice;
And ſince the law allows as much to me
As ſhe can challenge, let the milder ſentence,
Which beſt becomes a mother, and a Queen,
Now overcome, nor let your wiſdom ſuffer:
In doing right to her, I in my wrong
Endure a ſecond raviſhment.

Bel. You can free him
Only from that which does concern yourſelf,
Not from the puniſhment that's due to me;
Your injuries you may forgive, not mine;
I plead mine own juſt wreak, which will right both,
Where that which you deſire robs me of juſtice:
'Tis that which I appeal to.

Mer. Bloody woman,
Doſt thou deſire his puniſhment? Let him live then;
For any man to marry where he likes not
Is ſtill a lingring torment.

Bel. For one rape
One death's ſufficient; that way cannot catch me.

Mer. To you I fly then, to your mercy, madam!
Exempting not your juſtice, be but equal;
And ſince in no regard I come behind her,
Let me not ſo be undervalued in
Your highneſs' favour, that the world take notice
You ſo preferr'd her, that in her behalf
You kill'd that ſon you would not ſave for me;
Mercy, oh, mercy, madam!

Bel. Great Queen, juſtice!

Age. With what a maſculine conſtancy the grave
    lady
Hath heard them both!

Leo. Yet how unmov'd fhe fits
In that which moft concerns her !
   Con. Now fhe rifes ;
And, having well weigh'd both their arguments,
Refolves to fpeak.
   Euph. And yet again fhe paufes :
Oh, Conon, fuch a refolution once
A Roman told me he had feen in Cato
Before he kill'd himfelf.
   Queen. 'Tis now determin'd.
Merione, I could wifh I were no Queen,
To give you fatisfaction ; no mother,
Beliza, to content you ; and would part
Even with my being, both might have their wifhes ;
But fince that is impoffible, in few words
I will deliver what I am refolv'd on :
The end for which all profitable laws
Were made looks two ways only, the reward
Of innocent good men, and the punifhment
Of bad delinquents : Ours, concerning rapes,
Provided that fame latter claufe of marriage
For him that had fall'n once, not then forefeeing
Mankind could prove fo monftrous, to tread twice
A path fo horrid. The great law-giver
Draco, that for his ftrange feverity
Was faid to write his ftern decrees in blood,
Made none for parricides, prefuming that
No man could be fo wicked : Such might be
Lycurgus' anfwer (did he live) for this.
But fince I find that in my fon which was not
Doubted in any elfe, I will add to it :
He cannot marry both, but for both dying,
Both have their full revenge.—You fee, Beliza,
You have your wifh. With you, Merione,
I'll fpend a tear or two. So, Heaven forgive thee !
   The. Upon my knees I do approve your judgment,
And beg that you would put it into act
With all fpeed poffible ; only that I may,
Having already made peace with myfelf,

               Part

Part so with all the world. Princely Agenor,
I ask your pardon. Yours, my lord Euphanes.
And, Crates, with the rest too, I forgive you;
Do you the like for me. Yours, gracious mother,
I dare not ask; and yet if that my death
Be like a son of yours, tho' my life was not,
Perhaps you may vouchsafe it. Lastly, that
Both these whom I have wrong'd may wish my ashes
No heavy burden, ere I suffer death,
For the restoring of Merione's honour,
Let me be married to her; and then die
For you, Beliza.

  Queen. Thou hast made in this
Part of amends to me, and to the world:
Thy suit is granted. Call a Flamen forth
To do this holy work; with him a headsman.

Enter Flamen and Executioner.

Raise up thy weeping eyes, Merione;
With this hand I confirm thy marriage,
Wishing that now the gods would shew some miracle,
That this might not divorce it.

  Cra. To that purpose
I am their minister. Stand not amaz'd;
To all your comforts, I will do this wonder.
Your majesty (with your pardon I must speak it)
Allow'd once heretofore of such a contract,
Which you repenting afterwards, revok'd it,
Being fully bent to match her with Agenor;
The griev'd prince knowing this, and yet not daring
To cross what you determin'd, by an oath
Bound me and these his followers to do something
That he might once enjoy her; we, sworn to it,
And easily persuaded, being assur'd
She was his wife before the face of Heaven,
Altho' some ceremonious forms were wanting,
Committed the first rape, and brought her to him,
Which broke the marriage; but when we perceiv'd
He purpos'd to abuse our ready service

In

In the fame kind, upon the chafte Beliza,
Holding ourfelves lefs tied to him than goodnefs,
I made difcovery of it to my brother,
Who can relate the reft.

    Euph. It is moft true.

    Queen. I would it were !

    Euph. In ev'ry circumftance
It is, upon my foul : For this known to me,
I won Merione, in my lady's habit
To be again (but willingly) furpriz'd ;
But with Agenor, and her noble brother,
With my approv'd friend Conon, with fuch fpeed
She was purfued, that, the lewd act fcarce ended,
The prince (affur'd he had enjoy'd Beliza,
For all the time Merione's face was cover'd)
Was apprehended and brought to your **prefence**,
But not 'till now difcover'd, in refpect
I hop'd the imminent danger of the prince,
To which his loofe unquenched heats had brought him,
Being purfued unto the lateft trial,
Would work in him compunction, which it has done ;
And **thefe two** ladies, in their feign'd contentions,
To your delight I hope have ferv'd as mafquers
To their own nuptials.

    Queen. My choice was worthy
When firft I look'd on thee : As thou haft order'd,
All fhall be done ; and not the meaneft that
Play'd in this unexpected comedy,
But fhall partake our bounty. And, my lord,
That with the reft you may feem fatisfied,
If you dare venture on a Queen, not yet
So far in debt to years but that fhe may
Bring you a lufty boy, I offer up
Myfelf and kingdom, during my life, to you.

    Age. It is a bleffing which I durft not hope for,
But with all joy receive.

    All. We all applaud it.

    Queen. Then on unto the temple, where the rites
Of marriage ended, we'll find new delights. [*Exeunt.*

THE TRAGEDY OF BONDUCA.

Ye powerful gods of Britain, hear our prayers,
Hear us, ye great revengers! — Act III.

J. Bewdet del.   C. Grignion sc.

Published as the Act directs, by T. Sherlock, in Bow Street, March 20, 1777.

THE

TRAGEDY

OF

BONDUCA.

─────────────

This Tragedy was first printed in the folio edition of 1647. In the year 1696, a friend of George Powell the player, but whose name is now unknown, made many alterations in it, and particularly in the first two acts. It was then acted at the Theatre-Royal, and printed in quarto in the same year. Since that time, two other plays on the same subject have been brought on the stage; one by Charles Hopkins, at the Theatre-Royal in Lincoln's Inn, in the succeeding year 1697; and the other by Richard Glover, Esq. at Drury-Lane Theatre, in the year 1753, under the title of Boadicea.

DRAMATIS

M E N.

Caratach, *general of the Britons, cousin to Bonduca.*

Nennius, *a great soldier, a British commander.*

Hengo, *a brave boy, nephew to Caratach.*

Suetonius, *general to the Roman army in Britain.*

Penius, *a brave Roman commander, but stubborn to the general.*

Junius, *a Roman captain, in love with Bonduca's daughter.*

Petillius, *another Roman captain.*

Demetrius, }
Decius, } *Roman commanders.*

Regulus, ⎫
Drusius, ⎬ *Roman officers.*
Macer, ⎪
Curius, ⎭

Judas, *a corporal, a cowardly hungry knave.*

Herald.

Druids.

Soldiers.

W O M E N.

Bonduca, *queen of the Iceni, a brave virago.*
Her two Daughters, *by Prasutagus* [1].

Scene, BRITAIN.

---

[1] *Bonduca, queen of the Iceni, a brave virago,* by Prosutagus.
  Her two daughters.] Thus runs the folio of 1679, from which the editor of the octavo inconsiderately copied. The reader will see by the course of the play, that the alteration made here is undoubtedly what the drawer-up of the *Dramatis Personæ* intended. *Sympson.*

THE

THE

TRAGEDY

OF

BONDUCA.

ACT I. SCENE I.

Enter Bonduca, Daughters, Hengo, Nennius, and Soldiers.

Bonduca. THE hardy Romans? Oh, ye gods of
     Britain,
    The ruft of arms, the blufhing
 fhame of foldiers!
Are thefe the men that conquer by inheritance?
The fortune-makers? thefe the Julians,

Enter Caratach.

That with the fun meafure the end of nature,
Making the world but one Rome, and one Cæfar?
Shame, how they flee! Cæfar's foft foul dwells in 'em,
Their mothers got 'em fleeping, Pleafure nurs'd em;
Their bodies fweat with fweet oils, love's allurements,
Not lufty arms. Dare they fend thefe to feek us,
Thefe Roman girls? is Britain grown fo wanton?
           Twice

Twice we have beat 'em, Nennius, fcatter'd 'em;
And thro' their big-bon'd Germans, on whofe pikes
The honour of their actions fits in triumph,
Made themes for fongs to fhame 'em: And a woman,
A woman beat 'em, Nennius; a weak woman,
A woman, beat thefe Romans!

 Car. So it feems;
A man would fhame to talk 'fo.

 Bond. Who's that?

 Car. I.

 Bond. Coufin, d'you grieve my fortunes?

 Car. No, Bonduca;
If I grieve, 'tis the bearing of your fortunes:
You put too much wind to your fail; difcretion
And hardy valour are the twins of honour,
And, nurs'd together, make a conqueror;
Divided, but a talker. 'Tis a truth,
That Rome has fled before us twice, and routed;
A truth we ought to crown the gods for, lady,
And not our tongues; a truth is none of ours,
Nor in our ends, more than the noble bearing;
For then it leaves to be a virtue, lady,
And we that have been victors, beat ourfelves,
When we infult upon our honour's fubject.

 Bond. My valiant coufin, is it foul to fay
What liberty and honour bid us do,
And what the gods allow us?

 Car. No, Bonduca;
So what we fay exceed not what we do.
You call the Romans ' fearful, fleeing Romans,
' And Roman girls, the lees of tainted pleafures:'
Does this become a doer? are they fuch?

 Bond. They are no more.

 Car. Where is your conqueft then?
Why are your altars crown'd with wreaths of flowers?
The beafts with gilt horns waiting for the fire?
The holy Druides compofing fongs
Of everlafting life to victory?
Why are thefe triumphs, lady? for a May-game?

          For

For hunting a poor herd of wretched Romans?
Is it no more? Shut up your temples, Britons,
And let the husbandman redeem his heifers,
Put out our holy fires, no timbrel ring,
Let's home and sleep; for such great overthrows,
A candle burns too bright a sacrifice,
A glow-worm's tail too full of flame. Oh, Nennius,
Thou hadst a noble uncle knew a Roman,
And how to speak him, how to give him weight
In both his fortunes.

   Bond. By the gods, I think
You dote upon these Romans, Caratach !

   Car. Witness these wounds, I do ; they were fairly
          giv'n :
I love an enemy ; I was born a soldier ;
And he that in the head on's troop defies me,
Bending my manly body with his sword,
I make a mistress. Yellow-tressed Hymen
Ne'er tied a longing virgin with more joy,
Than I am married to that man that wounds me :
And are not all these Roman? Ten struck battles
I suck'd these honour'd scars from, and all Roman;
Ten years of bitter nights and heavy marches,
(When many a frozen storm sung thro' my cuirass,
And made it doubtful whether that or I
Were the more stubborn metal) have I wrought thro',
And all to try these Romans. Ten times a-night
I've swam the rivers, when the stars[2] of Rome
Shot at me as I floated, and the billows
Tumbled their watry ruins on my shoulders,
Charging my batter'd sides with troops of agues ;
And still to try these Romans, whom I found
(And, if I lie, my wounds be henceforth backward,
And be you witness, gods, and all my dangers)

----

   [2] *When the* stars *of Rome.*] Mr. Theobald in his margin gives us *shafts* or *darts*, as thinking the place corrupted. I have not, however, ventured to disturb the text ; as thinking the passage right as it stands.   *Sympson.*

   We think Theobald's conjecture very plausible.

As ready, and as full of that I brought,
(Which was not fear, nor flight) as valiant,
As vigilant, as wise, to do and suffer,
Ever advanc'd as forward as the Britons,
Their sleeps as short, their hopes as high as ours,
Ay, and as subtle, lady. 'Tis dishonour,
And, follow'd, will be impudence, Bonduca,
And grow to no belief, to taint these Romans.
Have not I seen the Britons——

 Bond. What?

 Car. Dishearten'd,
Run, run, Bonduca! not the quick rack ³ swifter;
The virgin from the hated ravisher
Not half so fearful; not a flight ⁴ drawn home,
A round stone from a sling, a lover's wish,
E'er made that haste that they have. By the gods,
I've seen these Britons, that you magnify,
Run as they would have out-run time, and roaring,
Basely for mercy roaring; the light shadows,
That in a thought scur o'er the fields of corn,
Halted on crutches to 'em.

 Bond. Oh, ye powers,
What scandals do I suffer!

 Car. Yes, Bonduca,
I've seen thee run too; and thee, Nennius;
Yea, run apace, both; then when Penius
(The Roman girl!) cut thro' your armed carts,
And drove 'em headlong on ye, down the hill;
Then when he hunted ye like Britain foxes,
More by the scent than fight; then did I see
These valiant and approved men of Britain,
Like boding owls, creep into tods of ivy,
And hoot their fears to one another nightly.

 Nen. And what did you then, Caratach?

 Car. I fled too,

---

³ *The* quick rack.] *i. e.* The *clouds.*

⁴ *Not a* flight] Here means *arrow.* So Shakespeare in Much
Ado about Nothing, act i. sc. i. makes Beatrice say,
 He (Benedick) *challeng'd Cupid at the* flight. *Sympson.*

             But

But not so fast; your jewel had been lost then,
Young Hengo there; he trasht me, Nennius [5];
For when your fears out-run him, then stept I,
And in the head of all the Roman fury
Took him, and, with my tough belt, to my back
I buckled him; behind him, my sure shield;
And then I follow'd. If I say I fought
Five times in bringing off this bud of Britain,
I lie not, Nennius. Neither had you heard
Me speak this, or ever seen the child more,
But that the son of Virtue, Penius,
Seeing me steer thro' all these storms of danger,
My helm still in my hand (my sword), my prow
Turn'd to my foe (my face), he cried out nobly,
Go, Briton, bear thy lion's whelp off safely;
Thy manly sword has ransom'd thee; grow strong,
And let me meet thee once again in arms;
Then if thou stand'st, thou'rt mine. I took his offer,
And here I am to honour him.

   Bond. Oh, cousin,
From what a flight of honour hast thou check'd me!
What wouldst thou make me, Caratach?

   Car. See, lady,
The noble use of others in our losses [6].

---

   5 *He trasht me, Nennius.*] The more natural as well as usual word in this place, should have been *trac'd, i. e.* followed, and probably the line run so in the Authors MSS. for if I remember right *trash* absolutely taken, is not to be met with in the sense here required.

                                        Sympson.

   To TRASH a *hound* is a term of hunting still used in the north, and perhaps not uncommon in other parts of England: It is, to *correct*, to *rate.*—Caratach says, ' It is very true, Nennius, that I fled from the ' Romans. But recollect, I did not run so fast as you pretend: I ' soon stood still, to defend your favourite youth Hengo: HE STOPPED ' my *flight*, and I saved his life.' In this passage, where *trash* properly signifies *check*, the commentators substitute *trace*; a correction which entirely destroys the force of the context, and the spirit of the reply.   *Warton.*

   6 ————————— *see, lady,*
   The noble use of others in our losses.] *i. e.* Observe the noble *behaviour* of the Romans when they conquer.

Does

Does this afflict you? Had the Romans cried this,
And, as we have done theirs, sung out these fortunes,
Rail'd on our base condition, hooted at us,
Made marks as far as th' earth was ours, to shew us
Nothing but sea could stop our flights, despis'd us,
And held it equal whether banqueting
Or beating of the Britons were more business,
It would have gall'd you.

   Bond. Let me think we conquer'd.

   Car. Do; but so think, as we may be conquer'd;
And where we have found virtue, tho' in those
That came to make us slaves, let's cherish it.
There's not a blow we gave since Julius landed,
That was of strength and worth, but, like records,
They file to after-ages. Our registers
The Romans are, for noble deeds of honour;
And shall we brand their mentions with upbraidings[7]?

   Bond. No more; I see myself. Th' hast made me,
            cousin,
More than my fortunes durst, for they abus'd me,
And wound me up so high, I swell'd with glory:
Thy temperance has cur'd that tympany,
And giv'n me health again, nay more, discretion.
Shall we have peace? for now I love these Romans.

   Car. Thy love and hate are both unwise ones, lady.

   Bond. Your reason?

   Nen. Is not peace the end of arms?

   Car. Not where the cause implies a general
            conquest:
Had we a diff'rence with some petty isle,
Or with our neighbours, lady, for our landmarks,
The taking in of some rebellious lord,
Or making head against commotions,
After a day of blood, peace might be argued;
But where we grapple for the ground we live on,
The liberty we hold as dear as life,
The gods we worship, and next those, our honours,

---

7 *And shall we burn their mentions.*] The variation in the text,
proposed by Sympson.

                         And

And with thofe fwords that know no end of battle:
Thofe men, befide themfelves, allow no neighbour;
Thofe minds that where the day is, claim inheritance,
And where the fun makes ripe the fruits, their harveft,
And where they march, but meafure out more ground
To add to Rome, and here i'th' bowels on us;
It muft not be.   No, as they are our foes,
And thofe that muft be fo until we tire 'em;
Let's ufe the peace of honour, that's fair dealing,
But in our ends our fwords[8].   That hardy Roman
That hopes to graft himfelf into my ftock,
Muft firft begin his kindred under-ground,
And be allied in afhes.
   Bond. Caratach,
As thou haft nobly fpoken, fhall be done;
And Hengo to thy charge I here deliver:
The Romans fhall have worthy wars.
   Car. They fhall:
And, little Sir, when your young bones grow ftiffer,
And when I fee you able in a morning
To beat a dozen boys, and then to breakfaft,
I'll tie you to a fword.
   Hengo. And what then, uncle?
   Car. Then you muft kill, Sir, the next valiant
      Roman
That calls you knave.
   Hengo. And muft I kill but one?
   Car. An hundred, boy, I hope.
   Hengo. I hope five hundred.
   Car. That is a noble boy! Come, worthy lady,
Let's to our feveral charges, and henceforth
Allow an enemy both weight and worth.   [*Exeunt.*

---

   [8] Ends *our fwords.*]   The fenfe feems to labour here; what I have
offer'd [*bands* for *ends*] is clear and abfolute.   Let us ufe the peace
of honour, but not tamely and fubmiffively defire it: No, let us feek
it with our fwords in our *bands,* as tho' we cou'd carve it out for ourfelves, if the conditions effer'd are not honourable.   *Sympfon.*
   Ends here means *purpofes:* 'We may deal honourably, but our *end*
' muft be war.' This is the fum of the whole fpeech; and the pro-
priety of this interpretation is confirmed by Bonduca afterwards faying.
   The Romans fhall have WORTHY WARS.

SCENE

SCENE II.

Enter Junius and Petillius.

Pet. What ail'st thou, man? dost thou want meat?

Jun. No.

Pet. Cloaths?

Jun. Neither. For Heav'ns love, leave me!

Pet. Drink?

Jun. You tire me.

Pet. Come, it is drink; I know 'tis drink.

Jun. 'Tis no drink.

Pet. I say, 'tis drink; for what affliction
Can light so heavy on a soldier,
To dry him up as thou art, but no drink?
Thou shalt have drink.

Jun. Prithee, Petillius——

Pet. And, by mine honour, much drink, valiant
   drink:
Never tell me, thou shalt have drink. I see,
Like a true friend, into thy wants; 'tis drink;
And when I leave thee to a desolation,
Especially of that dry nature, hang me.

Jun. Why do you do this to me?

Pet. For I see,
Altho' your modesty would fain conceal it,
Which sits as sweetly on a soldier
As an old side-saddle——

Jun. What do you see?

Pet. I see as fair as day [9], that thou want'st drink.
Did I not find thee gaping like an oyster
For a new tide? Thy very thoughts lie bare,
Like a low ebb; thy soul, that rid in sack,
Lies moor'd for want of liquor. Do but see
Into thyself; for, by the gods, I do;
For all thy body's chap'd and crack'd like timber,
For want of moisture: What is't thou want'st there,
  Junius,

---

[9] *As far as day.*] Amended in 1750.

An if it be not drink?

Jun. You have too much on't.

Pet. It may be a whore too; say it be; come, meecher[10],
Thou shalt have both; a pretty valiant fellow,
Die for a little lap and lechery?
No, it shall ne'er be said in our country,
Thou diedst o'th' chin-cough. Hear, thou noble Roman,
The son of her that loves a soldier,
Hear what I promis'd for thee! thus I said:
Lady, I take thy son to my companion;
Lady, I love thy son, thy son loves war,
The war loves danger, danger drink, drink discipline,
Which is society and lechery;
These two beget commanders: Fear not, lady;
Thy son shall lead.

Jun. 'Tis a strange thing, Petillius,
That so ridiculous and loose a mirth
Can master your affections.

Pet. Any mirth,
And any way, of any subject, Junius,
Is better than unmanly mustiness.
What harm's in drink? in a good wholesome wench?
I do beseech you, Sir, what error? Yet
It cannot out of my head handsomely,
But thou wouldst fain be drunk; come, no more fooling;
The general has new wine, new come over.

Jun. He must have new acquaintance for it too,
For I will none, I thank ye.

Pet. 'None, I thank you?'
A short and touchy answer! 'None, I thank you?'
You do not scorn it, do you?

Jun. Gods defend, Sir!
I owe him still more honour.

Pet. 'None, I thank you?'
No company, no drink, no wench, 'I thank you?'
You shall be worse entreated, Sir.

Jun. Petillius,
As thou art honest, leave me!

Pet. 'None, I thank you?'

---

[10] *Meecher.*] See note 55 on the Scornful Lady.

A modest and a decent resolution,
And well put on. Yes; I will leave you, Junius,
And leave you to the boys, that very shortly
Shall all salute you, by your new sirname
Of Junius ' None I thank you.' I would starve now,
Hang, drown, despair, deserve the forks ", lie open
To all the dangerous passes of a wench,
Bound to believe her tears, and wed her aches,
Ere I would own thy follies. I have found you,
Your lays, and out-leaps, Junius, haunts, and lodges;
I've view'd you, and I've found you by my skill
To be a fool o'th' first head, Junius,
And I will hunt you: You're in love, I know it;
You are an ass, and all the camp shall know it;
A peevish idle boy, your dame shall know it;
A wronger of my care, yourself shall know it.

Enter Judas and four Soldiers.

Judas. A bean? a princely diet, a full banquet,
To what we compass.
   1 Sold. Fight like hogs for acorns?
   2 Sold. Venture our lives for pig-nuts?
   Pet. What ail these rascals?
   3 Sold. If this hold, we're starv'd.
   Judas. For my part, friends,
Which is but twenty beans a-day, (a hard world
For officers, and men of action!)
And those so clipt by master Mouse, and rotten—
(For understand 'em French beans, where the fruits
Are ripen'd like the people, in old tubs)
For mine own part, I say, I'm starv'd already,
Not worth another bean, consum'd to nothing,
Nothing but flesh " and bones left, miserable:

" *Forks.*] i. e. The *gallows.*   *Sympson.*

" Flesh *and bones left.*] This is really a merry description of a
man hunger-starved; he was reduced to flesh and bones! Why what
would he be at? Would he be more than so? Modes of speech are
strangely altered, if we should not read and the Poets have wrote,
      Skin *and bones.*   *Sympson.*

It is meant to be *a merry description,* as the rest of the scene proves.
                                     Now

Now if this musty provender can prick me
To honourable matters of atchievement, Gentlemen,
Why, there's the point.

4 Sold. I'll fight no more.

Pet. You'll hang then!
A sovereign help for hunger. Ye eating rascals,
Whose gods are beef and brewis! whose brave angers
Do execution upon these, and chibbals [1]!
Ye dog's heads in the porridge-pot! ye fight no more?
Does Rome depend upon your resolution
For eating mouldy pie-crust?

3 Sold. 'Would we had it!

Judas. I may do service, captain.

Pet. In a fish-market.
You, corporal Curry-comb, what will your fighting
Profit the commonwealth? d' you hope to triumph?
Or dare your vamping valour, goodman Cobler,
Clap a new sole to th' kingdom? 'Sdeath, ye dog-
   whelps,
You fight, or not fight?

Judas. Captain!

Pet. Out, ye flesh-flies!
Nothing but noise and nastiness!

Judas. Give us meat,
Whereby we may do.

Pet. Whereby hangs your valour?

Judas. Good bits afford good blows.

Pet. A good position:
How long is't since thou eat'st last? Wipe thy mouth,

---

[1] *Chibbals.*] A sort of onions. So Ben Johnson, in his Gipsies Metamorphosed.

 ' Where the cacklers, but no grunters,
 ' Shall uncas'd be for the hunters:
 ' Those we still must keep alive;
 ' I, and put them out to thrive
 ' In the parks, and in the chases,
 ' And the finer walled places;
 ' As Saint James's, Greenwich, Tibbals,
 ' Where the acorns plump as *chibbals,*
 ' Soon shall change both kind and name,
 ' And proclaim 'em the king's game.' *Sympson.*

And

And then tell truth.

Judas. I have not eat to th' purpose——

Pet. ' To th' purpose?' what's that? half a cow,
    and garlick?

Ye rogues, my company eat turf, and talk not;
Timber they can digeft, and fight upon't;
Old mats, and mud with fpoons, rare meats. Your
    fhoes, flaves;

Dare ye cry out for hunger, and thofe extant?
Suck your fword-hilts, ye flaves; if ye be valiant,
Honour will make 'em marchpane. ' To the purpofe?'
A grievous penance! Doft thou fee that gentleman,
That melancholy monfieur?

Jun. Pray you, Petillius!

Pet. He has not eat thefe three weeks.

2 Sold. H' has drunk the more then.

3 Sold. And that's all one.

Pet. Nor drunk nor flept thefe two months.

Judas. Captain, we do befeech you, as poor foldiers,
Men that have feen good days, whofe mortal ftomachs
May fometime feel afflictions——   [*To Junius.*

Jun. This, Petillius,
Is not fo nobly done.

Pet. 'Tis common profit;
Urge him to th' point, he'll find you out a food
That needs no teeth nor ftomach; a ftrange furmity
Will feed you up as fat as hens i' th' foreheads,
And make ye fight like fichoks; to him.

Judas. Captain——

Jun. Do you long to have your throats cut?

Pet. See what mettle
It makes in him: Two meals more of this melancholy,
And there lies Caratach.

Judas. We do befeech you——

2 Sold. Humbly befeech your valour——

Jun. Am I only
Become your fport, Petillius?

Judas. But to render
In way of general good, in prefervation——

                              Jun.

Jun. Out of my thoughts, ye flaves!

4 *Sold.* Or rather pity——

3 *Sold.* Your warlike remedy againft the maw-worms.

Judas. Or notable receipt to live by nothing.

Pet. Out with your table-books!

Jun. Is this true friendfhip?
And muft my killing griefs make others May-games?
Stand from my fword's point, flaves! your poor ftarv'd fpirits
Can make me no oblations; elfe, oh, Love,
Thou proudly-blind deftruction, I would fend thee
Whole hecatombs of hearts, to bleed my forrows.

Judas. Alas, he lives by love, Sir. [*Exit Junius.*

Pet. So he does, Sir;
And cannot you do fo too? All my company
Are now in love; ne'er think of meat, nor talk
Of what provant is: *Aymes*, and hearty *hey-hoes*
Are fallads fit for foldiers. Live by meat?
By larding up your bodies? 'tis lewd, and lazy,
And fhews ye merely mortal, dull, and drives ye
To fight, like camels, with bafkets at your nofes.
Get ye in love! Ye can whore well enough,
That all the world knows; faft ye into famine,
Yet ye can crawl like crabs to wenches; handfomely
Fall but in love now, as ye fee example,
And follow't but with all your thoughts, *probatum*,
There's fo much charge fav'd, and your hunger's
        ended. [*Drum afar off.*
Away! I hear the general. Get ye in love all,
Up to the ears in love, that I may hear
No more of thefe rude murmurings; and difcretely
Carry your ftomachs, or I prophefy
A pickled rope will choke ye. Jog, and talk not!
                            [*Exeunt.*

Enter Suetonius, Demetrius, Decius, drum and colours.

Suet. Demetrius, is the meffenger difpatch'd
To Penius, to command him to bring up
The Volans regiment?

                                           Dem.

Dem. He's there by this time.

Suet. And are the horſe well view'd we brought
from Mona [14]?

Dec. The troops are full and luſty.

Suet. Good Petillius,

Look to thoſe eating rogues, that bawl for victuals,
And ſtop their throats a day or two: Proviſion
Waits but the wind to reach us.

Pet. Sir, already

I have been tampering with their ſtomachs, which I find
As deaf as adders to delays: Your clemency
Hath made their murmurs, mutinies; nay, rebellions;
Now, an they want but muſtard, they're in uproars!
No oil but Candy, Luſitanian figs,
And wine from Leſbos, now can ſatisfy 'em;
The Britiſh waters are grown dull and muddy,
The fruit diſguſtful; Orontes [15] muſt be ſought for,
And apples from the Happy Iſles; the truth is,
They are more curious now in having nothing,
Than if the ſea and land turn'd up their treaſures.
This loſt the colonies, and gave Bonduca
(With ſhame we muſt record it) time and ſtrength
To look into our fortunes; great diſcretion
To follow offer'd vict'ry; and laſt, full pride
To brave us to our teeth, and ſcorn our ruins.

Suet. Nay, chide not, good Petillius! I confeſs
My will to conquer Mona, and long ſtay
To execute that will, let in theſe loſſes:
All ſhall be right again, and as a pine
Rent from Oeta by a ſweeping tempeſt,
Jointed again, and made a maſt, defies

---

[14] *Mona.*] i. e. The Iſle of Angleſea.

[15] *Orontes.*] Our Poets are ſadly out here in their choice of pleaſant waters for drinking. Mr. Maundrell ſays, the waters of this
river are thick and turbid, as unfit to be drunk, as its fiſh to be eaten.
Choaſpes was undoubtedly what they would have ſaid, but truſting to
memory they made this miſtake. The waters of this river were
famous for their fineneſs, &c. and as Ælian tells us were drunk by
the Perſian monarchs, let 'em be in what part of their dominions
they would. *Sympſon.*

Those angry winds that split him ; so will I,
Piec'd to my never-failing strength and fortune,
Steer thro' these swelling dangers, plow their prides up,
And bear like thunder thro' their loudest tempests.
They keep the field still?

Dem. Confident and full.

Pet. In such a number, one would swear they grew:
The hills are wooded with their partizans [16],
And all the vallies overgrown with darts,
As moors are with rank rushes ; no ground left us
To charge upon, no room to strike. Say fortune
And our endeavours bring us into 'em,
They are so infinite, so ever-springing,
We shall be kill'd with killing ; of desperate women,
That neither fear or shame e'er found, the devil
Has rank'd amongst 'em multitudes ; say the men fail,
They'll poison us with their petticoats ; say they fail,
They've priests enough to pray us into nothing.

Suet. These are imaginations, dreams of nothing;
The man that doubts or fears ——

Dec. I'm free of both.

Dem. The self-same I.

Pet. And I as free as any ;
As careless of my flesh, of that we call life,
So I may lose it nobly, as indifferent
As if it were my diet. Yet, noble general,
It was a wisdom learn'd from you, I learn'd it,
And worthy of a soldier's care, most worthy,
To weigh with most deliberate circumstance
The ends of accidents, above their offers ;
How to go on and get [17]; to save a Roman,

---

[16] *Partizans.*] Pikes or halberts.

[17] *Go on and get.*] *To go on and get* is a little favouring of tauto-
logy ; for if a man *goes on,* in the sense of this passage, he cannot
chuse but *get.* But *to go on, and yet not lose a Roman,* is an expression
which the words immediately following would induce us to believe
the Poets wrote here. I have not however disturbed the text, and
only humbly offer this innovation to the judgment of the reader.
                                                      Sympson.

   To go on and get is, we think, right, and means simply *to proceed
with advantage.*

Whose

Whofe one life is more worth in way of doing,
Than millions of thefe painted wafps; how, viewing,
To find advantage out; how, found, to follow it
With counfel and difcretion, left mere fortune
Should claim the victory.

    Suet. 'Tis true, Petillius,
And worthily remember'd: The rule is certain,
Their ufes no lefs excellent; but where time
Cuts off occafions, danger, time and all
Tend to a prefent peril[18], 'tis requir'd
Our fwords and manhoods be beft counfellors,
Our expeditions, precedents. To win is nothing,
Where Reafon, Time, and Counfel are our camp-
            mafters:
But there to bear the field, then to be conquerors,
Where pale Deftruction takes us, takes us beaten,
In wants and mutinies, ourfelves but handfulls,
And to ourfelves our own fears, needs a new way,
A fudden and a defperate execution:
Here, how to fave, is lofs; to be wife, dangerous;
Only a prefent well-united ftrength,
And minds made up for all attempts, difpatch it:
Difputing and delay here cool the courage;
Neceffity gives time for doubts[19]; (things infinite,
According to the fpirit they are preach'd to:)
Rewards like them[20], and names for after-ages,
Muft fteel the foldier, his own fhame help to arm him:
And having forc'd his fpirit, ere he cools,
Fling him upon his enemies; fudden and fwift,
Like tigers amongft foxes, we muft fight for't:

---

[18] —— danger, *time and all*
    Tend to a prefent peril.] i. e. *Danger* tends to a prefent *danger.*
Our Poets might have been guilty of fuch inaccuracy, and they might
not. *Evil* is very near in letters to *peril,* taking away the *p,* and
might probably have been the word.   *Seward.*

[19] *Neceffity gives time for doubts.*] The whole context feems to
require *gives* NO *time for doubts:*
    DISPUTING *and* DELAY *here cool the courage.*
See the whole fpeech.

[20] *Rewards* LIKE THEM.] This feems to be corrupt; or, which
is more probable, there feems to be a line loft here.

                                Fury

Fury muft be our fortune; fhame we've loft
Spurs ever in our fides to prick us forward:
There is no other wifdom nor difcretion
Due to this day of ruin, but deftruction;
The foldier's order firft, and then his anger.

Dem. No doubt they dare redeem all.

Suet. Then no doubt
The day muft needs be ours. That the proud woman
Is infinite in number better likes me,
Than if we dealt with fquadrons; half her army
Shall choke themfelves, their own fwords dig their
    graves.
I'll tell ye all my fears; one fingle valour,
The virtues of the valiant Caratach,
More doubts me than all Britain: He's a foldier
So forg'd out, and fo temper'd for great fortunes,
So much man thruft into him, fo old in dangers,
So fortunate in all attempts, that his mere name
Fights in a thoufand men, himfelf in millions,
To make him Roman: But no more. Petillius,
How ftands your charge?

Pet. Ready for all employments,
To be commanded too, Sir.

Suet. 'Tis well govern'd;
Tomorrow we'll draw out, and view the cohorts:
I' th' mean time, all apply their offices.
Where's Junius?

Pet. In's cabin, fick o' th' mumps, Sir.

Suet. How?

Pet. In love, indeed in love, moft lamentably
   loving,
To the tune of Queen Dido.

Dec. Alas poor gentleman!

Suet. 'Twill make him fight the nobler. With
   what lady?
I'll be a fpokefman for him.

Pet. You'll fcant fpeed, Sir.

Suet. Who is't?

Pet. The devil's dam, Bonduca's Daughter,

            Her

Her youngeft, crack'd i' th' ring.

   Suet. I'm forry for him:

But fure his own difcretion will reclaim him;

He muft deferve our anger elfe. Good captains,

Apply yourfelves in all the pleafing forms

Ye can, unto the foldiers; fire their fpirits,

And fet 'em fit to run this action;

Mine own provifions fhall be fhar'd amongft 'em,

'Till more come in; tell 'em, if now they conquer,

The fat of all the kingdom lies before 'em.

Their fhames forgot, their honours infinite,

And want for ever banifh'd. Two days hence,

Our fortunes, and our fwords, and gods be for us!

                             [*Exeunt.*

ACT II. SCENE I.

Enter Penius, Regulus, Macer, and Drufius.

Pen. I MUST come?

   Macer. So the general commands, Sir.

   Pen. I *muft* bring up my regiment?

   Macer. Believe, Sir,

I bring no lie.

   Pen. But did he fay, I *muft* come?

   Macer. So delivered.

   Pen. How long is't, Regulus, fince I commanded

In Britain here?

   Reg. About five years, great Penius.

   Pen. The general fome five months. Are all my

        actions

So poor and loft, my fervices fo barren,

That I'm remember'd in no nobler language

But *muft* come up?

   Macer. I do befeech you, Sir,

Weigh but the time's eftate.

   Pen. Yes, good lieutenant,

                        I do,

I do, and his that fways it. *Muſt* come up?
Am I turn'd bare centurion? *Muſt*, and *ſhall*,
Fit embaſſies to court my honour?

Macer. Sir——

Pen. Set me to lead a handful of my men
Againſt an hundred thouſand barbarous ſlaves
That have march'd name by name with Rome's beſt
     doers?
Serve 'em up ſome other meat; I'll bring no food
To ſtop the jaws of all thoſe hungry wolves;
My regiment's mine own. I *muſt*, my language?

Enter Curius.

Cur. Penius, where lies the hoſt?
Pen. Where Fate may find 'em.
Cur. Are they ingirt?
Pen. The battle's loſt.
Cur. So ſoon?
Pen. No; but 'tis loſt, becauſe it muſt be won;
The Britons muſt be victors. Whoe'er ſaw
A troop of bloody vultures hovering
About a few corrupted carcaſſes,
Let him behold the ſilly Roman hoſt,
Girded with millions of fierce Britain's ſwains,
With deaths as many as they have had hopes;
And then go thither, he that loves his ſhame!
I ſcorn my life, yet dare not loſe my name.

Cur. Do not you hold it a moſt famous end,
When both our names and lives are ſacrific'd
For Rome's encreaſe?

Pen. Yes, Curius; but mark this too:
What glory is there, or what laſting fame
Can be to Rome or us, what full example,
When one is ſmother'd with a multitude,
And crouded in amongſt a nameleſs preſs?
Honour got out of flint, and on their heads
Whoſe virtues, like the ſun, exhal'd all valours[21],

---

[21] *Like the ſun, exhal'd all* valours.] The ſimile, and the argument, both ſeem to require us to read *vapours.*

Muſt

Muft not be loft in mifts and fogs of people,
Notelefs, and out of name, both rude and naked [22] :
Nor can Rome tafk us with impoffibilities,
Or bid us fight againft a flood ; we ferve her,
That fhe may proudly fay fhe has good foldiers,
Not flaves to choke all hazards. Who but fools,
That make no diff'rence betwixt certain dying,
And dying well, would fling their fames and fortunes
Into this Britain gulf, this quickfand ruin,
That, finking, fwallows us ? what noble hand
Can find a fubject fit for blood there ? or what fword
Room for his execution ? what air to cool us,
But poifon'd with their blafting breaths and curfes,
Where we lie buried quick above the ground,
And are with labouring fweat, and breathlefs pain,
Kill'd like to flaves, and cannot kill again ?

    Druf. Penius, mark antient wars, and know that then
A captain weigh'd an hundred thoufand men [23].

    Pen. Drufius, mark antient wifdom, and you'll find
        then,
He gave the overthrow that fav'd his men.
I muft not go.

    Reg. The foldiers are defirous,
Their eagles all drawn out, Sir.

    Pen. Who drew up, Regulus ?
Ha ? fpeak ! did you ? whofe bold will durft attempt
        this ?
Drawn out ? why, who commands, Sir ? on whofe
        warrant

---

[22] But *rude and naked*] Amended by Sympfon.

[23] ―――― *that then*

    Captains weigh'd.] The corruption here is very evident, but
little trouble will fet all right. We may read thus,

    ―――― *that then*
       Ten captains weigh'd.

Or thus, ―――― *that ten*

    Captains out-*weigh'd*—The number has either been dropt
upon us, or the verb fuffered a mutilation of its firft fyllable : I am
for the firft, and have altered the text accordingly. *Sympfon.*

  We do not like either of thefe conjectures, and hope our reading
will meet with approbation.

                               Durft

Durſt they advance?

Reg. I keep mine own obedience.

Druſ. 'Tis like the general cauſe, their love of
    honour,

Relieving of their wants——

  Pen. Without my knowledge?

Am I no more? my place but at their pleaſures?

Come, who did this?

  Druſ. By Heaven, Sir, I am ignorant.

    [*Drum ſoftly within, then enter Soldiers with drum
    and colours.*

  Pen. What! am I grown a ſhadow?—Hark! they
    march.

I'll know, and will be myſelf. Stand! Diſobedience?

He that advances one foot higher, dies for't.

Run thro' the regiment, upon your duties,

And charge 'em, on command, beat back again;

By Heaven, I'll tithe 'em all elſe!

  Reg. We'll do our beſt.   [*Exe. Druſ. and Reg.*

  Pen. Back! ceaſe your bawling drums there,

I'll beat the tubs about your brains elſe. Back!

Do I ſpeak with leſs fear than thunder to ye?

Muſt I ſtand to beſeech ye? Home, home!—Ha!

D'ye ſtare upon me? Are thoſe minds I moulded,

Thoſe honeſt valiant tempers I was proud

To be a fellow to, thoſe great diſcretions

Made your names fear'd and honour'd, turn'd to wild-
    fires?

Oh, gods, to diſobedience? Command, farewell!

And ye be witneſs with me, all things ſacred,

I have no ſhare in theſe mens' ſhames! March, ſoldiers,

And ſeek your own ſad ruins; your old Penius

Dares not behold your murders.

  1 *Sold.* Captain!

  2 *Sold.* Captain!

  3 *Sold.* Dear, honour'd captain!

  Pen. Too, too dear-lov'd ſoldiers,

Which made ye weary of me, and Heav'n yet knows,

Tho' in your mutinies, I dare not hate you;

                   Take

Take your own wills ! 'tis fit your long experience
Should now know how to rule yourfelves; I wrong ye,
In wifhing ye to fave your lives and credits,
To keep your necks whole from the axe hangs o'er ye :
Alas, I much difhonour'd ye ; go, feek the Britons,
And fay ye come to glut their facrifices ;
But do not fay I fent ye. What ye have been,
How excellent in all parts, good, and govern'd,
Is only left of my command, for ftory ;
What now ye are, for pity. Fare ye well !

Enter Drufius and Regulus.

Druf. Oh, turn again, great Penius ! fee the foldier
In all points apt for duty.

Reg. See his forrow
For's difobedience, which he fays was hafte,
And hafte, he thought, to pleafe you with. See,
    captain,
The toughnefs of his courage turn'd to water;
See how his manly heart melts.

Pen. Go; beat homeward ;
There learn to eat your little with obedience ;
And henceforth ftrive to do as I direct ye.

Macer. My anfwer, Sir.   [*Exeunt foldiers.*

Pen. Tell the great general,
My companies are no faggots to fill breaches ;
Myfelf no man that *muft*, or *fhall*, can carry :
Bid him be wife, and where he is, he's fafe then ;
And when he finds out poffibilities,
He may command me. Commend me to the captains.

Macer. All this I fhall deliver.

Pen. Farewell, Macer !   [*Exit.*

Cur. Pray gods this breed no mifchief !

Reg. It muft needs,
If ftout Suetonius win ; for then his anger,
Befides the foldiers' lofs of due and honour,
Will break together on him.

Druf. He's a brave fellow ;
And but a little hide his haughtinefs,

(Which

(Which is but sometimes neither, on some causes)
He shews the worthiest Roman this day living.
You may, good Curius, to the general
Make all things seem the best.

   Cur. I shall endeavour.
Pray for our fortunes, gentlemen; if we fall,
This one farewell serves for a funeral.
The gods make sharp our swords, and steel our hearts!

   Reg. We dare, alas, but cannot fight our parts [14].
                             [*Exeunt.*

SCENE II.

Enter Junius, Petillius, and a Herald.

   Pet. Let him go on. Stay; now he talks.
   Jun. Why,
Why should I love mine enemy? what's beauty?
Of what strange violence, that, like the plague,
It works upon our spirits? Blind they feign him;
I'm sure, I find it so——

   Pet. A dog shall lead you.
   Jun. His fond affections blinder——
   Pet. Hold you there still!
   Jun. It takes away my sleep——
   Pet. Alas, poor chicken!
   Jun. My company, content, almost my fashion——
   Pet. Yes, and your weight too, if you follow it.
   Jun. 'Tis sure the plague, for no man dare come
          near me
Without an antidote; 'tis far worse, hell.———
   Pet. Thou'rt damn'd without redemption then.
   Jun. The way to't
Strew'd with fair Western smiles, and April blushes,
Led by the brightest constellations; eyes,
And sweet proportions, envying Heaven; but from
          thence

---

[14] *We dare, alas, &c.*] This has hitherto been made a continuation
of *Curius*'s speech; but it is impossible that this line and that which
precedes it should belong to any one person. *Curius* is going to the
engagement, therefore properly speaks the former, but the latter must
be spoke by either *Drusius* or *Regulus* (who are subordinate to Penius),
and is expressive of their discontent at being kept from the field.

No way to guide, no path, no wifdom brings us.

Pet. Yes, a fmart water, Junius.

Jun. Do I fool?
Know all this, and fool ftill? Do I know further,
That when we have enjoy'd our ends we lofe 'em,
And all our appetites are but as dreams
We laugh at in our ages?——

Pet. Sweet philofopher!

Jun. Do I know on ftill, and yet know nothing?
          Mercy, gods!
Why am I thus ridiculous?

Pet. Motley on thee!
Thou art an arrant afs.

Jun. Can red and white,
An eye, a nofe, a cheek——

Pet. But one cheek, Junius?
An half-fac'd miftrefs?

Jun. With a little trim,
That wanton fools call fafhion, thus abufe me?
Take me beyond my reafon? Why fhould not I
Dote on my horfe well trapt, my fword well hatch'd?
They are as handfome things, to me more ufeful,
And poffible to rule too. Did I but love,
Yet 'twere excufable, my youth would bear it;
But to love there, and that no time can give me,
Mine honour dare not afk (fhe has been ravifh'd),
My nature muft not know (fhe hates our nation),
Thus to difpofe my fpirit!

Pet. Stay a little; he will declaim again.

Jun. I will not love! I am a man, have reafon,
And I will ufe it; I'll no more tormenting,
Nor whining for a wench; there are a thoufand——

Pet. Hold thee there, boy!

Jun. A thoufand will entreat me.

Pet. Ten thoufand, Junius.

Jun. I am young and lufty,
And to my fafhion valiant; can pleafe nightly.

Pet. I'll fwear thy back's *probatum*, for I've known
          thee

Leap

THE TRAGEDY OF BONDUCA. 305

Leap at fixteen like a ftrong ftallion.

Jun. I will be man again.

Pet. Now mark the working!

The devil and the fpirit tug for't : Twenty pound
Upon the devil's head!

Jun. I muft be wretched!

Pet. I knew I'd won.

Jun. Nor have I fo much power
To fhun my fortune.

Pet. I will hunt thy fortune
With all the fhapes imagination breeds,   [*Mufick.*
But I will fright thy devil. Stay, he fings now.

[*Song, by Junius, and Petillius after him in mockage.*

Jun. Muft I be thus abus'd?

Pet. Yes, marry muft you.

Let's follow him clofe : Oh, there he is ; now read it.

Herald [*reading*]. It is the general's command,
that all fick perfons, old and unable, retire within
the trenches ; he that fears has liberty to leave the
field[25] : Fools, boys, and cowards[26] muft not come
near the regiments, for fear of their infeЄtions ; efpecially thofe cowards they call lovers.

Jun. Ha?

Pet. Read on.

Herald [*reading*]. If any common foldier love an
enemy, he's whip'd and made a flave : If any captain[27], caft, with lofs of honours, flung out of the
army, and made unable ever after to bear the name
of a foldier.

Jun. The pox confume ye all, rogues!   [*Exit.*

Pet. Let this work ;
H'has fomething now to chew upon. He's gone ;
Come, fhake no more.

---

[25] *He that fears his liberty.*] Amended by Sympfon.

[26] *Fools, boys, and* lovers.] Sympfon, to avoid the repetition of
lovers, reads *cowards.*

[27] *Captain,* waft.] The reftoring of the verb here to its ancient
undoubted right, makes full and compleat fenfe, which it could not be
faid to be before this infertion.   *Sympfon.*

Sympfon reads, HE's *caft*; but the verb may be very well *underftood.*

VOL. VI.   U   *Herald.*

Herald. Well, Sir, you may command me,
But not to do the like again for Europe;
I would have given my life for a bent two-pence.
If I e'er read to lovers whilst I live again,
Or come within their confines———

Pet. There's your payment,
And keep this private.

Herald. I am school'd for talking. [*Exit.*

Enter Demetrius.

Pet. How now, Demetrius? are we drawn?

Dem. 'Tis doing;
Your company stands fair. But pray you, where's Junius?
Half his command are wanting, with some forty
That Decius leads.

Pet. Hunting for victuals.
Upon my life, free-booting rogues! their stomachs
Are like a widow's lust, ne'er satisfied.

Dem. I wonder how they dare stir, knowing the enemy
Master of all the country.

Pet. Resolute hungers
Know neither fears nor faiths; they tread on ladders,
Ropes, gallows, and overdo all dangers [28].

Dem. They may be hang'd tho'.

Pet. There's their joyful supper;
And no doubt they are at it.

Dem. But, for Heaven's sake,
How does young Junius?

Pet. Drawing on, poor gentleman.

Dem. What, to his end?

Pet. To the end of all flesh, woman.

Dem. This love has made him a stout soldier.

Pet. Oh, a great one,

---

[28] *Ropes, gallows, and overdo all dangers.*] The verse and the sense here both seem to labour: I hope I have supplied the one, and remedied the other. *To overdo a danger* is an expression I don't remember, but *to overlook one* common. *Sympson.*

Sympson reads, *ropes, gallows's, and overlook all danger.* To OVERDO *all danger* is to *run more risques than the occasion requires.* We see no need of altering the old text.

Fit

Fit to command young goslings. But what news?

Dem. I think the messenger's come back from Penius
By this time; let's go know.

Pet. What will you say now
If he deny to come, and take exceptions
At some half syllable, or sound deliver'd
With an ill accent, or some stile left out?

Dem. I cannot think he dare.

Pet. He dare speak treason,
Dare say what no man dares believe, dares do———
But that's all one: I'll lay you my black armour
To twenty crowns, he comes not.

Dem. Done.

Pet. You'll pay?

Dem. I will.

Pet. Then keep thine old use, Penius!
Be stubborn and vainglorious, and I thank thee.
Come, let's go pray for six hours; most of us
I fear will trouble Heav'n no more: Two good blows
Struck home at two commanders of the Britons,
And my part's done.

Dem. I do not think of dying.

Pet. 'Tis possible we may live; but, Demetrius,
With what strange legs, and arms, and eyes, and noses,
Let carpenters and copper-smiths consider.
If I can keep my heart whole, and my windpipe,
That I may drink yet like a soldier———

Dem. Come, let's have better thoughts; mine's on
your armour.

Pet. Mine's in your purse, Sir; let's go try the
wager! [*Exeunt.*

SCENE III.

*Enter Judas and his four companions (halters about
their necks), Bonduca, her Daughters, and Nennius
following.*

Bond. Come, hang 'em presently.

Nen. What made your rogueships
U 2   Harrying

Harrying [29] for victuals here? are we your friends?
Or do you come for spies? Tell me directly,
Would you not willingly be hang'd now? Don't ye
      long for't?

   Judas. What say ye? shall we hang in this vein?
      Hang we must,
And 'tis as good to dispatch it merrily,
As pull an arse like dogs to't.

   1 *Sold.* Any way,
So it be handsome.

   3 *Sold.* I had as lieve 'twere toothsome too:
But all agree, and I'll not stick out, boys [30].

   4 *Sold.* Let us hang pleasantly.

   Judas. Then pleasantly be't:
Captain, the truth is, we had as lieve hang
With meat in our mouths, as ask your pardon empty.

   Bond. These are brave hungers.
What say you to a leg of beef now, sirrah?

   Judas. Bring me acquainted with it, and I'll tell ye.

   Bond. Torment 'em, wenches, (I must back) then
      hang 'em.   [*Exit.*

   Judas. We humbly thank your Grace!

   1 *Daugh.* The rogues laugh at us.

   2 *Daugh.* Sirrah, what think you of a wench now?

   Judas. A wench, lady?
I do beseech your ladyship, retire;
I'll tell you presently: You see the time's short;
One crash, even to the settling of my conscience.

   Nen. Why, is't no more but up, boys?

   Judas. Yes, ride too, captain;
Will you but see my seat?

   1 *Daugh.* Ye shall be set, Sir,
Upon a jade shall shake ye.

   Judas. Sheets, good madam,
Will do it ten times better.

   1 *Daugh.* Whips, good soldier,

---

[29] *Harrying.*] To *harry* is to *plunder* or *oppress.*   *Johnson.*
[30] *I'll not out, boys.*] Here seems to be a deficiency in the expression,
which by the insertion of a monosyllable, I hope I have made up.
                              Sympson.

                                       Which

Which you shall taste before you hang, to mortify you;
'Tis pity you should die thus desperate.

2 Daugh. These are the merry Romans, the brave
        madcaps:
'Tis ten to one we'll cool your resolutions.
Bring out the whips.

Judas. 'Would your good ladyships
Would exercise 'em too!

4 Sold. Surely, ladies [11],
We'll shew you a strange patience.

Nen. Hang 'em, rascals!
They'll talk thus on the wheel.

Enter Caratach.

Car. Now, what's the matter?
What are these fellows? what's the crime committed,
That they wear necklaces?

Nen. They're Roman rogues,
Taken a-foraging.

Car. Is that all, Nennius?

Judas. 'Would I were fairly hang'd! This is the devil,
The kill-cow Caratach.

Car. And you would hang 'em?

Nen. Are they not enemies?

1 Sold. My breech makes buttons.

1 Daugh. Are they not our tormentors?

Car. Tormentors? flea-traps!
Pluck off your halters, fellows.

Nen. Take heed, Caratach;
Taint not your wisdom.

Car. Wisdom, Nennius?
Why, who shall fight against us, make our honours,
And give a glorious day into our hands,
If we dispatch our foes thus? What's their offence?
Stealing a loaf or two to keep out hunger?
A piece of greasy bacon, or a pudding?
Do these deserve the gallows? They are hungry,
Poor hungry knaves, no meat at home left, starv'd:

---

[11] Surely, *ladies.*] Seward reads, *Securely, ladies.*

Art

Art thou not hungry?

Judas. Monſtrous hungry.

Car. He looks

Like Hunger's ſelf. Get 'em ſome victuals,

And wine to cheer their hearts; quick! Hang up
       poor pilchers?

2 Sold. This is the braveſt captain——

Nen. Caratach,

I'll leave you to your will.

Car. I'll anſwer all, Sir.

2 Daugh. Let's up and view his entertainment of 'em!

I am glad they're ſhifted any way; their tongues elſe

Would ſtill have murder'd us.

1 Daugh. Let's up and ſee it!   *[Exeunt.*

Enter Hengo.

Car. Sit down, poor knaves! Why, where's this wine
       and victuals?

Who waits there?

Serv. [*within.*] Sir, 'tis coming.

Hengo. Who are theſe, uncle?

Car. They are Romans, boy.

Hengo. Are theſe they

That vex mine aunt ſo? can theſe fight? they look

Like empty ſcabbards all, no mettle in 'em;

Like men of clouts, ſet to keep crows from orchards:

Why, I dare fight with theſe.

Car. That's my good chicken!—

And how d'ye? how d'ye feel your ſtomachs?

Judas. Wondrous apt, Sir;

As ſhall appear when time calls.

Car. That's well; down with't.

A little grace will ſerve your turns. Eat ſoftly!

You'll choke, ye knaves, elſe. Give 'em wine!

Judas. Not yet, Sir;

We're even a little buſy.

Hengo. Can that fellow

Do any thing but eat? Thou fellow!

Judas. Away, boy;

Away;

Away; this is no boy's play.

Hengo. By Heaven, uncle,

If his valour lie in's teeth, he's the moſt valiant.

Car. I am glad to hear you talk, Sir.

Hengo. Good uncle, tell me,

What's the price of a couple of cramm'd Romans?

Car. Some twenty Britons, boy; theſe are good
foldiers.

Hengo. Do not the cowards eat hard too?

Car. No more, boy.

Come, I'll fit with you too. Sit down by me, boy.

Judas. Pray bring your diſh then.

Car. Hearty knaves! more meat there.

1 *Sold.* That's a good hearing.

Car. Stay now, and pledge me.

Judas. This little piece, Sir.

Car. By Heaven, ſquare eaters!

More meat, I ſay! Upon my conſcience,

The poor rogues have not eat this month! how terribly

They charge upon their victuals! Dare ye fight thus?

Judas. Believe it, Sir, like devils.

Car. Well ſaid, Famine!

Here's to thy general.

Judas. Moſt excellent captain,

I will now pledge thee.

Car. And tomorrow-night, ſay to him,

His head is mine.

Judas. I can aſſure you, captain,

He will not give it for this waſhing.

Car. Well ſaid.   [*Daughters above.*

1 *Daugh.* Here's a ſtrange entertainment: How
the thieves drink!

2 *Daugh.* Danger is dry; they look'd for colder
liquor.

Car. Fill 'em more wine; give 'em full bowls.
Which of you all now,

In recompenſe of this good, dare but give me

A ſound knock in the battle?

Judas. Delicate captain,

          To

To do thee a fufficient recompenfe,
I'll knock thy brains out.

 Car. Do it.

 Hengo. Thou dar'ft as well
Be damn'd! thou knock his brains out? thou fkin
  of man?
Uncle, I will not hear this.

 Judas. Tie up your whelp.

 Hengo. Thou kill my uncle? 'Would I had but a fword
For thy fake, thou dried dog!

 Car. What a mettle
This little vermin carries!

 Hengo. Kill mine uncle?

 Car. He fhall not, child.

 Hengo. He cannot; he's a rogue,
An only eating rogue! kill my fweet uncle?
Oh, that I were a man!

 Judas. By this wine, which I
Will drink to captain Junius, who loves
The queen's moft excellent majefty's little daughter
Moft fweetly, and moft fearfully, I'll do it.

 Hengo. Uncle, I'll kill him with a great pin.

 Car. No more, boy!
I'll pledge thy captain. To ye all, good fellows!

 2 Daugh. In love with me? that love fhall coft your
  lives all.
Come, fifter, and advife me; I have here
A way to make an eafy conqueft of 'em,
If fortune favour me.   [*Exeunt Daughters.*

 Car. Let's fee you fweat
Tomorrow blood and fpirit, boys, this wine
Turn'd to ftern valour.

 1 Sold. Hark you, Judas;
If he fhould hang us after all this?

 Judas. Let him:
I'll hang like a gentleman, and a Roman.

 Car. Take away there;
They have enough.

 Judas. Captain, we thank you heartily

For

For your good cheer; and if we meet tomorrow,
One of us pays for't.

Car. Get 'em guides; their wine
Has over-master'd 'em.

Enter Second Daughter and a Servant.

2 Daugh. That hungry fellow
With the red beard there, give it him, and this,
To see it well deliver'd.

Car. Farewell, knaves !
Speak nobly of us; keep your words tomorrow,

Enter a Guide.

And do something worthy your meat. Go, guide 'em,
And see 'em fairly onward.

Judas. Meaning me, Sir ?

Serv. The same.
The youngest daughter to the queen entreats you
To give this privately to captain Junius ;
This for your pains !

Judas. I rest her humble servant ;
Commend me to thy lady. Keep your files, boys.

Serv. I must instruct you further.

Judas. Keep your files there !
Order, sweet friends; faces about [31] now.

Guide. Here, Sir ;
Here lies your way.

Judas. Bless the founders, I say !
Fairly, good soldiers, fairly march now; close, boys!
[*Exeunt.*

SCENE IV.

Enter Suetonius, Petillius, Demetrius, Decius, and Macer.

Suet. Bid me be wise, and keep me where I am,
And so be safe ? not come, because commanded ?
Was it not thus ?

---

[31] *Faces about.*] See note 63, on Scornful Lady.

Macer.

Macer. It was, Sir.

Pet. What now think you?

Suet. Muſt *come* ſo heinous to him, ſo diſtaſteful?

Pet. Give me my money.

Dem. I confeſs 'tis due, Sir,
And preſently I'll pay it.

Suet. His obedience
So blind at his years and experience,
It cannot find where to be tender'd?

  Macer. Sir,
The regiment was willing, and advanc'd too,
The captains at all points ſteel'd up; their preparations
Full of reſolve and confidence; youth and fire,
Like the fair breaking of a glorious day,
Gilded their phalanx; when the angry Penius
Stept like a ſtormy cloud 'twixt them and hopes.

  Suet. And ſtopt their reſolutions.

  Macer. True; his reaſon
To them was odds, and odds ſo infinite,
Diſcretion durſt not look upon.

  Suet. Well, Penius,
I cannot think thee coward yet; and treacherous
I dare not think; th' haſt lopt a limb off from me;
And let it be thy glory, thou was ſtubborn,
Thy wiſdom, that thou lefr'ſt thy general naked!
Yet, ere the ſun ſet, I ſhall make thee ſee
All valour dwells not in thee, all command
In one experience. Thou'lt too late repent this,
And wiſh ' I *muſt* come up' had been thy bleſſing.

  Pet. Let's force him.

  Suet. No, by no means; he's a torrent
We cannot eaſily ſtem.

  Pet. I think, a traitor.

  Suet. No ill words! let his own ſhame firſt revile
    him.
That wine I have, ſee it, Demetrius,
Diſtributed amongſt the ſoldiers,
To make 'em high and luſty; when that's done,
Petillius, give the word thro', that the eagles

May

May prefently advance; no man difcover,
Upon his life, the enemies' full ftrength,
But make it of no value. Decius,
Are your ftarv'd people yet come home?

Dec. I hope fo.

Suet. Keep 'em in more obedience: This is no time
To chide, I could be angry elfe, and fay more to you;
But come, let's order all. Whofe fword is fharpeft,
And valour equal to his fword this day,
Shall be my faint.

Pet. We fhall be holy all then.   [*Exeunt.*

Manet Decius. Enter Judas and his company.

Judas. Captain, captain, I've brought 'em off again;
The drunkenneft flaves!

Dec. Pox confound your roguefhips!
I'll call the general, and have ye hang'd all.

Judas. Pray who will you command then?

Dec. For you, firrah,
That are the ringleader to thefe devices,
Whofe maw is never cramm'd, I'll have an engine—

Judas. A wench, fweet captain.

Dec. Sweet Judas, even the forks,
Where you fhall have two lictors with two whips
Hammer your hide.

Judas. Captain, good words, fair words,
Sweet words, good captain; if you like not us,
Farewell! we have employment.

Dec. Where haft thou been?

Judas. There where you dare not be, with all your
      valour.

Dec. Where's that?

Judas. With the beft good fellow living.

1 Sold. The king of all good fellows.

Dec. Who's that?

Judas. Caratach.
Shake now, and fay, we have done fomething worthy!
Mark me, with Caratach; by this Heaven, Caratach!
Do you as much now, an you dare. Sweet Caratach!

                You

You talk of a good fellow, of true drinking;
Well, go thy ways, old Caratach! Befides the drink,
    captain,
The braveft running banquet of black puddings,
Pieces of glorious beef——

  Dec. How fcap'd ye hanging?

  Judas. Hanging's a dog's death, we are gentlemen;
And I fay ftill, old Caratach!

  Dec. Belike then,
You are turn'd rebels all.

  Judas. We're Roman boys all,
And boys of mettle. I muft do that, captain,
This day, this very day——

  Dec. Away, ye rafcal!

  Judas. Fair words, I fay again!

  Dec. What muft you do, Sir?

  Judas. I muft do that my heart-ftrings yern to do;
But my word's paft.

  Dec. What is it?

  Judas. Why, kill Caratach.
That's all he afk'd us for our entertainment.

  Dec. More than you'll pay.

  Judas. 'Would I had fold myfelf
Unto the fkin I had not promis'd it!
For fuch another Caratach——

  Dec. Come, fool,
Have you done your country fervice?

  Judas. I've brought that
To captain Junius——

  Dec. How?

  Judas. I think will do all;
I cannot tell; I think fo.

  Dec. How! to Junius?
I'll more enquire of this. You'll fight now?

  Judas. Promife,
Take heed of promife, captain!

  Dec. Away, and rank then.

  Judas. But, hark ye, captain; there is wine
    diftributing

                   I would

I would fain know what fhare I have.

Dec. Be gone;
You have too much.

Judas. Captain, no wine, no fighting:
There's one call'd Caratach that has wine.

Dec. Well, Sir,
If you'll be rul'd now, and do well——

Judas. Do excellent.

Dec. You fhall have wine, or any thing. Go file;
I'll fee you have your fhare. Drag out your dormife,
And ftow 'em fomewhere, where they may fleep hand-
            fomely;
They'll hear a hunts-up fhortly.

Judas. Now I love thee;
But no more forks nor whips!

Dec. Deferve 'em not then.
Up with your men; I'll meet you prefently;
And get 'em fober quickly.

Judas. Arm, arm, bullies!
All's right again and ftraight; and, which is more,
More wine, more wine. Awake, ye men of Memphis.
Be fober and difcreet; we've much to do, boys.
                                    [*Exeunt.*

A C T   III.   S C E N E   I.

Enter a Meffenger.

Mef. PREPARE there for the facrifice! the
            queen comes.

*Mufick. Enter in folemnity the Druids finging, the
    Second Daughter ftrewing flowers; then Bonduca,
    Caratach, Nennius, and others.*

Bond. Ye powerful gods of Britain, hear our prayers;
Hear us, ye great revengers; and this day
Take pity from our fwords, doubt from our valours;
                                    Double

Double the fad remembrance of our wrongs
In every breaft; the vengeance due to thofe
Make infinite and endlefs! On our pikes
This day pale Terror fit, horrors and ruins
Upon our executions; claps of thunder
Hang on our armed carts; and 'fore our troops
Defpair and Death; Shame beyond thefe attend 'em!
Rife from the duft, ye relicks of the dead,
Whofe noble deeds our holy Druids fing;
Oh, rife, ye valiant bones! let not bafe earth
Opprefs your honours, whilft the pride of Rome
Treads on your ftocks, and wipes out all your ftories!

   Nen. Thou great Tiranes[33], whom our facred priefts,
Armed with dreadful thunder, place on high
Above the reft of the immortal gods,
Send thy confuming fires and deadly bolts,
And fhoot 'em home; ftick in each Roman heart
A fear fit for confufion; blaft their fpirits,
Dwell in 'em to deftruction; thro' their phalanx
Strike, as thou ftrik'ft a proud tree; fhake their bodies,
Make their ftrengths totter, and their toplefs[34] fortunes
Unroot, and reel to ruin!

   1 *Daugh.* Oh, thou god,
Thou feared god, if ever to thy juftice
Infulting wrongs, and ravifhments of women,
(Women deriv'd from thee) their fhames[35], the
       fufferings

---

  [33] *Thou great* Tiranes.] Thus wrote our Authors, though the antiquarians of latter days have not follow'd their example.

  Mr. Sammes in his Britannia Antiqua Illuftrata, calls this god *Taramis:* Toland in his Remains, *Taramis* or *Taranis*, but Mr. Baxter allows neither the one or the other. *Jupiter Tonans verò five* Tanarus *Lucano* Taranis *Gallorum lingua dicitur. Nam vitiofum effe* Taramis, *Britannorum hodierna lingua clariffimo eft argumento, cui* Tonitrua *dicuntur* Taraneu, *ut fit fingulari numero* Taran. *Vid.* Gloffar. Antiq. Britannic. in voc. Tanarus. From fo great a choice of names as I have here ferv'd up, the reader may take which pleafes him beft.   *Sympfon.*

  [34] *Their* toplefs *fortunes.*] This epithet is by no means agreeable to the context; probably we fhould read *faplefs.*

  [35] Their *fhames.*] Sympfon and Seward, THE *fhames.*

Of

Of thofe that daily fill'd thy facrifice
With virgin incenfe, have accefs, now hear me!
Now fnatch thy thunder up, now on thefe Romans,
Defpifers of thy power, of us defacers,
Revenge thyfelf; take to thy killing anger,
To make thy great work full, thy juftice fpoken,
An utter rooting from this blefled ifle
Of what Rome is or has been!

    Bond. Give more incenfe!
The gods are deaf and drowfy, no happy flame
Rifes to raife our thoughts. Pour on.

    2 *Daugh.* See, Heav'n,
And all you pow'rs that guide us, fee and fhame,
We kneel fo long for pity. O'er your altars,
Since 'tis no light oblation that you look for,
No incenfe-offering, will I hang mine eyes;
And as I wear thefe ftones with hourly weeping,
So will I melt your powers into compaffion.
This tear for Profutagus my brave father;
(Ye gods, now think on Rome!) this for my mother,
And all her miferies; yet fee, and fave us!
But now ye muft be open-ey'd. See, Heaven,
Oh, fee thy fhow'rs ftol'n from thee; our difhonours,
                [*A fmoke from the altar.*
Oh, fifter, our difhonours! Can ye be gods,
And thefe fins fmother'd?

    Bond. The fire takes.

    Car. It does fo,
But no flame rifes. Ceafe your fretful prayers,
Your whinings, and your tame petitions;
The gods love courage arm'd with confidence,
And prayers fit to pull them down: Weak tears
And troubled hearts, the dull twins of cold fpirits,
They fit and fmile at. Hear how I falute em:
Divine Andate[16], thou who holdft the reins

16 *Divine* Andate.] The real name of this goddefs, fays Mr.
Baxter from Xiphilin, is not *Andate* but *Andrafta*; and fo I have
ventured to alter the text.   *Sympfon.*
    Whether the real name of the goddefs was *Andate* or *Andrafta*, there
can be little doubt but that the Authors wrote *Andate*; and therefore
                                      it

Of furious battles, and disorder'd war,
And proudly roll'st thy swarty chariot-wheels
Over the heaps of wounds and carcasses,
Sailing thro' seas of blood; thou sure-steel'd stern-
          ness,
Give us this day good hearts, good enemies,
Good blows o' both sides, wounds that fear or flight
Can claim no share in; steel us both with angers
And warlike executions fit thy viewing;
Let Rome put on her best strength, and thy Britain,
Thy little Britain, but as great in fortune,
Meet her as strong as she, as proud, as daring!
And then look on, thou red-ey'd god [37]; who does best,
Reward with honour; who despair makes fly,
Unarm for ever, and brand with infamy!
Grant this, divine Andate! 'tis but justice;
And my first blow thus on thy holy altar
I sacrifice unto thee.   [*A flame arises.*

Bond. It flames out.   [*Musick.*
Car. Now sing, ye Druids.   [*Song.*
Bond. It is out again.
Car. H'has giv'n us leave to fight yet; we ask no
      more;
The rest hangs in our resolutions:
Tempt him no more.
  Bond. I would know further, cousin.
  Car. His hidden meaning dwells in our endeavours,
Our valours are our best gods. Chear the soldier,
And let him eat.
  Mes. He's at it, Sir.
  Car. Away then;

---

it is scarce warrantable to alter it. We cannot but observe, that
Mr. Glover, who wrote a tragedy on this story, follows the Authors
in their name of the goddess, act i. scene i.

    ' May stern *Andate*, war's victorious goddess,
    ' Again resign me to your impious rage,
    ' If e'er I blot my sufferings from remembrance.'   R.

[37] *Thou red-ey'd God.*] As the Greeks use Θεὸς, and the Latins
Deus, both for god and goddess; so our Poets here have taken the
same liberty, and call Andrasta *red-ey'd God,* though she was really a
goddess.   *Sympson.*
                                               When

When he has done, let's march. Come, fear not, lady;
This day the Roman gains no more ground here,
But what his body lies in.

    Bond. Now I'm confident.   [*Exeunt. Recorders.*

SCENE II.

Enter Junius, Curius, and Decius.

    Dec. We dare not hazard it; befide our lives,
It forfeits all our underftandings.

    Jun. Gentlemen,
Can ye forfake me in fo juft a fervice,
A fervice for the commonwealth, for honour?
Read but the letter; you may love too.

    Dec. Read it.
If there be any fafety in the circumftance,
Or likelihood 'tis love, we will not fail you:
Read it, good Curius.

    Cur. Willingly.

    Jun. Now mark it.

    Cur. [*reading.*] Health to thy heart, my honour'd
           Junius,
And all thy love requited! I am thine,
Thine everlaftingly; thy love has won me;
And let it breed no doubt, our new acquaintance
Compels this; 'tis the gods' decree to blefs us.
The times are dangerous to meet, yet fail not;
By all the love thou bear'ft me I conjure thee,
Without diftruft of danger, to come to me!
For I have purpos'd a delivery
Both of myfelf and fortune this blefs'd day
Into thy hands, if thou think'ft good. To fhew thee
How infinite my love is, ev'n my mother
Shall be thy prifoner, the day yours without hazard;
For I beheld your danger like a lover,
A juft affecter of thy faith: Thy goodnefs,
I know, will ufe us nobly; and our marriage,
If not redeem [18], yet leffen Rome's ambition:

    18 *Redeem.*] Probably we fhould read, *reclaim.* In this place,
redeem is hardly fenfe.

I'm weary of thefe miferies. Ufe my mother
(If you intend to take her) with all honour;
And let this difobedience to my parent
Be laid on love, not me. Bring with thee, Junius,
Spirits refolv'd to fetch me off, the nobleft,
Forty will ferve the turn, juft at the joining
Of both the battles; we will be weakly guarded,
And for a guide, within this hour, fhall reach thee
A faithful friend of mine. The gods, my Junius,
Keep thee, and me to ferve thee! Young Boavica.

 Cur. This letter carries much belief, and moft
    objeftions
Anfwer'd [19], we muft have doubted.

 Dec. Is that fellow
Come to you for a guide yet?

 Jun. Yes.

 Dec. And examin'd?

 Jun. Far more than that; he has felt tortures, yet
He vows he knows no more than this truth.

 Dec. Strange!

 Cur. If fhe mean what fhe writes, as't may be
    probable,
'Twill be the happieft vantage we can lean to.

 Jun. I'll pawn my foul fhe means truth.

 Dec. Think an hour more;

---

39 ———— *and moft objeftions*
 Anfwer'd, we muft have doubted.] This is not grammar, without being made an imperfect fentence: But I believe the original ran thus,
   ———*and thofe objeftions*
 Anfwers, we muft have doubted.
or, ———*and thofe*
  Objeftions anfwers, which we muft have doubted.
The former makes the following verfes moft complete. *Seward.*
 Perhaps we fhould read,
  This letter carries much belief, and moft
  Objeftions anfwer'd, elfe we muft have doubted.
The fimpleft mode of correction is by inferting the word *that,*
which was probably dropt at prefs,
  This letter carries much belief, and moft
  Objeftions anfwer'd that we muft have doubted;
are is underftood, according to the elliptical ftile of our Authors.

             Then

Then if your confidence grow ftronger on you,
We'll fet in with you.

Jun. Nobly done! I thank ye.
Ye know the time.

Cur. We will be either ready
To give you prefent counfel, or join with you.

Enter Suetonius, Petillius, Demetrius, and Macer.

Jun. No more, as ye are gentlemen. The general!

Suet. Draw out apace; the enemy waits for us.
Are ye all ready?

Jun. All our troops attend, Sir.

Suet. I'm glad to hear you fay fo, Junius;
I hope you're difpoffefs'd.

Jun. I hope fo too, Sir.

Suet. Continue fo. And, gentlemen, to you now!
To bid you fight is needlefs; ye are Romans,
The name will fight itfelf: To tell ye who
You go to fight againft, his power, and nature,
But lofs of time; ye know it ⁴⁰, know it poor,
And oft have made it fo: To tell ye further,
His body fhews more dreadful than it has done,
To him that fears lefs poffible to deal with,
Is but to ftick more honour on your actions,
Load ye with virtuous names, and to your memories
Tie never-dying Time and Fortune conftant.
Go on in full affurance! draw your fwords
As daring and as confident as juftice;
The gods of Rome fight for ye; loud Fame calls ye,
Pitch'd on the toplefs Apennine⁴¹, where the fnow dwells,

---

⁴⁰ Yet *know it.*] Mr. Theobald, Mr. Seward and myfelf, all
concurred in this flight alteration of the text: Not that I fhould have
taken notice of fo fmall a matter, but out of a defire that the world
fhould know the very minuteft thing that Mr. Theobald had done in
his intended edition of our Authors. *Sympfon.*
  Very kind to Mr. Theobald's memory indeed! and very honourable to themfelves! fince the word YE is not an ' alteration of the
' text,' but the lection of the old books. For an account of other
falfhoods in the annotations on this play, fee p. 329.
  ⁴¹ ————*loud fame calls ye,*
Pitch'd on the toplefs Apennine, and blows

And blows to all the under-world, all nations,
The feas and unfrequented defarts; wakens
The ruin'd monuments; and there where nothing
But eternal death and fleep is, informs again
The dead bones with your virtues. Go on, I fay:
Valiant and wife rule Heav'n, and all the great
Afpects! attend 'em, do but blow upon
This enemy, who but that we want foes,
Cannot deferve that name; and like a mift,
A lazy fog, before your burning valours
You'll find him fly to nothing. This is all,
We've fwords, and are the fons of antient Romans,
Heirs to their endlefs valours; fight and conquer!

   Dec. Dem. It is done.

   Pet. That man that loves not this day,
And hugs not in his arms the noble danger,
May he die famelefs and forgot!

   Suet. Sufficient!
Up to your troops, and let your drums beat thunder;
March clofe and fudden, like a tempeft: All executions
                                 [March.

Done without fparkling [42] of the body; keep your
        phalanx
Sure lin'd, and piec'd together, your pikes forward,
And fo march like a moving fort. Ere this day run,
We fhall have ground to add to Rome, well won. *[Exe.*

To all the under world, all nations,
The feas, and unfrequented defarts, where the fnow dwells;
Wakens the ruin'd monuments, and there
Where nothing but eternal death and fleep is,
Informs again the dead bones With your virtues,
Go on, I fay: Valiant and wife, rule Heav'n,
And all the great afpects attend 'em. Do but blow
Upon this enemy, who, but that we want foes, &c.] So run the
former editions.—The words, *where the fnow dwells,* feem by fome
accident to have got out of their place. Their tranfpofition, the new
arrangement of the verfes, and punctuation, we hope will be allowed
to throw new beauties on the paffage. The abolition of the period
after the words *dead bones* is alfo recommended by Mr. Seward in his
Preface.

   [42] *Sparkling.*] i. e. *Scattering.* See note 12 on the Loyal Subject;
and note 6 on the Humorous Lieutenant.

                         S C E N E

SCENE III.

Enter Caratach and Nennius.

Nen. The Roman is advanc'd; from yond' hill's brow
We may behold him, Caratach.   [*A march.*
  Car. Let's thither; [*Drums within at one place afar off.*
I see the dust fly. Now I see the body.
Observe 'em, Nennius; by Heaven, a handsome body,
And, of a few, strongly and wisely jointed!
Suetonius is a soldier.
  Nen. As I take it,
That's he that gallops by the regiments,
Viewing their preparations.
  Car. Very likely;
He shews no less than general. See how bravely
The body moves, and in the head how proudly
The captains stick like plumes; he comes apace on.
Good Nennius, go, and bid my stout lieutenant
Bring on the first square body to oppose 'em,
And, as he charges, open to enclose 'em;
The queen move next with hers, and wheel about,
To gain their backs, in which I'll lead the vanguard!
We shall have bloody crowns this day, I see by't.
Haste thee, good Nennius; I'll follow instantly.
                              [*Exit Nennius.*
How close they march, as if they grew together,
                              [*March.*
No place but lin'd alike, sure from oppression!
They will not change this figure; we must charge 'em,
And charge 'em home at both ends, **van** and rear;
                    [*Drums in another place afar off.*
They never totter else. I hear our musick,
And must attend it: Hold, good sword, but this day,
And bite hard where I hound thee! and hereafter
I'll make a relick of thee, for young soldiers
To come like pilgrims to, and kiss for conquests.
                              [*Exit.*
        X 3   SCENE

SCENE IV.

Enter Junius, Curius, and Decius.

Jun. Now is the time ; the fellow ftays.
Dec. What think ye ?
Cur. I think 'tis true.
Jun. Alas, if 'twere a queftion,
If any doubt or hazard fell into't,
D'ye think mine own difcretion fo felf-blind,
My care of ye fo naked, to run headlong ?
   Dec. Let's take Petillius with us !
   Jun. By no means ;
He's never wife but to himfelf, nor courteous,
But where the end's his own : We're ftrong enough,
If not too many. Behind yonder hill,
The fellow tells me, fhe attends, weak guarded,
Her mother and her fifter.
   Cur. I would venture.
   Jun. We fhall not ftrike five blows for't. Weigh
       the good,
The general good may come.
   Dec. Away ! I'll with ye ;
But with what doubt——
   Jun. Fear not ; my foul for all !
     [*Exeunt. Alarms, drums and trumpets in feveral*
     places afar off, as at a main battle.

SCENE V.

Enter Drufius and Penius above.

  Druf. Here you may fee 'em all, Sir ; from this hill
The country fhews off level.
   Pen. Gods defend me,
What multitudes they are, what infinites !
The Roman power fhews like a little ftar

                   Hedg'd

Hedg'd with a double halo [41].—Now the knell rings:

[Loud shouts.

Hark, how they shout to th' battle! how the air
Totters and reels, and rends apieces, Drusius,
With the huge-vollied clamours!

Druf. Now they charge
(Oh, gods!) of all sides, fearfully.

Pen. Little Rome,
Stand but this growing Hydra one short hour,
And thou haft out-done Hercules!

Druf. The duft
Hides 'em; we cannot fee what follows.

Pen. They're gone,
Gone, swallow'd, Drusius; this eternal fun
Shall never fee 'em march more.

Druf. Oh, turn this way,
And fee a model of the field! fome forty,
Against four hundred!

Pen. Well fought, bravely follow'd!
Oh, nobly charg'd again, charg'd home too! Drusius,
They feem to carry it. Now they charge all; *[Loud shouts.*
Close, close, I fay! they follow it. Ye gods,
Can there be more in men? more daring spirits?
Still they make good their fortunes. Now they're
                    gone too,
For ever gone! fee, Drusius, at their backs
A fearful ambush rises. Farewell, valours,
Excellent valours! oh, Rome, where's thy wisdom?

Druf. They're gone indeed, Sir.

Pen. Look out toward the army;
I'm heavy with these slaughters.

Druf. 'Tis the same still,
Cover'd with duft and fury.

---

[41] —— *little star*

Hedg'd with a double hollow.] Thus the octavo of 1711:
The folio of 1679 has *hollo*, that of 1647 *halloa*; which last led me
to conjecture the real word was *halo*, a well-known term in astro-
nomy, and to my great pleasure I found afterward, Mr. Theobald
had placed this very correction in his margin.   *Simpson.*

Enter

Enter the two Daughters, with Junius, Curius, Decius,
Soldiers, and Servants.

2 *Daugh.* Bring 'em in;
Tie 'em, and then unarm 'em.

1 *Daugh.* Valiant Romans,
Ye're welcome to your loves!

2 *Daugh.* Your death, fools!

Dec. We deserve 'em;
And, women, do your worst.

1 *Daugh.* Ye need not beg it.

2 *Daugh.* Which is kind Junius?

Serv. This.

2 *Daugh.* Are you my sweetheart?
It looks ill on't! How long is't, pretty soul,
Since you and I first lov'd? Had we not reason
To dote extremely upon one another?
How does my love? This is not he; my chicken
Could prate finely, sing a love-song.

Jun. Monster——

2 *Daugh.* Oh, now it courts!

Jun. Arm'd with more malice
Than he that got thee has, the devil.

2 *Daugh.* Good!
Proceed, sweet chick.

Jun. I hate thee; that's my last.

2 *Daugh.* Nay, an you love me, forward!—No?
Come, sister,
Let's prick our answers on our arrows' points,
And make 'em laugh a little. Ye damn'd lechers,
Ye proud improvident fools, have we now caught ye?
Are ye i'th' noose? Since ye're such loving creatures,
We'll be your Cupids: Do ye see these arrows?
We'll send them to your wanton livers, goats.

1 *Daugh.* Oh, how I'll trample on your hearts, ye
villains,
Ambitious salt-itch slaves, Rome's master-sins!
The mountain-rams tupt your hot mothers.

2 *Daugh.* Dogs,

To

To whofe brave founders a falt whore gave fuck!
Thieves, honour's hangmen, do ye grin? Perdition
Take me for ever, if in my fell anger [44],
I do not out-do all example.

Enter Caratach.

Car. Where,
Where are thefe ladies? Ye keep noble quarter!
Your mother thinks you dead or taken, upon which
She will not move her battle.—Sure thefe faces
I have beheld and known; they're Roman leaders!
How came they here?

  2 Daugh. A trick, Sir, that we us'd;
A certain policy conducted 'em
Unto our fnare: We've done you no fmall fervice.
Thefe us'd as we intend, we are for th' battle.

  Car. As you intend? Taken by treachery?

  1 Daugh. Is't not allow'd?

  Car. Thofe that fhould gild our conqueft,
Make up a battle worthy of our winning,
Catch'd up by craft?

  2 Daugh. By any means that's lawful.

  Car. A woman's wifdom in our triumphs? Out!
Out, out, ye fluts [45], ye follies! From our fwords
Filch our revenges bafely?—Arm again, gentlemen!
Soldiers, I charge ye help 'em.

  2 Daugh. By Heaven, Uncle,
We will have vengeance for our rapes!

---

44 *My felf-anger.*] *Fell,* as I have corrected the text, and as Mr. Seward likewife reads, is undoubtedly the genuine lection. *Sympfon.*

Sympfon may be credited in the affertion that FELL is 'undoubtedly 'the genuine lection,' though not in the other, that he has 'cor-'rected the text;' fince the firft folio reads FELL, not SELF!—In the fame ftile, he tells us, that he and Seward join'd in making Sue-tonius (p. 331) fpeak of *Honour's golden* FACE, inftead of FATE, when the firft folio exhibits FACE!—And alfo, that 'the other copies' make Caratach fay to Hengo, (p 333) THE *fortune's mine,* and he and Seward 'agreed in correcting the place,' by altering THE to THY; though the firft folio reads THY!

45 *Out, ye fluts.*] We have added the word *out* here, which we have no doubt was dropt by the compofitor or tranfcriber.

Car.

Car. By Heaven,
Ye fhould have kept your legs clofe then. Difpatch
    there !
   1 *Daugh.* I will not off thus !
  Car. He that ftirs to execute,
Or fhe, tho' it be yourfelves, by him that got me,
Shall quickly feel mine anger ! One great day given us,
Not to be fnatch'd out of our hands but bafely,
And muft we fhame the gods from whence we have it,
With fetting fnares for foldiers ? I'll run away firft,
Be hooted at, and children call me coward,
Before I fet up ftales for victories [46].
Give 'em their fwords.
   2 *Daugh.* Oh, Gods !
  Car. Bear off the women
Unto their mother !
   2 *Daugh.* One fhot, gentle uncle !
  Car. One cut her fiddle-ftring ! Bear 'em off, I fay.
   1 *Daugh.* The devil take this fortune !
  Car. Learn to fpin,   [*Exeunt Daughters.*
And curfe your knotted hemp !—Go, gentlemen,
Safely go off, up to your troops ; be wifer ;
There thank me like tall foldiers: I fhall feek ye. [*Ex.*
  Cur. A noble worth !
  Dec. Well, Junius ?
  Jun. Pray ye, no more !
  Cur. He blufhes ; do not load him.
  Dec. Where's your love now ? [*Drums loud again.*
  Jun. Puff ! there it flies. Come, let's redeem our
    follies. [*Exeunt Junius, Curius, and Decius.*
  Druf. Awake, Sir ; yet the Roman body's whole ;
I fee 'em clear again.
  Pen. Whole ? 'tis not poffible ;
Drufius, they muft be loft.
  Druf. By Heav'n, they're whole, Sir,
And in brave doing ; fee, they wheel about
To gain more ground.
  Pen. But fee there, Drufius, fee,

---

[46] *Set up* ſcales *for* victories.] Amended in 1750.

                    See

See that huge battle moving from the mountains!
Their gilt coats shine like dragons' scales, their march
Like a rough tumbling storm; see 'em, and view 'em,
And then see Rome no more. Say they fail, look,
Look where the armed carts stand; a new army!
Look how they hang like falling rocks! as murdering
Death rides in triumph, Drusius, fell Destruction
Lashes his fiery horse, and round about him
His many thousand ways to let out souls.
Move me again when they charge, when the mountain
Melts under their hot wheels, and from their ax'trees
Huge claps of thunder plough the ground before 'em!
'Till then, I'll dream what Rome was.

Enter Suetonius, Petillius, Demetrius, and Macer.

Suet. Oh, bravely fought!
Honour 'till now ne'er shew'd her golden face
I'th' field : Like lions, gentlemen, you've held
Your heads up this day. Where's young Junius,
Curius and Decius?
   Pet. Gone to Heav'n, I think, Sir.
   Suet. Their worths go with 'em! Breathe a while.
       How do ye?
   Pet. Well; some few scurvy wounds; my heart's
       whole yet.
   Dem. 'Would they would give us more ground!
   Suet Give? we'll have it.
   Pet. Have it, and hold it too, despite the devil.

Enter Junius, Decius, and Curius.

   Jun. Lead up to th' head, and line sure! The
       queen's battle
Begins to charge like wildfire. Where's the general?
   Suet. Oh, they are living yet. Come, my brave
       soldiers,
Come, let me pour Rome's blessing on ye: Live,
Live, and lead armies all! Ye bleed hard.
   Jun. Best;
We shall appear the sterner to the foe.
                         Dec.

Dec. More wounds, more honour.

Pet. Lose no time.

Suet. Away then;

And stand this shock, ye've stood the world.

Pet. We'll grow to't.

Is not this better now than lowsy loving?

Jun. I am myself, Petillius.

Pet. 'Tis I love thee [47].   [*Exeunt Romans.*

Enter Bonduca, Caratach, Daughters, and Nennius.

Car. Charge 'em i' th' flanks! Oh, you have play'd
          the fool,

The fool extremely, the mad fool!

Bond. Why, cousin?

Car. The woman fool! Why did you give the word

Unto the carts to charge down, and our people,

In grofs before the enemy? We pay for't;

Our own swords cut our throats! Why, pox on't!

Why do you offer to command? The devil,

The devil, and his dam too! who bid you

Meddle in mens' affairs?

Bond. I'll help all.

Car. Home,   [*Exeunt Queen, &c.*

Home and spin, woman, spin, go spin! you trifle.

Open before there, or all's ruin'd!—How?

                              [*Shouts within.*

Now comes the tempest on ourselves, by Heaven!

Within. Victoria!

Car. Oh, woman, scurvy woman, beastly woman!

          [*Exeunt omnes præter Drusius and Penius.*

Druf. Victoria, victoria!

Pen. How's that, Drusius?

Druf. They win, they win, they win! Oh, look,
          look, look, Sir,

For Heav'n's sake, look! The Britons fly, the Britons
          fly! Victoria!

---

[47] *'Tis I love thee.*] So the former copies. Mr. Seward and
myself agreed in filling up the deficiency of the sense by the insertion
of *now* into the present text.   *Sympson.*

They read, *'Tis now I love thee*; but the former copies are right,
as Petillius means to oppose *his* love to that of Bonvica.

                                        Enter

Enter Suetonius, Soldiers, and Captains.

Suet. Soft, soft, pursue it soft, excellent soldiers!
Close, my brave fellows, honourable Romans!
Oh, cool thy mettle, Junius; they are ours,
The world cannot redeem 'em: Stern Petillius,
Govern the conquest nobly. Soft, good soldiers!
[*Exeunt.*

Enter Bonduca, Daughters, and Britons.

Bond. Shame! whither fly ye, ye unlucky Britons?
Will ye creep into your mothers' wombs again? Back,
  cowards!
Hares, fearful hares, doves in your angers! leave me?
Leave your queen desolate? her hapless children,

Enter Caratach and Hengo.

To Roman rape again, and fury?
  Car. Fly, ye buzzards!
Ye've wings enough, ye fear! Get thee gone, woman,
  [*Loud shout within.*
Shame tread upon thy heels! All's lost, all's lost!
  Hark,
Hark how the Romans ring our knells! [*Ex. Bond. &c.*
  Hengo. Good uncle,
Let me go too.
  Car. No, boy; thy fortune's mine;
I must not leave thee. Get behind me; shake not;

Enter Petillius, Junius, and Decius.

I'll breech you, if you do, boy.—Come, brave Romans!
All is not lost yet.
  Jun. Now I'll thank thee, Caratach. [*Fight. Drums.*
  Car. Thou art a soldier; strike home, home! have at
    you!
  Pen. His blows fall like huge sledges on an anvil.
  Dec. I'm weary.
  Pet. So am I.
                                                    Car.

Car. Send more fwords to me.

Jun. Let's fit and reft.   [*Sit down.*

Druf. What think you now?

Pen. Oh, Drufius,

I've loft mine honour, loft my name, loft all
That was my light: Thefe are true Romans, and I
A Briton coward, a bafe coward! Guide me
Where nothing is but defolation,
That I may never more behold the face
Of man, or mankind know me! Oh, blind Fortune,
Haft thou abus'd me thus!

Druf. Good Sir, be comforted;
It was your wifdom rul'd you.   Pray you go home;
Your day is yet to come, when this great fortune
Shall be but foil unto it.   [*Retreat.*

Pen. Fool, fool, coward! [*Exe. Penius and Drufius.*

Enter Suetonius, Demetrius, foldiers, drum and colours.

Suet. Draw in, draw in!—Well have you fought,
          and worthy

Rome's noble recompenfe.   Look to your wounds;
The ground is cold and hurtful.   The proud queen
Has got a fort, and there fhe and her daughters
Defy us once again: Tomorrow morning
We'll feek her out, and make her know our fortunes
Stop at no ftubborn walls.   Come, fons of Honour,
True Virtue's heirs, thus hatch'd with Britain blood,
Let's march to reft, and fet in gules like funs.
Beat a foft march, and each one eafe his neighbours!
                              [*Exeunt.*

ACT IV. SCENE I.

Enter Petillius, Junius, Decius, and Demetrius, singing.

Pet. SMOOTH was his cheek,
   Dec. And his chin it was fleek,
Jun. With, whoop, he has done wooing!
Dem. Junius was this captain's name,
   A lad for a lafs's viewing.
Pet. Full black his eye, and plump his thigh,
Dec. Made up for love's purfuing.
Dem. Smooth was his cheek,
Pet. And his chin it was fleek,
Jun. With, whoop, he has done wooing!

Pet. Oh, my vex'd thief, art thou come home again?
Are thy brains perfect?
Jun. Sound as bells.
Pet. Thy back-worm
Quiet, and caft his fting, boy?
Jun. Dead, Petillius,
Dead to all folly, and now my anger only——
   Pet. Why, that's well faid; hang Cupid and his
     quiver,
A drunken brawling boy! Thy honour'd faint
Be thy ten fhillings, Junius; there's the money,
And there's the ware; fquare dealing: This but fweats
   thee
Like a nefh nag[48], and makes thee look pin-buttock'd;

---

   [48] *Like a* nefh *nag.*] *Nefh,* i. e. *tender, delicate,* from the *A. S.* nefe,
mollis, delicatus.   *Sympfon.*
   So in Chaucer's Court of Love,
    ' Than flatiry befpake and faid iwis,
      ' Se fo fhe goth on patins faire and fete,
   ' It doth right well, what pretty man is this,
      ' That romith here? now truly drink ne mete
      ' Nede I not have, mine herte for joy doth bete
   ' Him to beholde, fo is he godely frefhe,
   ' It femeth for love his herte is tendre and *nefihe.*
                                  R.
                                  The

The other runs thee whining up and down
Like a pig in a ftorm, fills thy brains full of ballads,
And fhews thee like a long Lent, thy brave body
Turn'd to a tail of green fifh without butter.

   Dec. When thou lov'ft next, love a good cup of wine,
A miftrefs for a king! fhe leaps to kifs thee,
Her red and white's her own, fhe makes good blood,
Takes none away; what fhe heats fleep can help,
Without a groping furgeon.

   Jun. I am counfel'd;
And henceforth, when I dote again——

   Dem. Take heed;
Y'had almoft paid for't.

   Pet. Love no more great ladies;
Thou can'ft not ftep amifs then; there's no delight in
      'em:
All's in the whiftling of their fnatcht-up filks;
They're only made for handfome view, not handling;
Their bodies of fo weak and wafh a temper,
A rough-pac'd bed will fhake them all to pieces;
A tough hen pulls their teeth out, tires their fouls;
Plenæ rimarum funt, they're full of rennet,
And take the fkin off where they're tafted: Shun 'em;
They live in culiffes, like rotten cocks,
Stew'd to a tendernefs that holds no tack;
Give me a thing I may crufh.

   Jun. Thou fpeak'ft truly:
The wars fhall be my miftrefs now.

   Pet. Well chofen!
For fhe's a bouncing lafs; fhe'll kifs thee at night, boy,
And break thy pate i' th' morning.

   Jun. Yefterday
I found thofe favours infinite.

   Dem. Wench good enough,
But that fhe talks too loud.

   Pet. She talks to th' purpofe,
Which never woman did yet. She'll hold grappling,
And he that lays on beft is her beft fervant;
All other loves are mere catching of dottrels,
                       Stretching

Stretching of legs out only, and trim lazinefs.
Here comes the general.

Enter Suetonius, Curius, and Macer.

Suet. I'm glad I've found ye:
Are thofe come in yet that purfued bold Caratach?
  Pet. Not yet, Sir, for I think they mean to lodge him;
Take him I know they dare not, 'twill be dangerous.
  Suet. Then hafte, Petillius, hafte to Penius:
I fear the ftrong conceit of what difgrace
H' has pull'd upon himfelf, will be his ruin;
I fear his foldiers' fury too: Hafte prefently;
I would not lofe him for all Britain. Give him, Petillius——
  Pet. That that fhall choke him.   [*Afide.*
  Suet. All the noble counfel,
His fault forgiven too, his place, his honour——
  Pet. For me, I think, as handfome——   [*Afide.*
  Suet. All the comfort;
And tell the foldier, 'twas on our command
He drew not to the battle.
  Pet. I conceive, Sir,
And will do that fhall cure all.
  Suet. Bring him with you
Before the queen's fort, and his forces with him;
There you fhall find us following of our conqueft.
Make hafte!
  Pet. The beft I may.   [*Exit.*
  Suet. And, noble gentlemen,
Up to your companies! we'll prefently
Upon the queen's purfuit. There's nothing done
'Till fhe be feiz'd; without her, nothing won.
    [*Exeunt. Short flourifh.*

SCENE II.

Enter Caratach and Hengo.

  Car. How does my boy?

Hengo. I would do well; my heart's well;
I do not fear.

Car. My good boy!

Hengo. I know, uncle,
We muſt all die; my little brother died,
I ſaw him die, and he died ſmiling; ſure
There's no great pain in't, uncle. But pray tell me,
Whither muſt we go when we're dead?

Car. Strange queſtions!—
Why, to the bleſſed'ſt place, boy—Ever-ſweetneſs
And happineſs dwells there.

Hengo. Will you come to me?

Car. Yes, my ſweet boy.

Hengo. Mine aunt too, and my couſins?

Car. All, my good child.

Hengo. No Romans, uncle?

Car. No, boy.

Hengo. I ſhould be loath to meet them there.

Car. No ill men,
That live by violence, and ſtrong oppreſſion,
Come thither; 'tis for thoſe the gods love, good men.

Hengo. Why, then, I care not when I go, for ſurely
I am perſuaded they love me: I never
Blaſphem'd 'em uncle, nor tranſgreſs'd my parents[49];
I always ſaid my prayers.

Car. Thou ſhalt go then,
Indeed thou ſhalt.

Hengo. When they pleaſe.

Car. That's my good boy!
Art thou not weary, Hengo?

Hengo. Weary, uncle?
I've heard you ſay you've march'd all day in armour.

Car. I have, boy.

Hengo. Am not I your kinſman?

---

[49] *Tranſgreſs'd my parents.*] The ſenſe here is clear, though the
phraſe be unuſual: However we find it occur again in Women Pleas'd,
act iii. ſc. i. Belvidere ſays to her mother the Ducheſs,
  —— *You are too royal to me,*
  To me that have ſo fooliſhly tranſgreſs'd you. *Sympſon.*

Car.

Car. Yes.

Hengo. And am not I as fully allied unto you
In thofe brave things, as blood?

Car. Thou art too tender.

Hengo. To go upon my legs? they were made to
   bear me.
I can play twenty mile a-day; I fee no reafon,
But, to preferve my country and myfelf,
I fhould march forty.

Car. What wouldft thou be living
To wear a man's ftrength?

Hengo. Why, a Caratach,
A Roman-hater, a fcourge fent from Heaven
To whip thefe proud thieves from our kingdom.
   Hark,   [*Drum.*
Hark, uncle, hark! I hear a drum.

  Enter Judas and his people to the door.

Judas. Beat foftly,
Softly, I fay; they're here. Who dare charge?

 1 *Sold.* He
That dares be knock'd o' th' head: I'll not come
   near him.

Judas. Retire again, and watch then. How he
   ftares!
H' has eyes would kill a dragon. Mark the boy well;
If we could take or kill him—A pox on ye,
How fierce ye look! See, how he broods the boy?
The devil dwells in's fcabbard. Back, I fay!
Apace, apace! h' has found us. [*They retire.*

 Car. Do ye hunt us?

 Hengo. Uncle, good uncle, fee! the thin ftarv'd
   rafcal,
The eating Roman, fee where he thrids the thickets:
Kill him, dear uncle, kill him! one good blow
To knock his brains into his breech; ftrike's head off,
That I may pifs in's face.

 Car. Do ye make us foxes?
Here, hold my charging-ftaff, and keep the place, boy!
     Y 2   I am

I am at bay, and like a bull I'll bear me.
Stand, ſtand, ye rogues, ye ſquirrels!   [*Exit.*

  Hengo. Now he pays 'em;
Oh, that I had a man's ſtrength!

Enter Judas, &c.

  Judas. Here's the boy;
Mine own, I thank my fortune.
  Hengo. Uncle, uncle!
Famine[50] is fall'n upon me, uncle.
  Judas. Come, Sir,
Yield willingly, (your uncle's out of hearing)
I'll tickle your young tail elſe.
  Hengo. I defy thee,
Thou mock-made man of mat! Charge home,
      ſirrah!
Hang thee, baſe ſlave, thou ſhak'ſt.
  Judas. Upon my conſcience,
The boy will beat me! how it looks, how bravely,
How confident the worm is! a ſcab'd boy
To handle me thus! Yield, or I cut thy head off.
  Hengo. Thou dar'ſt not cut my finger; here 'tis,
      touch it.
  Judas. The boy ſpeaks ſword and buckler! Prithee
      yield, boy;
Come, here's an apple, yield.
  Hengo. By Heav'n, he fears me!
I'll give you ſharper language: When, ye coward,
When come ye up?
  Judas. If he ſhould beat me——
  Hengo. When, Sir?
I long to kill thee! Come, thou canſt not ſcape me;
I've twenty ways to charge thee, twenty deaths
Attend my bloody ſtaff.
  Judas. Sure 'tis the devil,
A dwarf devil in a doublet!
  Hengo. I have kill'd

---

    50 *Famine.*] Meaning Judas, whom he before calls, *the thin*
ſtarv'd raſcal, and afterwards, *Hunger.*

                           A captain,

A captain, firrah, a brave captain, and when I've done,
I've kick'd him thus. Look here; fee how I charge
This ftaff!

    Judas. Moft certain this boy will cut my throat
          yet.

Enter two Soldiers running.

    1 *Sold.* Flee, flee! he kills us.
    2 *Sold.* He comes, he comes!
    Judas. The devil take the hindmoft!
                      [*Exeunt Judas, &c.*
    Hengo. Run, run, ye rogues, ye precious rogues,
          ye rank rogues!
A comes, a comes, a comes, a comes! that's he, boys!
What a brave cry they make!

Enter Caratach, with a head.

    Car. How does my chicken?
    Hengo. 'Faith, uncle, grown a foldier, a great
          foldier;
For, by the virtue of your charging-ftaff,
And a ftrange fighting face I put upon't,
I've out-brav'd Hunger.
    Car. That's my boy, my fweet boy!
Here, here's a Roman's head for thee.
    Hengo. Good provifion!
Before I ftarve, my fweet-fac'd gentleman,
I'll try your favour.
    Car. A right complete foldier!
Come, chicken, let's go feek fome place of ftrength
(The country's full of fcouts) to reft a while in;
Thou wilt not elfe be able to endure
The journey to my country. Fruits and water
Muft be your food a while, boy.
    Hengo. Any thing;
I can eat mofs, nay, I can live on anger,
To vex thefe Romans. Let's be wary, uncle.
    Car. I warrant thee; come cheerfully.
    Hengo. And boldly!   [*Exeunt.*
        Y 3   SCENE

SCENE III.

Enter Penius, Drusius, and Regulus.

Reg. The soldier shall not grieve you.

Pen. Pray ye forsake me;
Look not upon me, as ye love your honours!
I am so cold a coward, my infection
Will choke your virtues like a damp else.

Drus. Dear captain!

Reg. Most honour'd Sir!

Pen. Most hated, most abhorr'd!
Say so, and then ye know me, nay, ye please me.
Oh, my dear credit, my dear credit!

Reg. Sure
His mind is dangerous.

Drus. The good gods cure it!

Pen. My honour got thro' fire, thro' stubborn
     breaches,
Thro' battles that have been as hard to win as Heaven,
Thro' Death himself, in all his horrid trims,
Is gone for ever, ever, ever, gentlemen!
And now I'm left to scornful tales and laughters,
To hootings at, pointing with fingers, ' That's he,
' That's the brave gentleman forsook the battle,
' The most wise Penius, the disputing coward.'
Oh, my good sword, break from my side, and kill me;
Cut out the coward from my heart!

Reg. You are none.

Pen. He lies that says so; by Heaven, he lies, lies basely,
Baser than I have done! Come, soldiers, seek me;
I've robb'd ye of your virtues! Justice seek me;
I've broke my fair obedience! last[50], Shame take me,
Take me, and swallow me, make ballads of me,
Shame, endless Shame! and pray do you forsake me!

Drus. What shall we do?

Pen. Good gentlemen, forsake me;

---

[50] *Obedience,* lost: *shame take me.*] This seems an evident corruption, which the alteration of one letter rectifies.

You were not wont to be commanded. Friends, pray
  do it,
And do not fear ; for as I am a coward
I will not hurt myself, (when that mind takes me,
I'll call to you, and afk your help) I dare not.
    [Throws himself upon the ground.

Enter Petillius.

 Pet. Good-morrow, gentlemen! Where's the tri-
  bune ?
Reg. There.
Druf. Whence come you, good Petillius ?
Pet. From the general.
Druf. With what, for Heaven's fake ?
Pet. With good counfel, Drufius,
And love, to comfort him.
 Druf. Good Regulus,
Step to the foldier and allay his anger ;
For he is wild as winter.   *[Exeunt Druf. and Reg.*
 Pet. Oh, are you there? have at you!—Sure he's
  dead,
It cannot be he dare out-live this fortune ;
He muft die, 'tis moft neceffary ; men expect it,
And thought of life in him goes beyond coward.
Forfake the field fo bafely ? Fy upon't !
So poorly to betray his worth, fo coldly
To cut all credit from the foldier ? Sure
If this man mean to live, (as I fhould think it
Beyond belief) he muft retire where never
The name of Rome, the voice of arms, or honour,
Was known or heard of yet. He's certain dead,
Or ftrongly means it ; he's no foldier elfe,
No Roman in him ; all h' has done but outfide,
Fought either drunk or defp'rate. Now he rifes.—
How does lord Penius ?
 Pen. As you fee.
 Pet. I'm glad on't ;
Continue fo ftill. The lord general,
The valiant general, great Suetonius——
     Y 4   *Pen.*

Pen. No more of me is fpoken; my name's perifh'd.

Pet. He that commanded fortune and the day,
By his own valour and difcretion,
(When, as fome fay, Penius refus'd to come,
But I believe 'em not) fent me to fee you.

Pen. Ye're welcome; and pray fee me, fee me well;
You fhall not fee me long.

Pet. I hope fo, Penius.—
The gods defend, Sir!

Pen. See me and underftand me: This is he
Left to fill up your triumph; he that bafely
Whiftled his honour off to th' wind, that coldly
Shrunk in his politick head, when Rome, like reapers,
Sweat blood and fpirit for a glorious harveft,
And bound it up, and brought it off; that fool,
That having gold and copper offer'd him,
Refus'd the wealth, and took the wafte; that foldier,
That being courted by loud Fame and Fortune,
Labour in one hand that propounds us gods,
And in the other Glory that creates us,
Yet durft doubt and be damn'd!

Pet. It was an error.

Pen. A foul one, and a black one.

Pet. Yet the blackeft
May be wafh'd white again.

Pen. Never.

Pet. Your leave, Sir;
And I befeech you note me, for I love you,
And bring along all comfort: Are we gods,
Allied to no infirmities? are our natures
More than mens' natures? When we flip a little
Out of the way of virtue, are we loft?
Is there no medicine call'd fweet mercy?

Pen. None, Petillius;
There is no mercy in mankind can reach me,
Nor is it fit it fhould; I've finn'd beyond it,

Pet. Forgivenefs meets with all faults.

Pen. 'Tis all faults,
All fins I can commit, to be forgiven;

'Tis

'Tis lofs of whole man in me, my difcretion,
To be fo ftupid, to arrive at pardon!

Pet. Oh, but the general——

Pen. He's a brave gentleman,
A valiant, and a loving; and I dare fay
He would, as far as Honour durft direct him,
Make even with my fault; but 'tis not honeft,
Nor in his power: Examples that may nourifh
Neglect and difobedience in whole bodies,
And totter the eftates and faiths of armies,
Muft not be play'd withal; nor out of pity
Make a general forget his duty;
Nor dare I hope more from him than is worthy.

Pet. What would you do?

Pen. Die.

Pet. So would fullen children,
Women that want their wills, flaves difobedient,
That fear the law. Die? Fy, great captain! you
A man to rule men, to have thoufand lives
Under your regiment, and let your paffion
Betray your reafon? I bring you all forgivenefs,
The noblest kind commends, your place, your honour——

Pen. Prithee no more; 'tis foolifh. Didft not thou
(By Heaven, thou didft; I over-heard thee, there,
There where thou ftand'ft now) deliver me for rafcal,
Poor, dead, cold coward, miferable, wretched,
If I out-liv'd this ruin?

Pet. I?

Pen. And thou didft it nobly,
Like a true man, a foldier; and I thank thee,
I thank thee, good Petillius, thus I thank thee!

Pet. Since you're fo juftly made up, let me tell you,
'Tis fit you die indeed.

Pen. Oh, how thou lov'ft me!

Pet. For fay he had forgiven you, fay the peoples'
whifpers
Were tame again, the time run out for wonder,
What muft your own command think, from whofe
fwords

You've

You've taken off the edges, from whofe valours
The due and recompenfe of arms; nay, made it doubtful
Whether they knew obedience? muft not thefe kill you?
Say they are won to pardon you, by mere miracle
Brought to forgive you, what old valiant foldier,
What man that loves to fight, and fight for Rome,
Will ever follow you more? Dare you know thefe
    ventures?
If fo, I bring you comfort; dare you take it?

Pen. No, no, Petillius, no.

Pet. If your mind ferve you,
You may live ftill; but how? yet pardon me:
You may out-wear all too; but when? and certain
There is a mercy for each fault, if tamely
A man will take't upon conditions.

  Pen. No, by no means: I'm only thinking now, Sir,
(For I'm refolv'd to go) of a moft bafe death,
Fitting the bafenefs of my fault. I'll hang.

  Pet. You fhall not; you're a gentleman I honour,
I would elfe flatter you, and force you live,
Which is far bafer. Hanging? 'tis a dog's death,
An end for flaves.

Pen. The fitter for my bafenefs.

Pet. Befides, the man that's hang'd preaches his end,
And fits a fign for all the world to gape at[51].

Pen. That's true; I'll take a fitter; poifon.

Pet. No,
'Tis equal ill; the death of rats and women,
Lovers, and lazy boys, that fear correction;
Die like a man.

Pen. Why, my fword then.

Pet. Ay, if your fword be fharp, Sir.
There's nothing under Heaven that's like your fword;
Your fword's a death indeed!

  Pen. It fhall be fharp, Sir.

---

[51] *And fits a fign.*] This reading is certainly againft all the notions
any one can have of a man's being hanged. *To fet a fign* bids faireft
for the true lection, though I have not dared to difturb the text.
           Sympfon.

              Pet.

Pet. Why, Mithridates was an arrant afs
To die by poifon [52], if all Bofphorus
Could lend him fwords: Your fword muft do the deed:
'Tis fhame to die choak'd, fame to die and bleed.

Pen. Thou haft confirm'd me; and, my good
          Petillius,
Tell me no more I may live.

Pet. 'Twas my commiffion;
But now I fee you in a nobler way,
A way to make all even.

Pen. Farewell, captain!
Be a good man, and fight well; be obedient;
Command thyfelf, and then thy men. Why fhakeft
          thou?

Pet. I do not, Sir.

Pen. I would thou hadft, Petillius!
I would find fomething to forfake the world with
Worthy the man that dies: A kind of earthquake
Thro' all ftern valours but mine own.

Pet. I feel now
A kind of trembling in me.

Pen. Keep it ftill;
As thou lov'ft virtue, keep it.

Pet. And, brave captain,
The great and honour'd Penius!——

Pen. That again!
Oh, how it heightens me! again, Petillius!

Pet. Moft excellent commander!——

Pen. Thofe were mine,
Mine, only mine!

Pet. They are ftill.

Pen. Then, to keep 'em
For ever falling more, have at ye! Heavens,

---

[52] *Mithridates was an arrant afs*
  To die by poifon, *if all Bofphorus*
  Could lend him fwords.] The affertion in this paffage is a manifeft
contradiction to the truth of hiftory. For Mithridates did not end
his days by poifon, but by the fword. Another inftance this of inattention in our Authors, or trufting too much to an *uninfallible* memory.   *Sympfon.*

Ye

Ye everlasting powers, I'm yours: The work is done,

         [Kills himself.

That neither fire, nor age, nor melting envy [53],

Shall ever conquer. Carry my last words

To the great gen'ral: Kiss his hands, and say,

My soul I give to Heav'n, my fault to justice,

Which I have done upon myself; my virtue,

If ever there was any in poor Penius,

Made more, and happier, light on him! (I faint)

And where there is a foe, I wish him fortune.

I die: Lie lightly on my ashes [54], gentle earth! *[Dies.*

 Pet. And on my sin! Farewell, great Penius!

The soldier is in fury; now I'm glad *[Noise within.*

'Tis done before he comes. This way for me,

The way of toil; for thee, the way of honour! *[Exit.*

   Enter Drusius and Regulus, with Soldiers.

 Sold. Kill him, kill him, kill him!

 Drus. What will ye do?

 Reg. Good soldiers, honest soldiers——

---

[53] Melting *envy.*] This epithet seems a little stiff and obscure. It was a custom of the Romans to deface the marble, and melt down the brazen statues of those who were become detestable to them; and to the melting of these brazen ones this epithet must refer. *Seward.*

We do not enter into Seward's explanation of this epithet. The Poets seem to mean to refer to Ovid's,

  ——*quod nec Jovis ira, nec* IGNIS,

 Nec poterit ferrum, nec edax abolere vetustas.

[54] *Lie lightly on my ashes, gentle earth*] In the beautiful Ode to the Memory of Col. George Villiers, drowned in the river Piava, in the county of Friuli, 1703, the Author, Mr. Prior, seems to have been indebted to this line for the thought in the following:

 ' Lay the dead hero graceful in a grave;

 ' (The only honour he can now receive)

 ' And fragrant mould upon his body throw;

 ' And plant the warrior laurel o'er his brow:

 ' *Light lie the earth*; and flourish green the bough.

So also Mr. Pope, in the Elegy to the Memory of an Unfortunate Lady:

 ' What tho' no sacred earth allow thee room,

 ' Nor hallow'd dirge be mutter'd o'er thy tomb,

 ' Yet shall thy grave with rising flow'rs be drest,

 ' And the green *turf lie lightly on thy breast.*'   R.

                 Sold.

Sold. Kill him, kill him, kill him!

Druf. Kill us firft; we command too.

Reg. Valiant foldiers,
Confider but whofe life ye feek.—Oh, Drufius,
Bid him be gone; he dies elfe.—Shall Rome fay,
Ye moft approved foldiers, her dear children
Devoured the fathers of the fights? fhall rage
And ftubborn fury guide thofe fwords to flaughter,
To flaughter of their own, to civil ruin?

   Druf. Oh, let 'em in; all's done, all's ended,
      Regulus;
Penius has found his laft eclipfe. Come, foldiers,
Come, and behold your miferies; come bravely,
Full of your mutinous and bloody angers,
And here beftow your darts. Oh, only Roman,
Oh, father of the wars!

   Reg. Why ftand ye ftupid?
Where be your killing furies? whofe fword now
Shall firft be fheath'd in Penius? Do ye weep?
Howl out, ye wretches, ye have caufe; howl ever!
Who fhall now lead ye fortunate? whofe valour
Preferve ye to the glory of your country?
Who fhall march out before ye, coy'd and courted
By all the miftreffes of war, care, counfel,
Quick-ey'd experience, and victory twin'd to him?
Who fhall beget ye deeds beyond inheritance
To fpeak your names, and keep your honours living,
When children fail, and Time, that takes all with him,
Build houfes for ye to oblivion?

   Druf. Oh, ye poor defp'rate fools, no more now
      foldiers,
Go home, and hang your arms up; let ruft rot 'em;
And humble your ftern valours to foft prayers!
For ye have funk the frame of all your virtues;
The fun that warm'd your bloods is fet for ever,—
I'll kifs thy honour'd cheek. Farewell, great Penius,
Thou thunder-bolt, farewell!—Take up the body:
Tomorrow mourning [55] to the camp convey it,

---

[55] *Tomorrow* morning.] The variation in the text is recommended in the edition of 1750.

There

There to receive due ceremonies. That eye
That blinds himself with weeping, gets moft glory.

[*Exeunt with a dead march.*

S C E N E IV.

Enter Suetonius, Junius, Decius, Demetrius, Curius, and
Soldiers: Bonduca, two Daughters, and Nennius above.
Drum and colours.

Suet. Bring up the catapults, and fhake the wall;
We will not be out-brav'd thus.

Nen. Shake the earth,
Ye cannot fhake our fouls. Bring up your rams,
And with their armed heads make the fort totter,
Ye do but rock us into death. [*Exit Nen.*

Jun. See, Sir,
See the Icenian queen in all her glory,
From the ftrong battlements proudly appearing,
As if fhe meant to give us lafhes!

Dec. Yield, queen.

Bond. I'm unacquainted with that language, Roman.

Suet. Yield, honour'd lady, and expect our mercy;
We love thy noblenefs. [*Exit Decius.*

Bond. I thank ye! ye fay well;
But mercy and love are fins in Rome and hell.

Suet. You cannot 'fcape our ftrength; you muft
yield, lady;
You muft adore and fear the power of Rome.

Bond. If Rome be earthly, why fhould any knee
With bending adoration worfhip her?
She's vicious; and, your partial felves confefs,
Afpires the height of all impiety;
Therefore 'tis fitter I fhould reverence
The thatched houfes where the Britons dwell
In carelefs mirth; where the blefs'd houfhold gods
See nought but chafte and fimple purity.
'Tis not high power that makes a place divine,
Nor that the men from gods derive their line;
But facred thoughts, in holy bofoms ftor'd,
Make people noble, and the place ador'd.

Suet.

Suet. Beat the wall deeper!

Bond. Beat it to the centre,

We will not sink one thought.

Suet. I'll make ye.

Bond. No.

2 *Daugh.* Oh, mother, these are fearful hours;
      speak gently

Enter Petillius, who whispers Suetonius.

To these fierce men, they will afford ye pity.

Bond. Pity? Thou fearful girl, 'tis for those
      wretches

That misery makes tame. Wouldst thou live less?

Wast not thou born a princess? Can my blood,

And thy brave father's spirit, suffer in thee

So base a separation from thyself,

As mercy from these tyrants? Thou lov'st lust sure,

And long'st to prostitute thy youth and beauty

To common slaves for bread. Say they had mercy,

The devil a relenting conscience,

The lives of kings rest in their diadems,

Which to their bodies lively souls do give,

And, ceasing to be kings, they cease to live.

Shew such another fear, and, by the Gods,

I'll fling thee to their fury.

Suet. He is dead then?

Pet. I think so certainly; yet all my means, Sir,

Even to the hazard of my life——

Suet. No more:

We must not seem to mourn here.

Enter Decius.

Dec. There's a breach made;

Is it your will we charge, Sir?

Suet. Once more, mercy,

Mercy to all that yield!

Bond. I scorn to answer;

Speak to him, girl, and hear thy sister.

1 *Daugh.* General,

Hear

Hare me, and mark me well, and look upon me,
Directly in my face, my woman's face,
Whose only beauty is the hate it bears ye;
See with thy narrowest eyes, thy sharpest wishes,
Into my soul, and see what there inhabits;
See if one fear, one shadow of a terror,
One paleness dare appear but from my anger,
To lay hold on your mercies. No, ye fools,
Poor fortune's fools, we were not born for triumphs,
To follow your gay sports, and fill your slaves
With hoots and acclamations.

Pet. Brave behaviour!

1 *Daugh.* The children of as great as Rome, as noble,
Our names before her, and our deeds her envy,
Must we gild o'er your conquest, make your state,
That is not fairly strong, but fortunate?
No, no, ye Romans, we have ways to scape ye,
To make ye poor again, indeed our prisoners,
And stick our triumphs full.

Pet. 'Sdeath, I shall love her.

1 *Daugh.* To torture ye with suffering, like our slaves;
To make ye curse our patience, wish the world
Were lost again, to win us only, and esteem
The end of all ambitions.

Bond. Do ye wonder?
We'll make our monuments in spite of fortune;
In spite of all your eagles' wings, we'll work
A pitch above ye; and from our height we'll stoop
As fearless of your bloody soars, and fortunate,
As if we prey'd on heartless doves.

Suet. Strange stiffness!
Decius, go charge the breach.   [*Exit Decius.*

Bond. Charge it home, Roman;
We shall deceive thee else. Where's Nennius?

Enter Nennius.

Nen. They've made a mighty breach.

Bond. Stick in thy body,
And make it good but half an hour.

                                             Nen.

Nen. I'll do it.

1 *Daugh.* And then be sure to die.

Nen. It shall go hard else.

Bond. Farewell, with all my heart! We shall meet
    yonder,
Where few of these must come.

Nen. Gods take thee, lady!   [*Exit Nennius.*

Bond. Bring up the swords, and poison.

    Enter one with swords and a great cup.

2 *Daugh.* Oh, my fortune!

Bond. How, how, ye whore?

2 *Daugh.* Good mother, nothing to offend you.

Bond. Here, wench.
Behold us, Romans!

Suet. Mercy yet.

Bond. No talking!
Puff! there goes all your pity. Come, short prayers,
And let's dispatch the business! You begin;
Shrink not, I'll see you do't.

2 *Daugh.* Oh, gentle mother!
Oh, Romans! oh, my heart! I dare not.

Suet. Woman, woman,
Unnatural woman!

2 *Daugh.* Oh, persuade her, Romans!
Alas, I'm young, and would live. Noble mother,
Can ye kill that ye gave life? Are my years
Fit for destruction?

Suet. Yield, and be a queen still,
A mother, and a friend.

Bond. Ye talk!—Come, hold it,
And put it home.

1 *Daugh.* Fy, sister, fy!
What would you live to be?

Bond. A whore still?

2 *Daugh.* Mercy!

Suet. Hear her, thou wretched woman!

2 *Daugh.* Mercy, mother!
Oh, whither will you send me? I was once

Your darling, your delight.

 Bond. Oh, gods! fear in my family?
Do it, and nobly.

 2 Daugh. Oh, do not frown then.

 1 Daugh. Do it, worthy fifter;
'Tis nothing; 'tis a pleafure: We'll go with you.

 2 Daugh. Oh, if I knew but whither!

 1 Daugh. To the bleffed;
Where we fhall meet our father——

 Suet. Woman!

 Bond. Talk not.

 1 Daugh. Where nothing but true joy is————

 Bond. That's a good wench!
Mine own fweet girl! put it clofe to thee.

 2 Daugh. Oh,
Comfort me ftill, for Heav'n's fake.

 1 Daugh. Where eternal
Our youths are, and our beauties; where no wars
  come,
Nor luftful flaves to ravifh us.

 2 Daugh. That fteels me;
A long farewell to this world!   [*Dies.*

 Bond. Good; I'll help thee.

 1 Daugh. The next is mine. Shew me a Roman
  lady
In all your ftories, dare do this for her honour;
They are cowards, eat coals like compell'd cats:
Your great faint, Lucrece,
Died not for honour; Tarquin tupt her well,
And, mad fhe could not hold him, bled.

 Pet. By Heaven,
I am in love! I'd give an hundred pound now
But to lie with this woman's behaviour. Oh, the devil!

 1 Daugh. Ye fhall fee me example: All your Rome,
If I were proud and lov'd ambition,
If I were luftful, all your ways of pleafure,
If I were greedy, all the wealth ye conquer————

 Bond. Make hafte.

 1 Daugh. I will.—Could not entice to live,

          But

But two short hours, this frailty. Would ye learn
How to die bravely, Romans, to fling off
This case of flesh, lose all your cares for ever?
Live as we have done, well, and fear the gods;
Hunt honour, and not nations, with your swords;
Keep your minds humble, your devotions high;
So shall ye learn the noblest part, to die.   [*Dies.*

 Bond. I come, wench.—To ye all, Fate's hangmen, you
That ease the aged destinies, and cut
The threads of kingdoms as they draw 'em! here,
Here is a draught would ask no less than Cæsar
To pledge it for the glory's sake!

 Cur. Great lady!
 Suet. Make up your own conditions.
 Bond. So we will.
 Suet. Stay!
 Dem. Stay!
 Suet. Be any thing.
 Bond. A faint, Suetonius,
When thou shalt fear, and die like a slave. Ye fools,
Ye should have tied up death first, when ye conquer'd;
Ye sweat for us in vain else: See him here,
He's ours still, and our friend; laughs at your pities;
And we command him with as easy reins
As do our enemies.—I feel the poison.—
Poor vanquish'd Romans, with what matchless tortures
Could I now rack ye! But I pity ye,
Desiring to die quiet: Nay, so much
I hate to prosecute my victory,
That I will give ye counsel ere I die:
If you will keep your laws and empire whole,
Place in your Roman flesh a Briton soul.   [*Dies.*

Enter Decius.

 Suet. Desperate and strange!
 Dec. 'Tis won, Sir, and the Britons
All put to th' sword.
 Suet. Give her fair funeral;
She was truly noble, and a queen.

       Z 2   *Pet.*

Pet. Pox take it,
A love-mange grown upon me? What a spirit!
Jun. I'm glad of this! I've found you.
Pet. In my belly,
Oh, how it tumbles!
Jun. Ye good gods, I thank ye!   [*Exeunt.*

ACT V. SCENE I.

Caratach upon a rock, and Hengo by him sleeping.

Car. THUS we afflicted Britons climb for safeties,
     And to avoid our dangers, seek destructions;
Thus we awake to sorrows. Oh, thou woman,
Thou agent for adversities, what curses
This day belong to thy improvidence!
To Britaine, by thy means, what sad millions
Of widows' weeping eyes! The strong man's valour
Thou hast betray'd to fury, the child's fortune
To fear, and want of friends; whose pieties
Might wipe his mournings off, and build his sorrows
A house of rest by his bless'd ancestors:
The virgins thou hast robb'd of all their wishes,
Blasted their blowing hopes, turned their songs,
Their mirthful marriage-songs, to funerals;
The land th' hast left a wildernefs of wretches.—
The boy begins to stir; thy safety made,
'Would my soul were in Heav'n!
Hengo. Oh, noble uncle,
Look out; I dream'd we were betray'd.
Car. No harm, boy;   [*A soft dead march within.*
'Tis but thy emptiness that breeds these fancies:
Thou shalt have meat anon.
Hengo. A little, uncle,
And I shall hold out bravely.—What are those,
(Look, uncle, look!) those multitudes that march there?
They come upon us stealing by.
                                        Car.

Car. I fee 'em ;
And prithee be not fearful.

Hengo. Now you hate me ;
'Would I were dead!

Car. Thou know'ft I love thee dearly.

Hengo. Did I e'er fhrink yet, uncle ? Were I a man
now,
I fhould be angry with you.

*Enter Drufius, Regulus, and Soldiers, with Penius's
bearfe, drums and colours.*

Car. My fweet chicken!—
See, they have reach'd us ; and, as it feems, they bear
Some foldier's body, by their folemn geftures,
And fad folemnities ; it well appears too
To be of eminence.—Moft worthy foldiers,
Let me entreat your knowledge to inform me
What noble body that is which you bear
With fuch a fad and ceremonious grief,
As if ye meant to wooe the world and Nature
To be in love with death ? Moft honourable
Excellent Romans, by your ancient valours,
As ye love fame, refolve me !

Sold. 'Tis the body
Of the great captain Penius, by himfelf
Made cold and fpiritlefs.

Car. Oh, ftay, ye Romans,
By the religion which ye owe thofe gods
That lead ye on to victories ! by thofe glories
Which made even pride a virtue in ye !

Druf. Stay.
What's thy will, Caratach ?

Car. Set down the body,
The body of the nobleft of all Romans ;
As ye expect an offering at your graves
From your friends' forrows, fet it down awhile,
That with your griefs an enemy may mingle,
(A noble enemy, that loves a foldier)
And lend a tear to Virtue ! Ev'n your foes,

Your wild foes, as you call'd us, are yet ftor'd
With fair affections, our hearts frefh, our fpirits,
Tho' fometime ftubborn, yet, when Virtue dies,
Soft and relenting as a virgin's prayers :
Oh, fet it down !

Druf. Set down the body, foldiers.

Car. Thou hallow'd relick, thou rich diamond
Cut with thine own duft ; thou for whofe wide fame
The world appears too narrow, man's all thoughts,
Had they all tongues, too filent ; thus I bow
To thy moft honour'd afhes ! Tho' an enemy,
Yet friend to all thy worths, fleep peaceably ;
Happinefs crown thy foul, and in thy earth
Some laurel fix his feat, there grow and flourifh,
And make thy grave an everlafting triumph !
Farewell all glorious wars, now thou art gone,
And honeft arms adieu ! All noble battles,
Maintain'd in thirft of honour, not of blood,
Farewell for ever !

Hengo. Was this Roman, uncle,
So good a man ?

Car. Thou never knew'ft thy father.

Hengo. He died 'fore I was born.

Car. This worthy Roman
Was fuch another piece of endlefs honour,
Such a brave foul dwelt in him ; their proportions
And faces were not much unlike, boy. Excellent nature !
See how it works into his eyes ! mine own boy !

Hengo. The multitudes of thefe men, and their
    fortunes,
Cou'd never make me fear yet ; one man's goodnefs—

Car. Oh, now thou pleafeft me ; weep ftill, my child,
As if thou faw'ft me dead ! with fuch a flux
Or flood of forrow, ftill thou pleafeft me.
And, worthy foldiers, pray receive thefe pledges,
Thefe hatchments of our griefs, and grace us fo much
To place 'em on his hearfe. Now, if ye pleafe,
Bear off the noble burden ; raife his pile
High as Olympus, making Heav'n to wonder

         To

To see a star upon earth out-shining theirs:
And ever-loved, ever-living be
Thy honour'd and most sacred memory!

Druf. Thou haft done honeftly, good Caratach;
And when thou dieft, a thoufand virtuous Romans
Shall fing thy foul to Heaven. Now march on, foldiers.

[*Exeunt. A dead march.*

Car. Now dry thine eyes, my boy.

Hengo. Are they all gone?
I could have wept this hour yet.

Car. Come, take cheer;
And raife thy fpirit, child; if but this day
Thou canft bear out thy faintnefs, the night coming
I'll fafhion our efcape.

Hengo. Pray fear not me;
Indeed I'm very hearty.

Car. Be fo ftill;
His mifchiefs leffen, that controls his ill.   [*Exeunt.*

S C E N E   II.

Enter Petillius.

Pet. What do I ail, i' th' name of Heav'n? I did but
        fee her,
And fee her die; fhe ftinks by this time ftrongly,
Abominably ftinks.   She was a woman,
A thing I never car'd for; but to die fo,
So confidently, bravely, ftrongly—Oh, the devil,
I have the bots! by Heaven, fhe fcorn'd us ftrangely,
All we could do, or durft do; threaten'd us
With fuch a noble anger, and fo govern'd
With fuch a fiery fpirit—The plain bots [56]!
A pox upon the bots, the love-bots! Hang me,
Hang me ev'n out o' th' way, directly hang me!
Oh, penny pipers, and moft painful penners
Of bountiful new ballads, what a fubject,
What a fweet fubject for your filver founds,

---

[56] *Bots.*] See note 50 on the Humourous Lieutenant.

Is

Is crept upon ye [57] !

Enter Junius.

Jun. Here is he; have at him!   [*Sings.*

  She set the sword unto her breast,
    Great pity it was to see,
  That three drops of her life-warm blood,
    Run trickling down her knee.

Art thou there, bonny boy? And i'faith how dost thou?

Pet. Well, gramercy; how dost thou? H'as found me,
Scented me out; the shame the devil ow'd me,
H'as kept his day with. And what news, Junius?

Jun. It was an old tale ten thousand times told,
  Of a young lady was turn'd into mould,
  Her life it was lovely, her death it was bold.

Pet. A cruel rogue! now he has drawn pursuit on me [58],
He hunts me like a devil. No more singing!
Th'hast got a cold: Come, let's go drink some sack,
    boy.

Jun. Ha, ha, ha, ha, ha, ha!

Pet. Why dost thou laugh?
What mare's nest hast thou found?

Jun. Ha, ha, ha!
I cannot laugh alone: Decius! Demetrius!
Curius! oh, my sides! ha, ha, ha, ha!
The strangest jest!

Pet. Prithee no more.

Jun. The admirablest fooling!

Pet. 'Thou art the prettiest fellow!

Jun. Sirs!

Pet. Why, Junius,
Prithee away, sweet Junius!

Jun. Let me sing then.

---

[57] *Crept upon ye.*] Sympson calls this nonsense, and reads, *crept upon* ME; for, says he, ' Love was not crept upon *them*, but *himself*.' Petillius means, ' What a sweet subject is fallen in *your* way.'

[58] *H'as drawn* pursue IT *on me.*] What strange stuff is this? By a small change of letters and a comma, I hope I have restor'd this place to its ancient purity.   *Seward.*
First folio says, *now h'has drawn* pursue *on me.*

                                      Pet.

Pet. Whoa, here's a ftir now! Sing a fong o' fixpence!
By Heaven, if—prithee—pox on't, Junius!

Jun. I muft either fing or laugh.

Pet. And what's your reafon?

Jun. What's that to you?

Pet. And I muft whiftle.

Jun. Do fo.
Oh, I hear 'em coming.

Pet. I've a little bufinefs.

Jun. Thou fhalt not go, believe it: What! a
      gentleman
Of thy fweet converfation?

Pet. Captain Junius,
Sweet captain, let me go with all celerity!
Things are not always one; and do not queftion,
Nor jeer, nor gibe: None of your doleful ditties,
Nor your fweet converfation; you will find then
I may be anger'd.

Jun. By no means, Petillius;
Anger a man that never knew paffion?
'Tis moft impoffible: A noble captain,
A wife and generous gentleman?

Pet. Tom Puppy,
Leave this way to abufe me: I have found you,
But, for your mother's fake, I will forgive you.
Your fubtile underftanding may difcover,
As you think, fome trim toy to make you merry,
Some ftraw to tickle you; but do not truft to't;
You're a young man, and may do well; be fober,
Carry yourfelf difcreetly.

    Enter Decius, Demetrius, and Curius.

Jun. Yes, forfooth.

Dem. How does the brave Petillius?

Jun. Monftrous merry.
We two were talking what a kind of thing
I was when I was in love; what a ftrange monfter
For little boys and girls to wonder at;
How like a fool I look'd!

                    Dec.

Dec. So they do all,
Like great dull flavering fools.

    Jun. Petillius faw too.

    Pet. No more of this; 'tis fcurvy; peace!

    Jun. How naftily,
Indeed how beaftly, all I did became me!
How I forgot to blow my nofe! There he ftands,
An honeft and a wife man; if himfelf
(I dare avouch it boldly, for I know it)
Should find himfelf in love——

    Pet. I'm angry.

    Jun. Surely
His wife felf would hang his beaftly felf;
His underftanding felf fo mawl his afs felf——

    Dec. He's bound to do it; for he knows the follies,
The poverties, and bafenefs, that belongs to't;
H'has read upon the reformations long.

    Pet. He has fo.

    Jun. 'Tis true, and he muft do't: Nor is it fit indeed
Any fuch coward——

    Pet. You'll leave prating?

    Jun. Should dare
Come near the regiments, efpecially
Thofe curious puppies (for believe there are fuch)
That only love behaviours: Thofe are dog-whelps,
Dwindle away becaufe a woman dies well;
Commit with paffions only; fornicate
With the free fpirit merely. You, Petillius,
For you have long obferv'd the world——

    Pet. Doft thou hear?
I'll beat thee damnably within thefe three hours!
Go pray; may be I'll kill thee. Farewell, Jack-daws!

    Dec. What a ftrange thing he's grown! [*Exit Pet.*

    Jun. I'm glad he is fo;
And ftranger he fhall be before I leave him.

    Cur. Is't poffible her mere death——

    Jun. I obferv'd him,
And found him taken, infinitely taken,
With her bravery; I have follow'd him,

And

And seen him kiss his sword since, court his scabbard,
Call *dying* dainty dear, her *brave mind* mistress;
Casting a thousand ways to give those forms,
That he might lie with 'em, and get old armours.
He had got me o'th' hip once; it shall go hard, friends,
But he shall find his own coin.

Enter Macer.

Dec. How now, Macer?
Is Judas yet come in?

Enter Judas.

Macer. Yes, and has lost
Most of his men too. Here he is.
Cur. What news?
Jun. I've lodg'd him; rouse him, he that dares!
Dem. Where, Judas?
Judas. On a steep rock i'th' woods, the boy too
    with him;
And there he swears he'll keep his Christmas, gentlemen,
But he will come away with full conditions,
Bravely, and like a Briton. He paid part of us;
Yet I think we fought bravely: For mine own part,
I was four several times at half-sword with him,
Twice stood his partizan; but the plain truth is,
He's a mere devil, and no man. I'th' end, he swing'd us,
And swing'd us soundly too: He fights by witchcraft;
Yet for all that I saw him lodg'd.
  Jun. Take more men,
And scout him round. Macer, march you along.
What victuals has he?
  Judas. Not a piece of biscuit,
Not so much as will stop a tooth, nor water
More than they make themselves: They lie
Just like a brace of bear-whelps, close, and crafty,
Sucking their fingers for their food.
  Dec. Cut off then
All hope of that way; take sufficient forces.
  Jun. But use no foul play, on your lives! that man
That does him mischief by deceit, I'll kill him.
  Macer. He shall have fair play; he deserves it.
                         Judas.

Judas. Hark ye!
What fhould I do there then? You are brave captains,
Moft valiant men: Go up yourfelves; ufe virtue;
See what will come on't; pray the gentleman
To come down, and be taken. Ye all know him,
I think ye've felt him too: There ye fhall find him,
His fword by's fide, plums of a pound weight by him,
Will make your chops ache: You'll find it a more labour
To win him living, than climbing of a crow's neft.

Dec. Away, and compafs him; we fhall come up
I'm fure within thefe two hours. Watch him clofe.

Macer. He fhall flee thro' the air, if he efcape us.

Jun. What's this loud lamentation? [*Sad noife within.*

Macer. The dead body
Of the great Penius is new come to th' camp, Sir.

Dem. Dead?

Macer. By himfelf, they fay.

Jun. I fear'd that fortune.

Cur. Peace guide him up to Heaven!

Jun. Away, good Macer. [*Exe. Macer and Judas.*

Enter *Suetonius, Drufius, Regulus,* and *Petillius.*

Suet. If thou be'ft guilty,
Some fullen plague, thou hat'ft moft, light upon thee!
The regiment return on Junius;
He well deferves it.

Pet. So!

Suet. Draw out three companies,
(Yours, Decius, Junius, and thou, Petillius)
And make up inftantly to Caratach;
He's in the wood before ye: We fhall follow,
After due ceremony done to th' dead,
The noble dead. Come, let's go burn the body.
[*Exeunt all but Petillius.*

Pet. The regiment giv'n from me? difgrac'd openly?
In love too with a trifle to abufe me?
A merry world, a fine world! ferv'd feven years
To be an afs o' both fides? fweet Petillius,
You've brought your hogs to a fine market! You are
wife, Sir,

Your

Your honourable brain-pan full of crotchets,
An underſtanding gentleman; your projects
Caſt with aſſurance ever! Wouldſt not thou now
Be bang'd about the pate, Petillius?
Anſwer to that, ſweet ſoldier! ſurely, ſurely,
I think you would; pull'd by the noſe, kick'd?
       Hang thee,
Thou art the arrant'ſt raſcal! Truſt thy wiſdom
With any thing of weight? the wind with feathers!
Out, you blind puppy! you command? you govern?
Dig for a groat a-day, or ſerve a ſwine-herd,
Too noble for thy nature too!—I muſt up;
But what I ſhall do there, let time diſcover.   [Exit.

SCENE III.

Enter Macer and Judas, with meat and a bottle.

Macer. Hang it o'th' ſide o'th' rock, as tho' the Britons
Stole hither to relieve him: Who firſt ventures
To fetch it off, is ours. I cannot ſee him.

Judas. He lies cloſe in a hole above, I know it,
Gnawing upon his anger. Ha! no; 'tis not he.

Macer. 'Tis but the ſhaking of the boughs.

Judas. Pox ſhake 'em!
I'm ſure they ſhake me ſoundly.—There!

Macer. 'Tis nothing.

Judas. Make no noiſe; if he ſtir, a deadly tempeſt
Of huge ſtones falls upon's. 'Tis done! away, cloſe!
                             [Exeunt.

Enter Caratach.

Car. Sleep ſtill, ſleep ſweetly, child; 'tis all thou
     feed'ſt on!
No gentle Briton near, no valiant charity,
To bring thee food? Poor knave, thou'rt ſick, ex-
     treme ſick,
Almoſt grown wild for meat; and yet thy goodneſs
Will not confeſs, nor ſhew it. All the woods
Are double lin'd with ſoldiers; no way left us
To make a noble 'ſcape. I'll ſit down by thee,
                             And,

And, when thou wak'ſt, either get meat to ſave thee,
Or loſe my life i' th' purchaſe; good Gods comfort thee!

  Enter Junius, Decius, Petillius, and Guide.
 Guide. You are not far off now, Sir.
 Jun. Draw the companies
The cloſeſt way thro' the woods; we'll keep on this
   way.
 Guide. I will, Sir: Half a furlong more you'll come
Within the ſight o' th' rock. Keep on the left ſide;
You'll be diſcover'd elſe: I'll lodge your companies
In the wild vines beyond ye.
 Dec. Do you mark him?
 Jun. Yes, and am ſorry for him.
 Pet. Junius,
Pray let me ſpeak two words with you.
 Jun. Walk afore;
I'll overtake you ſtraight.
 Dec. I will.   [*Exit.*
 Jun. Now, captain?
 Pet. You have oft told me, you have lov'd me, Junius.
 Jun. Moſt ſure I told you truth then.
 Pet. And that love
Should not deny me any honeſt thing.
 Jun. It ſhall not.
 Pet. Dare you ſwear it?
I have forgot all paſſages between us
That have been ill, forgiven too; forget you [59].
 Jun. What would this man have?—By the Gods,
   I do, Sir,
So it be fit to grant you.
 Pet. 'Tis moſt honeſt.
 Jun. Why, then I'll do it.
 Pet. Kill me.
 Jun. How!
 Pet. Pray kill me.
 Jun. Kill you?
 Pet. Ay, kill me quickly, ſuddenly;
Now kill me.

---

[59] Forgot *you.*] Amended in 1750.

             Jun.

Jun. On what reason? You amaze me!

Pet. If you do love me, kill me; afk me not why:
I would be kill'd, and by you.

Jun. Mercy on me!
What ails this man? Petillius!

Pet. Pray you difpatch me;
You are not fafe whilft I live: I am dangerous,
Troubled extremely, ev'n to mifchief, Junius,
An enemy to all good men. Fear not, 'tis juftice;
I fhall kill you elfe.

Jun. Tell me but the caufe,
And I will do it.

Pet. I'm difgrac'd, my fervice
Slighted and unrewarded by the general,
My hopes left wild and naked; befides thefe,
I'm grown ridiculous, an afs, a folly,
I dare not truft myfelf with: Prithee, kill me!

Jun. All thefe may be redeem'd as eafily
As you would heal your finger.

Pet. Nay——

Jun. Stay, I'll do it;
You fhall not need your anger. But firft, Petillius,
You fhall unarm yourfelf; I dare not truft
A man fo bent to mifchief.

Pet. There's my fword,
And do it handfomely.

Jun. Yes, I will kill you,
Believe that certain; but firft I'll lay before you
The moft extreme fool you have play'd in this,
The honour purpos'd for you, the great honour
The general intended you.

Pet. How?

Jun. And then I'll kill you,
Becaufe you fhall die miferable. Know, Sir,
The regiment was giv'n me, but 'till time
Call'd you to do fome worthy deed, might ftop
The peoples' ill thoughts of you for lord Penius,
I mean his death. How foon this time's come to you,
And hafted by Suetonius! Go, fays he,
Junius and Decius, and go thou, Petillius,

(Diftinctly,

(Diftinctly, *thou*, *Petillius*) and draw up,
To take ftout Caratach; there's the deed purpos'd,
A deed to take off all faults, of all natures:
And *thou*, *Petillius*, mark it! there's the honour;
And that done, all made even.

    Pet. Stay!

    Jun. No, I'll kill you.
He knew thee abfolute, and full in foldier,
Daring beyond all dangers, found thee out
According to the boldnefs of thy fpirit,
A fubject, fuch a fubject——

    Pet. Hark you, Junius!
I will live now.

    Jun. By no means.—Woo'd thy worth,
Held thee by the chin up, as thou funk'ft, and fhew'd
      thee
How Honour held her arms out. Come, make ready,
Since you will die an afs.

    Pet. Thou wilt not kill me?

    Jun. By Heaven, but I will, Sir. I'll have no man
      dangerous
Live to deftroy me afterward. Befides, you have gotten
Honour enough; let young men rife now. Nay,
I do perceive too by the general, (which is
One main caufe you fhall die, howe'er he carry it)
Such a ftrong doting on you, that I fear
You fhall command in chief; how are we paid then?
Come, if you'll pray, difpatch it.

    Pet. Is there no way?

    Jun. Not any way to live.

    Pet. I will do any thing,
Redeem myfelf at any price: Good Junius,
Let me but die upon the rock, but offer
My life up like a foldier!

    Jun. You will feek then
To out-do every man.

    Pet. Believe it, Junius,
You fhall go ftroke by ftroke with me.

    Jun. You'll leave off too,
As you are noble, and a foldier,

For

For ever thefe mad fancies.

Pet. Dare you truſt me?
By all that's good and honeſt——

Jun. There's your ſword then;
And now, come on a new man: Virtue guide thee! [*Exe.*

Enter Caratach and Hengo, on the rock.

Car. Courage, my boy! I have found meat: Look,
    Hengo,
Look where ſome bleſſed Briton, to preſerve thee,
Has hung a little food and drink: Cheer up, boy;
Do not forſake me now!

Hengo. Oh, uncle, uncle,
I feel I cannot ſtay long; yet I'll fetch it,
To keep your noble life. Uncle, I'm heart-whole,
And would live.

Car. Thou ſhalt, long I hope.

Hengo. But my head, uncle!
Methinks the rock goes round.

Enter Macer and Judas.

Macer. Mark 'em well, Judas.

Judas. Peace, as you love your life!

Hengo. Do not you hear
The noiſe of bells?

Car. Of bells, boy? 'Tis thy fancy;
Alas, thy body's full of wind.

Hengo. Methinks, Sir,
They ring a ſtrange ſad knell, a preparation
To ſome near funeral of ſtate: Nay, weep not,
Mine own ſweet uncle! you will kill me ſooner.

Car. Oh, my poor chicken!

Hengo. Fy, faint-hearted uncle!
Come, tie me in your belt, and let me down.

Car. I'll go myſelf, boy.

Hengo. No, as you love me, uncle!
I will not eat it, if I do not fetch it;
The danger only I deſire; pray tie me.

Car. I will, and all my care hang o'er thee! Come, child,
My valiant child!

Hengo. Let me down apace, uncle,

And you fhall fee how like a daw I'll whip it
From all their policies; for 'tis moft certain
A Roman train: And you muft hold me fure too,
You'll fpoil all elfe. When I have brought it, uncle,
We'll be as merry——

 Car. Go, i' th' name of Heav'n, boy!

 Hengo. Quick, quick, uncle! I have it.—Oh!

 Car. What ail'ft thou?   [*Judas fhoots Hengo.*

 Hengo. Oh, my beft uncle, I am flain!

 Car. I fee you,   [*Car. kills Judas with a ftone.*
And Heav'n direct my hand!—Deftruction
Go with thy coward foul!—How doft thou, boy?——
Oh, villain, pocky villain!

 Hengo. Oh, uncle, uncle,
Oh, how it pricks me (am I preferv'd for this?)
Extremely pricks me!

 Car. Coward, rafcal coward!
Dogs eat thy flefh!

 Hengo. Oh, I bleed hard; I faint too; out upon't,
How fick I am!—The lean rogue, uncle!

 Car. Look, boy;
I've laid him fure enough.

 Hengo. Have you knock'd his brains out?

 Car. I warrant thee for ftirring more: Cheer up, child.

 Hengo. Hold my fides hard; ftop, ftop; oh, wretched
   fortune,
Muft we part thus? Still I grow ficker, uncle.

 Car. Heaven look upon this noble child!

 Hengo. I once hop'd
I fhould have liv'd to have met thefe bloody Romans
At my fword's point, to have reveng'd my father,
To have beaten 'em, Oh, hold me hard! But, uncle—

 Car. Thou fhalt live ftill I hope, boy. Shall I draw it?

 Hengo. You draw away my foul then; I would live
A little longer, (fpare me, Heavens!) but only
To thank you for your tender love! Good uncle,
Good noble uncle, weep not!

 Car. Oh, my chicken,
My dear boy, what fhall I lofe?

 Hengo. Why, a child,

That

That muſt have died however; had this 'ſcap'd me,
Fever or famine——I was born to die, Sir.

Car. But thus unblown, my boy?

Hengo. I go the ſtraighter
My journey to the gods. Sure I ſhall know you
When you come, uncle?

Car. Yes, boy.

Hengo. And I hope
We ſhall enjoy together that great bleſſedneſs
You told me of.

Car. Moſt certain, child.

Hengo. I grow cold;
Mine eyes are going.

Car. Lift 'em up!

Hengo. Pray for me;
And, noble uncle, when my bones are aſhes,
Think of your little nephew! Mercy!

Car. Mercy!
You bleſſed angels, take him!

Hengo. Kiſs me! ſo.
Farewell, farewell!   [*Dies.*

Car. Farewell the hopes of Britain!
Thou royal graft, farewell for ever!—Time and Death,
Ye've done your worſt. Fortune, now ſee, now proudly
Pluck off thy veil, and view thy triumph: Look,
Look what th'haſt brought this land to. Oh, fair flower,
How lovely yet thy ruins ſhew, how ſweetly
Ev'n death embraces thee! The peace of Heaven,
The fellowſhip of all great ſouls, be with thee!

Enter Petillius and Junius on the rock.

Ha! Dare ye, Romans? Ye ſhall win me bravely.
Thou'rt mine!   [*Fight.*

Jun. Not yet, Sir.

Car. Breathe ye, ye poor Romans,
And come up all, with all your antient valours;
Like a rough wind I'll ſhake your ſouls, and ſend 'em—

Enter Suetonius, and all the Roman captains.

Suet. Yield thee, bold Caratach! By all the gods,
As I am ſoldier, as I envy thee,

I'll

I'll ufe thee like thyfelf, the valiant Briton.

Pet. Brave foldier, yield, thou ftock of arms and
        honour,
Thou filler of the world with fame and glory!

Jun. Moft worthy man, we'll wooe thee, be thy
        prifoners.

Suet. Excellent Briton, do me but that honour,
That more to me than conquefts, that true happinefs,
To be my friend!

Car. Oh, Romans, fee what here is!
Had this boy liv'd——

Suet. For Fame's fake, for thy fword's fake,
As thou defir'ft to build thy virtues greater!
By all that's excellent in man, and honeft——

Car. I do believe. Ye've had me a brave foe;
Make me a noble friend, and from your goodnefs,
Give this boy honourable earth to lie in!

Suet. He fhall have fitting funeral.

Car. I yield then;
Not to your blows, but your brave courtefies.

Pet. Thus we conduct then to the arms of peace
The wonder of the world!

Suet. Thus I embrace thee;   [*Flourifh.*
And let it be no flatt'ry that I tell thee,
Thou art the only foldier!

Car. How to thank ye,
I muft hereafter find upon your ufage,
I am for Rome?

Suet. You muft.

Car. Then Rome fhall know
The man that makes her fpring of glory grow.

Suet. Petillius, you have fhewn much worth this day,
Redeem'd much error; you have my love again;
Preferve it. Junius, with you I make him
Equal in the regiment.

Jun. The elder and the nobler;
I will give place, Sir.

Suet. You fhew a friend's foul.
March on, and thro' the camp, in every tongue,
The virtues of great Caratach be fung!   [*Exeunt.*

Ralph. *Speak what thou art, and how thou hast been us'd,*
    That I may give him condign punishment.
I.Knight *I am a Knight* ———   *Act III*.

THE KNIGHT OF THE

BURNING PESTLE.

―――――*Quod si*
Judicium subtile, videndis artibus illud
Ad libros & ad hæc Musarum dona vocares:
Bœotum in crasso jurares aëre natum.

Horat. in Epist. ad Oct. Aug.

―――――――――――――

This Play was first printed in quarto, in the year 1613. *The title-page,*
edit. 1635, *ascribes it to both Authors: The preface and the prologue,*
however, attribute it to one only. Langbaine says, it was in vogue
some years since, being revived at the King's House, and a new pro-
logue, instead of the old one in prose, spoken by Mrs. Ellen Guin.
He likewise conjectures, that the idea of bringing the Citizen and
his Wife upon the stage was in imitation of Ben Jonson's Staple of
News. We do not know of any revival of it since the time Lang-
baine mentions above.

TO THE READERS OF THIS COMEDY.

GENTLEMEN, the world is fo nice in thefe our times, that for apparel there is no fafhion; for mufick (which is a rare art, though now flighted) no inftrument; for diet, none but the French *quelque chofe* that are delicate; and for plays, no invention but that which now runneth an invective way, touching fome particular perfons, or elfe it is contemned before it is thoroughly underftood. This is all that I have to fay, That the Author had no intent to wrong any one in this Comedy; but, as a merry paffage, here and there interlaced it with delight, which he hopes will pleafe all, and be hurtful to none.

PROLOGUE.

PROLOGUE.

WHERE the bee can suck no honey, she leaves her sting behind; and where the bear cannot find *origanum* to heal his grief, he blasteth all other leaves with his breath. We fear, it is like to fare so with us; that seeing you cannot draw from our labours sweet content, you leave behind you a sour mislike, and with open reproach blame our good meaning, because you cannot reap the wonted mirth. Our intent was at this time to move inward delight, not outward lightness; and to breed (if it might be) soft smiling, not loud laughing; knowing it, to the wise, to be a great pleasure to hear counsel mixed with wit, as, to the foolish, to have sport mingled with rudeness. They were banished the theatre of Athens, and from **Rome** hissed, that brought parasites on the stage with apish actions, or fools with uncivil habits, or courtezans with immodest words. We have endeavoured to be as far from unseemly speeches, to make your ears glow, as we hope you will be free from unkind reports, or mistaking the author's intention, who never aimed at any one particular in this play, to make our cheeks blush. And thus I leave it, and thee to thine own censure, to like or dislike. *Vale* [1].

---

[1] *And thus I leave it,* &c.] These words seem more addressed to the *reader* than *spectator*, to whom this Address rather would apply as an *epilogue*.

DRAMATIS

DRAMATIS PERSONÆ.

M E N.

Speaker of the Prologue.

Citizen.

Ralph, *his apprentice*, the Knight of the Burning Peſtle.

Merchant, *father of Luce*.

Jaſper, *his apprentice*.

Maſter Humphrey, *a fooliſh ſuitor to Luce*.

Old Merrythought, *father of Jaſper and Michael*.

Michael, *favourite ſon of Mrs. Merrythought*.

Tim, *acting as ſquire* ⎱ *to Ralph*.
George, *acting as dwarf* ⎰

Hoſt.

Barber.

Tapſter.

Three ſuppoſed Knights.

Sergeant.

Soldiers.

Boy.

W O M E N.

Wife *to the Citizen*.

Luce, *beloved of and loving Jaſper*.

Mrs. Merrythought.

Woman *captive*.

T H E

THE KNIGHT OF THE

BURNING PESTLE.

Enter Speaker of the Prologue.

Prologue. FROM all that's near the court, from
all that's great
Within the compass of the city-walls,
We now have brought our scene——

Enter Citizen.

Cit. Hold your peace, goodman boy!

Prol. What do you mean, Sir?

Cit. That you have no good meaning: This seven
years there hath been plays at this house, I have ob-
serv'd it, you have still girds at citizens; and now you
call your play, ' The London Merchant.' Down
with your title, boy, down with your title!

Prol. Are you a member of the noble city?

Cit. I am.

Prol. And a freeman?

Cit. Yea, and a grocer.

Prol. So, grocer; then, by your sweet favour, we
intend no abuse to the city.

Cit. No, Sir? yes, Sir; if you were not resolv'd
to play the Jacks, what need you study for new subjects, purposely to abuse your betters? Why could
not you be contented, as well as others, with the legend

of Whittington, or the Life and Death of Sir Thomas Grefham? with the building of the Royal Exchange? or the ftory of Queen Eleanor, with the rearing of London-Bridge upon wool-facks?

Prol. You feem to be an underftanding man; what would you have us do, Sir?

Cit. Why, prefent fomething notably in honour of the commons of the city.

Prol. Why, what do you fay to the Life and Death of fat Drake, or the Repairing of Fleet Privies?

Cit. I do not like that; but I will have a citizen, and he fhall be of my own trade.

Prol. Oh, you fhould have told us your mind a month fince; our play is ready to begin now.

Cit. 'Tis all one for that; I will have a grocer, and he fhall do admirable things.

Prol. What will you have him do?

Cit. Marry, I will have him——

Wife [*below*]. Hufband, hufband!

Ralph [*below*]. Peace, miftrefs!

Wife. Hold thy peace, Ralph; I know what I do, I warrant you. Hufband, hufband!

Cit. What fay'ft thou, cony?

Wife. Let him kill a lion with a Peftle, hufband; let him kill a lion with a Peftle!

Cit. So he fhall; I'll have him kill a lion with a Peftle.

Wife. Hufband! fhall I come up, hufband?

Cit. Ay, cony. Ralph, help your miftrefs this way. Pray, gentlemen, make her a little room; I pray you, Sir, lend me your hand to help up my wife: I thank you, Sir; fo!

Wife. By your leave, gentlemen all! I'm fomething troublefome; I'm a ftranger here; I was ne'er at one of thefe plays, as they fay, before; but I fhould have feen Jane Shore² once; and my hufband hath promifed

---

² *Jane Shore.*] Probably, ' The Firft and Second Parts of King
' Edward the Fourth, containing his merry paftime with the Tanner
' of Tamworth, as alfo his love to fair miftriffe *Shore*, her great
' promotion, fall and miferie, and laftly the lamentable death of
                                                              ' both

me any time this twelvemonth, to carry me to the Bold Beauchams, but in truth he did not. I pray you bear with me.

Cit. Boy, let my wife and I have a couple of ſtools, and then begin ; and let the grocer do rare things.

Prol. But, Sir, we have never a boy to play him: Every one hath a part already.

Wife. Huſband, huſband, for God's ſake, let Ralph play him : Beſhrew me, if I do not think he will go beyond them all.

Cit. Well remember'd, wife. Come up, Ralph! I'll tell you, gentlemen ; let them but lend him a ſuit of reparrel, and neceſſaries, and, by gad, if any of them all blow wind in the tail on him, I'll be hang'd.

Wife. I pray you, youth, let him have a ſuit of reparrel ! I'll be ſworn, gentlemen, my huſband tells you true : He will act you ſometimes at our houſe, that all the neighbours cry out on him ; he will fetch you up a couraging part ſo in the garret, that we are all as fear'd I warrant you, that we quake again. We'll fear our children with him ; if they be never ſo unruly, do but cry, ' Ralph comes, Ralph comes,' to them, and they'll be as quiet as lambs. Hold up thy head, Ralph ; ſhew the gentlemen what thou canſt do ; ſpeak a huffing part; I warrant you the gentlemen will accept of it.

Cit. Do, Ralph, do.

Ralph. By Heaven, methinks [1], it were an eaſy leap
To pluck bright honour from the pale-fac'd moon,
Or dive into the bottom of the ſea,
Where never fathom-line touch'd any ground,
And pluck up drowned honour from the lake of hell.

Cit. How ſay you, gentlemen, is it not as I told you?

Wife. Nay, gentlemen, he hath play'd before, my

' both her and her huſband, &c. as it hath divers times been publickly
' played by the right honourable the earle of Derbie his ſervants.'
B. L. quarto.   R.

[1] *By Heaven, methinks, &c.*] This ſpeech (with very little variation) is taken from Shakeſpeare's Firſt Part of Henry IV.

huſband

huſband ſays, Muſidorus[4], before the wardens of our company.

Cit. Ay, and he ſhould have plaid Jeronimo[5] with a ſhoemaker for a wager.

Prol. He ſhall have a ſuit of apparel, if he will go in.

Cit. In, Ralph, in, Ralph! and ſet out the grocery in their kind, if thou lov'ſt me.

Wife. I warrant our Ralph will look finely when he's dreſs'd.

Prol. But what will you have it call'd?

Cit. ' The Grocers' Honour.'

Prol. Methinks ' The Knight of the Burning Peſtle' were better.

Wife. I'll be ſworn, huſband, that's as good a name as can be.

Cit. Let it be ſo; begin, begin; my wife and I will ſit down.

Prol. I pray you do.

Cit. What ſtately muſick have you? you have ſhaums[6]?

Prol. Shaums? No.

Cit. No? I'm a thief if my mind did not give me ſo. Ralph plays a ſtately part, and he muſt needs have ſhaums: I'll be at the charge of them myſelf, rather than we'll be without them.

Prol. So you are like to be.

Cit. Why, and ſo I will be: There's two ſhillings;

---

[4] *Muſidorus.*] This Play was printed in the year 1598, and afterwards in 1610, 1615, 1629, and 1668. The title to the edition of 1629 is the following: ' A moſt pleaſant Comedy of *Mucedorus*, ' the King's Sonne of Valentia, and Amadine the King's Daughter ' of Aragon; with the merry conceits of Mouſe Amplified, with ' new additions, as it was acted before the King's Majeſty at White- ' hall, on Shrove-Sunday night, by his Highneſſe Servants uſually ' playing at the Globe.' In a volume now in the poſſeſſion of Mr. Garrick, and which formerly belonged to King Charles, this Play is aſcribed to Shakeſpeare.

[5] *Jeronimo.*] See note 36 on the Chances.

[6] *Shaums.*] Muſical inſtruments mentioned in ſcripture, probably from *pſeaume*, French for *pſalms*, to which they were accompaniments. Some editions read, *ſhawnes*.

let's

let's have the waits of Southwark! they are as rare
fellows as any are in England, and that will fetch them
all o'er the water, with a vengeance, as if they were mad.

Prol. You ſhall have them. Will you ſit down then?

Cit. Ay. Come, wife.

Wife. Sit you merry all, gentlemen; I'm bold to
ſit amongſt you for my eaſe.

Prol. From all that's near the court, from all that's
   great
Within the compaſs of the city-walls,
We now have brought our ſcene: Fly far from hence
All private taxes, all immodeſt phraſes [7],
Whatever may but ſhew like vicious!
For wicked mirth never true pleaſure brings,
But honeſt minds are pleaſ'd with honeſt things.—
 Thus much for that we do; but, for Ralph's part,
you muſt anſwer for yourſelf [8].

Cit. Take you no care for Ralph; he'll diſcharge
himſelf, I warrant you.

Wife. I'faith, gentlemen, I'll give my word for Ralph.

---

7 *All private taxes, immodeſt phraſes,*
 Whate'er may but ſhew—] The variations were preſcribed by
an anonymous correſpondent of Mr. Sympſon.

 8 *For Ralph's part you muſt anſwer for yourſelf.*] I once thought
that this latter *for* was to be ſtruck out as redundant; but upon exa-
mination we ſhall find it not a redundancy, but a deficiency, and
ſhould read thus, *anſwer for't yourſelf.*   *Sympſon.*

 The old reading is eaſy, and correct enough for common
converſation.

ACT I.

Enter Merchant and Jasper.

Merch. SIRRAH, I'll make you know you are
my 'prentice,
And whom my charitable love redeem'd
Even from the fall of fortune; gave thee heat
And growth, to be what now thou art, new caft thee;
Adding the truft of all I have, at home,
In foreign ftaples, or upon the fea,
To thy direction; tied the good opinions
Both of myfelf and friends to thy endeavours;
So fair were thy beginnings: But with thefe,
As I remember, you had never charge
To love your mafter's daughter; and even then
When I had found a wealthy hufband for her;
I take it, Sir, you had not: But, however,
I'll break the neck of that commiffion,
And make you know you're but a merchant's factor.

Jafp. Sir, I do liberally confefs I'm yours,
Bound both by love and duty to your fervice,
In which my labour hath been all my profit;
I have not loft in bargain, nor delighted
To wear your honeft gains upon my back;
Nor have I given a penfion to my blood,
Or lavifhly in play confum'd your ftock:
Thefe, and the miferies that do attend them,
I dare with innocence proclaim are ftrangers
To all my temperate actions. For your daughter,
If there be any love to my defervings
Borne by her virtuous felf, I cannot ftop it;
Nor am I able to refrain her wifhes:
She's private to herfelf, and beft of knowledge
Whom fhe will make fo happy as to figh for.

Befides,

Befides, I cannot think you mean to match her
Unto a fellow of fo lame a prefence,
One that hath little left of nature in him.

Merch. 'Tis very well, Sir; I can tell your wifdom
How all this fhall be cur'd.

Jafp. Your care becomes you.

Merch. And thus it fhall be, Sir: I here difcharge
      you
My houfe and fervice; take your liberty;
And when I want a fon I'll fend for you.   [*Exit.*

Jafp. Thefe be the fair rewards of them that love.
Oh, you that live in freedom never prove
The travel of a mind led by defire!

Enter Luce.

Luce. Why, how now, friend? ftruck with my
      father's thunder?

Jafp. Struck, and ftruck dead, unlefs the remedy
Be full of fpeed and virtue; I am now,
What I expected long, no more your father's.

Luce. But mine?

Jafp. But yours, and only yours I am;
That's all I have to keep me from the ftatute.
You dare be conftant ftill?

Luce. Oh, fear me not!
In this I dare be better than a woman.
Nor fhall his anger nor his offers move me,
Were they both equal to a prince's power.

Jafp. You know my rival?

Luce. Yes, and love him dearly;
E'en as I love an ague, or foul weather:
I prithee, Jafper, fear him not!

Jafp. Oh, no;
I do not mean to do him fo much kindnefs.
But to our own defires [10]: You know the plot
We both agreed on?

Luce. Yes, and will perform
My part exactly.

10 *But to our own* defires.] Probably *defigns.*

                               Jafp.

Jasp. I defire no more.
Farewell, and keep my heart; 'tis yours.

Luce. I take it;
He muft do miracles, make me forfake it. [*Exeunt.*

Cit. Fy upon 'em, little infidels! what a matter's
here now? Well, I'll be hang'd for a halfpenny, if
there be not fome abomination knavery in this play.
Well; let 'em look to't; Ralph muft come, and if
there be any tricks a-brewing——

Wife. Let 'em brew and bake too, hufband, a
God's name; Ralph will find all out, I warrant you,
an they were older than they are. I pray, my pretty
youth, is Ralph ready?

Boy. He will be prefently.

Wife. Now I pray you make my commendations
unto him, and withal, carry him this ftick of licorice;
tell him his miftrefs fent it him; and bid him bite a
piece; 'twill open his pipes the better, fay.

Enter Merchant and Mafter Humphrey.

Merch. Come, Sir, fhe's yours; upon my faith, fhe's
      yours;
You have my hand: For other idle letts,
Between your hopes and her, thus with a wind
They're fcatter'd, and no more. My wanton 'prentice,
That like a bladder blew himfelf with love,
I have let out, and fent him to difcover
New mafters yet unknown.

Hum. I thank you, Sir,
Indeed I thank you, Sir; and ere I ftir,
It fhall be known, however you do deem,
I am of gentle blood, and gentle feem.

Merch. Oh, Sir, I know it certain.

Hum. Sir, my friend,
Altho', as writers fay, all things have end,
And that we call a pudding hath his two,
Oh, let it not feem ftrange, I pray to you,
If in this bloody fimile I put
My love, more endlefs than frail things or gut.

                                      Wife.

Wife. Husband, I prithee, sweet lamb, tell me one thing; but tell me truly.—Stay, youths, I beseech you, till I question my husband.

Cit. What is it, mouse?

Wife. Sirrah, didst thou ever see a prettier child? how it behaves itself, I warrant ye! and speaks and looks, and perts up the head! I pray you, brother, with your favour, were you never none of Mr. Moncaster's scholars?

Cit. Chicken, I prithee heartily contain thyself; the childer are pretty childer; but when Ralph comes, lamb——

Wife. Ay, when Ralph comes, cony! Well, my youth, you may proceed.

Merch. Well, Sir; you know my love, and rest, I hope,
Assur'd of my consent; get but my daughter's,
And wed her when you please. You must be bold,
And clap in close unto her; come, I know
You've language good enough to win a wench.

Wife. A whoreson tyrant! hath been an old stringer in his days, I warrant him!

Hum. I take your gentle offer, and withal
Yield love again for love reciprocal.

Merch. What, Luce! within there!

Enter Luce.

Luce. Call'd you, Sir?

Merch. I did;
Give entertainment to this gentleman;
And see you be not froward. To her, Sir!
My presence will but be an eye-sore to you. [*Exit.*

Hum. Fair mistress Luce, how do you? are you well?
Give me your hand, and then I pray you tell
How doth your little sister, and your brother?
And whether you love me or any other?

Luce. Sir, these are quickly answer'd.

Hum. So they are,
Where women are not cruel. But how far

Is it now diftant from the place we are-in,
Unto that bleffed place, your father's warren.

Luce. What makes you think of that, Sir?

Hum. E'en that face;
For ftealing rabbits whilome in that place,
God Cupid, or the keeper, I know not whether,
Unto my coft and charges brought you thither,
And there began——

Luce. Your game, Sir?

Hum. Let no game,
Or any thing that tendeth to the fame,
Be ever more remember'd, thou fair killer,
For whom I fate me down and brake my tiller[11].

Wife. There's a kind gentleman, I warrant you;
when will you do as much for me, George?

Luce. Befhrew me, Sir, I'm forry for you loffes;
But, as the proverb fays, ' I cannot cry;'
I would you had not feen me!

Hum. So would I,
Unlefs you had more maw to do me good.

Luce. Why, cannot this ftrange paffion[12] be with-
ftood?
Send for a conftable, and raife the town.

Hum. Oh, no, my valiant love will batter down
Millions of conftables, and put to flight
E'en that great watch of Midfummer, day at night[13].

___

[11] *Tiller.*] See note 14 on Philafter.

[12] *This* ftrange *paffion.*] Sympfon fays, ' To fend for a *conftable*
' *and raife a town*, to withftand a STRANGE *paffion*, borders feem-
' ingly near upon nonfenfe;' he would therefore read, STRONG
paffion: But we fee no reafon why fhe may not go from one metaphor
to another.

[13] *That great watch of Midfummer day at night.*] What is alluded
to here is probably the following cuftom: On the vigil of St. John
the Baptift, it was formerly ufual, after fun-fetting, for the principal
citizens to make bonfires before their doors, and alfo to fet out tables
furnifhed with meat and drink, of which they invited their neighbours and paffengers to partake. At the fame time a marching watch,
confifting of about 2000 men, furnifhed with lights, perambulated
from St. Paul's Gate to Aldgate, and back again, when they broke
up. Part of this watch was provided at the expence of the city of
London, and other part of the feveral parifhes. The cuftom continued

Luce. Befhrew me, Sir, 'twere good I yielded then;
Weak women cannot hope, where valiant men
Have no refiftance. ·

Hum. Yield then; I am full
Of pity, tho' I fay it, and can pull
Out of my pocket thus a pair of gloves.
Look, Lucy, look; the dog's tooth, nor the doves,
Are not fo white as thefe; and fweet they be,
And whipt about with filk, as you may fee.
If you defire the price, fhoot from your eye
A beam to this place, and you fhall efpy
F S, which is to fay, my fweeteft honey,
They coft me three and two-pence, or no money.

Luce. Well, Sir, I take them kindly, and I thank you:
What would you more?

Hum. Nothing.

Luce. Why then, farewell!

Hum. Nor fo, nor fo; for, lady, I muft tell,
Before we part, for what we met together;
God grant me time, and patience, and fair weather!

Luce. Speak and declare your mind in terms fo brief.

Hum. I fhall; then firft and foremoft, for relief
I call to you, if that you can afford it;
I care not at what price, for on my word, it
Shall be repaid again, altho' it coft me
More than I'll fpeak of now; for love haft tofs'd me
In furious blanket like a tennis-ball,
And now I rife aloft, and now I fall.

Luce. Alas, good gentleman, alas the day!

Hum. I thank you heartily; and, as I fay,
Thus do I ftill continue without reft,
I' th' morning like a man, at night a beaft,
Roaring and bellowing mine own difquiet,
That much I fear, forfaking of my diet,
Will bring me prefently to that quandary,

---

nued until the time of Henry VIII. when it was prohibited by him.
In 1548 it was again revived; but being found to be the means of
collecting diforderly people together, and occafioning great riots, it
was in the year 1569 laid afide, and has ever fince been difcontinued.
See Stow's Survey.   *R.*

I fhall

I shall bid all adieu.

Luce. Now, by St. Mary,
That were great pity!

Hum. So it were, beshrew me;
Then ease me, lusty Luce, and pity shew me.

Luce. Why, Sir, you know my will is nothing worth
Without my father's grant; get his consent,
And then you may with full assurance try me [14].

Hum. The worshipful your sire will not deny me;
For I have ask'd him, and he hath replied,
' Sweet master Humphrey, Luce shall be thy bride.'

Luce. Sweet master Humphrey, then I am content.

Hum. And so am I, in truth.

Luce. Yet take me with you;
There is another clause must be annex'd,
And this it is: I swore, and will perform it,
No man shall ever 'joy me as his wife,
But he that stole me hence: If you dare venture,
I'm yours (you need not fear; my father loves you)
If not, farewell for ever!

Hum. Stay, nymph, stay;
I have a double gelding, colour'd bay,
Sprung by his father from Barbarian kind,
Another for myself, tho' somewhat blind,
Yet true as trusty tree.

Luce. I'm satisfied;
And so I give my hand. Our course must lie
Thro' Waltham-Forest, where I have a friend
Will entertain us. So farewell, Sir Humphrey,
And think upon your business! [*Exit Luce.*

Hum. Tho' I die,
I am resolv'd to venture life and limb,
For one so young, so fair, so kind, so trim. [*Exit Hum.*

Wife. By my faith and troth, George, and as I am
virtuous, it is e'en the kindest young man that ever
trod on shoe-leather. Well, go thy ways; if thou
hast her not, 'tis not thy fault, i'faith.

---

[14] *You may with assurance try me.*] The measure assisted by
Sympson.

Cit.

Cit. I prithee, mouse, be patient! a shall have her, or I'll make some of 'em smoke for't.

Wife. That's my good lamb George. Fy! this stinking tobacco[15] kills men[16]! 'would there were none in England! Now I pray, gentlemen, what good does this stinking tobacco do you? nothing, I warrant you; make chimnies a your faces!—Oh, husband, husband, now, now! there's Ralph, there's Ralph!

Enter Ralph, like a grocer in his shop, with two apprentices, reading Palmerin of England.

Cit. Peace, fool! let Ralph alone. Hark you, Ralph; do not strain yourself too much at the first. Peace! Begin Ralph.

Ralph. ' Then Palmerin and Trineus[17]', snatching
' their lances from their dwarfs, and clasping their
' helmets, gallop'd amain after the giant; and Pal-
' merin having gotten a sight of him, came posting
' amain, saying, ' Stay, traiterous thief! for thou
" mayst not so carry away her, that is worth the
" greatest lord in the world;' and with these words
' gave him a blow on the shoulder, that he struck him
' besides his elephant. And Trineus coming to the
' knight that had Agricola behind him, set him soon
' besides his horse, with his neck broken in the fall;
' so that the princess getting out of the throng,
' between joy and grief said, ' All happy knight,
" the mirror of all such as follow arms, now may I
" be well assured of the love thou bearest me." I

---

[15] *Tobacco.*] At the time our Authors wrote (we learn from Prynne, in his Histriomastrix, p. 322) *tobacco*, wine, and beer, were the usual accommodations in the theatre, as the two latter are still at Sadler's Wells. See also Percy's Reliques of Ancient Poetry, vol. i.   *R.*

[16] *Kills men.*] Sympson reads, *kills* ME.

[17] *Then Palmerin and Trineus, &c.*] This passage is taken, with some slight variations, from ' Palmerin D'Oliva, the Mirrour of
' Nobilitie, Mappe of Honor, Anotamie of Rare Fortunes, Heroycall
' President of Love, Wonder of Chivalrie, and most accomplished
' Knight in all Perfections.' 4to. 1588. B. L. p. 131.   *R.*

wonder why the kings do not raise an army of fourteen or fifteen hundred thousand men, as big as the
army that the prince of Portigo brought against
Rosicler, and destroy these giants; they do much hurt
to wandering damsels, that go in quest of their knights.

Wife. Faith, husband, and Ralph says true; for
they say the king of Portugal cannot sit at his meat,
but the giants and the ettins[18] will come and snatch
it from him.

Cit. Hold thy tongue. On, Ralph!

Ralph. And certainly those knights are much to be
commended, who, neglecting their possessions, wander
with a squire and a dwarf through the desarts, to relieve poor ladies.

Wife. Ay, by my faith are they, Ralph; let 'em
say what they will, they are indeed. Our knights
neglect their possessions well enough, but they do not
the rest.

Ralph. There are no such courteous and fair well-
spoken knights in this age: They will call one the
son of a whore, that Palmerin of England would have
called *fair Sir*; and one that Rosicler would have
called *right beauteous damsel*, they will call *damn'd bitch*.

Wife. I'll be sworn will they, Ralph; they have
called me so an hundred times, about a scurvy pipe of
tobacco.

Ralph. But what brave spirit could be content to
sit in his shop, with a flapet of wood, and a blue
apron before him, selling Methridatam and dragons'
water to visited houses, that might pursue feats of
arms, and, through his noble atchievements, procure
such a famous history to be written of his heroick
prowess?

Cit. Well said, Ralph; some more of those words,
Ralph!

---

[18] *Ettins.*] The good woman is here a little tautological, as at
other times she is nonsensical, (unless I mistake her meaning in this
place) for giants and *ettins*, or *etins*, are giants and giants, *eten* in
Saxon signifying so.   *Sympson.*

Ettins, quasi *heathens*; it is not probable she thought of *Saxon.*

Wife.

Wife. They go finely, by my troth.

Ralph. Why should I not then pursue this course, both for the credit of myself and our company? for amongst all the worthy books of atchievements, I do not call to mind that I yet read of a Grocer-Errant: I will be the said Knight.—Have you heard of any that hath wandered unfurnished of his squire and dwarf? My elder 'prentice Tim shall be my trusty squire, and little George my dwarf. Hence, my blue apron! Yet, in remembrance of my former trade, upon my shield shall be pourtrayed a Burning Pestle, and I will be called the Knight of the Burning Pestle.

Wife. Nay, I dare swear thou wilt not forget thy old trade; thou wert ever meek.

Ralph. Tim!

Tim. Anon.

Ralph. My beloved squire, and George my dwarf, I charge you that from henceforth you never call me by any other name, but the *Right courteous and valiant Knight of the Burning Pestle*; and that you never call any female by the name of a woman or wench, but *fair lady*, if she have her desires; if not, *distressed damsel*; that you call all forests and heaths *desarts*, and all horses, *palfries!*

Wife. This is very fine!—Faith, do the gentlemen like Ralph, think you, husband?

Cit. Ay, I warrant thee; the players would give all the shoes in their shop for him.

Ralph. My beloved squire Tim, stand out: Admit this were a desart, and over it a knight-errant pricking[19], and I should bid you enquire of his intents, what would you say?

Tim. 'Sir, my master sent me to know whither 'you are riding?'

Ralph. No! thus; 'Fair Sir! the *Right courteous* 'and valiant *Knight of the Burning Pestle* commanded 'me to enquire upon what adventure you are bound;

---

[19] *Pricking.*] i. e. *Riding. A gentle knight was* pricking *on the* plain, is the first line of Spenser's Fairy Queen.

'whether

' whether to relieve some distressed damsels, or other-
' wise.'

Cit. Whoreson blockhead cannot remember!

Wife. I'faith, and Ralph told him on't before; all
the gentlemen heard him; did he not, gentlemen?
did not Ralph tell him on't?

*George. Right courteous and valiant Knight of the
Burning Pestle,* here is a distressed damsel, to have a
halfpenny-worth of pepper.

Wife. That's a good boy! see, the little boy can
hit it; by my troth, it's a fine child.

Ralph. Relieve her, with all courteous language.
Now shut up shop; no more my 'prentice, but my
trusty Squire and Dwarf. I must bespeak my shield,
and arming Pestle.

Cit. Go thy ways, Ralph! As I am a true man,
thou art the best on 'em all.

Wife. Ralph, Ralph!

Ralph. What say you, mistress?

Wife. I prithee come again quickly, sweet Ralph.

Ralph. Bye-and-bye. [*Exit.*

Enter Jasper and Mrs. Merrythought.

Mrs. Mer. Give thee my blessing? No, I'll never
give thee my blessing; I'll see thee hang'd first; it
shall ne'er be said I gave thee my blessing: Thou art
thy father's own son, of the blood of the Merry-
thoughts; I may curse the time that e'er I knew thy
father; he hath spent all his own, and mine too, and
when I tell him of it, he laughs and dances, and
sings, and cries ' A merry heart lives long-a.' And
thou art a waste-thrift, and art run away from thy
master, that loved thee well, and art come to me;
and I have laid up a little for my younger son Michael,
and thou thinkest to bezzle that, but thou shalt never
be able to do it. Come hither, Michael; come,
Michael; down on thy knees: Thou shalt have my
blessing.

Enter

Enter Michael.

Mich. I pray you, mother, pray to God to bleſs me!

Mrs. Mer. God bleſs thee! but Jaſper ſhall never have my bleſſing; he ſhall be hang'd firſt, ſhall he not, Michael? how ſayſt thou?

Mich. Yes, forſooth, mother, and grace of God.

Mrs. Mer. That's a good boy!

Wife. I'faith, it's a fine-ſpoken child!

Jaſp. Mother, tho' you forget a parent's love,
I muſt preſerve the duty of a child.
I ran not from my maſter, nor return
To have your ſtock maintain my idleneſs.

Wife. Ungracious child, I warrant him! hark, how he chops logick with his mother: Thou hadſt beſt tell her ſhe lies; do, tell her ſhe lies.

Cit. If he were my ſon, I would hang him up by the heels, and flea him, and ſalt him, whoreſon halter-ſack!

Jaſp. My coming only is to beg your love,
Which I muſt ever, tho' I never gain it;
And, howſoever you eſteem of me,
There is no drop of blood hid in theſe veins,
But I remember well belongs to you,
That brought me forth, and would be glad for you
To rip them all again, and let it out.

Mrs. Mer. I'faith, I had ſorrow enough for thee (God knows); but I'll hamper thee well enough. Get thee in, thou vagabond, get thee in, and learn of thy brother Michael.

Mer. [*within.*] Noſe, noſe, jolly red noſe,
    And who gave thee this jolly red noſe?

Mrs. Mer. Hark, my huſband! he's ſinging and hoiting; and I'm fain to cark and care, and all little enough. Huſband! Charles! Charles Merrythought!

Enter Old Merrythought.

Mer. Nutmegs and ginger, cinnamon, and cloves;
    And they gave me this jolly red noſe.

Mrs.

Mrs. Mer. If you would confider your eftate, you would have little lift to fing, I wis.

Mer. It fhould never be confider'd, while it were an eftate, if I thought it would fpoil my finging.

Mrs. Mer. But how wilt thou do, Charles? thou art an old man, and thou canft not work, and thou haft not forty fhillings left, and thou eateft good meat, and drinkeft good drink, and laugheft.

Mer. And will do.

Mrs. Mer. But how wilt thou come by it, Charles?

Mer. How? Why, how have I done hitherto thefe forty years? I never came into my dining-room, but, at eleven and fix o'clock, I found excellent meat and drink o' th' table; my cloaths were never worn out, but next morning a taylor brought me a new fuit; and without queftion it will be fo ever! Ufe makes perfectnefs; if all fhould fail, it is but a little ftraining myfelf extraordinary, and laugh myfelf to death.

Wife. It's a foolifh old man this; is not he, George?

Cit. Yes, cony.

Wife. Give me a penny i'th' purfe while I live, George.

Cit. Ay, by'r lady, cony, hold thee there!

Mrs. Mer. Well, Charles; you promis'd to provide for Jafper, and I have laid up for Michael: I pray you pay Jafper his portion; he's come home, and he fhall not confume Michael's ftock; he fays his mafter turned him away, but I promife you truly I think he ran away.

Wife. No, indeed, miftrefs Merrythought, tho' he be a notable gallows, yet I'll affure you his mafter did turn him away, even in this place; 'twas, i'faith, within this half-hour, about his daughter; my hufband was by.

Cit. Hang him, rogue! he ferv'd him well enough: Love his mafter's daughter? By my troth, cony, if there were a thoufand boys, thou wouldft fpoil them all, with taking their parts; let his mother alone with him.

Wife.

Wife. Ay, George, but yet truth is truth.

Mer. Where is Jasper? he's welcome, however. Call him in; he shall have his portion. Is he merry?

Mrs. Mer. Ay, foul chive him, he is too merry. Jasper! Michael!

Enter Jasper and Michael.

Mer. Welcome, Jasper! tho' thou run'st away, welcome! God bless thee! 'Tis thy mother's mind thou shouldst receive thy portion; thou hast been abroad, and I hope hast learn'd experience enough to govern it; thou art of sufficient years; hold thy hand: One, two, three, four, five, six, seven, eight, nine, there is ten shillings for thee; thrust thyself into the world with that, and take some settled course: If Fortune cross thee, thou hast a retiring place; come home to me; I have twenty shillings left. Be a good husband; that is, wear ordinary cloaths, eat the best meat, and drink the best drink; be merry, and give to the poor, and, believe me, thou hast no end of thy goods.

Jasp. Long may you live free from all thought of ill, And long have cause to be thus merry still! But, father——

Mer. No more words, Jasper; get thee gone! Thou hast my blessing; thy father's spirit upon thee! Farewell, Jasper!

But yet, or ere you part (oh, cruel!)
   Kiss me, kiss me, sweeting,
   Mine own dear jewel!

So; now begone; no words! *[Exit Jasper.*

Mrs. Mer. So, Michael; now get thee gone too.

Mich. Yes forsooth, mother; but I'll have my father's blessing first.

Mrs. Mer. No, Michael; 'tis no matter for his blessing; thou hast my blessing; be gone. I'll fetch my money and jewels, and follow thee: I'll stay no longer with him, I warrant thee. Truly, Charles, I'll be gone too.

Mer.

Mer. What! you will not?

Mrs. Mer. Yes indeed will I.

Mer. Hey-ho, farewell, Nan!

I'll never truft wench more again, if I can.

Mrs. Mer. You fhall not think (when all your own is gone) to fpend that I have been fcraping up for Michael.

Mer. Farewell, good wife! I expect it not; all I have to do in this world, is to be merry; which I fhall, if the ground be not taken from me; and if it be,

When earth and feas from me are reft,
The fkies aloft for me are left. [*Exeunt.*

[*Boy danceth. Mufick.*

FINIS ACTUS PRIMI.

Wife. I'll be fworn he's a merry old gentleman, for all that. Hark, hark, hufband, hark! fiddles, fiddles! now furely they go finely. They fay 'tis prefent death for thefe fiddlers to tune their rebecks [20] before the great Turk's grace; is't not, George? But look, look! here's a youth dances! now, good youth, do a turn o' th' toe. Sweetheart, i'faith I'll have Ralph come and do fome of his gambols; he'll ride the wild-mare, gentlemen, 'twould do your hearts good to fee him. I thank you, kind youth; pray bid Ralph come.

Cit. Peace, cony! Sirrah, you fcurvy boy, bid the players fend Ralph; or, by God's wounds, an they do not, I'll tear fome of their perriwigs befide their heads; this is all riff-raff.

---

[20] *Rebecks.*] A *rebeck* was an inftrument with three ftrings, re- fembling a modern fiddle.   *R.*

It is mentioned in Milton's *Allegro.*

A C T II.

Enter Merchant and Master Humphrey.

Merch. AND how, faith, how goes it now, son
Humphrey?

Hum. Right worshipful, and my beloved friend
And father dear, this matter's at an end.

Merch. 'Tis well; it should be so: I'm glad the girl
Is found so tractable.

Hum. Nay, she must whirl
From hence, (and you must wink; for so, I say,
The story tells) tomorrow before day.

Wife. George, dost thou think in thy conscience
now 'twill be a match? tell me but what thou think'st,
sweet rogue: Thou seest the poor gentleman (dear
heart!) how it labours and throbs, I warrant you,
to be at rest: I'll go move the father for't.

Cit. No, no; I prithee sit still, honeysuckle;
thou'lt spoil all: If he deny him, I'll bring half-a-
dozen good fellows myself, and in the shutting of an
evening knock it up, and there's an end.

Wife. I'll buss thee for that, i'faith, boy! Well,
George, well, you have been a wag in your days, I
warrant you; but God forgive you, and I do with
all my heart.

Merch. How was it, son? you told me that tomorrow
Before day-break, you must convey her hence.

Hum. I must, I must; and thus it is agreed:
Your daughter rides upon a brown-bay steed,
I on a sorrel, which I bought of Brian,
The honest host of the red roaring Lion,
In Waltham situate: Then if you may,
Consent in seemly sort; lest by delay,
The fatal sisters come, and do the office,
And then you'll sing another song.

Merch. Alas,
Why should you be thus full of grief to me,

That

That do as willing as yourfelf agree
To any thing, fo it be good and fair?
Then fteal her when you will, if fuch a pleafure
Content you both; I'll fleep and never fee it,
To make your joys more full.   But tell me why
You may not here perform your marriage?

Wife. God's blefling o' thy foul, old man! i'faith
thou art loath to part true hearts.   I fee a has her,
George; and I'm as glad on't! Well, go thy ways,
Humphrey, for a fair-fpoken man; I believe thou haft
not thy fellow within the walls of London; an I
fhould fay the fuburbs too, I fhould not lie.   Why
doft not thou rejoice with me, George?

Cit. If I could but fee Ralph again, I were as
merry as mine hoft, i'faith.

Hum. The caufe you feem to afk, I thus declare:
(Help me, oh, mufes nine!) Your daughter fware
A foolifh oath, the more it was the pity;
Yet no one but myfelf [21] within this city
Shall dare to fay fo, but a bold defiance
Shall meet him, were he of the noble fcience.
And yet fhe fware, and yet why did fhe fwear?
Truly I cannot tell, unlefs it were
For her own eafe; for fure fometimes an oath,
Being fworn thereafter, is like cordial broth:
And this it was fhe fwore, never to marry,
But fuch a one whofe mighty arm could carry
(As meaning me, for I am fuch a one)
Her bodily away, thro' ftick and ftone,
'Till both of us arrive, at her requeft,
Some ten miles off, in the wild Waltham-Foreft.

Merch. If this be all, you fhall not need to fear
Any denial in your love; proceed;
I'll neither follow, nor repent the deed.

Hum. Good night, twenty good nights, and twenty
    more,
And twenty more good nights, that makes threefcore!
                                            [*Exeunt.*

---

[21] *Yet none but myfelf.*] The reading in the text is Theobald's.
Sympfon's anonymous correfpondent propofes, *None but I myfelf.*

                                            Enter

Enter Mrs. Merrythought and Michael.

Mrs. Mer. Come, Michael; art thou not weary, boy?

Mich. No forſooth, mother, not I.

Mrs. Mer. Where be we now, child?

Mich. Indeed forſooth, mother, I cannot tell, unleſs we be at Mile-End: Is not all the world Mile-End, mother?

Mrs. Mer. No, Michael, not all the world, boy; but I can aſſure thee, Michael, Mile-End is a goodly matter: There has been a pitchfield, my child, between the naughty Spaniels and the Engliſhmen; and the Spaniels ran away, Michael, and the Engliſhmen followed. My neighbour Coxſtone was there, boy, and kill'd them all with a birding-piece.

Mich. Mother, forſooth!

Mrs. Mer. What ſays my white boy?

Mich. Shall not my father go with us too?

Mrs. Mer. No, Michael, let thy father go ſnick-up; he ſhall never come between a pair of ſheets with me again, while he lives; let him ſtay at home and ſing for his ſupper, boy. Come, child, ſit down, and I'll ſhew my boy fine knacks, indeed: Look here, Michael; here's a ring, and here's a brooch, and here's a bracelet, and here's two rings more, and here's money and gold by th' eye, my boy!

Mich. Shall I have all this, mother?

Mrs. Mer. Ay, Michael, thou ſhalt have all, Michael.

Cit. How lik'ſt thou this, wench?

Wife. I cannot tell; I would have Ralph, George; I'll ſee no more elſe, indeed-la; and I pray you let the youths underſtand ſo much by word of mouth; for I will tell you truly, I'm afraid o' my boy. Come, come, George, let's be merry and wiſe; the child's a fatherleſs child, and ſay they ſhould put him into a ſtrait pair of gaſkins, 'twere worſe than knot-graſs[13], he would never grow after it.

---

[13] *Knot-graſs.*]——'Get you gone, you dwarf,
'You Minimus, of hindring *knot-graſs* made.'
　　　　　Midſummer-Night's Dream, act iii. ſcene ii.
Upon which paſſage the laſt editor obſerves, 'It appears that
　　　　　　　　　　　　　　　　　　　　　　　'knot-

Enter Ralph, Tim, and George.

Cit. Here's Ralph, here's Ralph!

Wife. How do you, Ralph? you are welcome, Ralph, as I may fay; it's a good boy! hold up thy head, and be not afraid; we are thy friends, Ralph. The gentlemen will praife thee, Ralph, if thou play'ft thy part with audacity. Begin, Ralph, a God's name!

Ralph. My trufty Squire, unlace my helm; give
          me my hat.
Where are we, or what defart might this be?

George. Mirror of knighthood, this is, as I take it, The perilous Waltham-Down; in whofe bottom ftands
The enchanted valley.

Mrs. Mer. Oh, Michael, we are betray'd, we are betray'd! here be giants! Fly, boy, fly, boy, fly!
          [*Exit with Michael, leaving a cafket.*

Ralph. Lace on my helm again! What noife is this?
A gentle lady, flying the embrace
Of fome uncourteous knight? I will relieve her.
Go, Squire, and fay, the Knight that wears this
          Peftle
In honour of all ladies, fwears revenge
Upon that recreant coward that purfues her;
Go comfort her, and that fame gentle fquire
That bears her company.

Tim. I go, brave Knight.

Ralph. My trufty Dwarf and friend, **reach me my**
          fhield;
And hold it while I fwear, firft, **by my knighthood;**
Then by the foul of Amadis de Gaul
(My famous anceftor); then by my fword
The beauteous Brionella girt **about me;**
By this bright burning Peftle, of mine honour
The living trophy; and by all refpect
Due to diftreffed damfels; here I vow

' *knot grafs* was anciently fuppofed to prevent the growth of any
' animal or child;' and produces this paffage, and the following from
the Coxcomb, in proof of his obfervation: ' We want a boy ex-
' tremely for this function, kept under for a year with milk and
' *knot-grafs.*'   R.

                                                        Never

Never to end the queft of this fair lady,
And that forfaken fquire, 'till by my valour
I gain their liberty!   [*Exit.*

George. Heav'n blefs the Knight
That thus relieves goor errant gentlewomen! [*Exit.*

Wife. Ay marry, Ralph, this has fome favour in't;
I would fee the proudeft of them all offer to carry his
books after him. But, George, I will not have him
go away fo foon; I fhall be fick if he go away, that
I fhall; call Ralph again, George, call Ralph again;
I prithee, fweetheart, let him come fight before me,
and let's ha' fome drums, and trumpets, and let him
kill all that comes near him, an thou lov'ft me, George!

Cit. Peace a little, bird! he fhall kill them all, an
they were twenty more on 'em than there are.

Enter Jafper.

Jafp. Now, Fortune, (if thou be'ft not only ill)
Shew me thy better face, and bring about
Thy defperate wheel, that I may climb at length,
And ftand; this is our place of meeting,
If love have any conftancy. Oh, age,
Where only wealthy men are counted happy!
How fhall I pleafe thee, how deferve thy fmiles,
When I am only rich in mifery?
My father's bleffing, and this little coin,
Is my inheritance; a ftrong revenue!
From earth thou art, and unto earth I give thee:
There grow and multiply, whilft frefher air
Breeds me a frefher fortune.—How! illufion!
                         [*Spies the cafket.*
What, hath the devil coin'd himfelf before me?
'Tis metal good; it rings well; I am waking,
And taking too, I hope. Now God's dear bleffing
Upon his heart that left it here! 'tis mine;
Thefe pearls, I take it, were not left for fwine. [*Exit.*

Wife. I do not like that this unthrifty youth fhould
embezzle away the money; the poor gentlewoman his
mother will have a heavy heart for it, God knows.

Cit. And reason good, sweetheart.

Wife. But let him go; I'll tell Ralph a tale in's ear, shall fetch him again with a wanion, I warrant him, if he be above ground; and besides, George, here be a number of sufficient gentlemen can witness, and myself, and yourself, and the musicians, if we be call'd in question. But here comes Ralph; George, thou shalt hear him speak, as he were an emperal.

Enter Ralph and George.

Ralph. Comes not Sir Squire again?

George. Right courteous Knight,
Your Squire doth come, and with him comes the lady.

Enter Mrs. Merrythought, Michael, and Tim.

Ralph. Fair! and the Squire of Damsels [24], as I
    take it!
Madam, if any service or devoir
Of a poor errant Knight may right your wrongs,
Command it; I am prest [25] to give you succour;
For to that holy end I bear my armour.

Mrs. Mer. Alas, Sir, I am a poor gentlewoman,
and I have lost my money in this forest.

Ralph. Desart, you would say, lady; and not lost
Whilst I have sword and lance. Dry up your tears,
Which ill befit the beauty of that face,

---

[24] *Your squire doth come, and with him comes the lady.*
    Enter Mrs. Merrythought, &c.
For *and the squire of damsels as I take it.*
    Ralph. *Madam, &c.*] Sympson omits the period at the end of the first line, and alters *for* to *fair*; we think him right in the alteration of the word; but we must go further before this passage is cleared of corruption, since, by giving the *first* and *third* lines to one speaker, the *third* appears a bald and needless repetition of the sense of the *first*, which is complete in itself. We have therefore made *Ralph's* speech begin at the third line instead of the fourth; and apprehend that he first addresses himself both to Mrs. Merrythought and Michael: Her he calls *Fair!* and him *Squire of Damsels!* as he names him afterwards, *this gentle Squire.* This is quite in his character, and the only reading that gives spirit, or even tolerable sense, to the third line; after which he proceeds to comfort them separately.

[25] *Prest.*] i. e. *Ready.* See note 46 on the Wild-Goose Chace.

And

And tell the ſtory, if I may requeſt it,
Of your diſaſtrous fortune.

Mrs. Mer. Out, alas! I left a thouſand pound, a
thouſand pound, e'en all the money I had laid up for
this youth, upon the ſight of your maſterſhip, you
look'd ſo grim, and, as I may ſay it, ſaving your preſence, more like a giant than a mortal man.

Ralph. I am as you are, lady; ſo are they,
All mortal. But why weeps this gentle ſquire?

Mrs. Mer. Has he not cauſe to weep, do you think,
when he has loſt his inheritance?

Ralph. Young hope of valour, weep not; I am here
That will confound thy foe, and pay it dear
Upon his coward head, that dare deny
Diſtreſſed ſquires and ladies equity.
I have but one horſe[16], upon which ſhall ride
This lady fair behind me, and before
This courteous ſquire: Fortune will give us more
Upon our next adventure. Fairly ſpeed
Beſide us, Squire and Dwarf, to do us need! [*Exeunt.*

Cit. Did not I tell you, Nell, what your man would
do? by the faith of my body, wench, for clean action
and good delivery, they may all caſt their caps at him.

Wife. And ſo they may, i'faith; for I dare ſpeak it
boldly, the twelve companies of London cannot match
him, timber for timber. Well, George, an he be not
inveigled by ſome of theſe paltry players, I ha' much
marvel; but, George, we ha' done our parts, if the
boy have any grace to be thankful.

Cit. Yes, I warrant you, duckling.

Enter Maſter Humphrey and Luce.

Hum. Good miſtreſs Luce, however I in fault am
For your lame horſe, you're welcome unto Waltham;
But which way now to go, or what to ſay,
I know not truly, 'till it be broad day.

Luce. Oh, fear not, maſter Humphrey; I am guide
For this place good enough,

---

[16] *I have but one horſe,* on *which.*] The variation is Sympſon's.

Hum.

Hum. Then up and ride;
Or, if it pleafe you, walk for your repofe;
Or fit, or, if you will, go pluck a rofe:
Either of which fhall be indifferent,
To your good friend and Humphrey, whofe confent
Is fo entangled ever to your will,
As the poor harmlefs horfe is to the mill.

Luce. Faith, an you fay the word, we'll e'en fit down,
And take a nap.

Hum. 'Tis better in the town,
Where we may nap together; for, believe me,
To fleep without a fnatch would mickle grieve me.

Luce. You're merry, mafter Humphrey.

Hum. So I am,
And have been ever merry from my dam.

Luce. Your nurfe had the lefs labour.

Hum. Faith, it may be,
Unlefs it were by chance I did bewray me.

Enter Jafper.

Jafp. Luce! dear friend Luce!

Luce. Here, Jafper.

Jafp. You are mine.

Hum. If it be fo, my friend, you ufe me fine:
What do you think I am?

Jafp. An arrant noddy.

Hum. A word of obloquy! Now, by God's body,
I'll tell thy mafter; for I know thee well.

Jafp. Nay, an you be fo forward for to tell,
Take that, and that; and tell him, Sir, I gave it:
And fay I paid you well.   [*Beats him.*

Hum. Oh, Sir, I have it,
And do confefs the payment. Pray, be quiet!

Jafp. Go, get you to your night-cap and the diet,
To cure your beaten bones.

Luce. Alas, poor Humphrey!
Get thee fome wholefome broth, with fage and cumfry;
A little oil of rofes, and a feather
To 'noint thy back withal.

Hum.

Hum. When I came hither,
'Would I had gone to Paris with John Dory [27]!

Luce. Farewell, my pretty Nump! I'm very forry
I cannot bear thee company.

Hum. Farewell!

The devil's dam was ne'er fo bang'd in hell. [*Exeunt.*

Manet Humphrey.

Wife. This young Jafper will prove me another
things, a my confcience, an he may be fuffered. George,
doft not fee, George, how a fwaggers, and flies at the
very heads a folks, as he were a dragon? Well, if I do
not do his leffon for wronging the poor gentleman I am
no true woman. His friends that brought him up
might have been better occupied, I wis, than have
taught him thefe fegaries: He's e'en in the high way
to the gallows, God blefs him!

Cit. You're too bitter, cony; the young man may
do well enough for all this.

Wife. Come hither, mafter Humphrey; has he hurt
you? now befhrew his fingers for't! Here, fweetheart, here's fome green ginger for thee. Now befhrew
my heart, but a has pepper-nel in's head, as big as a
pullet's egg! Alas, fweet lamb, how thy temples beat!
Take the peace on him, fweetheart, take the peace on
him.

Enter Boy.

Cit. No, no; you talk like a foolish woman! I'll

---

[27] *John Dory.*] Sir John Hawkins, in his Hiftory of Mufic, fays,
'The fong of *John Dory*, with the tune to it, is printed in the
'Deuteromelia, or the fecond part of Mufick's Melodie, 1609.
'The legend of this perfon is, that being a fea-captain, or perhaps
'a pirate, he engaged to the king of France to bring the crew of an
'Englifh fhip bound as captives to Paris, and that accordingly he at-
'tempted to make prize of an Englifh veffel, but was himfelf taken
'prifoner. The fong of *John Dory*, and the tune to it, were a long
'time popular in England: In the comedy of the Chances, written
'by Beaumont and Fletcher, Antonio, a humorous old man, receives
'a wound, which he will not fuffer to be dreffed but upon condition
'that the fong of *John Dory* be fung the while.'——The Song is
alfo printed in Sir John's Appendix, No. 27.

ha'

ha' Ralph fight with him, and fwinge him up well-
favour'dly. Sirrah, Boy; come hither: Let Ralph
come in and fight with Jafper.

Wife. Ay, and beat him well; he's an unhappy boy.

Boy. Sir, you muft pardon us; the plot of our play
lies contrary; and 'twill hazard the fpoiling of our play.

Cit. *Plot* me no *plots!* I'll ha' Ralph come out; I'll
make your houfe too hot for you elfe.

Boy. Why, Sir, he fhall; but if any thing fall out
of order, the gentlemen muft pardon us.

Cit. Go your ways, goodman Boy! I'll hold him a
penny, he fhall have his belly full of fighting now.
Ho! here comes Ralph! no more!

*Enter Ralph, Mrs. Merrythought, Michael, Tim and
George.*

Ralph. What knight is that, Squire? afk him if he keep
The paffage, bound by love of lady fair,
Or elfe but prickant.

Hum. Sir, I am no knight,
But a poor gentleman, that this fame night
Had ftolen from me, upon yonder green,
My lovely wife, and fuffer'd (to be feen
Yet extant on my fhoulders) fuch a greeting,
That whilft I live, I fhall think of that meeting.

Wife. Ay, Ralph, he beat him unmercifully, Ralph;
an thou fpar'ft him, Ralph, I would thou wert hang'd.

Cit. No more, Wife, no more!

Ralph. Where is the caitiff wretch hath done this
deed?
Lady, your pardon! that I may proceed
Upon the queft of this injurious knight.
And thou, fair Squire, repute me not the worfe,
In leaving the great venture of the purfe,

Enter Jafper and Luce.

And the rich cafket, 'till fome better leifure.

Hum. Here comes the broker hath purloin'd my
treafure.

Ralph.

Ralph. Go, Squire, and tell him I am here,
An errant Knight at arms, to crave delivery
Of that fair lady to her own knight's arms.
If he deny, bid him take choice of ground,
And fo defy him.

Tim. From the Knight that bears
The Golden Peſtle, I defy thee, Knight;
Unleſs thou make fair reſtitution
Of that bright lady.

Jaſp. Tell the Knight that ſent thee
He is an aſs; and I will keep the wench,
And knock his head-piece.

Ralph. Knight, thou art but dead,
If thou recall not thy uncourteous terms.

Wife. Break his pate, Ralph; break his pate, Ralph,
foundly!

Jaſp. Come, Knight; I'm ready for you.—Now your
　　　　Peſtle　　　　[*Snatches away his Peſtle.*
Shall try what temper, Sir, your mortar's of.
With that he ſtood upright in his ſtirrups, and gave
the knight of the calves-ſkin ſuch a knock, that he
forſook his horſe, and down he fell; and then he
leaped upon him, and plucking off his helmet——

Hum. Nay, an my noble Knight be down ſo ſoon,
Tho' I can ſcarcely go, I needs muſt run.

　　　　　　[*Exeunt Humphrey and Ralph.*

Wife. Run, Ralph, run, Ralph; run for thy life,
boy; Jaſper comes, Jaſper comes!

Jaſp. Come, Luce, we muſt have other arms for you;
Humphrey, and Golden Peſtle, both adieu! [*Exeunt.*

Wife. Sure the devil, God bleſs us, is in this
ſpringald! Why, George, didſt ever ſee ſuch a fire-
drake? I am afraid my boy's miſcarried; if he be,
though he were maſter Merrythought's ſon a thouſand
times, if there be any law in England, I'll make ſome
of them ſmart for't.

Cit. No, no; I have found out the matter, ſweetheart; Jaſper is enchanted; as ſure as we are here, he
is enchanted: He could no more have ſtood in Ralph's

　　　　　　　　　hands,

hands, than I can stand in my lord-mayor's. I'll have a ring to discover all enchantments, and Ralph shall beat him yet: Be no more vex'd, for it shall be so.

Enter Ralph, Tim, George, Mrs. Merrythought, and Michael.

Wife. Oh, husband, here's Ralph again! Stay, Ralph; let me speak with thee: How dost thou, Ralph? Art thou not shrewdly hurt? the foul great lungies laid unmercifully on thee; there's some sugar-candy for thee. Proceed; thou shalt have another bout with him.

Cit. If Ralph had him at the fencing-school, if he did not make a puppy of him, and drive him up and down the school, he should ne'er come in my shop more.

Mrs. Mer. Truly, master Knight of the Burning Pestle, I am weary.

Mich. Indeed-la, mother, and I'm very hungry.

Ralph. Take comfort, gentle dame, and your fair
        Squire!
For in this desart there must needs be plac'd
Many strong castles, held by courteous knights;
And 'till I bring you safe to one of those
I swear by this my order ne'er to leave you.

Wife. Well said, Ralph! George, Ralph was ever comfortable, was he not?

Cit. Yes, duck.

Wife. I shall ne'er forget him: When we had lost our child, (you know it was stray'd almost, alone, to Puddle-Wharf, and the criers were abroad for it, and there it had drown'd itself but for a sculler) Ralph was the most comfortablest to me! Peace, mistress, says he, let it go! I'll get you another as good. Did he not, George? did he not say so?

Cit. Yes, indeed did he, mouse.

George. I would we had a mess of pottage, and a pot of drink, Squire, and were going to-bed.

Tim. Why, we are at Waltham-town's end, and that's the Bell Inn.

George.

George. Take courage, valiant Knight, damſel, and
       Squire!
I have diſcover'd, not a ſtone's caſt off,
An antient caſtle held by the old knight
Of the moſt holy order of the Bell,
Who gives to all knights-errant entertain:
There plenty is of food, and all prepar'd
By the white hands of his own lady dear.
He hath three ſquires that welcome all his gueſts:
The firſt, hight Chamberlino [28] ; who will ſee
Our beds prepar'd, and bring us ſnowy ſheets,
Where never footman ſtretch'd his butter'd hams.
The ſecond, hight Tapſtero; who will ſee
Our pots full filled, and no froth therein.
The third, a gentle ſquire, Oſtlero hight,
Who will our palfries ſlick with whiſps of ſtraw,
And in the manger put them oats enough,
And never greaſe their teeth with candle-ſnuff.

Wife. That ſame Dwarf's a pretty boy, but the
Squire's a grout-nold.

1 *Ralph.* Knock at the gates, my Squire, with ſtately
      lance!

Enter Tapſter.

Tap. Who's there? You're welcome, gentlemen!
will you ſee a room?

George. Right courteous and valiant Knight of the
Burning Peſtle, this is the ſquire Tapſtero.

Ralph. Fair ſquire Tapſtero! I, a wandering Knight,
Hight of the Burning Peſtle, in the queſt

---

[28] *The firſt high Chamberlain*
    — *hight* Tapſtro
    — *ſquire Oſtlero height.*] The correction of *hight* for
high, is from Mr. Theobald's conjecture, but he did not go to the
bottom of the grievance, for Chamberlain is not quantity, and ſo can't
ſtand in the verſe. *Chamberlino* is from the ſaid quarto of 1613.
Tapſtro, octavo, *Taſtero*, quarto, I have alter'd to *Tapſtero*. *Oſtlero*
hight is from the firſt quarto too.   *Sympſon.*

   Hight is no amendment, being in old book ; as is alſo *Chamberlino*.
The ſubſtituting *Tapſtero* for *Taſtero* (if to be called an amendment)
is the only one.

Of

Of this fair lady's casket and wrought purse,
Losing myself in this vast wilderness,
Am to this castle well by fortune brought;
Where hearing of the goodly entertain
Your knight of holy order of the Bell,
Gives to all damsels, and all errant knights,
I thought to knock, and now am bold to enter.

Tap. An't please you see a chamber, you are very
welcome. [*Exeunt.*

Wife. George, I would have something done, and I
cannot tell what it is.

Cit. What is it, Nell?

Wife. Why, George, shall Ralph beat nobody
again? Prithee, sweetheart, let him!

Cit. So he shall, Nell; and if I join with him, we'll
knock them all.

Enter Master Humphrey and Merchant.

Wife. Oh, George, here's master Humphrey again
now, that lost mistress Luce; and mistress Luce's father.
Master Humphrey will do somebody's errand, I
warrant him.

Hum. Father, it's true in arms I ne'er shall clasp her;
For she is stol'n away by your man Jasper.

Wife. I thought he would tell him.

Merch. Unhappy that I am, to lose my child!
Now I begin to think on Jasper's words,
Who oft hath urg'd to me thy foolishness:
Why didst thou let her go? thou lov'st her not,
That wouldst bring home thy life, and not bring her.

Hum. Father, forgive me; I shall tell you true;
Look on my shoulders, they are black and blue:
Whilst to and fro fair Luce and I were winding,
He came and basted me with a hedge-binding.

Merch. Get men and horses straight! we will be there
Within this hour. You know the place again?

Hum. I know the place where he my loins did
swaddle;
I'll get six horses, and to each a saddle.

Merch.

THE BURNING PESTLE.

Merch. Mean time, I will go talk with Jasper's father.

[Exeunt.

Wife. George, what wilt thou lay with me now, that master Humphrey has not mistress Luce yet? speak, George, what wilt thou lay with me?

Cit. No, Nell; I warrant thee, Jasper is at Puckeridge with her by this.

Wife. Nay, George, you must consider mistress Luce's feet are tender; and besides, 'tis dark; and I promise you truly, I do not see how he should get out of Waltham-Forest with her yet.

Cit. Nay, cony, what wilt thou lay with me that Ralph has her not yet?

Wife. I will not lay against Ralph, honey, because I have not spoken with him. But look, George; peace! here comes the merry old gentleman again.

Enter Old Merrythought.

Mer. When it was grown to dark midnight,
    And all were fast asleep,
In came Margaret's grimly ghost,
    And stood at William's feet [29].

I have money, and meat, and drink, before-hand, till tomorrow at noon; why should I be sad? Methinks I have half-a-dozen jovial spirits within me; ' I am ' three merry men [30]', and three merry men!'—To what end should any man be sad in this world? Give me a man that when he goes to hanging cries, ' Troul ' the black bowl to me!' and a woman that will sing a catch in her travel! I have seen a man come by my door with a serious face, in a black cloak, without a hatband, carrying his head as if he look'd for pins in the street: I have look'd out of my window half-a-year after, and have spied that man's head upon London-Bridge: 'Tis vile; never trust a taylor that does not sing at his work! his mind is on nothing but filching.

---

[29] *When it was grown,* &c.] This stanza is printed in Percy's Reliques of Ancient Poetry, vol. iii. p. 120.

[30] *Three merry men,* &c.] See vol. v. p. 137, 138, of this Work.

Wife,

Wife. Mark this, George! 'tis worth noting: Godfrey, my taylor, you know, never fings, and he had fourteen yards to make this gown; and I'll be fworn, miftrefs Peniftone the draper's wife had one made with twelve.

   Mer. 'Tis mirth that fills the veins with blood,
      More than wine, or fleep, or food;
      Let each man keep his heart at eafe,
      No man dies of that difeafe.
      He that would his body keep
      From difeafes, muft not weep;
      But whoever laughs and fings,
      Never he his body brings
      Into fevers, gouts, or rheums,
      Or lingringly his lungs confumes;
      Or meets with achés in the bone,
      Or catarrhs, or griping ftone:
      But contented lives for aye;
      The more he laughs, the more may.

   Wife. Look, George; how fayft thou by this, George? Is't not a fine old man? Now God's blefſing a thy fweet lips! when wilt thou be fo merry, George? Faith, thou art the frowningft little thing, when thou art angry, in a country.

Enter Merchant.

   Cit. Peace, cony! thou fhalt fee him took down too, I warrant thee. Here's Luce's father come now.

   Mer. As you came from Walfingham,
      From the Holy Land,
    There met you not with my true love
      By the way as you came[31]?

   Merch. Oh, mafter Merrythought, my daughter's
      gone!
This mirth becomes you not; my daughter's gone!

   Mer. Why, an if fhe be, what care I?
      Or let her come, or go, or tarry.

[31] *As you came,* &c.] From a ballad printed in Percy's Reliques of Antient Poetry, vol. ii. p. 94.

Merch. Mock not my mifery; it is your fon
(Whom I have made my own, when all forfook him)
Has ftol'n my only joy, my child, away.

Mer. He fet her on a milk-white fteed,
  And himfelf upon a grey;
 He never turn'd his face again,
  But he bore her quite away.

Merch. Unworthy of the kindnefs I have fhewn
To thee, and thine; too late, I well perceive,
Thou art confenting to my daughter's lofs.

Mer. Your daughter? what a ftir's here wi' your
daughter? Let her go, think no more on her, but
fing loud. If both my fons were on the gallows, I
would fing,

  Down, down, down; they fall
  Down, and arife they never fhall.

Merch. Oh, might I behold her once again,
And fhe once more embrace her aged fire!

Mer. Fy, how fcurvily this goes!
' And fhe once more embrace her aged fire?'
You'll make a dog on her, will ye? fhe cares much
for her aged fire, I warrant you.

  She cares not for her daddy, **nor**
  She cares not for her mammy, **for**
   She is, fhe is, fhe is
  My lord of Lowgave's laffy.

Merch. For this thy fcorn I will purfue that fon
Of thine to death.

Mer. Do; and when you ha' kill'd him,

Give him flowers enow, Palmer, give him flowers
   enow!
Give him red and white, and blue, green, and yellow.

Merch. I'll fetch my daughter——

Mer. I'll hear no more o' your daughter; it fpoils
my mirth.

Merch. I fay, I'll fetch my daughter.

       Mer.

Mer. Was never man for lady's fake[32],

        Down, down,

   Tormented as I Sir Guy,

        De derry down,

For Lucy's fake, that lady bright,

        Down, down,

As ever men beheld with eye!

        De derry down.

Merch. I'll be reveng'd, by Heaven!   [*Exeunt.*

    FINIS ACTUS SECUNDI.   [*Mufic.*

Wife. How doft thou like this, George?

Cit. Why, this is well, cony; but if Ralph were hot once, thou fhouldft fee more.

Wife. The fidlers go again, hufband.

Cit. Ay, Nell; but this is fcurvy mufick. I gave the whorefon gallows money, and I think he has not got me the waits of Southwark: If I hear 'em not anon[33], I'll twinge him by the ears. You muficians, play Baloo[34]!

Wife. No, good George, let's ha' Lachrymæ!

Cit. Why this is it, cony.

Wife. It's all the better, George. Now, fweet lamb, what ftory is that painted upon the cloth? the confutation of St. Paul?

Cit. No, lamb; that's Ralph and Lucrece.

Wife. Ralph and Lucrece? which Ralph? our Ralph?

Cit. No, moufe; that was a Tartarian.

Wife. A Tartarian? Well, I would the fidlers had done, that we might fee our Ralph again!

---

[32] *Was never man, &c.*] From the Legend of Sir Guy. Percy's Reliques of Antient Poetry, vol. iii. p. 102.

[33] *If I hear him not.*] Amended by Sympfon.

[34] *Baloo.*] See Percy's Reliques of Antient Poetry, vol. ii. p. 196. Lady Anne Bothwell's Lamentation; in which the concluding lines of each ftanza are thefe:

   ' *Balow,* my babe, lie ftil and fleipe!

   ' It grieves me fair to fee thee weepe.'

                   A C T

A C T III.

Enter Jasper and Luce.

Jasp. COME, my dear dear! tho' we have lost
                our way,
We have not lost ourselves. Are you not weary
With this night's wandring, broken from your rest?
And frighted with the terror that attends
The darkness of this wild unpeopled place?

Luce. No, my best friend; I cannot either fear,
Or entertain a weary thought, whilst you
(The end of all my full desires) stand by me:
Let them that lose their hopes, and live to languish
Amongst the number of forsaken lovers,
Tell the long weary steps, and number time,
Start at a shadow, and shrink up their blood,
Whilst I (possess'd with all content and quiet)
Thus take my pretty love, and thus embrace him.

Jasp. You've caught me, Luce, so fast, that whilst
                I live
I shall become your faithful prisoner,
And wear these chains for ever. Come, sit down,
And rest your body, too, too delicate
For these disturbances. So! will you sleep?
Come, do not be more able than you are;
I know you are not skilful in these watches,
For women are no soldiers: Be not nice,
But take it; sleep, I say.

Luce. I cannot sleep;
Indeed I cannot, friend.

Jasp. Why then we'll sing,
And try how that will work upon our senses.

Luce. I'll sing, or say, or any thing but sleep.

Jasp. Come, little mermaid, rob me of my heart
With that enchanting voice.

Luce. You mock me, Jasper.

                    S O N G.

SONG.

Jasp. Tell me, dearest, what is love [35] ?
Luce. 'Tis a lightning from above ;
　　　'Tis an arrow, 'tis a fire,
　　　'Tis a boy they call Desire.
　　　　'Tis a smile
　　　　Doth beguile
Jasp. The poor hearts of men that prove.

　　Tell me more, are women true?
Luce. Some love change, and so do you.
Jasp. 　Are they fair, and never kind?
Luce. 　Yes, when men turn with the wind.
Jasp. 　　Are they froward?
Luce. 　　　Ever toward
　　Those that love, to love anew.

Jasp. Dissemble it no more ; I see the god
Of heavy sleep lay on his heavy mace
Upon your eye-lids.
　Luce. I am very heavy.
　Jasp. Sleep, sleep ; and quiet rest crown thy sweet
　　　thoughts !
Keep from her fair blood all distempers [36], startings,
Horrors and fearful shapes ! let all her dreams
Be joys, and chaste delights, embraces, wishes,
And such new pleasures as the ravish'd soul
Gives to the senses ! So ; my charms have took.
Keep her, ye powers divine, whilst I contemplate
Upon the wealth and beauty of her mind !
She's only fair, and constant, only kind,
And only to thee, Jasper. Oh, my joys !
Whither will you transport me ? let not fullness
Of my poor buried hopes come up together,
And over-charge my spirits ; I am weak !
Some say (however ill) the sea and women
Are govern'd by the moon ; both ebb and flow,

---

[35] *Tell me, dearest, what is love.*] This song, with a little variation, is also in the Captain.

[36] *Keep from her fair blood distempers, startings.*] Sympson, to assist the measure, added the word ALL.

Both

Both full of changes; yet to them that know,
And truly judge, these but opinions are,
And heresies, to bring on pleasing war
Between our tempers, that without these were
Both void of after-love, and present fear;
Which are the best of Cupid. Oh, thou child
Bred from despair, I dare not entertain thee,
Having a love without the faults of women,
And greater in her perfect goods than men;
Which to make good, and please myself the stronger,
Tho' certainly I'm certain of her love,
I'll try her, that the world and memory
May sing to after-times her constancy.
Luce! Luce! awake!

Luce. Why do you fright me, friend,
With these distemper'd looks? what makes your sword
Drawn in your hand? who hath offended you?—
I prithee, Jasper, sleep; thou'rt wild with watching.

Jasp. Come, make your way to Heaven, and bid
                    the world,
With all the villainies that stick upon it,
Farewell; you're for another life.

Luce. Oh, Jasper,
How have my tender years committed evil,
Especially against the man I love,
Thus to be cropp'd untimely?

Jasp. Foolish girl,
Canst thou imagine I could love his daughter
That flung me from my fortune into nothing?
Discharged me his service, shut the doors
Upon my poverty, and scorn'd my prayers,
Sending me, like a boat without a mast,
To sink or swim? Come; by this hand, you die!
I must have life and blood, to satisfy
Your father's wrongs.

Wife. Away, George, away! raise the watch at
Ludgate, and bring a mittimus from the justice for
this desperate villain! Now I charge you, gentlemen,
see the king's peace kept! Oh, my heart, what a

varlet's this, to offer manslaughter upon the harmless
gentlewoman!

Cit. I warrant thee, sweetheart, we'll have him
hampered.

Luce. Oh, Jasper, be not cruel!
If thou wilt kill me, smile, and do it quickly,
And let not many deaths appear before me!
I am a woman made of fear and love,
A weak, weak woman; kill not with thy eyes!
They shoot me thro' and thro'. Strike! I am ready;
And dying still I love thee.

Enter Merchant, Master Humphrey, and men.

Merch. Whereabouts?

Jasp. No more of this; now to myself again.

Hum. There, there he stands, with sword, like
        martial knight,
Drawn in his hand; therefore beware the fight,
You that are wise; for, were I good Sir Bevis,
I would not stay his coming. By your leaves [37].

Merch. Sirrah, restore my daughter!

Jasp. Sirrah, no.

Merch. Upon him then!

Wife. So; down with him, down with him, down
with him! cut him i'the leg, boys, cut him i'the leg!

Merch. Come your ways, minion! I'll provide a
cage for you, you're grown so tame. Horse her away!

Hum. Truly, I'm glad your forces have the day.
                          [*Exeunt.*

Manet Jasper.

Jasp. They're gone, and I am hurt; my love is lost,
Never to get again. Oh, me unhappy!
Bleed, bleed and die.—I cannot. Oh, my folly,
Thou hast betray'd me! Hope, where art thou fled?
Tell me, if thou be'st any where remaining,

---

[37] *By your* leaves.] This must be pronounced as two syllables;
'tis in the taste of Chaucer and our old English Poets: 'Tis a licence
however our Poets seldom take, and I don't remember above three
or four instances of it throughout the edition.   *Sympson.*

Shall I but see my love again? Oh, no!
She will not deign to look upon her butcher,
Nor is it fit she should; yet I must venture.
Oh, Chance, or Fortune, or whate'er thou art,
That men adore for powerful, hear my cry,
And let me loving live, or losing die!　　　　[*Exit.*

Wife. Is a gone, George?

Cit. Ay, cony.

Wife. Marry, and let him go, sweetheart! By the
faith a my body, a has put me into such a fright, that
I tremble (as they say) as 'twere an aspen-leaf: Look
a my little finger, George, how it shakes! Now in
truth every member of my body is the worse for't.

Cit. Come, hug in mine arms, sweet mouse; he
shall not fright thee any more. Alas, mine own dear
heart, how it quivers!

*Enter Mrs. Merrythought, Ralph, Michael, Tim, George,
Host, and a Tapster.*

Wife. Oh, Ralph! how dost thou Ralph? How hast
thou slept to-night? has the knight us'd thee well?

Cit. Peace, Nell; let Ralph alone!

Tap. Master, the reckoning is not paid.

Ralph. Right courteous Knight, who, for the
　　　　order's sake
Which thou hast ta'en, hang'st out the holy Bell,
As I this flaming Pestle bear about,
We render thanks to your puissant self,
Your beauteous lady, and your gentle squires,
For thus refreshing of our wearied limbs,
Stiffen'd with hard atchievements in wild desart.

Tap. Sir, there is twelve shillings to pay.

Ralph. Thou merry squire Tapstero, thanks to thee
For comforting our souls with double jug!
And if adventurous Fortune prick thee forth,
Thou jovial squire, to follow feats of arms,
Take heed thou tender every lady's cause,
Ev'ry true knight, and ev'ry damsel fair!
But spill the blood of treacherous Saracens,

　　　　And

And false enchanters, that with magick spells
Have done to death full many a noble knight.

Hoft. Thou valiant Knight of the Burning Peftle,
give ear to me; there is twelve fhillings to pay, and,
as I am a true Knight, I will not bate a penny.

Wife. George, I prithee tell me, muft Ralph pay
twelve fhillings now?

Cit. No, Nell, no; nothing but the old Knight is
merry with Ralph.

Wife. Oh, is't nothing elfe? Ralph will be as
merry as he.

Ralph. Sir Knight, this mirth of yours becomes you
      well;
But, to requite this liberal courtefy,
If any of your fquires will follow arms,
He fhall receive from my heroick hand,
A knighthood, by the virtue of this Peftle.

Hoft. Fair Knight, I thank you for your noble offer;
Therefore, gentle Knight,
Twelve fhillings you muft pay, or I muft cap you.

Wife. Look, George! did not I tell thee as much?
the Knight of the Bell is in earneft. Ralph fhall not
be beholding to him: Give him his money, George,
and let him go fnick-up.

Cit. Cap Ralph? No; hold your hand, Sir Knight
of the Bell! There's your money; have you any thing
to fay to Ralph now? Cap Ralph?

Wife. I would you fhould know it, Ralph has
friends that will not fuffer him to be capt for ten times
fo much, and ten times to the end of that. Now take
thy courfe, Ralph!

Mrs. Mer. Come, Michael; thou and I will go
home to thy father; he hath enough left to keep us
a day or two, and we'll fet fellows abroad to cry our
purfe and cafket: Shall we, Michael?

Mich. Ay, I pray, mother; in truth my feet are
full of chilblains with travelling.

Wife. Faith, and thofe chilblains are a foul trouble.
Miftrefs Merrythought, when your youth comes home,

let

let him rub all the foles of his feet, and his heels, and
his ancles, with a moufe-fkin; or, if none of you can
catch a moufe, when he goes to-bed, let him roll his
feet in the warm embers, and I warrant you he fhall
be well; and you may make him put his fingers
between his toes, and fmell to them; it's very fove-
reign for his head, if he be coftive.

Mrs. Mer. Mafter Knight of the Burning Peftle,
my fon Michael and I bid you farewell: I thank your
worfhip heartily for your kindnefs.

Ralph. Farewell, fair lady, and your tender fquire!
If pricking thro' thefe defarts, I do hear
Of any trait'rous knight, who thro' his guile
Hath lit upon your cafket and your purfe,
I will defpoil him of them and reftore them.

Mrs. Mer. I thank your worfhip.

                      [*Exit with Michael.*

Ralph. Dwarf, bear my fhield; Squire, elevate
      my lance;
And now, farewell, you Knight of holy Bell!

Cit. Ay, ay, Ralph, all is paid.

Ralph. But yet, before I go, fpeak, worthy knight,
If aught you do of fad adventures know,
Where errant-knight may thro' his prowefs win
Eternal fame, and free fome gentle fouls
From endlefs bonds of fteel and ling'ring pain.

Hoft. Sirrah, go to Nick the barber, and bid him
prepare himfelf, as I told you before, quickly.

Tap. I am gone, Sir.   [*Exit.*

Hoft. Sir Knight, this wildernefs affordeth none
But the great venture, where full many a knight
Hath tried his prowefs, and come off with fhame;
And where I would not have you lofe your life,
Againft no man, but furious fiend of hell.

Ralph. Speak on, Sir Knight; tell what he is, and
      where:
For here I vow upon my blazing badge,
Never to blaze a day in quietnefs;
But bread and water will I only eat,

                  And

And the green herb and rock shall be my couch,
'Till I have quell'd that man, or beast, or fiend,
That works such damage to all errant-knights.

Host. Not far from hence, near to a craggy cliff,
At the north end of this distressed town,
There doth stand a lowly house,
Ruggedly builded, and in it a cave
In which an ugly giant now doth won[38],
Ycleped Barbaroso; in his hand
He shakes a naked lance of purest steel,
With sleeves turn'd up; and him before he wears
A motly garment, to preserve his cloaths
From blood of those knights which he massacres,
And ladies gent; without his door doth hang
A copper bason, on a prickant spear;
At which no sooner gentle knights can knock
But the shrill sound fierce Barbaroso hears,
And rushing forth, brings in the errant-knight,
And sets him down in an enchanted chair:
Then with an engine, which he hath prepar'd,
With forty teeth, he claws his courtly crown,
Next makes him wink, and underneath his chin
He plants a brazen piece of mighty bore[40],
And knocks his bullets round about his cheeks;
Whilst with his fingers, and an instrument
With which he snaps his hair off, he doth fill
The wretch's ears with a most hideous noise.
Thus every knight-adventurer he doth trim,
And now no creature dares encounter him.

Ralph. In God's name, I will fight with him:
    Kind Sir,

---

[38] *Won.*] Old word for *dwell.*   *Sympson.*

[40] *A brazen piece of mighty* board.] So the octavo; the first quarto,
of mighty bord. Both of which are foreign to the places they occupy.
I conjecture the Poets intended to say *bore*; so the cavity of a gun,
cannon, &c. is commonly called: And though the anachronism of
making ordnance, contemporary with knight-errantry may be allowed,
yet nonsense has, or can have no claim to the like privilege.
                                                           Sympson.

Go but before me to this difmal cave
Where this huge giant Barbarofo dwells,
And, by that virtue that brave Roficler
That damned brood of ugly giants flew,
And Palmerin Frannarco overthrew,
I doubt not but to curb this traitor foul,
And to the devil fend his guilty foul.

Hoft. Brave-fprighted Knight, thus far I will perform
This your requeft; I'll bring you within fight
Of this moft loathfome place, inhabited
By a more loathfome man; but dare not ftay,
For his main force fwoops all he fees away.

Ralph. Saint George! Set on; before march, Squire
and Page! [*Exeunt.*

Wife. George, doft think Ralph will confound the
giant?

Cit. I hold my cap to a farthing he does: Why,
Nell, I faw him wreftle with the great Dutchman, and
hurl him.

Wife. Faith, and that Dutchman was a goodly man,
if all things were anfwerable to his bignefs. And yet
they fay there was a Scottifhman higher than he, and
that they two on a night met [41], and faw one another
for nothing. But of all the fights that ever were in
London, fince I was married, methinks the little child
that was fo fair grown about the members was the
prettieft; that and the hermaphrodite.

Cit. Nay, by your leave, Nell, Ninivie was better.

Wife. Ninivie? Oh, that was the ftory of Joan and
the wall [42], was it not, George?

Cit. Yes, lamb.

---

[41] *That they two and a Knight met.*] The correction in the prefent edition I hope will be allowed by every candid and judicious
reader: *Night* being the time when thefe *men-monfters* remove from
place to place, thereby to prevent fpoiling their market, by expofing
to common view, what they would have the world pay dearly for
the fight of. *Sympfon.*

[42] *Story of* Joan *and the* wall.] Affected blunder for *Jonah* and
the *whale.* *Theobald.*

Enter

Enter Mrs. Merrythought.

Wife. Look, George; here comes miftrefs Merrythought again! and I would have Ralph come and
fight with the giant; I tell you true, I long to fee't.

Cit. Good miftrefs Merrythought, be gone, I pray
you, for my fake! I pray you forbear a little; you
fhall have audience prefently; I have a little bufinefs.

Wife. Miftrefs Merrythought, if it pleafe you to
refrain your paffion a little, till Ralph have difpatch'd
the giant out of the way, we fhall think ourfelves much
bound to thank you: I thank you, good miftrefs
Merrythought.   [*Exit Mrs. Merrythought.*

Enter a Boy.

Cit. Boy, come hither; fend away Ralph and this
whorefon giant quickly.

Boy. In good faith, Sir, we cannot; you'll utterly
fpoil our play, and make it to be hifs'd; and it coft
money; you will not fuffer us to go on with our plots.
I pray, gentlemen, rule him!

Cit. Let him come now and difpatch this, and I'll
trouble you no more.

Boy. Will you give me your hand of that?

Wife. Give him thy hand, George, do; and I'll
kifs him. I warrant thee the youth means plainly.

Boy. I'll fend him to you prefently.   [*Exit Boy.*

Wife. I thank you, little youth. Feth, the child hath
a fweet breath, George; but I think it be troubled
with the worms; Carduus Benedictus and mare's milk
were the only thing in the world for't. Oh, Ralph's
here, George! God fend thee good luck, Ralph!

Enter Ralph, Hoft, Tim, and George.

Hoft. Puiffant knight, yonder his manfion is.
Lo, where the fpear and copper bafon are!
Behold the ftring on which hangs many a tooth,
Drawn from the gentle jaw of wandring knights!
I dare not ftay to found; he will appear.   [*Exit.*
Ralph.

Ralph. Oh, faint not, heart! Sufan, my lady dear,
The cobler's maid in Milk-Street, for whose fake
I take these arms, oh, let the thought of thee
Carry thy knight thro' all th' adventurous deeds;
And, in the honour of thy beauteous self,
May I destroy this monster Barbaroso!
Knock, Squire, upon the bason, 'till it break
With the shrill strokes, or 'till the giant speak.

Enter Barber.

Wife. Oh, George, the giant, the giant! Now, Ralph, for thy life!

Bar. What fond unknowing wight is this, that dares
So rudely knock at Barbaroso's cell,
Where no man comes, but leaves his fleece behind?

Ralph. I, traiterous caitiff, who am sent by Fate
To punish all the sad enormities
Thou hast committed against ladies gent,
And errant-knights, traitor to God and men!
Prepare thyself; this is the dismal hour
Appointed for thee to give strict account
Of all thy beastly treacherous villainies.

Bar. Fool-hardy knight, full soon thou shalt aby
This fond reproach: Thy body will I bang;

[*He takes down his pole.*

And lo! upon that string thy teeth shall hang.
Prepare thyself, for dead soon shalt thou be.

Ralph. Saint George for me! [*They fight.*
Bar. Gargantua for me!
Wife. To him, Ralph, to him! hold up the giant; set out thy leg before, Ralph!
Cit. Falsify a blow, Ralph, falsify a blow! the giant lies open on the left side.
Wife. Bear't off, bear't off still: There, boy. Oh, Ralph's almost down, Ralph's almost down!
Ralph. Sufan, inspire me! now have up again.
Wife. Up, up, up, up, up! so, Ralph! down with him, down with him, Ralph!
Cit. Fetch him over the hip, boy!

Wife.

Wife. There, boy ! kill, kill, kill, kill, kill, Ralph !

Cit. No, Ralph ; get all out of him first.

Ralph. Presumptuous man ! see to what desperate end
Thy treachery hath brought thee : The just gods,
Who never prosper those that do despise them,
For all the villainies which thou hast done
To knights and ladies, now have paid thee home,
By my stiff arm, a knight adventurous.
But say, vile wretch, before I send thy soul
To sad Avernus, (whither it must go)
What captives holdst thou in thy sable cave ?

Bar. Go in, and free them all ; thou hast the day.

Ralph. Go, Squire and Dwarf, search in this dreadful cave,
And free the wretched prisoners from their bonds.

            [*Exeunt Tim and George.*

Bar. I crave for mercy, as thou art a Knight,
And scorn'st to spill the blood of those that beg.

Ralph. Thou shew'st no mercy, nor shalt thou have
any ;
Prepare thyself, for thou shalt surely die.

*Enter Tim leading one winking, with a bason under
his chin.*

Tim. Behold, brave Knight, here is one prisoner,
Whom this vile man hath used as you see[43].

Wife. This is the wisest word I heard the squire speak.

---

43 *Whom this wild man.*] Though all the copies agree in this reading, 'tis yet highly probable that a corruption has taken place here. In-
humanity and barbarity are the characteristics this giant is distinguished
by, and as such I would have what I take to be the right lection
restored, and make the line run thus,
    Whom this vilde man. &c.
Vilde for *vile* is the common lection both in Shakespear and Spencer,
and I am surprized that the great Oxford editor of Shakespear should
so frequently (I believe universally) alter this reading in his fine edition
of that poet, into the modern *vile.*   *Sympson.*

   We cannot conceive why Mr. Sympson should be surprized at this :
Himself confesses that it is only modernizing the orthography ; and
if that is not allowable in this word, why is it in any other ?

                        Ralph.

Ralph. Speak what thou art, and how thou haft been
    us'd,
That I may give him condign punifhment.

  1 *Knight.* I am a Knight that took my journey poft
Northward from London; and, in courteous wife,
This giant train'd me to his loathfome den,
Under pretence of killing of the itch;
And all my body with a powder ftrew'd,
That fmarts and ftings; and cut away my beard,
And my curl'd locks, wherein were ribands tied;
And with a water wafh'd my tender eyes,
(Whilft up and down about me ftill he fkipt)
Whofe virtue is, that 'till my eyes be wip'd
With a dry cloth, for this my foul difgrace,
I fhall not dare to look a dog i' th' face.

  Wife. Alas, poor Knight! Relieve him, Ralph;
relieve poor knights, whilft you live.

  Ralph. My trufty Squire, convey him to the town,
Where he may find relief. Adieu, fair Knight!

                               [Exit Knight.

Enter George, leading one with a patch over his nofe.

  George. Puiffant Knight, o' th' Burning Peftle hight,
See here another wretch, whom this foul beaft
Hath fcotch'd [44] and fcor'd in this inhuman wife.

  Ralph. Speak me thy name, and eke thy place of
    birth,
And what hath been thy ufage in this cave.

  2 *Knight.* I am a Knight, Sir Pockhole is my name,
And by my birth I am a Londoner,
Free by my copy, but my anceftors
Were Frenchmen all; and riding hard this way,
Upon a trotting horfe, my bones did ache;
And I, faint Knight, to eafe my weary limbs,
Lit at this cave; when ftraight this furious fiend,

---

[44] Scorch'd *and* fcor'd.] The account that the Knight, here
handed out by the Dwarf, gives of himfelf a little after, makes much
againft the reading of *fcorch'd*, but naturally agrees with the alteration
Mr. Theobald and myfelf have advanced.   *Sympfon.*

                                        With

With sharpest instrument of purest steel,
Did cut the gristle of my nose away,
And in the place this velvet plaister stands :
Relieve me, gentle Knight, out of his hands !

Wife. Good Ralph, relieve Sir Pockhole, and send him away; for in truth his breath stinks.

Ralph. Convey him straight after the other Knight. Sir Pockhole, fare you well !

2 Knight. Kind Sir, good night !　　　　　[*Exit.*
Man [*within*]. Deliver us !　　　　[*Cries within.*
Woman [*within*]. Deliver us !

Wife. Hark, George, what a woful cry there is ! I think some woman lies-in there.

Man. Deliver us !
Woman. Deliver us !

Ralph. What ghastly noise is this ? speak, Barbaroso; Or, by this blazing steel, thy head goes off !

Bar. Prisoners of mine, whom I in diet keep.
Send lower down into the cave,
And in a tub that's heated smoaking hot,
There may they find them, and deliver them.

Ralph. Run, Squire and Dwarf; deliver them with
　　　　speed.　　　　[*Exeunt Tim and George.*

Wife. But will not Ralph kill this giant ? Surely I am afraid, if he let him go he will do as much hurt as ever he did.

Cit. Not so, mouse, neither, if he could convert him.

Wife. Ay, George, if he could convert him; but a giant is not so soon converted as one of us ordinary people. There's a pretty tale of a witch, that had the devil's mark about her, God bless us ! that had a giant to her son, that was call'd Lob-lie-by-the-fire; didst never hear it, George?

Enter Tim leading Third Knight, with a glass of lotion in his hand, and George leading a Woman, with diet-bread and drink.

Cit. Peace, Nell; here comes the prisoners.

George. Here be these pined wretches, manful Knight,
　　　　　　　　　　　　　　　　　That

That for this six weeks have not seen a wight.

Ralph. Deliver what you are, and how you came
To this sad cave, and what your usage was?

3 Knight. I am an errant-Knight [45] that follow'd arms,
With spear and shield; and in my tender years
I strucken was with Cupid's fiery shaft,
And fell in love with this my lady dear,
And stole her from her friends in Turnball-street [46],
And bore her up and down from town to town,
Where we did eat and drink, and musick hear;
'Till at the length at this unhappy town
We did arrive, and coming to this cave,
This beast us caught, and put us in a tub,
Where we this two months sweat, and should have done
Another month, if you had not reliev'd us.

Woman. This bread and water hath our diet been,
Together with a rib cut from a neck
Of burned mutton; hard hath been our fare!
Release us from this ugly giant's snare!

3 Knight. This hath been all the food we have
  receiv'd;
But only twice a-day, for novelty, [*Pulls out a siringe.*
He gave a spoonful of this hearty broth
To each of us, thro' this same slender quill.

Ralph. From this infernal monster you shall go,
That useth knights and gentle ladies so.
Convey them hence. [*Exeunt Third Knight and Woman.*

Cit. Cony, I can tell thee the gentlemen like Ralph.

Wife. Ay, George, I see it well enough. Gentlemen,
I thank you all heartily for gracing my man Ralph;
and I promise you, you shall see him oftener.

Bar. Mercy, great Knight! I do recant my ill,
And henceforth never gentle blood will spill.

Ralph. I give thee mercy; but yet thou shalt swear
Upon my Burning Pestle, to perform

---

45 *Man. I am an errant* Knight.] Surely then this character should
be called THIRD *Knight*, as well as the others FIRST and SECOND
Knights.   M. R.

46 *Turnbal.-Street.*] See note 46 on the Scornful Lady.

Thy

Thy promise utter'd.

Bar. I fwear and kifs.

Ralph. Depart then, and amend!
Come, Squire and Dwarf; the fun grows towards his
   fet,
And we have many more adventures yet.   [*Exeunt.*

Cit. Now Ralph is in this humour, I know he would
ha' beaten all the boys in the houfe, if they had been
fet on him.

Wife. Ay, George, but it is well as it is : I warrant
you the gentlemen do confider what it is to overthrow
a giant. But look, George; here comes miftrefs Merrythought, and her fon Michael : Now you are welcome,
miftrefs Merrythought; now Ralph has done, you may
go on.

Enter Mrs. Merrythought and Michael.

Mrs. Mer. Micke, my boy?

Mich. Ay, forfooth, mother!

Mrs. Mer. Be merry, Micke; we are at home now;
where I warrant you, you fhall find the houfe flung out
of the windows. Hark! hey dogs, hey! this is the
old world i'faith with my hufband : I get in among
them, I'll play them fuch a leffon, that they fhall have
little lift to come fcraping hither again!—Why,
mafter Merrythought! hufband! Charles Merrythought!

Mer. [*within.*] If you will fing, and dance, and laugh,
  And hollow, and laugh again!
 And then cry, there boys, there; why then,
  One, two, three, and four,
 We fhall be merry within this hour.

Mrs. Mer. Why, Charles! do you not know your
own natural wife? I fay, open the door, and turn me
out thofe mangy companions; 'tis more than time that
they were fellow-like with you : You are a gentleman,
Charles, and an old man, and father of two children;
and I myfelf, (though I fay it) by my mother's fide,
          niece

niece to a worſhipful gentleman, and a conductor; he has been three times in his majeſty's ſervice at Cheſter; and is now the fourth time, God bleſs him, and his charge, upon his journey.

Mer. Go from my window, love, go;
 Go from my window, my dear:
  The wind and the rain
  Will drive you back again,
 You cannot be lodged here.

Hark you, miſtreſs Merrythought, you that walk upon adventures, and forſake your huſband, becauſe he ſings with never a penny in his purſe; what, ſhall I think myſelf the worſe? Faith no, I'll be merry.

 You come not here, here's none but lads of mettle,
 Lives of a hundred years, and upwards,
 Care never drunk their bloods, nor want made them
  warble.
 Hey-ho, my heart is heavy.

Mrs. Mer. Why, maſter Merrythought, what am I, that you ſhould laugh me to ſcorn thus abruptly? am I not your fellow-feeler, as we may ſay, in all our miſeries? your comforter in health and ſickneſs? have I not brought you children? are they not like you, Charles? Look upon thine own image, hard-heated man! and yet for all this——

Mer. Begone, begone, my juggy, my puggy,
 Begone, my love, my dear!
  The weather is warm,
  'Twill do thee no harm;
 Thou canſt not be lodged here.

Be merry, boys! ſome light muſick, and more wine!

Wife. He's not in earneſt, I hope, George; is he?

Cit. What if he be, ſweetheart?

Wife. Marry if he be, George, I'll make bold to tell him he's an ingrant old man[47], to uſe his bedfellow ſo ſcurvily.

---

[47] *Ingrant*] Is the reading of all the copies but that of 1711, which exhibits *ignorant*; of which word it may be a vitiation, as
        ingrum

Cit. What! how does he use her, honey?

Wife. Marry come up, Sir Saucebox! I think you'll take his part, will you not? Lord, how hot are you grown! you are a fine man, an you had a fine dog; it becomes you sweetly!

Cit. Nay, prithee, Nell, chide not; for as I am an honest man, and a true Christian grocer, I do not like his doings.

Wife. I cry you mercy then, George! you know we are all frail, and full of infirmities.—D'ye hear, master Merrythought? may I crave a word with you?

Mer. Strike up, lively lads!

Wife. I had not thought in truth, master Merrythought, that a man of your age and discretion, as I may say, being a gentleman, and therefore known by your gentle conditions, could have used so little respect to the weakness of his wife: For your wife is your own flesh, the staff of your age, your yoke-fellow, with whose help you draw through the mire of this transitory world; nay, she's your own rib. And again——

Mer. I come not hither for thee to teach,
I have no pulpit for thee to preach,
I would thou hadst kiss'd me under the breech,
As thou art a lady gay.

Wife. Marry, with a vengeance, I am heartily sorry for the poor gentlewoman! but if I were thy wife, i'faith, greybeard, i'faith——

Cit. I prithee, sweet honeysuckle, be content!

Wife. Give me such words, that am a gentlewoman born? hang him, hoary rascal! Get me some drink, George; I am almost molten with fretting: Now beshrew his knave's heart for it!

Mer. Play me a light lavalto. Come, be frolick; fill the good fellows wine!

Mrs. Mer. Why, master Merrythought, are you

---

ingrum is in Wit without Money (see note 77 on that play): *Ingrant* here seems to stand for *ingrateful.*

disposed

difpofed to make me wait here? You'll open, I hope;
I'll fetch them that fhall open elfe.

Mer. Good woman, if you will fing, I'll give you
you fomething; if not——

> You are no love for me, Margret,
> I am no love for you[47].

Come aloft, boys, aloft[48]!

Mrs. Mer. Now a churl's fart in your teeth, Sir!
Come, Micke, we'll not trouble him; a fhall not ding
us i' th' teeth with his bread and his broth, that he
fhall not. Come, boy; I'll provide for thee, I warrant thee: We'll go to mafter Venterwels, the
merchant; I'll get his letter to mine hoft of the Bell
in Waltham; there I'll place thee with the tapfter;
will not that do well for thee, Micke? and let me alone
for that old cuckoldly knave your father! I'll ufe him
in his kind, I warrant you!

FINIS ACTUS TERTII.

Wife. Come, George; where's the beer?

Cit. Here, love!

Wife. This old fornicating fellow will not out of
my mind yet. Gentlemen, I'll begin to you all; and
I defire more of your acquaintance, with all my heart.
Fill the gentlemen fome beer, George. [*Boy danceth.*]
Look, George, the little Boy's come again! methinks
he looks fomething like the prince of Orange in his
long ftocking, if he had a little harnefs about his
neck. George, I will have him dance Fading; Fading
is a fine jig[49], I'll affure you, gentlemen. Begin,
brother; now a capers, fweet heart! now a turn a th'
toe, and then tumble! Cannot you tumble, youth?

---

[47] *You are no love*, &c.] Thefe lines are to be found in Percy's
Reliques of Ancient Poetry, vol. iii. p. 120.

[48] *Come aloft, boys, aloft.*] This line has hitherto been printed as
part of the *fong*; to which we cannot think it belongs.

[49] Fading; fading *is a fine jig.*] This dance is mentioned by Ben
Jonfon, in the Irifh Mafque at Court: 'Daunfh a *fading* at te ved-
'ding;' and again, 'Show tee how teye can foot te *fading* and te
'fadow.'

VOL. VI.   E e   *Boy.*

Boy. No indeed, forſooth.

Wife. Nor eat fire?

Boy. Neither.

Wife. Why then, I thank you heartily; there's two-pence to buy you points withal.

A C T   IV[50].

Enter Jaſper and Boy.

Jaſp. THERE, boy; deliver this: But do it well.
Haſt thou provided me four luſty fellows,
Able to carry me? and art thou perfect
In all thy buſineſs?

Boy. Sir, you need not fear;
I have my leſſon here, and cannot miſs it:
The men are ready for you, and what elſe
Pertains to this employment.

Jaſp. There, my boy;
Take it, but buy no land.

Boy. Faith, Sir, 'twere rare
To ſee ſo young a purchaſer. I fly,
And on my wings carry your deſtiny.   [*Exit.*

Jaſp. Go, and be happy! Now, my lateſt hope,
Forſake me not, but fling thy anchor out,
And let it hold! Stand, fix'd, thou rolling ſtone,
'Till I enjoy my deareſt! Hear me, all
You powers, that rule in men, celeſtial!   [*Exit.*

Wife. Go thy ways; thou art as crooked a ſprig as
ever grew in London! I warrant him, he'll come to
ſome naughty end or other; for his looks ſay no leſs:
Beſides, his father (you know, George) is none of the
beſt; you heard him take me up like a Gill-flirt, and

---

50 *Act* IV.] All the copies concur in making this *act* begin with
the *Boy's dancing*; but as the *dance* was certainly introduced by way of
interlude, here as well as at the end of the firſt act, we have made this
act begin with a part of the real play, as all the others do.

ſing

fing bawdy fongs upon me; but i'faith, if I live,
George——

Cit. Let me alone, fweetheart! I have a trick in
my head fhall lodge him in the Arches for one year, and
make him fing *peccavi*, ere I leave him; and yet he
fhall never know who hurt him neither.

Wife. Do, my good George, do!

Cit. What fhall we have Ralph do now, Boy?

Boy. You fhall have what you will, Sir.

Cit. Why, fo, Sir; go and fetch me him then, and
let the fophy of Perfia come and chriften him a child.

Boy. Believe me, Sir, that will not do fo well; 'tis
ftale; it has been had before at the Red Bull[51].

Wife. George, let Ralph travel over great hills, and
let him be weary, and come to the king of Cracovia's
houfe, covered with black velvet[52], and there let the
king's daughter ftand in her window all in beaten gold,
combing her golden locks with a comb of ivory; and
let her fpy Ralph, and fall in love with him, and come
down to him, and carry him into her father's houfe,
and then let Ralph talk with her!

Cit. Well faid, Nell; it fhall be fo: Boy, let's ha't
done quickly.

Boy. Sir, if you will imagine all this to be done already, you fhall hear them talk together; but we cannot prefent a houfe covered with black velvet, and a
lady in beaten gold.

Cit. Sir Boy, let's ha't as you can then.

Boy. Befides, it will fhew ill-favouredly to have a
grocer's prentice to court a king's daughter.

Cit. Will it fo, Sir? You are well read in hiftories!

---

51 *The Red Bull.*] The *Red Bull* was one of the playhoufes in the
reigns of James I. and Charles I. It was fituated in St. John's Street.
R.

52 *Cracovia's houfe covered with velvet.*] I have inferted the colour
of the *velvet*, which was here wanting, from what the Boy fays the
fecond fpeech below, as to the impoffibility of their complying with
this requeft of the Citizen's Wife,
    But we can't prefent an houfe covered with black *velvet.*
                                                      Sympfon.

I pray

I pray you, what was Sir Dagonet [53]? Was not he prentice to a grocer in London? Read the play of the Four Prentices of London [54], where they toss their pikes so. I pray you fetch him in, Sir, fetch him in!

---

[53] *Sir Dagonet.*] In the Second Part of Shakespeare's Henry IV. act iii. scene iv. this character is mentioned by Justice Shallow: ' I ' remember at Mile-End Green, when I lay at Clement's Inn, I was ' *Sir Dagonet* in Arthur's Show;' upon which Mr. Warton remarks, ' Arthur's Show seems to have been a theatrical representation made ' out of the old romance of Morte Arthure, the most popular one of ' our Author's age. *Sir Dagonet* is king Arthur's squire.'

[54] *The Foure Prentices of London.*] The commentators on Beaumont and Fletcher's Knight of the Burning Pestle have not observed that the design of that play is founded upon a comedy called, ' The Four ' Prentices of London, with the Conquest of Jerusalem; as it hath ' been diverse times acted at the Red Bull, by the Queen's Majesty's ' Servants. Written by Tho. Heywood, 1612.' For as in Beaumont and Fletcher's play, a grocer in the Strand turns knight-errant, making his apprentice his squire, &c. so in Heywood's play four apprentices accoutre themselves as knights, and go to Jerusalem in quest of adventures. One of them, the most important character, is a goldsmith, another a grocer, another a mercer, and a fourth an haberdasher. But Beaumont and Fletcher's Play, though founded upon it, contains many satyrical strokes against Heywood's comedy; the force of which is entirely lost to those who have not seen that comedy.

Thus in Beaumont and Fletcher's Prologue, or first scene, a Citizen is introduced declaring that, in the play, he ' will have a grocer, and ' he shall do admirable things.'

Again, act i. scene i. Ralph says, ' Amongst all the worthy books ' of atchievements, I do not call to mind that I have yet read of a ' grocer-errant: I will be the said knight. Have you heard of any ' that hath wandered unfurnished of his squire and dwarf? My elder ' prentice Tim shall be my trusty squire, and George my dwarf.'

In the following passage the allusion to Heywood's comedy is demonstrably manifest, act iv. scene i.

' *Boy.* It will shew ill-favouredly to have a grocer's prentice court ' a king's daughter.

' *Cit.* Will it so, Sir? You are well read in histories; I pray you ' who was Sir Dagonet? Was he not prentice to a grocer in London? ' Read the play of *The Four Prentices*, where they toss their pikes so.'

In Heywood's comedy, Eustace the grocer's prentice is introduced courting the daughter of the king of France; and in the frontispiece the Four Prentices are represented in armour tilting with javelins. Immediately before the last-quoted speeches we have the following instances of allusion.

' *Cit.* Let the Sophy of Persia come, and christen him a child.

' *Boy.* Believe me, Sir, that will not do so well; 'tis flat; it has ' been before at the Red Bull.'

A circumstance

Boy. It fhall be done.—It is not our fault, gentlemen.

[*Exit.*

Wife. Now we fhall fee fine doings, I warrant thee, George. Oh, here they come! How prettily the king of Cracovia's daughter is dreffed.

Enter Ralph, Lady, Tim, and George.

Cit. Ay, Nell, it is the fafhion of that country, I warrant thee.

Lady. Welcome, Sir Knight, unto my father's
   court,
King of Moldavia; unto me, Pompiona,
His daughter dear! But fure you do not like
Your entertainment, that will ftay with us
No longer but a night.

 Ralph. Damfel right fair,
I am on many fad adventures bound,
That call me forth into the wildernefs:
Befides, my horfe's back is fomething gall'd,
Which will enforce me ride a fober pace.
But many thanks, fair lady, be to you,
For ufing errant-Knight with courtefy!

 Lady. But fay, brave Knight, what is your name
   and birth?

 Ralph. My name is Ralph, I am an Englifhman,
(As true as fteel, a hearty Englifhman)
And 'prentice to a grocer in the Strand,
By deed indent, of which I have one part:
But Fortune calling me to follow arms,
On me this holy order I did take
Of Burning Peftle, which in all mens' eyes
I bear, confounding ladies' enemies.

 Lady. Oft have I heard of your brave countrymen,
And fertile foil, and ftore of wholefome food;
My father oft will tell me of a drink

A circumftance in Heywood's comedy; which, as has been already
fpecified, was acted at the Red Bull. Beaumont and Fletcher's play
is pure burlefque. Heywood's is a mixture of the droll and ferious,
and was evidently intended to ridicule the reigning fafhion of reading
romances.   *Warton.*

In

In England found, and Nipitato call'd,
Which driveth all the forrow from your hearts.

Ralph. Lady, 'tis true; you need not lay your lips
To better Nipitato than there is.

Lady. And of a wild-fowl he will often fpeak,
Which powder'd beef and muftard called is:
For there have been great wars 'twixt us and you;
But truly, Ralph, it was not long of me.
Tell me then, Ralph, could you contented be
To wear a lady's favour in your fhield?

Ralph. I am a knight of a religious order,
And will not wear a favour of a lady
That trufts in Antichrift, and falfe traditions.

Cit. Well faid, Ralph! convert her, if thou canft.

Ralph. Befides, I have a lady of my own
In merry England; for whofe virtuous fake
I took thefe arms; and Sufan is her name,
A cobler's maid in Milk-Street; whom I vow
Ne'er to forfake, whilft life and Peftle laft.

Lady. Happy that cobling dame, whoe'er fhe be,
That for her own, dear Ralph, hath gotten thee!
Unhappy I, that ne'er fhall fee the day
To fee thee more, that bear'ft my heart away!

Ralph. Lady, farewell! I needs muft take my leave.

Lady. Hard-hearted Ralph, that ladies doft deceive!

Cit. Hark thee, Ralph! there's money for thee:
Give fomething in the king of Cracovia's houfe; be
not beholding to him.

Ralph. Lady, before I go, I muft remember
Your father's officers, who, truth to tell,
Have been about me very diligent:
Hold up thy fnowy hand, thou princely maid!
There's twelve-pence for your father's chamberlain;
And there's another fhilling for his cook,
For, by my troth, the goofe was roafted well;
And twelve-pence for your father's horfe-keeper,
For 'nointing my horfe-back, and for his butter
There is another fhilling; to the maid
That wafh'd my boot-hofe, there's an Englifh groat;
And

And two-pence to the boy that wip'd my boots!
And, laſt, fair lady, there is for yourſelf
Three-pence, to buy you pins at Bumbo-fair!

Lady. Full many thanks ; and I will keep them ſafe
'Till all the heads be off, for thy ſake, Ralph.

Ralph. Advance, my Squire and Dwarf! I cannot ſtay.

Lady. Thou kill'ſt my heart in parting thus away.
[*Exeunt.*

Wife. I commend Ralph yet, that he will not ſtoop
to a Cracovian ; there's properer women in London
than any are there, I wis. But here comes maſter
Humphrey and his love again ; now, George!

Cit. Ay, cony, peace!

Enter Merchant, Maſter Humphrey, Luce, and Boy.

Merch. Go, get you up! I will not be entreated.
And, goſſip mine, I'll keep you ſure hereafter
From gadding out again, with boys and unthrifts :
Come, they are womens' tears ; I know your faſhion.
Go, ſirrah, lock her in, and keep the key
[*Exeunt Luce and Boy.*
Safe, as you love your life [55]. Now, my ſon Humphrey,
You may both reſt aſſured of my love
In this, and reap your own deſire.

Hum. I ſee this love you ſpeak of, thro' your
daughter,
Altho' the hole be little ; and hereafter
Will yield the like in all I may or can,
Fitting a Chriſtian and a gentleman.

Merch. I do believe you, my good ſon, and thank
you ;

---

[55] *Safe as your life.*] We ought to read here, ſays the gentleman
quoted ſo often above, thus,

    Safe as you love your life.   *Sympſon.*

The reader will probably be ſurprized at Sympſon's ſaying, ' quoted
' SO OFTEN,' when we have mentioned the gentleman SO SELDOM :
The cauſe is, the gentleman ſcarcely ever propoſed a variation from
the old books, but (as in the preſent caſe ; for they exhibit the words
you love) recommended *reſtorations* from them ; which Sympſon,
from his wonderful inattention to the authorized copies, ſuppoſed
were *corrections.*

          For

For 'twere an impudence to think you flatter'd.

Hum. It were indeed ; but fhall I tell you why ?
I have been beaten twice about the lie.

Merch. Well, fon, no more of compliment. My
daughter
Is yours again ; appoint the time and take her :
We'll have no ftealng for it ; I myfelf
And fome few of our friends will fee you married.

Hum. I would you would, i'faith ! for be it known,
I ever was afraid to lie alone.

Merch. Some three days hence then——

Hum. Three days ? let me fee !
'Tis fomewhat of the moft ; yet I agree,
Becaufe I mean againft the 'pointed day
To vifit all my friends in new array.

Enter Servant.

Serv. Sir, there's a gentlewoman without would
fpeak with your worfhip.

Merch. What is fhe ?

Serv. Sir, I afk'd her not.

Merch. Bid her come in.

Enter Mrs. Merrythought and Michael.

Mrs. Mer. Peace be to your worfhip ! I come as a
poor fuitor to you, Sir, in the behalf of this child.

Merch. Are you not wife to Merrythought ?

Mrs. Mer. Yes, truly : 'Would I had ne'er feen his
eyes ! he has undone me and himfelf, and his children ;
and there he lives at home, and fings and hoits, and
revels among his drunken companions ! but, I warrant
you, where to get a penny to put bread in his mouth
he knows not : And therefore, if it like your worfhip, I would entreat your letter to the honeft hoft of
the Bell in Waltham, that I may place my child under
the protection of his tapfter, in fome fettled courfe
of life.

Merch. I'm glad the Heav'ns have heard my prayers!
Thy hufband,

When

When I was ripe in forrows, laugh'd at me;
Thy fon, like an unthankful wretch, I having
Redeem'd him from his fall, and made him mine,
To fhew his love again, firft ftole my daughter,
Then wrong'd this gentleman ; and, laft of all,
Gave me that grief had almoft brought me down
Unto my grave, had not a ftronger hand
Reliev'd my forrows : Go, and weep as I did,
And be unpitied ; for I here profefs
An everlafting hate to all thy name.

Mrs. Mer. Will you fo, Sir ? how fay you by that?
Come, Micke ; let him keep his wind to cool his
pottage ! We'll go to thy nurfe's, Micke ; fhe knits
filk ftockings, boy, and we'll knit too, boy, and be
beholding to none of them all. [*Exit with Michael.*

Enter a Boy with a letter.

Boy. Sir, I take it you are the mafter of this houfe.
Merch. How then, Boy ?
Boy. Then to yourfelf, Sir, comes this letter.
Merch. From whom, my pretty Boy ?
Boy. From him that was your fervant ; but no more
Shall that name ever be, for he is dead !
Grief of your purchas'd anger broke his heart :
I faw him die, and from his hand receiv'd
This paper, with a charge to bring it hither :
Read it, and fatisfy yourfelf in all.

Merch. [*reading.*] ' Sir, that I have wronged your
' love I muft confefs ; in which I have purchafed to
' myfelf, befides mine own undoing, the ill opinion
' of my friends. Let not your anger, good Sir, out-
' live me, but fuffer me to reft in peace with your
' forgivenefs : Let my body (if a dying man may fo
' much prevail with you) be brought to your daughter,
' that fhe may know my hot flames are now buried,
' and withal receive a teftimony of the zeal I bore her
' virtue. Farewell for ever, and be ever happy !
' Jafper.'

God's

God's hand is great in this! I do forgive him;
Yet I am glad he's quiet, where I hope
He will not bite again.   Boy, bring the body,
And let him have his will, if that be all.

Boy. 'Tis here without, Sir.

Merch. So, Sir; if you pleaſe,
You may conduct it in; I do not fear it!

Hum. I'll be your uſher, Boy; for, tho' I ſay it,
He ow'd me ſomething once, and well did pay it.

[*Exeunt.*

Enter Luce alone.

Luce. If there be any puniſhment inflicted
Upon the miſerable, more than yet I feel,
Let it together ſeize me, and at once
Preſs down my ſoul! I cannot bear the pain
Of theſe delaying tortures!—Thou that art
The end of all, and the ſweet reſt of all,
Come, come, oh, Death! bring me to thy peace,
And blot out all the memory I nouriſh
Both of my father and my cruel friend!
Oh, wretched maid, ſtill living to be wretched,
To be a ſay [56] to Fortune in her changes,
And grow to number times and woes together!
How happy had I been, if, being born,
My grave had been my cradle!

Enter Servant.

Serv. By your leave,
Young miſtreſs! Here's a boy hath brought a coffin;
What a would ſay I know not; but your father
Charg'd me to give you notice.   Here they come!

Enter two bearing a coffin, Jaſper in it.

Luce. For me I hope 'tis come, and 'tis moſt wel-
       come.

Boy. Fair miſtreſs, let me not add greater grief
To that great ſtore you have already.   Jaſper,

---

[56] *To be a ſay.*] *A ſay* ſeems corrupt; perhaps we ſhould read,
aſſay.

(That

(That whilft he liv'd was yours, now dead,
And here enclos'd) commanded me to bring
His body hither, and to crave a tear
From thofe fair eyes, (tho' he deferv'd not pity)
To deck his funeral, for fo he bid me
Tell her for whom he died.

Luce. He fhall have many. [*Exe. coffin-carriers and boy.*
Good friends, depart a little, whilft I take
My leave of this dead man, that once I lov'd.
Hold yet a little, life! and then I give thee
To thy firft heavenly being. Oh, my friend!
Haft thou deceiv'd me thus, and got before me?
I fhall not long be after. But, believe me,
Thou wert too cruel, Jafper, 'gainft thyfelf,
In punifhing the fault I could have pardon'd,
With fo untimely death: Thou didft not wrong me,
But ever wert moft kind, moft true, moft loving;
And I the moft unkind, moft falfe, moft cruel!
Didft thou but afk a tear? I'll give thee all,
Even all my eyes can pour down, all my fighs,
And all myfelf, before thou goeft from me:
Thefe are but fparing rites; but if thy foul
Be yet about this place, and can behold
And fee what I prepare to deck thee with,
It fhall go up, borne on the wings of peace,
And fatisfied: Firft will I fing thy dirge,
Then kifs thy pale lips, and then die myfelf,
And fill one coffin, and one grave together.

Come, you whofe loves are dead,
  And whiles I fing,
  Weep and ring
Every hand, and every head
Bind with cyprefs and fad yew;
Ribbons black and candles blue,
For him that was of men moft true!
Come with heavy moaning [57],
  And on his grave
  Let him have
Sacrifice of fighs and groaning;

---

57 *With heavy* mourning.] Amended in 1750.

Let

Let him have fair flowers enow,
White and purple, green and yellow,
For him that was of men moſt true!

Thou ſable cloth, ſad cover of my joys,
I lift thee up, and thus I meet with death.

Jaſp. And thus you meet the living.

Luce. Save me, Heaven!

Jaſp. Nay, do not fly me, fair; I am no ſpirit:
Look better on me; do you know me yet?

Luce. Oh, thou dear ſhadow of my friend!

Jaſp. Dear ſubſtance,
I ſwear I am no ſhadow; feel my hand!
It is the ſame it was; I am your Jaſper,
Your Jaſper that's yet living, and yet loving!
Pardon my raſh attempt, my fooliſh proof
I put in practice of your conſtancy!
For ſooner ſhould my ſword have drunk my blood,
And ſet my ſoul at liberty, than drawn
The leaſt drop from that body; for which boldneſs
Doom me to any thing! if death, I take it,
And willingly.

Luce. This death I'll give you for it! [*Kiſſes him.*
So; now I'm ſatisfied, you are no ſpirit,
But my own trueſt, trueſt, trueſt friend!
Why do you come thus to me?

Jaſp. Firſt, to ſee you;
Then to convey you hence.

Luce. It cannot be;
For I am lock'd up here, and watch'd at all hours,
That 'tis impoſſible for me to 'ſcape.

Jaſp. Nothing more poſſible: Within this coffin
Do you convey yourſelf; let me alone,
I have the wits of twenty men about me;
Only I crave the ſhelter of your cloſet
A little, and then fear me not. Creep in,
That they may preſently convey you hence.
Fear nothing, deareſt love! I'll be your ſecond;
Lie cloſe; ſo! all goes well yet. Boy!

Boy. At hand, Sir.

Jaſp. Convey away the coffin, and be wary.

Boy.

Boy. 'Tis done already.

Jasp. Now muſt I go conjure.   [*Exit.*

Enter Merchant.

Merch. Boy, Boy!

Boy. Your ſervant, Sir.

Merch. Do me this kindneſs, Boy; (hold; here's a crown)

Before thou bury the body of this fellow,

Carry it to his old merry father, and ſalute him

From me, and bid him ſing; h' hath cauſe.

Boy. I will, Sir.

Merch. And then bring me word what tune he is in,

And have another crown; but do it truly.

I've fitted him a bargain, now, will vex him.

Boy. God bleſs your worſhip's health, Sir!

Merch. Farewell, Boy!   [*Exeunt.*

Enter Old Merrythought.

Wife. Ah, old Merrythought, art thou there again?
Let's hear ſome of thy ſongs.

Mer. Who can ſing a merrier note
    Than he that cannot change a groat?

Not a denier left, and yet my heart leaps: I do wonder yet, as old as I am, that any man will follow a trade, or ſerve, that may ſing and laugh, and walk the ſtreets. My wife and both my ſons are I know not where; I have nothing left, nor know I how to come by meat to ſupper; yet am I merry ſtill; for I know I ſhall find it upon the table at ſix o'clock; therefore, hang thought!

    I would not be a ſerving-man
        To carry the cloak-bag ſtill,
    Nor would I be a falconer
        The greedy hawks to fill;
    But I would be in a good houſe,
        And have a good maſter too;
    But I would eat and drink of the beſt,
        And no work would I do.

This

This is that keeps life and soul together, mirth! This is the philofpher's ftone that they write fo much on, that keeps a man ever young!

Enter a Boy.

Boy. Sir, they fay they know all your money is gone, and they will truft you for no more drink.

Mer. Will they not? let 'em chufe! The beft is, I have mirth at home, and need not fend abroad for that; let them keep their drink to themfelves.

For Jillian of Berry fhe dwells on a hill,
And fhe hath good beer and ale to fell,
And of good fellows fhe thinks no ill,
And thither will we go now, now, now,
  And thither will we go now.
And when you have made a little ftay,
You need not know what is to pay,
But kifs your hoftefs, and go your way.
And thither, &c.

Enter another Boy.

2 Boy. Sir, I can get no bread for fupper.

Mer. Hang bread and fupper! let's preferve our mirth, and we fhall never feel hunger, I'll warrant you. Let's have a catch: Boy, follow me; come, fing this catch.

Ho, ho, nobody at home,
Meat, nor drink, nor money ha' we none?
  Fill the pot, Eedy,
  Never more need I.

Mer. So, boys; enough. Follow me: let's change our place, and we fhall laugh afrefh.   [*Exeunt.*

Wife. Let him go, George; a fhall not have any countenance from us; not a good word from any i'th' company, if I may ftrike ftroke in't.

Cit. No more a fhannot, love. But, Nell, I will have Ralph do a very notable matter now, to the eternal honour and glory of all grocers. Sirrah! you there! Boy! Can none of you hear?

Boy.

Boy. Sir, your pleasure?

Cit. Let Ralph come out on May-day in the morning, and speak upon a conduit, with all his scarfs
about him, and his feathers, and his rings, and his
knacks.

Boy. Why, Sir, you do not think of our plot;
what will become of that then?

Cit. Why, Sir, I care not what become on't! I'll
have him come out, or I'll fetch him out myself; I'll
have something done in honour of the city. Besides,
he hath been long enough upon adventures: Bring
him out quickly; or if I come amongst you——

Boy. Well, Sir, he shall come out; but if our
play miscarry, Sir, you are like to pay for't. [*Exit.*

Cit. Bring him away then!

Wife. This will be brave, i'faith! George, shall
not he dance the morris too, for the credit of the
Strand?

Cit. No, sweetheart, it will be too much for the
boy. Oh, there he is, Nell! he's reasonable well in
reparrel; but he has not rings enough.

Enter Ralph.

Ralph. London, to thee I do present
   The merry month of May;
Let each true subject be content
   To hear me what I say:
For from the top of Conduit-Head,
   As plainly may appear,
I will both tell my name to you,
   And wherefore I came here.
My name is Ralph, by due descent
   Tho' not ignoble I,
Yet far inferior to the flock
   Of gracious grocery;
And by the common counsel of
   My fellows in the Strand,
With gilded staff, and crossed scarf,
   The May-lord here I stand.

                    Rejoice,

Rejoice, oh, Englifh hearts, rejoice,
 Rejoice, oh, lovers dear;
Rejoice, oh, city, town, and country,
 Rejoice eke every fhire!
For now the fragrant flowers do fpring
 And fprout in feemly fort,
The little birds do fit and fing,
 The lambs do make fine fport;
And now the burchin-tree doth bud,
 That makes the fchoolboy cry,
The morrs rings, while hobby-horfe
 Doth foot it featuoufly;
The lords and ladies now abroad,
 For their difport and play,
Do kifs fometimes upon the grafs,
 And fometimes in the hay.
Now butter with a leaf of fage
 Is good to purge the blood,
Fly Venus and phlebotomy,
 For they are neither good!
Now little fifh on tender ftone
 Begin to caft their bellies,
And fluggifh fnails, that erft were mew'd [58],
 Do creep out of their fhellies.
The rumbling rivers now do warm,
 For little boys to paddle;
The fturdy fteed now goes to grafs,
 And up they hang his faddle.
The heavy hart, the blowing buck [59],
 The rafcal and the pricket,
Are now among the yeoman's peafe,
 And leave the fearful thicket.
And be like them, oh, you, I fay,
 Of this fame noble town,
And lift aloft your velvet heads,
 And flipping of your gown:

---

[58] *That erft were* mute.] Corrected by Sympfon.
[59] *The* blowing *buck.*] The firft quarto reads *bellowing.* The judicious are left to their choice.   *Sympfon.*
We cannot fuppofe any of the *judicious* will prefer *bellowing.*

              With

With bells on legs, and napkins clean
   Unto your shoulders tied,
With scarfs and garters as you please,
   And hey for our town cried.
March out and shew your willing minds,
   By twenty and by twenty,
To Hogsdon, or to Newington,
   Where ale and cakes are plenty!
And let it ne'er be said for shame,
   That we the youths of London,
Lay thrumming of our caps at home,
   And left our custom undone.
Up then, I say, both young and old,
   Both man and maid a-maying,
With drums and guns that bounce aloud,
   And merry tabor playing!
Which to prolong, God save our king,
   And send his country peace,
And root out treason from the land!
   And so, my friends, I cease.   [*Exit.*

FINIS ACTUS QUARTI.

ACT V.

Enter Merchant solus.

Merch. I Will have no great store of company at
the wedding; a couple of neighbours and
their wives; and we will have a capon in stewed broth,
with marrow, and a good piece of beef, stuck with
rosemary [60].

Enter Jasper, with his face mealed.

Jasp. Forbear thy pains, fond man! it is too late.
Merch. Heav'n bless me! Jasper?
Jasp. Ay, I am his ghost,

---

[60] *Rosemary.*] See note 33 on the Elder Brother.

Whom thou haſt injur'd for his conſtant love.
Fond worldly wretch! who doſt not underſtand
In death that true hearts cannot parted be.
Firſt know, thy daughter is quite borne away
On wings of angels, thro' the liquid air,
Too far out of thy reach, and never more
Shalt thou behold her face: But ſhe and I
Will in another world enjoy our loves;
Where neither father's anger, poverty,
Nor any croſs that troubles earthly men,
Shall make us ſever our united hearts.
And never ſhalt thou ſit, or be alone
In any place, but I will viſit thee
With ghaſtly looks, and put into thy mind
The great offences which thou didſt to me.
When thou art at thy table with thy friends,
Merry in heart, and fill'd with ſwelling wine,
I'll come in midſt of all thy pride and mirth,
Inviſible to all men but thyſelf⁶¹,
And whiſper ſuch a ſad tale in thine ear,
Shall make thee let the cup fall from thy hand,
And ſtand as mute and pale as death itſelf.

Merch. Forgive me, Jaſper! Oh, what might I do,
Tell me, to ſatisfy thy troubled ghoſt?

Jaſp. There is no means; too late thou think'ſt on
this.

Merch. But tell me what were beſt for me to do?

Jaſp. Repent thy deed, and ſatisfy my father,
And beat fond Humphrey out of thy doors. [*Exit.*

Enter Humphrey.

Wife. Look, George; his very ghoſt would have
folks beaten.

Hum. Father, my bride is gone, fair miſtreſs Luce.
My ſoul's the fount of vengeance, miſchief's ſluice.

Merch. Hence, fool, out of my ſight, with thy fond
paſſion!

---

⁶¹ *Inviſible to all men but thyſelf.*] This ſeems to be meant as a
ridicule on the appearance of Banquo's ghoſt in Macbeth.

Thou

Thou haſt undone me.

Hum. Hold, my father dear!
For Luce thy daughter's ſake, that had no peer.

Merch. Thy father, fool? There's ſome blows
    more; be gone!   *[Beats him.*
Jaſper, I hope thy ghoſt be well appeas'd
To ſee thy will performed. Now I'll go
To ſatisfy thy father for thy wrongs.   *[Exit.*

Hum. What ſhall I do? I have been beaten twice,
And miſtreſs Luce is gone? Help me, Device!
Since my true love is gone, I never more,
Whilſt I do live, upon the ſky will pore;
But in the dark will wear out my ſhoe-ſoles
In paſſion, in Saint Faith's church under Paul's. *[Exit.*

Wife. George, call Ralph hither; if you love me,
call Ralph hither! I have the braveſt thing for him to
do——George! prithee, call him quickly.

Cit. Ralph! why, Ralph, boy!

Enter Ralph.

Ralph. Here, Sir.

Cit. Come hither, Ralph; come to thy miſtreſs, boy.

Wife. Ralph, I would have thee call all the youths
together in battle-ray, with drums, and guns, and
flags, and march to Mile-End in pompous faſhion,
and there exhort your ſoldiers to be merry and wiſe,
and to keep their beards from burning, Ralph; and
then ſkirmiſh, and let your flags fly, and cry, ' kill,
kill, kill!' My huſband ſhall lend you his jerkin,
Ralph, and there's a ſcarf; for the reſt, the houſe
ſhall furniſh you, and we'll pay for't. Do it bravely,
Ralph; and think before whom you perform, and
what perſon you repreſent.

Ralph. I warrant you, miſtreſs; if I do it not, for
the honour of the city, and the credit of my maſter,
let me never hope for freedom!

Wife. 'Tis well ſpoken, i'faith! Go thy ways; thou
art a ſpark indeed.

Cit. Ralph, Ralph, double your files bravely, Ralph!
                       Ralph.

Ralph. I warrant you, Sir. [*Exit.*

Cit. Let him look narrowly to his service; I shall take him else. I was there myself a pike-man once, in the hottest of the day, wench; had my feather shot sheer away, the fringe of my pike burnt off with powder, my pate broken with a scouring-stick, and yet, I thank God, I am here. [*Drums within.*

Wife. Hark, George, the drums!

Cit. Ran, tan, tan, tan, ran, tan! Oh, wench, an thou hadst but seen little Ned of Aldgate, drum Ned, how he made it roar again, and laid on like a tyrant, and then struck softly till the ward came up, and then thundered again, and together we go? sa, sa, sa, bounce, quoth the guns! courage, my hearts, quoth the captains! Saint George, quoth the pike-men! and withal, here they lay, and there they lay! And yet for all this I am here, wench.

Wife. Be thankful for it, George; for indeed 'tis wonderful.

Enter Ralph and his company, with drums and colours.

Ralph. March fair, my hearts [61]! lieutenant, beat
the rear up.
Ancient, let your colours fly; but have
A great care of the butchers' hooks at Whitechapel;
They have been the death of many a fair ancient.
Open your files, that I may take a view
Both of your persons and munition.
Sergeant, call a muster.

Serg. A stand!—William Hamerton, pewterer!

Ham. Here, captain.

Ralph. A croslet and a Spanish pike! 'tis well;
Can you shake it with a terror?

Ham. I hope so, captain.

Ralph. Charge upon me.—'Tis with the weakest:
Put more strength, William Hamerton, more strength.

61 *March fair, my hearts,* &c.] As Ralph's part seems intended for metre (though this whole scene has hitherto been printed as prose), we have endeavoured to divide it accordingly, and hope it is settled tolerably right.

As

As you were again.   Proceed, Sergeant.

Serg. George Greengoose, poulterer!

Green. Here!

Ralph. Let me fee your piece, neighbour Greengoose;
When was fhe fhot in?

Green. An't like you, mafter captain, I made a fhot
even now, partly to fcour her, and partly for audacity.

Ralph. It fhould feem fo
Certainly; for her breath is yet inflamed.
Befides, there is a main fault in the touch-hole,
It runs and ftinketh:
And I tell you moreover, and believe it,
Ten fuch touch-holes would breed the pox i' th' army.
Get you a feather, neighbour, get you a feather,
Sweet oil, and paper, and your piece may do
Well enough yet.   Where's your powder?

Green. Here.

Ralph. What, in a paper?
As I'm a foldier and a gentleman,
It craves a martial court! You ought to die for't.
Where's your horn? Anfwer me to that.

Green. An't like you, Sir, I was oblivious.

Ralph. It likes me not it fhould be fo; 'tis a fhame
For you, and a fcandal to all our neighbours,
Being a man of worth and eftimation,
To leave your horn behind you: I'm afraid
'Twill breed example. But let me tell you no more on't.
Stand, till I view you all.   What's become
O' th' nofe of your flafk?

1 Sold. Indeed-la, captain, 'twas blown away with
powder.

Ralph. Put on a new one at the city's charge.
Where's the ftone of this piece?

2 Sold. The drummer took it out to light tobacco.

Ralph. 'Tis a fault, my friend; put it in again.
You want a nofe, and you a ftone; Sergeant, take a
        note on't,
For I mean to ftop it in the pay.   Remove and march!
Soft and fair, gentlemen, foft and fair! Double your files;

As you were! faces about [61]! Now, you with the sodden
    face,
Keep in there! Look to your match, sirrah,
It will be in your fellow's flask anon.
So; make a crescent now; advance your pikes;
Stand and give ear!—Gentlemen, countrymen,
Friends, and my fellow-soldiers, I have brought you
This day from the shops of security,
And the counters of content, to measure out
In these furious fields, honour by the ell,
And prowess by the pound.   Let it not,
Oh, let it not, I say, be told hereafter,
The noble issue of this city-fainted;
But bear yourselves in this fair action
Like men, valiant men, and free men! Fear not
The face of the enemy, nor the noise of the guns;
For believe me, brethren, the rude rumbling
Of a brewer's carr is more terrible,
Of which you have a daily experience:
Neither let the stink of powder offend you,
Since a more valiant stink is nightly with you.
To a resolved mind, his home is every where:
I speak not this to take away
The hope of your return; for you shall see
(I do not doubt it) and that very shortly,
Your loving wives again, and your sweet children,
Whose care doth bear you company in baskets.
Remember then whose cause you have in hand,
And, like a sort of true-born scavengers,
Scour me this famous realm of enemies.
I have no more to say but this:
Stand to your tacklings, lads, and shew to th' world,
You can as well brandish a sword
As shake an apron. Saint George, and on, my hearts!
    Omnes. Saint George, Saint George!   [*Exeunt.*
    Wife. 'Twas well done, Ralph! I'll send thee a cold
capon a-field, and a bottle of March beer; and, it
may be, come myself to see thee.

---

[61] *Faces about*] See note 63 on the Scornful Lady.

                                                        Cit.

Cit. Nell, the boy hath deceiv'd me much! I did not think it had been in him. He has perform'd such a matter, wench, that, if I live, next year I'll have him captain of the gallifoilt, or I'll want my will.

Enter Old Merrythought.

Mer. Yet, I thank God, I break not a wrinkle more than I had. Not a ftoop, boys? Care, live with cats; I defy thee! My heart is as found as an oak; and tho' I want drink to wet my whiftle, I can fing,

Come no more there, boys, come no more there;
For we fhall never whilft we live come any more there.

Enter a Boy, with a coffin.

Boy. God fave you, Sir!

Mer. It's a brave boy. Canft thou fing?

Boy. Yes, Sir, I can fing; but 'tis not fo neceffary at this time.

Mer. Sing we, and chaunt it,
    Whilft love doth grant it.

Boy. Sir, Sir, if you knew what I have brought you, you would have little lift to fing.

Mer. Oh, the mimon round,
    Full long I have thee fought,
        And now I have thee found,
    And what haft thou here brought?

Boy. A coffin, Sir, and your dead fon Jafper in it.

Mer. Dead? Why, farewell he!
    Thou waft a bonny boy,
        And I did love thee.

Enter Jafper.

Jafp. Then I pray you, Sir, do fo ftill.

Mer. Jafper's ghoft?
    Thou art welcome from Stygian-lake fo foon;
        Declare to me what wondrous things
    In Pluto's court are done.

Jafp.

Jasp. By my troth, Sir, I ne'er came there; 'tis too hot for me, Sir.

Mer. A merry ghost, a very merry ghost!

And where is your true love? Oh, where is yours?

Jasp. Marry, look you, Sir! [*Heaves up the coffin.*

Mer. Ah, ha! art thou good at that, i'faith?

With hey trickfy terlerie-whifkin,
The world it runs on wheels.
When the young man's ——
Up goes the maiden's heels.

Mrs. Merrythought and Michael within.

Mrs. Mer. What, master Merrythought! will you not let's in? What do you think shall become of us?

Mer. What voice is that that calleth at our door?

Mrs. Mer. You know me well enough; I am sure I have not been such a stranger to you.

Mer. And some they whistled, and some they sung,
Hey down, down!
And some did loudly say,
Ever as the lord Barnet's horn blew,
Away, Musgrave, away [64].

Mrs. Mer. You will not have us starve here, will you, master Merrythought?

Jasp. Nay, good Sir, be persuaded; she's my mother:
If her offences have been great against you,
Let your own love remember she is yours,
And so forgive her.

Luce. Good master Merrythought,
Let me entreat you; I will not be denied.

Mrs. Mer. Why, master Merrythought, will you be a vex'd thing still?

Mer. Woman, I take you to my love again;
But you shall sing before you enter; therefore

---

[64] *And some they whistled, &c.*] The ballad from which this stanza is taken is printed in Percy's Reliques of Ancient Poetry, vol. iii. p. 63. R.

Difpatch your fong, and fo come in.

Mrs. Mer. Well, you muft have your will, when all's done. Micke, what fong canft thou fing, boy?

Mich. I can fing none forfooth, but A Lady's Daughter of Paris, properly.

Mich. [*fings.*] It was a lady's daughter, &c.

Mer. Come, you're welcome home again.

If fuch danger be in playing,
    And jeft muft to earneft turn,
You fhall go no more a-maying——

Merch. [*within.*] Are you within, Sir? mafter Merrythought!

Jafp. It is my mafter's voice; good Sir, go hold him In talk whilft we convey ourfelves into Some inward room.

Mer. What are you? are you merry?
You muft be very merry, if you enter.

Merch. I am, Sir.

Mer. Sing then.

Merch. Nay, good Sir, open to me.

Mer. Sing, I fay,
Or, by the merry heart, you come not in!

Merch. Well, Sir, I'll fing.
        Fortune my foe ⁶⁵, &c.

Mer. You're welcome, Sir, you're welcome!
You fee your entertainment; pray you be merry.

Merch. Oh, mafter Merrythought, I'm come to afk you
Forgivenefs for the wrongs I offer'd you,
And your moft virtuous fon; they're infinite,
Yet my contrition fhall be more than they.
I do confefs my hardnefs broke his heart,
For which juft Heaven hath giv'n me punifhment
More than my age can carry; his wandring fpirit,
Not yet at reft, purfues me every where,
Crying, ' I'll haunt thee for thy cruelty.'

---

⁶⁵ *Fortune my foe.*] See note 2 on the Cuftom of the Country.

My

My daughter fhe is gone, I know not how,
Taken invifible, and whether living,
Or in the grave, 'tis yet uncertain to me.
Oh, mafter Merrythought, thefe are the weights
Will fink me to my grave! Forgive me, Sir.

Mer. Why, Sir, I do forgive you; and be merry!
And if the wag in's life-time play'd the knave,
Can you forgive him too?

Merch. With all my heart, Sir.

Mer. Speak it again, and heartily.

Merch. I do, Sir;
Now, by my foul, I do.

Mer. With that came out his paramour;
She was as white as the lilly flower,
Hey troul, troly, loly!

Enter Luce and Jafper.

With that came out her own dear knight,
He was as true as ever did fight, *&c.*
Sir, if you will forgive 'em, clap their hands
Together; there's no more to be faid i' th' matter.

Merch. I do, I do.

Cit. I do not like this: Peace, boys! Hear me, one
of you! every body's part is come to an end but
Ralph's, and he's left out.

Boy. 'Tis long of yourfelf, Sir; we have nothing
to do with his part.

Cit. Ralph, come away! Make an end on him [66], as
you have done of the reft, boys; come!

Wife. Now, good hufband, let him come out and die.

Cit. He fhall, Nell. Ralph, come away quickly,
and die, boy.

Boy. 'Twill be very unfit he fhould die, Sir, upon
no occafion; and in a comedy too.

Cit. Take you no care for that, Sir Boy; is not his
part at an end, think you, when he's dead? Come
away, Ralph!

---

[66] *Make on bim.*] The two words which we have added feem
abfolutely neceffary to the completion of the fenfe.

Enter

Enter Ralph, with a forked arrow through his head.

Ralph. When I was mortal [67], this my coftive corps
Did lap up figs and raifins in the Strand;
Where fitting, I efpied a lovely dame,
Whofe mafter wrought with lingell [68] and with awl,
And underground he vamped many a boot:
Straight did her love prick forth me, tender fprig,
To follow feats of arms in warlike wife,
Thro' Waltham-Defart; where I did perform
Many atchievements, and did lay on ground
Huge Barbarofo, that infulting giant,
And all his captives foon fet at liberty.
Then honour prick'd me from my native foil
Into Moldavia, where I gain'd the love
Of Pompiona, his beloved daughter;
But yet prov'd conftant to the black-thumb'd maid
Sufan, and fcorned Pompiona's love;
Yet liberal I was, and gave her pins,
And money for her father's officers.
I then returned home, and thruft myfelf
In action, and by all men chofen was
The lord of May; where I did flourifh it,
With fcarfs and rings, and pofy in my hand [69].
After this action I preferred was,
And chofen city-captain at Mile-End,
With hat and feather, and with leading ftaff,
And train'd my men, and brought them all off clean,
Save one man that bewray'd him with the noife.
But all thefe things I Ralph did undertake,
Only for my beloved Sufan's fake.
Then coming home, and fitting in my fhop

---

[67] *When I was mortal, &c.*] This fpeech is a parody on that of
the Ghoft of Andrea, at the beginning of the famous play of
Jeronimo:
   ' When this eternal fubftance of my foul
   ' Did live imprifon'd in my wonted flefh, &c.'   R.

[68] *Lingell*] A thread of hemp rubbed with rofin, &c. ufed by
ruftics for mending their fhoes.   *Percy.*

[69] *And poefie in my hand.*] The orthography varied by Sympfon
to *pofie.*

With

With apron blue, Death came unto my ftall
To cheapen *aquavitæ*; but ere I
Could take the bottle down, and fill a tafte,
Death caught a pound of pepper in his hand,
And fprinkled all my face and body o'er,
And in an inftant vanifhed away.

   Cit. 'Tis a pretty fiction, i'faith!

   Ralph. Then took I up my bow and fhaft in hand,
And walked in Moorfields to cool myfelf:
But there grim cruel Death met me again,
And fhot this forked arrow thro' my head;
And now I faint; therefore be warn'd by me,
My fellows every one, of forked heads!
Farewell, all you good boys in merry London!
Ne'er fhall we more upon Shrove-Tuefday meet,
And pluck down houfes of iniquity;
(My pain encreafeth) I fhall never more
Hold open, whilft another pumps both legs,
Nor daub a fattin gown with rotten eggs;
Set up a ftake, oh, never more I fhall!
I die! fly, fly, my foul, to Grocers' Hall! Oh,
      oh, oh, *&c.*

   Wife. Well faid, Ralph! do your obeifance to the
gentlemen, and go your ways. Well faid, Ralph!

                           [*Exit Ralph.*

   Mer. Methinks all we, thus kindly and unexpect-
edly reconciled, fhould not part without a fong.

   Merch. A good motion.

   Mer. Strike up then!

      Better mufick ne'er was known,
      Than a quire of hearts in one.
      Let each other, that hath been
      Troubled with the gall or fpleen,
      Learn of us to keep his brow
      Smooth and plain, as ours are now!
      Sing, tho' before the hour of dying;
      He fhall rife, and then be crying,
      ' Heyho, 'tis nought but mirth
      ' That keeps the body from the earth.'

                          [*Exeunt omnes.*

                    EPILOGUS.

EPILOGUS.

Cit. Come, Nell, ſhall we go? the play's done.

Wife. Nay, by my faith, George, I have more manners than ſo; I'll ſpeak to theſe gentlemen firſt. I thank you all, gentlemen, for your patience and countenance to Ralph, a poor fatherleſs child! and if I may ſee you at my houſe, it ſhould go hard but I would have a pottle of wine, and a pipe of tobacco for you; for truly I hope you like the youth; but I would be glad to know the truth: I refer it to your own diſcretions, whether you will applaud him or no; for I will wink, and, whilſt, you ſhall do what you will.—I thank you with all my heart. God give you good night! Come, George.

THE privy mark of irony, which runs through this play, not being underſtood, was the reaſon, ſays Walter Burre, [In his Dedication of the quarto of 1613, to his many ways endeared friend, maiſter Robert Keyſar] that it was ready to give up the ghoſt, and ran the danger of being ſmothered in perpetual oblivion, had not Mr. Keyſar been mov'd to relieve and cheriſh it. And that the Reader may not think the hint of ridiculing Romance-Writers was taken from Don Quixote, the ſame Burre aſſures us, in very ſtrong terms, that our Knight came out into the world above a full year before the Spaniard. If this be ſo, then the preſent play was wrote at leaſt in the year 1604, for Cervantes did not publiſh his firſt part before *A. D.* 1605.

However, this eight days performance has more gall in it than I could wiſh; and the Poet, againſt whom the keeneſt part of this ſatire is ſeemingly levell'd, deſerv'd better treatment than we find he has met with: And it might be owing perhaps to Spenſer's friends that this piece was ſuppreſſed for at leaſt the term of nine years, *i. e.* from 1604, in which it might be wrote, to *A. D.* 1613, when the firſt quarto copy came out into the world. *Simpſon.*

We by no means credit the aſſertion of Walter Burre, that ' our ' Knight came into the world' before Don Quixotte: It muſt be obvious to every attentive reader of both, that our Authors derived many principal hints from that ſource. But a much ſtronger proof of this play being of a later date than Burre aſſerts, is, that it followed Heywood's Four Prentices (the reference to which is fully proved by the very ingenious Mr. Warton, p. 436 of this volume) of which we have no account till the year 1612. It therefore appears probable, that Cervantes began the ridicule on Knight-Errantry; that Heywood followed his track; and that our Authors (even while they laughed at Heywood) burleſqued the ſame folly, in the ſucceeding year.

END OF THE SIXTH VOLUME.

www.ingramcontent.com/pod-product-compliance
Lightning Source LLC
Chambersburg PA
CBHW052346110726
47901CB00005B/1378